ALSO BY MAGGIE MCPHEE

Autumn In The Desert Series

Death In Autumn, prequel novella

Second Chances, Book 2

Never Too Late, Book 3

At Last, Book 4

RENAISSANCE

AUTUMN IN THE DESERT, BOOK 1

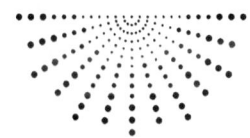

MAGGIE MCPHEE

Cover by: Zoran Petrovic/Fiverr.com name, visual arts

Map of Palm Lakes by: Maria Gandolfo/ Fiverr.com name, Renflowergrapx

ISBN: 978-0-9978816-2-2 (Ebook version)

ISBN: 978-0-9978816-1-5 (Paperback version)

Sixth Sense Books

150 Buck Run E

Dahlonega, GA 30533

Email address: authormaggiemcphee@gmail.com

For my husband, Nigel

CONTENTS

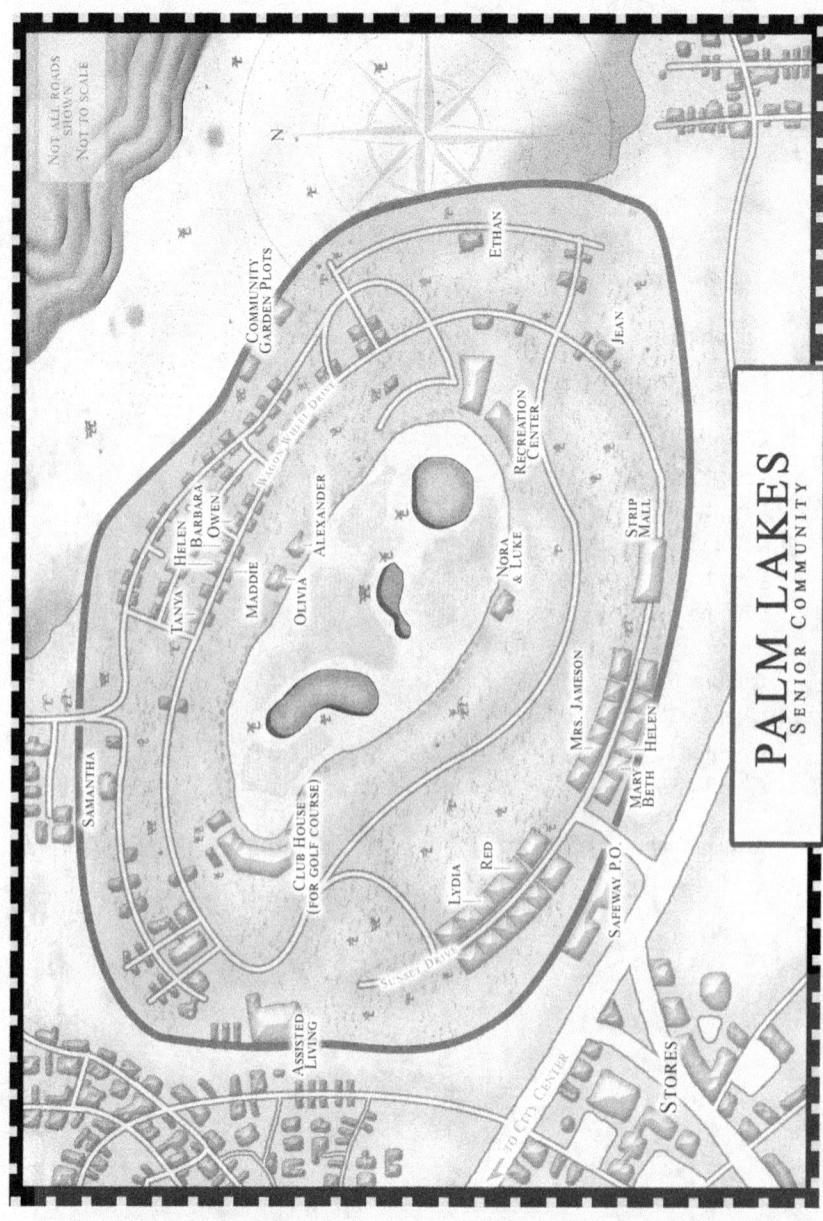

PALM LAKES
SENIOR COMMUNITY

CHARACTERS

Residents Of Palm Lakes
    Maddie and Stanley O'Neill
    Samantha Taylor, the O'Neills' daughter, and her husband Arthur
    Helen Mueller, recent widow
    Alexander Stirling, bachelor
    Serafina Costello, widowed
    Mary Beth Costello, daughter of Serafina, divorced & living temporarily with Mom, in spite of being too young to legally reside there
    Ethan Westerfield, widower and volunteer with The Helpers
    Barbara Blackstone and her husband Ben
    Red Johnson, member of The Posse
    Lydia Stern, divorcee
    Tanya Cooper and her husband
    Owen Schmidt, serial killer
    Jean Callahan and her husband Richard
    Bernie, a neighbor who is a widower

Wagon Wheel Drive residents (single family homes)
    Maddie and Stanley O'Neill
    Barbara and Ben Blackstone, their cat Fluffy and dog Jack

Tanya Cooper and husband
Owen Schmidt
Helen Mueller and her cat Sheba

Sunset Drive residents (condos)
Lydia Stern
Serafina and Mary Beth Costello
Later, Helen Mueller
Mrs. Jameson

Living along the golf course
Alexander Stirling

Nonresidents
Sally, Helen's daughter
Julio, landscaping contractor

* * *

ACKNOWLEDGMENTS

I enjoyed writing this, my first novel, but I could never have completed it without the support and help of my husband, who is my alpha reader. His editing skills vastly improved the story. Any remaining errors are mine.

A heartfelt thank you goes out from me to all my readers. It makes all the effort worthwhile to hear that you love reading about characters of mature years facing challenges much like your own. Boomer fiction or senior fiction isn't even a genre at the time of this writing, but hopefully, other authors will recognize the vitality of senior readers and provide them with stories to which they can easily relate, tales that give them hope and inspire them to know that life isn't over at 55, or even at 85. Life begins anew each day, offering opportunities for joy and fulfillment.

CHAPTER ONE

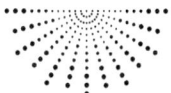

SATURDAY, JULY 22, 1995

Helen, 9:00am

*H*is ice blue eyes betrayed his intent, but she was paralyzed like a
fly in amber. Pain bloomed through her skull when his hand
struck her head, knocking her sideways. She recovered her balance and clumsily
ran for the front door, her only thought to put as much distance between them as
possible.

She grabbed for the doorknob, compensating when it appeared to swim to the
right as if the house were swaying in an earthquake. As she threw the door open,
she glanced back, relieved to see him rooted to the floor in the living room.

Until now, he'd only hit her where it didn't show. She wasn't sure if his loss
of control signaled a new phase in his ongoing abusiveness, or if it meant this
would be the day she would die. She wasn't going to wait around to find out.

Stumbling down the front steps like a drunk, she ran across the yard towards
the street, tripping when she lost the battle with the rolling side-to-side motion.
As she fled through the pines in the filtered moonlight, she berated herself for
pushing his buttons; if only she would be properly submissive, this wouldn't
happen.

The effort of thinking while running proved too much for her, and she
paused, cursing herself for a fool. There was nowhere to go. She needed a car to

escape, and no way could she drive in her condition, even if she could get around him.

The crunching of pine needles and twigs signaled his pursuit, and she took off again in a jagged run, but the determination she had briefly felt transformed into a familiar feeling of resignation. She would never get away.

He caught up with her and grabbed her arm roughly. "Where do you think you're going?"

"Anywhere but here," she snapped. She knew she was inviting more violence but couldn't help it.

"Don't be stupid! Get back in the house. How would it look if someone saw you wandering around at this time of night?"

"I don't care," she said weakly, but in truth, she did. Reason was returning. She couldn't leave the kids. What if he started hurting them? He'd made it clear she'd never take them away from him.

She turned in defeat and slowly trudged back to the house, her heart pounding from the adrenaline rush. In addition to the pain and dizziness, her ears were ringing. The persistent noise got louder and louder, finally blocking out the pain...

She shot into a sitting position, her hand over her pounding heart, trying to salvage some calm. *It's just the phone!* Instinctively her eyes sought the clock on her nightstand. 9:02am. *Warren, of course.*

Grateful that having the phone handy saved her the embarrassment of admitting she'd been asleep, Helen cleared her throat and picked up the handset.

"Mom. Hope I didn't disturb you. I wanted to touch base before I head out. How are you doing?"

"You don't need to call me every day anymore, Warren. I'm OK." She looked down at her hand, which was shaking slightly, no doubt an aftereffect of the nightmare. Good thing he couldn't see.

"You've never been on your own, Mom. It's a big shock, not having Dad to do things. And it's a big change being alone."

"I'm adjusting fine, Warren." She didn't sound convincing, even to herself. How could she prove to him that she was OK when being numb or asleep was the best part of her day?

"It's just that there were a lot of things Dad always did that are being forced on you now, and that's a lot of responsibility at a time like this."

"Warren, we've been through this before. Just because your Dad took care of finances doesn't mean I can't balance a checkbook, live on a budget or pay bills."

"It's not that I think you're incompetent, Mom. But why should you have to learn all that stuff and be alone when you have family you can rely on?"

She didn't hide her sigh as she anxiously bunched a handful of nightgown. She wasn't up to having this argument again. "If you're going to ask me to move back to Wisconsin, I've already told you a hundred times that I'll think about it, but it's too big a decision for me to make right now."

His sigh was nearly as big as hers. "Mom, we'd just feel so much better if we knew you were safe. You're out in the middle of the desert."

Exasperated at his total lack of empathy, she snapped at him. "Oh, for heaven's sake, Warren, it's not like there's a serial killer living down the street. This is a gated retirement community. We have additional security in the Posse. The crime rate is virtually zero. I'm safer here than I would be living with you in Wisconsin. And the winters are so much nicer." It was exhausting covering this ground over and over, especially since she wasn't really sure *what* she wanted, other than to have some peace and quiet.

"Lena and I both feel that at your age, with your health concerns, it would be better for everyone if you came back here to live. If you insist, you could live on your own near one of us. But you need to be near your family."

"I'll thank you not to refer to me as if I'm an invalid or cripple just because I had cancer several years ago. I'm probably healthier than you are."

She couldn't tell if his gusty sigh was a sign of relenting or annoyance. "OK, Mom, just remember we're concerned and think you'd be better off here. You know I can easily set up an apartment for you here at the old place. You'd have enough independence, but we'd be right here to help."

"You've made this generous offer many times in the past several weeks, Warren, and I appreciate it. But I'm not deciding now. You have a busy day, so I'll let you go." She'd run out of the patience required to deal with him, so before he could object, she pressed the 'off' button and shakily set the phone down.

She walked into the kitchen as if dragging a boulder behind her. She was so tired. She just wanted some peace. She stood looking around aimlessly while smoothing the shiny, worn surface of the nightgown as if soothing her ruffled feelings.

Her eyes fell on the half-empty bottle of wine stoppered on the counter. Too bad it was too early for that. And as much as she needed to wake up, her scrambled nerves just couldn't handle caffeine, so she poured a glass of orange juice, added an ice cube and walked out to the small patio, flicking the switch for the ceiling fan as she went through the door. It was hot outside (it was July in the desert, after all), but her patio was sheltered by a large citrus tree, so it was shady in spite of being hotter than she liked. The fan helped a bit, even though the moving air felt like it was escaping from an oven.

No one could see her, but she could see bits of sky and watch the hummingbirds come to the feeder. Before sitting down, she stepped beyond the edge of the patio and looked left and right. No walls surrounded her neighbors' back yards, so she had a clear view across them in both directions to the streets beyond. Not a person in sight, which was not surprising on a July day.

Her next door neighbor's calico cat Fluffy was walking into the yard two lots down. That wasn't good. Barbara had mentioned that Owen had lodged a complaint with the Homeowners' Association about her pets roaming. And that was *after* he had said a few nasty things directly to Barbara. Helen wondered why Barbara couldn't see that man was a very angry character. Should she call Barbara? No, Barbara had to have let the cat out. *Mind your own business, Helen...but what about the cat?*

Helen pushed the worry aside and sat in the padded chair as if she'd been on her feet for hours, wondering at the long sigh that escaped her lips. Why was she so tired? Not getting any answer, she sipped her cool juice and listened to the buzzing of the hummingbirds as they jockeyed for position at the feeder. Angry little dive bombers, they zipped back and forth from the patio to the tree. The occasional 'wahhhnn' of a quail punctuated the stillness. No other sounds marred the peace. The only breeze came from the ceiling fan.

A random thought invaded, as she recalled that a Saturday like this, back in Wisconsin, you'd hear someone mowing his lawn or working on a motorcycle in his driveway, revving the engine. Kids would be screaming as they ran wild through the neighborhood. The sounds of summer were so different here, if you could even call them sounds. Maddie, her neighbor across the street, had once said Palm Lakes was like a mausoleum. Maybe she was right. It sure was quiet.

Some minutes later, her glass empty, she was just beginning to feel comfortable when she heard the phone ringing. It couldn't be Warren; he never called back, and he had said he had somewhere to go. Nerves jangling, she reluctantly got up and went to the kitchen.

"Hi, Helen. It's Barbara. I tried to call sooner, but you must have been on the phone. How are you?"

"Sorry, Barbara. I should get call waiting with all the calls I've been having. I was talking with Warren. He calls every day. Nights during the week, but mornings on weekends."

"Isn't that considerate of him!"

Helen responded drily, "I think he has other motives."

After a brief silence, Barbara said, "What makes you say that?"

Regretting her impetuous comment, she forced herself to reply. "He wants me to come back to Wisconsin and live with him and let him run my life. He doesn't think I'm competent, safe or healthy enough to stay here without Lou. And he won't take 'no' for an answer. I don't want to go, not yet anyway, but I don't know what to do." She blurted the rest out without thinking. "I don't have enough money to stay in this house much longer anyway, now that Lou's gone."

She was horrified at herself. Barbara wasn't an intimate friend (not that she had *any* friends), and she probably didn't want to be bothered with such drama. Helen distractedly began to twist a handful of nightgown, hoping Barbara wouldn't think she was a whiner.

"Look, Helen, if you want to stay in Palm Lakes, maybe you can. You ought to talk to a realtor. I can refer you to a good one. Her name is Shari Lopez, and she's a real pro. The housing market is doing well. If you sell your home, you can move into a condo here in Palm Lakes. It's much less expensive, especially for utilities. And they take care of your landscaping as part of the fee. Would you like Shari's business card?"

Stunned at the suggestion, Helen brightened up. "Thank you, Barbara. Yes, please give me her card. I hadn't even thought of that option."

"I know the time often comes when people choose to go back 'home' and live with family. But if you don't want to, there's no reason you can't find a way to stay. We'd hate to lose you."

Helen wondered why Barbara would pay her such a compliment. "That's kind of you. You've done so much for me since Lou passed, and all I've ever been is the hermit next door. You've kept me going since the funeral. All those invitations to Sunday dinner and the casseroles you've brought to divert me from a diet of Twinkies and boxed wine. How will I ever repay you?"

Barbara laughed as if she didn't believe Helen would choose such a demented eating plan. "You haven't come over more than three times in seven weeks. That hardly constitutes a debt you need to repay. You shouldn't be alone all the time. We're here to help."

"I appreciate your suggesting the realtor. My mind hasn't been firing on all cylinders lately." It chilled her to realize how frighteningly true that statement was.

"Glad to help. How about coming to our place for dinner tomorrow? We're having fettucini alfredo. And I can give you Shari's card then."

"Thanks, I would like that very much. What time?"

"5:30 will be about right."

"Can I bring dessert or wine or something?"

"A bottle of wine would be lovely. Or a box." Her joke coaxed a small laugh from Helen. "See you then!"

As Helen placed the phone back in the base, Sheba came walking through the kitchen door, meowing for her meal. Helen picked her up and crooned at her.

"Hello, Princess! Did you sleep well? I love you so much." She snuggled in the long gray fur, feeling the soothing rumble of Sheba's loud purr.

Sheba quietly accepted the obeisance that was her due, but her pinned back ears said she was hungry and running out of patience.

"Mama's little treasure wants dinner? OK, I'll fix it for you."

Putting her down, Helen got Sheba's bowl and opened a can of her favorite cat chow. She placed it ceremoniously on the mat beside Sheba's crockery water bowl. "Here, Your Majesty. Your dinner is served."

Sheba began to chow down without further comment. Helen went to collect the empty glass from the patio table. As she returned to the kitchen, she reflected that Sheba seemed to be losing weight.

"Sheba, are you feeling OK? I know you're older and don't like to jump now, but are you hurting?"

Sheba stopped gulping food long enough to look at Helen with pale green eyes that glittered with an uncanny intelligence, but gave no answer beyond one meow.

The rest of the day played out like all the others since Lou died. She couldn't sit still long enough to read or watch TV. Nothing seemed interesting, yet she wanted to be distracted. She didn't feel like doing housework. She wasn't hungry, so she didn't eat. Life had become frustrating and confusing, like trying to eat soup with a fork. All hard work and no nourishment. At least she managed to shower and dress, though she put on no makeup or jewelry.

Early in the evening, Helen sat at the desk in the small office, staring at the pile of bills and other correspondence, annoyed at herself for ignoring them. There were more condolence letters and cards to answer. It was amazing how many people had written in support, and even more surprising how many had said nice things about Lou, given that he was an abusive bastard. Not that she'd ever told anyone, so what could she expect? It made it so hard to reply sincerely.

She looked at the to-do list on the note pad. She'd been looking at the same list for weeks, but once a month the bills *had* to get paid. Maybe she could focus long enough to get it done. She grabbed the checkbook, looked at the anemic total and felt the familiar clenching in her stomach. The savings account had a bit in it, but not a lot. How long could she put off making a decision about what to do with her life? She sighed and started writing checks.

It didn't take as long as she had feared. She put the last check into the proper envelope and stamped all of them. She carried the envelopes to the front room and put them into the little basket near the door so she'd remember to put them in the mailbox next time she went out. At least one onerous task was done. After a day without food, hunger was finally clawing its way into her consciousness, so she went to the kitchen to see what she could throw together.

The inside of the refrigerator was a nearly-empty white cavern. She'd finished the last of Barbara's most recent casserole two days ago. Some condiments, a container of half-and-half and a butter dish dominated the landscape. There was a partial pack of hot dogs, so she decided to fry some up and have some scrambled eggs with them.

She'd lost weight since Lou died, and she knew she needed to snap out of it, whatever 'it' was, but she felt so tired all the time. As much as she loved cooking, doing it for one seemed pointless, especially since she had no appetite. But she hadn't eaten all day, so she forced herself to go through the motions.

Not tasting a thing, she ate her dinner in front of the television while an old movie played in black and white, a reflection of her colorless mood. A few glasses of wine cloaked her in a welcome numbness. At some point, she realized the movie was over and got up and rinsed the dishes and put them in the dishwasher. It took a few days to fill it up enough to justify running it, but she didn't have the energy to hand wash them, even though that made the most sense. At least there was no one around to criticize her. Except herself.

Wrapped in a wine-fueled softness, she wandered into the office to journal before bed. For most of her marriage, journaling had been her therapy, keeping her sane when life threatened to spin out of control. Now it was the one spot of routine in the shifting landscape of her life. But the changing landscape had diminished her compulsion to write, so she'd sit and stare at an empty page wondering how to fill it. It was as if Lou had been her only inspiration, and now that he was gone, she had nothing to say. No, it felt worse than that. It was like by dying, he'd stolen from her the one thing that gave her joy. Which seemed just the opposite of how she should feel. Not that anything made sense anymore.

Sitting at her father-in-law's antique oak desk, she gazed at all the books she'd used for journals, which now held a place of honor on a nearby shelf. She ran her fingers along their spines, reminiscing about the escape they had offered from an existence that was close to incarceration, a sentence that had ended seven weeks ago when Lou died suddenly of a heart attack. Twenty-seven of them lined the shelf, a riot of sizes, colors and textures. There were bound journals, spiral notebooks and thick diaries. Some were gifts from her children, who knew she liked to write. Others were leftover school notebooks the kids hadn't used.

These books were the truest friends she ever had (besides Sheba), and it gave her a pang to admit that. At her age, she should have some human friends, but Lou hadn't wanted her to socialize, and she hadn't cared enough to fight him about it.

She pulled out the journal that was covered in cloth that looked like zebra skin and thumbed through its pages. That was the year Sally was born, and the book held stories of fear, pain and then, the wonder and joy of her youngest child's birth. It was hard to believe that was thirty years ago. She slipped the old journal back among the others and pulled out the thick purple book from the end.

She used to love writing in her journal, could hardly wait to pour her heart out. Now she felt nothing. Disturbed by her lack of motivation, she picked up the pen anyway and dated the next blank page.

July 22, 1995

I dreamt last night about the time Lou hit me in the head so hard I was dizzy for over a year. It was so long ago. Why dream about it now? It's not as if he'd been hitting me lately. He actually mellowed these last 10 years, as if he didn't have the energy to get physical.

I used to think he'd end up killing me. But I didn't see any way out when the kids were small, and by the time all of them were gone, he'd gotten a lot better. There were times I wished him dead, but I never really thought he'd die before me. I couldn't even picture being on my own.

It's been nearly two months, and I have no idea what to do with my life. I never made any plans. It would be easy to give in to Warren and put all the decisions on him. He'd be so pleased. I couldn't live with Lena, but maybe I could force myself to live with him.

And yet...I'm not eager to put myself under another man's thumb. I want to do what I want to do...but I don't know what that is.

It comes down to money. The house and car are paid for, but with Lou's retirement gone and so little savings, I know I can't go on living here much longer. He didn't make any plans for me to survive him. And it never occurred to me to ask.

Barbara made a kind suggestion, and it might be worth looking into. And maybe I should consider getting a part-time job. The one thing I have plenty of is time and the freedom to spend it however I wish. Now that I'm on my own, maybe I should participate in some of the clubs or courses they have here. It's strange to be able to choose...It's overwhelming.

Why do I feel so stuck now that I'm finally free? Why do I have to force myself to write? I was more functional when Lou was alive. Now I can barely eat, sleep or clean house. Or even take proper care of Sheba.

Feeling disgusted with herself, Helen put the pen down and closed the journal. Replacing the book on the shelf, she decided to turn in for the night. It was past midnight again, and tomorrow she needed to go to Barbara's for dinner.

A cricket chirped loudly from the master bedroom. *How do they get in, anyway?* Most of the time, you couldn't find them to remove them. Lou had hated the noise, but she found they made her feel less alone, especially at night, when the emptiness, which should have comforted her, was an aching, menacing presence that reminded her how alone and confused she was.

She carried Sheba into the master suite and laid her on the queen-sized bed. Sheba barely stirred (it was past her bedtime), but the purr was loud and soothing to Helen's nerves.

She dressed in her nightgown and climbed into bed and snuggled up beside Sheba. Between Sheba's purrs and loud chirps from Mr. Cricket, Helen drifted off to sleep in spite of her unanswered questions about the future.

* * *

Tanya, 9:06am

IGNORING the pounding headache that demanded her attention, Tanya scrutinized her reflection in the bathroom mirror. She ran a hand through her bleached hair, noting it could use another treatment. Suppressing both pain and annoyance, she wondered yet again why the skimpy black negligee had not done the trick last night.

She stepped back from the mirror to appraise her assets. The distance made her vision just hazy enough to take ten years off her age. Her skin was weathered from years of sun-worshipping, but her legs were shapely, and she had boobs that turned men's minds to mush. What real man would reject a body like hers, especially gift-wrapped in such an enticing negligee? She ran her hands down the silky fabric, unable to solve the puzzle.

Could he have a lover? The thought was ridiculous; he didn't have the balls. Unlike her. She wasn't afraid to go after what she wanted. Maybe it was time to go on the hunt again. If he didn't want her, she'd find someone who did.

Slipping into in her red silk robe, she headed to the kitchen, past the closed door of the guest bedroom where her husband always slept. She could hear him moving around as he got ready to go play golf. What a bore! It was all he ever did.

After filling a large mug with orange juice and a generous splash of vodka (she really needed to take the edge off after last night's rejection), she sat on the faux leopardskin couch in the living room ready to pounce on him when he came through.

She was primed and aching for a fight. Not that they ever really fought. She pictured a fight as being more aggressive, with a clear victor and passionate makeup sex afterwards. All they ever did was replay the same tedious arguments over and over, neither of them actually winning, and sex had become a rarity.

Sipping her drink and pumping herself up by replaying last night's drama in her head, she didn't have to wait long for him to appear. He tiptoed around the corner on his way to the garage door, unaware that she sat on the couch behind him. He looked like a skinny gray scarecrow in his unfashionable clothes.

"You coward! Were you going to slink out of the house without even apologizing for last night?"

He stopped and turned around, pulling himself to his full six feet of height, a surprising hint of disdain in his eyes. "I was unaware that I had done anything that called for an apology, Tanya."

She loathed it when he took that superior tone with her. "I dressed special for you, and you rejected me out of hand."

"I'd hardly call it special when you were three sheets to the wind from drinking. You know how I feel about your over-imbibing. It's unattractive."

His criticism stung her more than she wanted to admit. "I'm tired of you judging me, using fancy words to make me feel like you're better than me. I may not have gone to college, but I put you through law school so you could become a big-shot lawyer, and you owe me."

"I'm tired of the same old arguments. How many years will I have to suffer because you worked to put me through law school? I've never cheated on you. I've stayed with you through everything. God knows why." Disgust hung on him like an old jacket, a bedraggled but perfect fit. "I owe you nothing. I'm sick of your drinking and your abusive behavior."

Enraged at his judgment, she shrieked at him. "You spineless wimp! Go ahead and run off to your golf game. Or your whore. You think I'm stupid? You aren't interested in sex with me, so you must be getting it elsewhere. I'll find out and divorce you!"

Anger flashed across his face, but instead of responding to her taunts, he turned and walked out the door, slamming it behind him. Tanya slumped and reached for her drink. Drained but still thrumming with anger, she decided she deserved to be pampered for the way things had turned out last night. She'd go get a manicure. That always raised her spirits.

At the salon an hour later, her favorite tech Ashley worked on her nails, blonde head bent over Tanya's hands in concentration. "You know, Mrs. Cooper, seeing as how you're a professional, you know all the tricks of the nail trade, so I have to stay on my toes with you." Her blue eyes glanced up at Tanya, a hint of laughter in them.

Reminded of herself at that age, Tanya replied with uncharacteristic kindness, "You always do a good job, Ashley."

Smiling at the compliment, Ashley turned around and selected a bottle of scarlet nail polish, then placed it on the table in front of Tanya. "What do you think of this color?"

Nodding in approval, Tanya commented, "Actually, that reminds me of my first nail varnish. It was my favorite color."

Back at work and head bent, Ashley said, "Lots of people are doing nontraditional colors now, but I think the classics suit you best."

"I've always loved that shade of red. My old man wasn't too keen on it, though. He found me painting my nails, threw a fit and scraped it off with a pocket knife."

Ashley raised her head, her widened eyes searching Tanya's face sympathetically. "Why'd he do that?"

"He was a religious nut and called me a whore for painting my nails. I was 15."

Ashley bit her lower lip, obviously shocked. "That was harsh."

"It was the last straw for me. I got married as soon as I could and ended up working in a nail salon. He's probably turning over in his grave at how my life turned out. At least I hope he is." Tanya harrumphed in emphasis.

Tanya returned home from her outing in a good mood. By mid-afternoon, she had a pretty good buzz on, but she'd nearly run out of vodka. She poured the last bit of it into her travel mug and added some coffee to get her through her shopping trip.

Stiletto heels were a challenge to wear when she was tipsy, but she wasn't going to sacrifice fashion for comfort or safety. Her ensemble of lacy, low-cut black top and leopardskin tights showcased her figure. Not for the first time, she was done with trying to make her marriage work. Maybe she'd find a handsome man and leave her husband, or at least have an affair.

During the drive to the supermarket, she found it hard to focus on the road, and she nearly ran over an elderly woman who jaywalked in front of her. She yelled at the old bat and tried to steady her hands on the wheel. The near miss scared her sober, and worry suddenly overcame her. She had too many citations as it was, and another would be ammunition for her husband.

At the next stop light, she drank her vodka-laced coffee and gave herself a pep talk. *Stay focused!*

With no further incidents, she arrived and parked (pretty well) and wove her way into the market and took a cart; it was excellent support.

She'd gotten most of what she needed, including more vodka, and was perusing the items on a sale shelf when Owen Schmidt from down the street nearly ran into her with his cart, bringing a bit of sunshine into her gloomy thoughts. What a hunk he was. Not as tall as she'd like, but a beautifully sculpted body. "Owen! Fancy meeting you here!"

His reaction confused her. She gave him a good look at her boobs, and he couldn't take his eyes off them, which sent pleasure shooting through her. Then he acted tongue-tied and raced off. All she'd done was touch his arm. Was he shy or playing hard to get?

Owen's sudden exit did not deter Tanya's alcohol-fueled fantasy. She would seduce him. It would serve her husband right if she found another man, a real man who would appreciate her. She could picture it now, Owen's muscled, naked body wrapped around hers in a passionate embrace. She could tell he was a man who knew what to do with a woman.

* * *

Owen, 9:10am

THE AIR-CONDITIONING WAS BLASTING full force in Owen's new BMW M3 but wasn't making a dent in the accumulated heat of the past week. Not for the first time, he wished they had covered parking at the lot where he stored his RV, but it was the closest one to his home, so he wouldn't complain.

He watched the desert scenery fly by as the car effortlessly ate the road. The temperature outside was 95, headed to triple digits on a day when yet again, there wasn't a cloud in the sky.

Owen turned off the main road at the entrance to Palm Lakes, "Senior Living At Its Best," and slowed to pass through the entrance. His car's sticker showed he was a resident, and the bored uniform in the guardhouse waved him through. Some people's idea of security was pretty stupid, but that wasn't his problem. In fact, it usually was to his advantage.

The palm-tree-lined road wound sinuously around the edge of the golf course that was at the heart of the community. In most of Palm Lakes, all you could see were the nearest stuccoed homes, but along this stretch of road, you could see acres of well-tended grass with sparkling lakes interspersed, the whole thing framed by tall palms against a backdrop of purple mountains in the hazy distance. Golf carts zipped along the paths, making the scene look like a brochure for a happy retirement. Owen had no interest in golf, but anywhere that had palm trees said 'paradise' to him.

Keeping to the speed limit, he passed street after street of houses that looked alike. Sure, there were different models, but the styles and range of colors didn't vary enough to create dissonance. Palm Lakes had a uniformity that appealed to his sense of order.

The roads and yards were deserted, but it was July. The wimps who couldn't take the heat had fled to second homes up north and the Canadian snow birds had returned to their mother country. Everyone else was locked inside their homes with the air-conditioning on. And that was fine with him. He rather liked the post-Armageddon feeling he got from driving along the deserted summer streets.

After pulling into his garage, he entered his home through the laundry room, placing his travel bag on top of the drier, aligning it with the front edge. In the living room, light streamed through the transom windows above closed curtains. His favorite design feature of the house, they allowed total privacy while filling the room with light. It felt good to be home.

Opening the refrigerator, he grabbed a bottle of Coke. As he disposed of the cap in the covered trash bin, he noticed with disgust that the cover was dirty.

A flash of paranoia ripped through him, the hair on the back of his neck standing to attention. Had someone been in the house? He'd only been gone a week. There were no signs of forced entry, and no one else had a key. He forced himself to calm down and take a deep breath. No one knew. He had just overlooked it in his rush to get on the road.

Feeling calmer, he put his Coke down and reached for the rubber gloves that lay across the dish drain. Squirting some green washing liquid onto the new sponge, he began to scrub the soiled area as if he were preparing an operating room for surgery. Finally, he judged it to be clean enough.

Task completed, he reached for his cold drink, noting that the chill was pleasant on his bandaged right hand. The injury was still tender, but he had treated it properly, so he knew it wouldn't become infected.

"You really did it this time, Junior!" He flinched as the familiar voice stabbed at him.

"Oh, shut up, Mother!" Why couldn't she just leave him alone?

"How dare you address me in that fashion? You will not use such language when speaking to me!" He could picture her pointing an index finger at him and shaking it.

"What are you going to do, wash my mouth out with soap? You're dead! You've been dead for years! So shut up!" He slammed his half-empty Coke on the counter, and some liquid sloshed out. Immediately he grabbed his cleaning supplies and tried to ignore his mother's armor-piercing voice as he scrubbed away.

"You need to quit making stupid mistakes."

His ire rose a notch at her criticism. "What are you going to do? Put me in the closet like you used to? You can't touch me anymore!" Though his anger was threatening to spin out of control, he managed to push it back down.

He did feel bad, though, because she was right; he had made a mistake this time. When he wielded the knife, he cut himself as he cut the woman, and he surely left his own blood behind, and that was bad. He didn't fully understand the whole DNA thing, but he was pretty sure he had left some. At least the body was well disposed of. His mother had gone quiet. Thank heaven for small favors.

He went into the master bathroom and took a long, hot shower. Though traveling by RV gave him some anonymity and privacy, the shower in it left a lot to be desired. Steam wrapped around him in a warm embrace, filling his nostrils with the citrusy scent of the soap, taking the edge off his anxiety and washing away any lingering evidence of his recent activities, but there was still a bony finger of concern plucking at his nerves as he toweled himself dry.

He knew what would help. He had to put the house in order. After starting a load of laundry, he went into the living room and surveyed it. He'd been gone a week, so there was a thin layer of dust on the furniture, and he knew the carpet was equally filthy. His books and CDs filled shelves in orderly, alphabetized rows, but the haze of dust irritated him. He attacked the chores with relish, anticipating the relief he'd feel when the room was clean.

While he was meticulously vacuuming the living room carpet, a motion caught his eye. Through the curtains he'd opened in order to shed more light on the rug, he saw an animal creeping stealthily across his yard.

Barbara's cat was once again pissing or shitting on his property. He fumed while the cat dug through the fine gravel, pooped and then covered it up half-heartedly. Before the cat could finish, he impulsively slid the glass door open and said, "Come here, kitty." Surprisingly, the cat came in. He quickly closed the door and scanned the yard. The mature landscaping screened his back door from the neighbors, so no one could have seen him let the cat in. Finally, he could do whatever he wanted with her.

He knew it was a female because it was calico. Females of all species deserved judgment. This one had a lot to answer for. She'd been trespassing in his yard for a long time, and the stupid bitch owner ignored his polite requests. The HOA didn't have the teeth to do anything except warn her. A fat lot of good that had done.

Well, he could fix the problem for good now. Scooping the cat up, he took her into the spare bedroom and put her in the empty closet. He'd deal with her...he just needed to set things up so cleanup would be easy.

His mother's voice intruded, laced with atypical fear. "Junior, you can't do that. You mustn't ever do that here."

"It's a cat, Mother. This is way better than complaining over and over to the Home Owners' Association. Those morons didn't do anything."

"You're the moron, Junior. Who do you suppose they'll suspect when the cat goes missing? After the number of complaints you've filed, they'll come knocking on your door. Do you really want to get caught over a cat?"

"They won't send police out looking for clues about a lost cat. I know how to clean up. Do you always have to criticize me?"

Her lack of response caused him to smile. Barbara would wonder what happened to her cat, but she would never know. Served her right.

The afternoon sped by. It was always like that when he was doing one of his projects. The house had been cleaned spotless, the laundry was drying and the remains of the cat were in a trash bag that he would take to a dumpster after dark. It had really been quite easy and invigorating once he figured out how to keep her quiet. It made him feel so invincible that he was tempted to find ways to continue relieving the neighborhood of wayward pets.

The refrigerator needed restocking, so he made a grocery list and drove to the market just outside the entrance to Palm Lakes. Pushing his cart down the aisles and grabbing each item on his list, he had to dodge old farts standing in the middle of the narrow aisles, staring at the labels on canned goods as if they were discovering the mysteries of life. They irritated the hell out of him.

He rounded the end of the aisle and nearly plowed into Tanya from up the street. Like the other old farts, she was blocking his way, staring at stock on the end of the shelf. But unlike the typical grandmotherly residents of Palm Lakes, Tanya dressed provocatively. Leopardskin tights, low-cut black top and sparkly stiletto heels showed off a figure that owed a lot either to great genes or to plastic surgery. Large sunglasses and bleached blonde hair added an exotic aura as if she were a celebrity slumming at the Safeway.

Her gaze drifted to him. "Owen! Fancy meeting you here!" Through the lenses of her sunglasses, she eyed him like a hungry predator.

Temporarily paralyzed, he held still as she leaned towards him, the fragrances of perfume and alcohol wrapping around him like invisible chains. His eyes were riveted on the view down her top. She had on a bra, but there wasn't much to the top half of it, and he basked in the glow of her nearly naked, perfectly-shaped tits just inches from his face. A chorus of conflicting emotions clamored for his attention. A coherent reaction was impossible. He tried to take his eyes off her tits without success.

"Owen, you look stronger every time I see you. You must work out a lot to be so buff! Here, let me feel your biceps." She squeezed his arm and then stroked it seductively. Beginning to sweat in spite of the air-conditioning, he mumbled an excuse and fled towards the next aisle without looking back.

In spite of the pandemonium raging within him, Owen completed his shopping and drove home, obeying the speed limit and making a full stop at all stop signs. By the time he arrived home, he had pushed all the conflicting feelings aside.

He unloaded the bags and put his groceries away. Satisfied that everything was lined up neatly and alphabetically, he decided to spend some time with his model train set. It made him feel like the Creator, designing and engineering his own miniature world. The feelings of order and control soothed him, though lately, the effect wasn't lasting as long as it used to.

He walked back to the second bedroom, his hobby room. He paused in the doorway to admire the order and beauty of what he had spent a year creating. There was no furniture here except his ergonomic chair and the small table at which he did some of the finer work of modeling. The floor space was mostly taken up with a scale model of a village and steam railway, including mountains, tunnels and bridges. Lakes with Canada geese and forests with a few deer added to the natural beauty.

Truly at peace for the first time since returning from his trip, he knelt down to continue working on the village. He was adding some new businesses to the small Main Street. He began to hum tunelessly as he sank into an almost meditative state, all the events of the day forgotten.

CHAPTER TWO

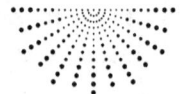

SATURDAY, AUGUST 12, 1995

Samantha , 9:00am

Samantha pulled up in front of Owen Schmidt's house for her 9am appointment. His large mesquite tree lay on its side, bare roots reaching for the sky like giant, alien fingers. It was another casualty of the monsoon storm that had ripped through town last night, taking off roofs and downing trees. If it was like most she'd seen today (she'd already had three appointments), there was no hope of propping it back up. But they always hated to hear that. They didn't believe the tree couldn't heal, no matter what she said. They told her things like "I don't have enough years left to start over." As if that would change the facts. Cruel Mother Nature had done her worst last night, and Samantha Taylor of Palo Verde Landscaping had to be the bearer of bad tidings.

She reached for her broad-brimmed straw hat and got out of the car, hoping this guy wouldn't shoot the messenger. His door opened not five seconds after she rang the bell. He didn't look happy.

She'd seen him from a distance a few times when visiting her parents across the street, but they'd never been introduced. "Mr. Schmidt, I'm Samantha from Palo Verde Landscaping. Shall we take a look at your tree?"

She turned and walked back to the tree without watching to see if he followed. Lots of these older guys weren't too keen on taking advice from a woman, especially one her age, and it seemed to help if she just took charge.

They stood on opposite sides of the gouged earth. The subtle message didn't escape her notice. She knew immediately the tree was a goner, but she'd learned not to pass that information on too quickly. So she squatted down on the edge of the hole, examining the mangled roots.

She glanced up at Owen, who stood watching with slitted eyes. He obviously wasn't an outdoors type, because he had no tan to speak of, in spite of his dark hair and brown eyes. Though his skin was pasty, his tank top revealed serious upper body sculpting. Maybe he lifted weights, possibly as compensation for his shorter-than-average height.

She brushed the dirt off her hands and stood up. He had a creepy vibe, but she wouldn't let him intimidate her. "Mr. Schmidt, this tree cannot be saved. I'm sorry."

Before she had a chance to explain anything, he cut her off. "Why can't you just prop it up. I see people do that all the time. I don't want to have to start over." He glared at her with mistrust.

Samantha suppressed a sigh and tried to be diplomatic. "Mr. Schmidt, there are some companies which would let you pay to prop this tree back up. It might not die. It has some roots still attached on one side. But very few, and propping it up won't regrow the roots that have been damaged. It will never be strong, and it won't take much of a wind to knock it over again. You're better off taking it out now and starting over. I can give you an estimate on a replacement, or I can make suggestions about other types of trees. The mesquite trees are quite prone to be damaged this way. I could suggest something sturdier if you like." She tried to smile but felt it turn to a grimace and chided herself for letting him get to her. The day was only starting; she needed to be thicker-skinned.

"Why did it happen to my tree, and not theirs?" He pointed diagonally across the street to her parents' gorgeous mesquite, apparently unaware of her relationship with his neighbors.

"Mr. Schmidt, there's no telling why the wind touched down here and not there. I can see that your tree hasn't been watered to encourage it to grow deep roots. If we plant a new tree for you, I can tell you how to

21

water it properly. Also, mesquites grow fast. They get top-heavy and need frequent pruning, or the canopy acts as a sail to the wind. If you go around town, you'll see that mesquites are about 75% of the downed trees, and I can guarantee you that over 90% of them haven't been properly watered and pruned."

He wasn't paying any attention to what she said. His mouth was an angry slash, and he made a dismissive sound and walked toward the house. "Come on in and give me an estimate."

Owen didn't wait for her or hold the door, but she didn't mind. At least they were still talking. The air-conditioning hit her like a breath of the arctic as she entered the house, which was meticulously clean and neat. This man was no hoarder like Mom. She saw no sign of a wife, but that didn't mean anything. She'd have to ask her parents. She didn't know many men who were such good housekeepers.

"Your home is lovely, Mr. Schmidt." She continued to notice impressive little details, like the total lack of dust and the shelf with alphabetically organized videotapes.

He looked surprised at the compliment but recovered quickly. "Thank you."

They discussed the particulars of planting the new tree. He was parsimonious with words, so it didn't take long. When they finished, Samantha got into her truck and drove the few feet to her parents' house, parking in their driveway. She couldn't say what it was, but something about Owen Schmidt made the hair on the back of her neck stand up.

She surveyed her parents' beautiful front yard as she got out of the truck. No storm damage was evident, but their mesquite tree needed pruning. She'd have to urge Mom to hire someone. At least it was being watered correctly, so that helped. The roof looked fine. Her boots crunched on the gravel as she walked along the side of the house to the back gate. The wrought iron fence was a lovely shade of brown that contrasted nicely with the cream stucco of the house. The hummingbird pattern on the gate always cheered her. Like her mother, she was fond of the hummers.

The gate creaked open and then latched shut behind her with a metallic clang. The back yard was in good order, the two citrus trees loaded with little fruitlets. The harvest would be good this winter. No damage that she could see.

Her Dad had designed the yard, and it was beautiful. She'd never thought of him as artistic, and it felt weird that he had done such a good job, never having shown any previous interest in gardening. Perhaps just as strange, he showed no interest in the maintenance of the yard once the plants were put in, leaving the details of that to her mother.

The heavy wrought iron screen door opened with a tug, and she let herself into the kitchen. She announced herself to avoid scaring her mother. "Mom, it's me." No one answered, but her folks were getting hard of hearing these days. She cruised through the kitchen into the small dining alcove then through the living room, patting Beau as he came to greet her, tail wagging. She finally found her mother in the guest bedroom sorting through jewelry supplies on the bed.

The room was packed tightly with furniture and assorted boxes of stuff lying against the walls. Every square inch of the bed was covered with the bits and pieces of her mother's jewelry hobby. Curtains covered the window, and the only lamp had a weak bulb that barely cast enough light to avoid tripping over the many obstacles.

Maddie O'Neill looked up at her daughter. Her eyeglasses were barely hanging onto the end of her nose. Her dirty-blonde hair, miraculously free of gray even though she was in her seventies, gave her a wild look; she cut it herself, and it was uneven in a punk sort of style that had to be unintentional, as she had no interest in fashion. The smile in her faded blue eyes was genuine but short-lived. Her wrinkled face spoke of the wear and tear of a stressful and unhappy life. Samantha hoped she wouldn't look as worn out in 30 years, then felt ashamed for thinking it.

Going back to her search, Mom waved her over. "Bring your young eyes over here. I need help finding something."

"Gee, Mom, my eyes aren't that young anymore, and it's so dark in here, I can't see anything."

"They're younger than mine, so give me a hand."

Samantha walked over and looked into the shoebox her mother was scooping through. It was loaded with beads of all colors, sizes and shapes. It wasn't going to be easy to find anything in that mess.

"Why are they are lumped together like this? You usually sort them and put them in boxes according to type. What exactly are you trying to find?"

Mom looked up briefly at the implied criticism and then went back to sifting through the beads. "These are the odd ones I don't have enough of to do anything with and that I don't intend to reorder, so I throw them in here. But it's getting so full, I can't find anything. My eyes don't distinguish as well as they used to. I'm looking for a 5/8 inch center-drilled bead of glass, shaped like a lizard and the color of red wine. Can you see anything like that?"

"Let me have the box, and I'll see if I can find it. But don't get your hopes up." Samantha smiled at her mother's reluctance to surrender the box to her. "Can we go out into the dining room where the light is better? I can't stay long, but I'll try to find it for you."

In the dining room, Samantha turned on the study light that sat on the table which was covered with jewelry supplies, partially finished projects and boxes of beads. They each took a seat. "Why don't I spill them out and we'll look together?"

Springing into action, Mom grabbed an old white tea towel and unfolded it on the table top. "Here, pour them on this cloth. The color contrast is helpful, and it might keep them from rolling onto the floor. We don't want Beau to eat them. You know he's not too discriminating."

The yellow lab in question padded quietly into the dining room and sat beside Samantha, who stroked him while pushing the beads apart with her other hand.

"I'm glad to see your yard and roof are OK. It's pretty bad around town."

"I saw on the news how much damage there was all over this side of the valley. There hasn't been a storm this bad in years." Mom continued to sort through the beads with her usual laser focus.

"Mom, even though you're watering your mesquite properly, it needs pruning. A storm like this could still blow it over. How about I set up an appointment for the guys to come by and do it?"

"You know I don't like them. They're too expensive. I'll do it myself."

"The tree is getting too big for you to do it. I wouldn't even undertake that job. Please don't try and do it yourself." Samantha shook her head, worried that she'd done more harm than good. Now Mom would try to prune the tree herself.

A flash of rebellion in her eyes, Mom said, "Never mind about the tree. Help me find the bead." They continued to spread the beads apart but didn't find what she wanted.

"How's Dad? I didn't see him when I came in. Is he home?"

"He may be in his study. You should go by and say hi before you leave."

"I will. I have an appointment soon. The brothers don't mind me visiting you during working hours, but I don't want to take advantage of their good will. I just wanted to see how you were doing after that bad storm."

"We're OK. Wait...I think I found it!" Mom held up a wine red lizard-shaped bead. It was very pretty.

"What are you using it for?"

"I'm replacing an earring that Barbara lost."

"You're so generous. The women around here are almost as loaded up with your jewelry as I am. That would make a pretty earring."

"I only had a few of these, and when I discovered how good they looked, there weren't any more for sale. I'm sorry I didn't make you a pair."

"You make me plenty of jewelry. I wasn't hinting or complaining."

"You never do. Go see your Dad before you leave." Mom had already started sweeping the other beads back into the box. There was no more time for small talk.

Samantha hugged her, petted Beau and went into her Dad's little office. The walls were lined floor to ceiling with bookshelves Mom had made to hold all of Dad's books, and in the center, there was just enough room for his desk and chair. Dad looked up. "I didn't hear you come in."

"I let myself in the back. I figured the front door was still locked, but you let Beau out, so the back would be open."

"Lots of trees down around town?" It was a rhetorical question, like so many of the scripted conversations she had with her parents, but that was OK, because she preferred staying on topics that didn't lead to conflict.

"Yes, it's pretty bad. We'll be busy for a while cleaning up and replacing trees. I'm glad you weren't affected. The yard looks good."

"It's doing OK. I need to talk with you about finances."

Not again. Has he forgotten he just went over this a week ago? "I can't stay now. I have an appointment. I just wanted to make sure you were all right after the storm. I had an appointment with your neighbor whose tree is down. Mr. Schmidt."

"Don't know much about him. He's quiet and lives alone. Keeps his yard clean. Doesn't make trouble, although Mom told me he complained to the HOA about Barbara's cat running free. He's right. She's an idiot for letting those animals out, with the coyotes around. Serve her right if it got eaten."

Samantha winced. "I'm sorry for the cat. She didn't mean anyone any harm."

"So when can you sit down with me for a few minutes?"

"We'll be over tomorrow afternoon."

"Fine." He went back to reading the book that lay open on the desk. She was dismissed and left to stare at the top of his head. His wavy hair was still thick, even though it was white. Stanley O'Neill was rather proud of having all his hair and teeth at nearly 84 years of age.

It struck her as strange to suddenly realize her parents were *old*. Of course they were, but she never thought of them as elderly in spite of their age. That was probably one reason she hated these little talks. She didn't want to think about either of them dying.

There was nothing else to say, so she turned and left, not looking forward to tomorrow. It had become a nearly weekly ritual for him to harangue her about how Mom was probably going to outlive him, and she wasn't fit to handle the money, and there wouldn't be very much, anyway. She didn't enjoy being in the middle of the decades-long war of her parents' marriage, nor did she like to contemplate having a mess to deal with after Dad died. She couldn't imagine her mother managing the practicalities of life without Dad, especially if money was scarce.

Thinking about their finances as she slipped out the back door, Samantha reflected on the alarm she felt every time he showed her the numbers. How had he let it get away from him so badly? Is was so contrary to his controlling personality to have so little savings, but she didn't dare ask him. He wanted an audience, not advice.

She started the truck, slid back into work mode and tried to let go of the nagging worry.

* * *

Jean, 9:53am

JEAN SAT at the stop light waiting for it to turn green, the air-conditioning blasting cool air in her face as she drifted back to what she had learned this morning. She was in shock. Sure, she and Richard had grown apart, but that hadn't seemed so terrible. They each had their interests, and she didn't begrudge him his golf or cards with the boys, and he never complained about her "New Age" pursuits and all the courses she was taking, even though she could tell he thought it was hogwash.

The sound of a car horn pierced her fog, bringing her back to present time. She forced herself to focus on the road and drove the rest of the way to class, fighting to break out of the miasma of sadness and confusion.

As she turned into the Community College's parking lot, she saw Lydia's car. She usually looked forward to being with Lydia. Lydia was so knowledgeable and enthusiastic, and just a bit eccentric, which made her even more interesting.

But today, she didn't feel like facing Lydia. She didn't believe in complaining about her spouse, but she was so down, she knew she'd never be able to hide it. Lydia would read her like a book and demand to know what was going on. (Sometimes she wondered if Lydia was psychic, but she'd never had the nerve to ask.) She didn't want to lie to her best friend, but she didn't know what to say, either.

She grabbed her purse and notebook, locked the car and walked reluctantly into the building. Stepping into the ladies' room, she applied new lipstick with a shaky hand, finger-combed her short, blonde hair and tried to calm her heart. It had been beating so fast for so long, she thought it might burst. What was she going to do? Obviously, nothing right now. She needed to focus on the class, Lydia, and having a good time. She'd figure out what to do about Richard later. Straightening her shoulders and putting on a faint smile, she went down the hall to the classroom.

The crystal healing course was being taught by a lovely woman in her 30s. Considering that retirees were mostly conservative types not interested in healing and metaphysics, the room was surprisingly full. Most of the 35 students were women.

Lydia had saved a seat for her, so she slipped along the back of the classroom and sat next to her, nodding a good morning. Lydia was dressed as usual in a flamboyant aging-hippie style, her sandals and long purple skirt topped by a tie-dyed blouse with a scooped neck that showed her ample cleavage to advantage. A necklace of shells clattered as she leaned down to get a pen out of her large cloth purse. Hooped gold earrings set off her olive skin and dark, curly hair, which cascaded lushly to her shoulders.

Jean fished in her purse for a pen, averting her gaze long enough to suppress the tears welling up in her eyes. It wouldn't do to cry in public. Then she'd have to explain for sure. The class hushed as the teacher began to speak. She'd have 50 minutes to compose herself. That should be enough.

It wasn't. When the class came to a close, she looked down at her notebook and wondered how she'd managed to take any notes. She had no recollection of what the teacher had said. The class had ended, and people were scrambling to collect their belongings and exit the classroom as if it were on fire. Lydia, typically atypical, was putting her belongings together slowly. They usually did a bit of shopping and then had lunch on class days. Jean didn't know if she could bear it today, but the idea of going home to Richard was even less attractive.

They walked in silence to the parking lot, and Lydia turned to her. "Let's take my car. You're too shook up to drive." Jean acquiesced with a nod and got into the passenger seat.

"Are you going to tell me, or are you going to make me beg?" The silence stretched as Jean tried to decide what was appropriate. The tears were welling up again, and as they began to spill over, she gave up trying to hold it all back.

"I had a shock today..."

28

"What sort of shock?"

"I found out Richard is into porn on the computer." Even though it was true, it didn't feel right telling anyone else. She didn't want sympathy. She just wanted to understand. Or maybe just get past it.

"Is that all? I thought maybe he was having an affair. I could tell you were really upset, but I knew it wasn't storm damage. You would have told me about that right off."

"I *am* really upset. It's bad enough we don't have a close relationship, but I don't like the idea of porn on our computer. It's disgusting. I would never have guessed he would do that." Jean bit her lower lip, wishing she hadn't said so much, but she knew Lydia wouldn't gossip. "I don't know what to do. I asked him not to do it anymore. He's an educated man. Why would he have to wallow in dirt like that? And what does it say about our marriage?"

"How did you discover this? Surely, he wasn't doing it in front of you?"

"Of course not. It was pure coincidence. There was an article in the paper today about clearing the browser history on your computer. I'm trying to become more savvy about it, and so I went and found what the History was...it shows what sites you've visited. And you can clear the record, but I never even knew about it. And Richard obviously didn't, either, because there were a bunch of porn sites listed. He's been visiting them frequently. I was stunned. I couldn't imagine him doing that. In fact, he never gave me the impression he knows much about the computer. When I confronted him, he acted guilty and ashamed. I asked him to stop doing it, and he promised that he would."

"So you believe he'll quit?" Lydia's tone implied she wouldn't make that assumption.

"Why would I mistrust him when he gave me his word? He knows I can forgive him this time, but lying to me would be unforgivable. We may not be that close anymore, but I can't imagine he'd lie to me."

Lydia reached over and patted her arm. "I hope you're right, honey. If he values you, he won't lie. I hope he realizes how lucky he is that you're forgiving him."

"It's not so much that I'm forgiving him. It's just that I don't want to dwell on what's wrong, and I'm hoping we can put things right. But I have to admit, I didn't have the nerve to ask him *why* he did it; how long he's been doing it; or whether it had anything to do with our marriage." She paused and shook her head as if trying to clear it. "Maybe I'm a fool. I was afraid to ask, I guess. And now I'm thinking I missed the opportunity." She put her hands over her face and started sobbing.

"Come on, Jean, honey. I'm taking you to an early lunch at the Mexican place. Double frozen margaritas for us both! You can't solve all the problems of life in one morning."

That's what Jean loved about Lydia. She always put things in perspective. They'd only known each other a few months, and they were so different, yet they were like sisters.

"Thanks, Lyd. I don't know what I'd do without you. I need to clear my head and not think about this." She let the cool air flow over her face as they trundled down the road to the restaurant.

After lunch, Lydia dropped Jean back at her car and she drove home, feeling much better for the companionship and compassion. But pulling into her garage in the stifling heat, she felt depression descend again, enervating her.

She was relieved to find the house empty. Richard's golf cart was in the garage, so a friend must have picked him up, or else he'd gone for a walk. There was no note saying where he was or when he'd be back. She wished he'd go away and never come back, then felt awful for having thought it. Her life had suddenly gotten so complicated. She wanted it to be as it was before. No conflicts. No fights. The freedom to learn new things.

Hoping to find a bit of peace, she poured herself a glass of cold, white wine and sat in the living room staring at the TV, even though it was off. Minutes or hours passed, she wasn't sure which. The glass was empty, and she couldn't find the energy to get up and refill it. It disturbed her to realize that when he came home, she wouldn't demand that they discuss what happened. She found she had somehow decided to give him a second chance, and so she would. They'd go on and try to get past this.

Tears welled in her eyes. She wasn't sure she could stand it, but it seemed the only choice. She heard the front door unlock and swiped her hands across her eyes. She didn't want Richard to see her crying.

* * *

Helen, 11:47am

HELEN OPENED ONE EYE, then the other, pushing through the pounding headache. The light peeking out around the edges of the curtains told her it was broad daylight. Turning over gingerly to check the bedside clock, she confirmed it was nearly noon. That wasn't nearly as big a surprise as her state of undress. She was lying naked on top of the covers, and that scared her. She always wore something to bed, but then, she didn't remember coming to bed last night. As her mind cast about for answers, panic seeped in. What had she done? She really couldn't remember.

Sheba lay sleeping soundly in her usual spot, and Helen reached over and petted her, trying to ground herself in normal reality. Sheba immediately began to purr loudly, which was very soothing to her frazzled nerves. Too bad she couldn't ask Sheba what had happened last night.

Finally she recalled that it was Saturday. Had Warren called, and she didn't even hear the phone ringing? She clutched her hands to her aching head. It just got worse and worse.

Taking care not to move too fast, she reached for the clothes that were strewn haphazardly across the foot of the bed, continuing to dig deep into her memory for what had happened last night. She remembered sitting and drinking a few glasses of wine with her movie as usual, but after that, it became a blank.

The best thing to do would be to get a shower and take a couple Tylenol. She pushed the crumpled clothes aside, got up and walked unsteadily into the bathroom. The shower washed away some of the bad feelings, brushing her teeth took the terrible taste out of her mouth and the Tylenol soon began to dim the headache. But she still couldn't remember last night, and that scared her.

After dressing in clean clothes, she went into the kitchen, followed by Sheba, who was protesting that it was way past feeding time. The meowing was hurtful in more ways than one, and she barked at Sheba. "Quit fussing. I'm moving as fast as I can!" She immediately felt guilty for being so unpleasant and bent down to pet Sheba in apology, but regretted it as a drumbeat hammered her fragile head.

She gingerly righted herself and turned towards the counter. A brief stab of paranoia and fear shot through her, but she quickly suppressed it. Of course no one had come into the house. She had the only key. So who had brought in those groceries that were lying on the counter? She picked up the tin of smoked oysters, then looked at the box of crackers that lay open on the counter, one sleeve partially empty with crumbs lying about. Turning towards the refrigerator, she opened the door and got slapped with shock again. The refrigerator was full. There were eggs, bacon, orange juice, meats and veggies. It was almost as if the good fairy had come and filled her fridge.

Not feeling like eating anything, she poured herself a large glass of orange juice and greedily drank it. Then she refilled it and set it on the counter, pausing long enough to feed Sheba. She grabbed the glass and went out to her spot on the patio, sinking into the chair. She'd forgotten to check the message machine. Oh well, she could do that later.

As she sipped her juice, she tried to reconstruct the previous evening. Try as she might, she couldn't remember a thing after the movie. She'd taken to drinking Sangria. It was cheap and tasty with ice, almost like drinking fruit juice. She never drank before 11am, and almost never drank much before 5 or 6pm. Most nights, it was 3 glasses of Sangria with a movie, then to bed. But yesterday, she'd had a glass at lunchtime...though no lunch; she hadn't been hungry (again). Then she had started drinking earlier than usual. By movie time, she was hungry, but there wasn't anything to eat (as usual). She remembered that much. She had watched the movie, but after that, it was blank.

Shame washed over her. She couldn't deny her drinking was a problem anymore. What was wrong with her? She'd never been a big drinker, and now she was acting like a lush. She finished her orange juice. Her head was still throbbing slightly, but she did feel somewhat stronger and more balanced. She got up and went into the house to check the message machine. She had one message. Punching the button, she listened to Warren's brief message. She'd call him later on when she felt better.

As she turned away from the machine, her gaze fell on the part of the living room she could see through the kitchen doorway. Her handbag and keys were sitting on the chair nearest the door to the garage. That's not where she usually left them.

It was all coming back to her now. She had been hungry for a snack, and she was frustrated there wasn't anything to eat, so she'd gone to the grocery store and stocked up...way more than she had intended. Now she had all the staples she could ask for and plenty of nice snacks, too. The problem was, she had no recollection, even now, of having gone to the store. She must have driven there in a drunken haze.

She was stunned and guilt-ridden. One thing she was sure of: she had to make a change, and she had to make it now. She'd also have to make sure she hadn't overdrawn her checking account; it was perilously low. Funny how her money fears, which had loomed so large, were now dwarfed by her concerns about the drinking. She stood there, shaking a bit with the realization that she could have killed herself or someone else.

The doorbell rang, adding another dissonant note to her day. *Who could that be?* She moved as fast as she dared towards the door to stop whoever it was from ringing the bell again. Not bothering to peer through the spy hole, she threw the door open with uncharacteristic carelessness.

A man stood framed in the door. He wasn't young, but he was tall and well-built. Very handsome in a Nordic way with his thinning gray-blonde hair and blue eyes. Obviously a Posse member, as he wore the uniform of the volunteer security personnel of Palm Lakes.

He held his ID up to the screen door. "Good afternoon, Mrs. Mueller. It is Mrs. Mueller, isn't it? I'm Red Johnson, with the Posse. Would it be possible for me to interview you about an incident that's been reported to us?"

Panic stabbed her in the chest, but she labored to hide it. "Certainly, Mr. Johnson. Yes, I'm Helen Mueller. I'll unlock the door." She reached for the key to the screen door which hung on a hook a couple feet from the door. Fortunately, it was out of his view, or he'd have seen how clumsy she was as she made two grabs for it. Could it be a mere coincidence for him to show up today? If only she could remember what had happened last night.

Unlocking the door with greater than usual deliberation, she ushered him in. "Would you like something to drink? Coffee? Tea? Water?" She was so nervous, she didn't know what to do. Even if he had come any other day, she'd still be nervous; she wasn't comfortable around strange men, especially big ones like this guy.

"Thanks, ma'am, but I'm fine. I just have a few questions to ask you." His voice was courteous and unthreatening, but she still couldn't calm down.

She preceded him into the living room and pointed him to a chair. Thank heaven the room was clean and tidy. It never got used, so aside from a bit of inevitable dust, it was fine for company. After he sat in the wing chair, she perched on the sofa, gathering her wits about her. "What can I help with, Mr. Johnson? Is everything okay in the neighborhood? I hope everyone is all right." Could he hear the guilt in her voice?

"Well, Mrs. Mueller, that was quite a storm last night, wasn't it?"

She tightened with fear at the non sequitur. Why was he asking that? She had no recollection of last night, including a storm. Her eyes darted left and right, and then she responded, "I haven't been out today or read the paper."

"Wow, you must be a heavy sleeper. There are trees down all over, even big ones. Parts of rooftops are torn off. Your neighbor down the street lost his tree. It's the biggest storm they've had in some years."

He looked searchingly at her, and she belatedly realized he was just making small talk. "I'm sorry; I'm just preoccupied today." She smiled weakly at him, hoping that would be enough.

"You're probably wondering why I'm here. I'm collecting information about a missing cat. Mrs. Blackstone's cat, to be exact; the one that went missing in late July. It's taken us a while to get around to it, but we'd like to see if we can give any closure to Mrs. Blackstone. Can you tell me anything that might help?"

Blessed relief washed over her. "Oh, dear, no. I know Fluffy went missing, but I guess we all assumed a coyote got her. Barbara told me the day after she disappeared. Coyotes seem to be a real hazard to pets here. I wish people wouldn't let their animals run loose...oh, please don't tell Barbara I said that. I'm not like Owen, all upset about Fluffy peeing in my yard." She had her wits about her enough to see his eyebrows shoot up when she mentioned Owen and immediately regretted it but pressed on. "I like animals. I have a cat of my own. I really never minded Fluffy coming into my yard. But I did always worry about her getting eaten by the coyotes or maybe getting hit by a car."

The officer wrote in his small notepad, then his blue eyes locked on her. "One reason we're following up on this lost cat is that there have been issues about it in the past. Your neighbor Owen Schmidt filed a complaint with the Homeowners' Association that Mrs. Blackstone's cat was running free, which is not only a violation of the law but against the covenants of Palm Lakes. This happened some months ago."

Uncomfortable with his scrutiny, she looked down. "Yes, Barbara told me that Owen was upset about Fluffy. She said he'd reported her to the HOA; that he had yelled at her once or twice about Fluffy before that."

"Yes, that's what I'm hearing from your neighbors. While it's most likely the cat was killed by predators, we have to rule out other causes. Would you have any reason to believe it could be anything else?"

She answered without even considering the ridiculous implication. "No. Of course not. I know Owen was upset, but I can't imagine he'd harm Fluffy...are you suggesting that?"

"No, ma'am. We just want to see if there's any reason to suspect foul play since there were obviously some bad feelings." He flashed her a Dennis Quaid smile with lots of wattage, and she felt herself relaxing.

Bringing her focus back, she suddenly remembered seeing Fluffy go into Owen's yard that morning long ago. When had Fluffy gone missing? It was just after that, wasn't it? But would it be fair to Owen to even mention that? She hesitated, wondering what she should do.

"Mrs. Mueller, did you remember something that might help my investigation?"

My, he is observant. "I'm not sure. I'm not convinced it will help, and I don't want to cause problems by saying something that might be meaningless."

He leaned forward a bit on the chair, obviously eager to hear what she had to say. "I respect your concern for keeping peace among the neighbors. But let me be the one to decide what's important. What you say will be kept confidential."

She took a deep breath and let it out. "OK. I remember the last time I saw Fluffy. It was a morning in late July, just before she disappeared. I was out on my patio, and I was enjoying looking around, and I saw her walk into Owen's yard. I remember thinking that he wouldn't be happy if he saw her because he had complained about her a number of times, not only to Barbara but to the HOA. I was wondering why Barbara let her loose. I even considered calling her, but I told myself, she must have let the cat out, and I didn't want to add to the judgment Owen had put on her. Now I'm wishing I had called her."

"It's not your fault, Mrs. Mueller. We don't know at this point what happened to the cat. We only know it disappeared after July 22nd. We're interviewing the neighbors to see if anyone saw the cat after that. So far, you seem to be the last person to see her alive."

"Have you learned anything from the other neighbors?"

"Not yet, but I still have some to interview."

"I imagine this is a pretty tame subject to be working on."

"I'd rather be doing this than investigating a homicide. Which is what I used to do." His disarming, boyish grin must be a deliberate attempt to soothe her into telling him everything he wanted to know. Well, it had worked.

She stood up in an attempt to end the interview. "I don't expect Fluffy will be found, and I feel bad for her and Barbara, but I suppose it was coyotes. They are everywhere, as you know. I wish people understood how dangerous they are."

He rose as she did, seemingly content with what she had told him. "You and me both. I've taken enough of your time. If you think of anything, here's my card. Just give me a call."

"Thanks, but I doubt I'll have anything to add. Good luck in the search. And thanks for helping." Locking the doors after he left, she went back into the kitchen and sank into a chair, exhausted from the feeling of having had a near miss.

By evening the hangover was largely gone and she was hungry for the first time in ages. For a change, there were all kinds of wonderful foods to work with. She fried up some bacon, then sautéed sliced shallots in the bacon grease and sliced an apple and put a couple pieces of chicken in the iron skillet with all the ingredients, threw in a few sprigs of thyme and put it all in the oven to roast. While it cooked, she mixed up a salad of greens, cucumber and tomatoes with some chopped fresh basil. She set the balsamic vinegar and olive oil out and went into her office to write in her journal while her dinner cooked.

Saturday, August 12, 1995

I lost some time last night. It wouldn't be so bad if I'd stayed home, but I went out to the grocery store when I was drunk. I've never been more ashamed in my life. The only good part is it appears no harm was done. Someone must have been watching over me. Even though the Posse guy showed up today, it wasn't to tell me I'd sideswiped a car or hit a pedestrian.

I guess the drinking started because I don't like being alone. The wine helped me sleep, kept me from listening to strange house noises or brooding in the middle of the night. But there must be other ways of getting a good night's sleep.

I commit to drinking responsibly from now on and spending time resolving how and where I'm going to live. And while I'm at it, I'm going to participate in some activities and accept invitations. I'm going to be so busy I won't feel alone anymore. The first class I'm going to take is the cooking class that starts next month. Maybe that will inspire me to eat more regularly.

Still weighed down by shame, she found she couldn't write any more. But at least she'd made a promise to herself that she'd make changes, and she was determined to keep that vow.

Later, after enjoying dinner for the first time in weeks, she watched a movie and had no inclination to drink wine. It was a start.

* * *

Red, 12:25pm

RED WALKED BACK to his cruiser, plowing through the hazy heat. The monsoon was well under way, and the humidity was up to 45%. He chuckled to himself. Forty-five percent wasn't that much, but it sure felt like it in the desert. As he slid into the broiling hot seat, he was grateful he had his uniform pants on instead of the shorts he wore when he was off duty. The reflectors he put in the window did little to make the car habitable, but they did keep the steering wheel from giving him third degree burns.

He reached into the small cooler for a bottle of water. Coffee was his nonalcoholic drink of choice, but in this weather, he had to have water in the afternoons. He drained the bottle while pondering the progress on this 'case.' Hardly worth being called a case, but at least it provided some variety from the petty thefts he usually dealt with, most of them because residents forgot to put their garage doors down. Plus, it was less stressful to be looking for a lost pet than an elderly person who wandered off due to Alzheimer's. In any case, it beat his old job as a homicide detective for low stress.

He took the micro-recorder out of his pocket so he could add his impressions from the interview. Old habits die hard, and he was meticulous about laying the groundwork in a case, rent-a-cop or not. "Mrs. Mueller seems to be a contradiction. She has an unusual innocence and youth about her, but she was hiding something. I'm sure of it. It may not be related to the lost cat; she smelled of alcohol under the soap and perfume. She may still be grieving; her neighbor told me she's a recent widow. Her deer-in-the-headlights look and the way she twisted her pants leg while she talked made her look anxious, if not suspicious. Maybe I'm reading too much into it. She doesn't seem the type to kill a cat. I know I tend to read too much into things when I'm bored, and let's face it, this job may be low stress, but it's boring."

He paused for a few seconds, thinking about the pretty woman's apparent fear of her neighbor. "She was concerned about Mr. Schmidt. She's scared of him. She didn't want it getting back to him that she saw the cat in his yard. So far, it appears she was the last person to see the cat alive. That isn't good for Schmidt. And she's far more credible as a witness than her neighbor Tanya Cooper." That, and she was far better looking than Tanya. Helen had the aura of a delicate flower, albeit one that hinted at having steel underneath.

Tanya, on the other hand, was brass on the outside and who knew what on the inside? When he'd knocked on her door at 9:30 this morning, she'd greeted him in a flimsy negligee with a drink in hand, leering at him. Boy did she have a rack on her! She reminded him so much of his second ex that he'd almost been afraid to go into the house. But he managed to ask his questions and escape unscathed.

It was obvious that Tanya had a thing for Owen Schmidt, the way she defended him when he mentioned the shouting match about the cat.

Maybe she was even sleeping with him. Palm Lakes was a desert version of Peyton Place, just with older players. People never ceased to amaze him. It didn't matter how old they got; they didn't get any smarter.

He sighed and pocketed the recorder. Retiring here had been a great idea, no matter what. Divorced three times, he could only afford a small condo, but he had golfing privileges and his Posse job kept him busy, if not entertained or challenged. Life was good, but sometimes he missed the chase. He'd been really good as a cop; lots of bad guys were locked up thanks to him. If only he'd been better at marriage. All three of his exes had the same complaint: he put work before them, working too many hours. Maybe if he'd hated his job, he'd still be married.

Tossing the empty plastic bottle into the small garbage bag that hung from the dashboard, he got out of the car and walked down to Owen Schmidt's house. This would be the most interesting interview for sure. Everyone he had talked to had mentioned that Owen didn't like the cat, and now the cat was missing and presumed dead. No one had anything bad to say about him, but no one had anything good to say, either; well, except for Tanya, and she didn't count. Was it a coincidence that the cat went missing? Or did Owen disappear the cat? He didn't really believe in coincidences, but he tried to keep an open mind.

He pressed the doorbell and waited for Schmidt to answer. The heat had accumulated in the southwest-facing alcove. His shirt was actually sticking to his back from the sweat.

The door opened to reveal a short, well-muscled man with thinning dark hair and brown eyes. He was obviously surprised to see Red, and a look of irritation flitted across his face before he could suppress it. "Can I help you, Officer?"

"Hi, I'm Red Johnson and I'm here to talk with Owen Schmidt. Is that you? I have a few questions."

"What's this about? Is everything all right?" For some reason, even though everyone asked him that question, it sounded different when Schmidt asked it, a bit too light, but at the same time concerned. Schmidt scanned the road outside as if he were waiting for someone.

Red asked, "Too bad about your tree. That was a hell of a storm last night."

Schmidt snorted briefly. "You got that right."

"I have a few routine questions I'm asking all the neighbors if you have time to answer them. I'd appreciate it, so I don't have to come back later." He didn't reveal further details. It sometimes was helpful to let subjects fill in the blanks on their own. This time, nothing happened, in spite of an awkward silence of ten seconds that seemed like years.

"Come on in, Officer. Get out of the heat." Schmidt finally opened the door and stepped back so Red could enter. It was amazing how cold 74 degrees felt when it was 110 outside. He never got over the contrast. With the sweat standing on his skin, it actually felt unpleasantly cold. He shrugged it off and followed the man into an impossibly clean living room. He thought *he* was a neat freak, but Schmidt had him outdone by a mile. He noticed CDs on the shelf by the stereo were arranged alphabetically, and there wasn't a speck of dust anywhere. Impressive. Maybe even pathological.

His short host sat in a recliner and watched with a hooded look as Red sat on the sofa and pulled out his notebook. It didn't escape Red's attention that he hadn't been offered any refreshments. Schmidt was at least a hostile witness, if not a perp. "I've been asking all the neighbors about a cat that was reported missing last month. Have you seen any cats wandering around lately?"

Schmidt appeared to be thinking. Finally, he spoke. "Well, I'm sure you know about the problem I had with my neighbor next door about her cat. In fact, both her pets are a nuisance. She lets them run free, and that's against the law, isn't it? There's a leash law in this county, right?"

"That is correct, Mr. Schmidt, but I'm not here to argue about whether it's legal for the cat to be running free. I just want to know if you have any information that might help us solve its disappearance. Do you remember how it looked?"

"Of course, it wasn't that long ago I saw it, but it was before the cat went missing. Barbara called me a couple days after and asked if I'd seen it. Must have been near the end of July." Schmidt's left bicep was twitching, and his mouth was clenched in a tight line that dipped down on the left side. No wonder Mrs. Mueller was scared of him. He was short, but his body said he pumped iron. He looked tightly wound and ready to explode.

Nodding and taking notes, Red continued, "Would you mind telling me the sequence of events leading to your altercation with Mrs. Blackstone about the cat?"

"I wouldn't call it an altercation exactly." Owen Schmidt's right hand reached up and swept back through his thinning hair in denial or exasperation. Maybe both.

Time to press him for details. "Well, Mrs. Blackstone said you raised your voice to her and threatened her about the cat messing in your yard. Do you deny that?"

Schmidt blinked, got up and went into the kitchen that bordered the living room. He got himself a glass of water, came back and sat down without offering Red anything. "I wouldn't say I threatened her. I told her I'd report her to the HOA because she was in violation of the covenants. I did report her the next time the cat came into my yard. But they didn't do anything besides tell her not to let the cat loose." He put his glass down and spread his hands apart as if asking what he could do. "She tried to tell me that she couldn't afford a fence, and the cat was used to roaming her property back wherever the hell she came from, and that she'd try to contain it, but she never did." He finished by clenching his jaw in a grimace.

Red gave him his complete attention. "When did you report her to the HOA?"

"A few months ago; I can't remember exactly. They keep records, don't they? Why don't you ask them?" The man's eyes dodged left and right, often a sign of prevarication or deflection.

Now was the time to apply even more pressure. "I'll do that, Mr. Schmidt. How did you feel about the cat continuing to roam free?" Red kept his voice light and smiled, hoping to disarm Schmidt or to trigger an outburst. Either one could help the case.

Schmidt paused and squirmed a bit. "No matter what I say, now that the cat is gone, it will look bad. Everyone knows I didn't like the cat coming into my yard and messing my property. But that doesn't mean I did anything to the cat. Probably a coyote got it. They're all over the place. The golf course is just a few blocks that way."

It was a reasonable assumption about the coyote, one that anyone would make, and the proximity to the golf course made it more likely. But Red wasn't buying it. Schmidt was hiding something. The question was, was he hiding something about the cat, or was he hiding something else, like Helen Mueller? Everyone had their secrets.

Red's cop antennae were tingling. Could he have killed the cat and disposed of its body? Anything was possible. But this late, it wouldn't be easy to find clues, and no one would bother with a search warrant without probable cause (especially for a missing cat), and pushing for that might make things worse between Schmidt and the neighbor lady.

"Well, that does it for me, Mr. Schmidt. Thanks for sharing your impressions. If you think of anything else, here's my card. Give me a call anytime." Holding the card like it was about to give him Ebola, Schmidt walked Red out to the door and sent him on his way.

Red sat in the car trying to put the pieces of the puzzle together. The timing of the complaints and the disappearance of the cat were circumstantial but highly suspicious. He took out his recorder. "Owen Schmidt appears to be a very fit individual who is repressing a lot of anger. While he has a right to be annoyed at his neighbor's unwillingness to keep her cat at home, he seems, in general, to be angrier than that alone would explain. He was also quite guarded when I interviewed him. Though many people are nervous when questioned by cops, it just felt wrong. His house was too clean. He doesn't have a wife, so it must be his preference to keep it so neat and tidy. I don't like him. He could have done it." He put the recorder away and looked at his watch. His shift was over in ninety minutes.

Sitting in the stuffy car, Red was already thinking of that first glass of scotch. The sound of the ice cubes dropping into the glass. The peaty taste. The air-conditioning cranked. Some Domino's pizza. A game he'd taped on the VCR. He had a nice evening ahead of him. He'd spend the rest of his shift cruising, letting the details of the case ferment in his mind. His intuition told him Schmidt bore watching, but gut feelings weren't enough. He needed some facts. And he knew just how he was going to get them.

After arriving home, he placed a call to an old friend at the Bureau. "Henry, how the hell are you? It's Red...Red Johnson."

"Why you old devil, what's up? I thought you'd retired."

Red laughed. "I did, but I'm doing a gig with the community patrol, and I have a favor to ask."

"Damn it, Red, you know the FBI doesn't do that kind of favor."

"I realize that, Henry, but we go back a long way. I could remind you of that case in '85."

"Don't you dare, you bastard! OK, what do you need?"

"I just want to check the background and record of a resident here. He gives me a bad vibe, but I have nothing on him and no access to records at this stage. If I give you a name and address, can you get back to me with information?"

"Sure, give me the details. I'll get back to you next week with what I can find. Just don't make a habit of this."

Later on, Red relaxed with his scotch. This investigation was stalled, but now that Schmidt was on his radar, he'd be swinging through his neighborhood more often. He didn't expect to find anything, but you never knew what following your intuition would lead to. And Henry might come up with something interesting to support or discount his feelings. Who knew where it would lead? Suddenly, retirement had just become a lot more interesting.

CHAPTER THREE

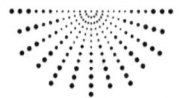

SATURDAY, AUGUST 19, 1995

Mary Beth, 10:35am

*D*ressing quickly in the clothes she had discarded the night before, Mary Beth stumbled into the bathroom and prepared herself to face another day. She looked in the mirror and winced. It was obvious that she'd put on weight since the divorce. She'd never been thin, but then again, she'd never been fat. The extra weight aged her, not that it mattered much in Palm Lakes, where everyone was older than she was. Her thick dark hair hadn't been cut in a couple of months due to lack of funds. Her green eyes, always her best feature, had bags under them. "You look like shit, girl."

She went and turned the water on in the shower, discarding her clothes in the hamper. At times like this, she was glad her mother set the thermostat at 85 degrees. It made sleeping a bitch, but when she stepped out of the shower wet, it felt like the beach on a summer's day.

Trying to ignore her craving for a cigarette, Mary Beth stepped into the shower and began to wash away the sweat from another night of tossing and turning. She'd been a strange combination of restless and stuck ever since Jason had divorced her, starting a domino effect that had demolished her life.

Mom cautioned her through the closed door, "Mary Beth, don't use up all the hot water. I have to wash clothes."

"Okay, Mom." No doubt her mother was annoyed at her staying in bed until 10:30. Mom was always up at 5am doing something like cleaning or cooking.

Pursued by ever-present Catholic guilt, she hurried through her shower, then went back to her small bedroom. She could hear Mom vacuuming the living room. It was a wonder there was any carpet left.

This is what her life boiled down to...living with her mother in a 2-bedroom condo that was way too small for both of them. Her tiny room consisted of a twin bed and a dresser, but this was her only option after losing her job. It was like as her worth shrank, her world shrank. Now she was living in borrowed space, begrudged borrowed space at that. Dressing quickly, she steeled herself for her mother's verbal assault and went out to the kitchen. As she passed the living room, Mom paused the vacuum and said, "So you're finally up, lazy head?"

"Yeah, Mom. I'm up. Just going to grab some breakfast."

"It's almost lunch time. When are you going to get on a regular schedule?"

"Shit, Mom, I don't know. Give me a break."

"Watch your mouth, Mary Beth."

"Yeah, Mom. Sure..." Mary Beth rooted around the sparkling kitchen and found some cereal and milk, and there was even a cup of coffee left in the pot Mom had made earlier. After she finished her meal, she put the dishes in the dishwasher. Her lower back was killing her, but she hated to take the pills. It had been years since the accident, and it seemed her back was getting worse, not better.

"What do you have planned today, Mary Beth?" There was a challenge in her mother's voice as she stood in the kitchen doorway holding a dust cloth.

"Not much, Mom." Mary Beth knew what was coming next. *Jesus, I've got to get out of here. She's driving me batshit crazy.*

"When are you going to *do* something with yourself? You can't sit around eating me out of house and home forever! I can't afford to support you."

45

"I know that, Mom. I've only been here a couple of weeks. I've contributed what I can. I didn't get much except debt in the divorce."

"Just about what I'd expect. That no-account Jason dumped you and ran off with another woman. Of course, he wouldn't live up to his obligations. Why didn't you fight for more?" Sighing, Mom sat in the chair nearest her, apparently breathless from her outburst.

"Mom, I've told you over and over. I didn't want alimony, and all we really had together was debt. If I had pressed for alimony, he might have been able to prove that my job paid more than his business, and he could have sued *me* for alimony." She looked at her mother, pleading for understanding, then sighed. "I wasn't thinking straight at the time, but I still feel it was right. I needed a complete break from him." She'd never admit it, but lately, she'd been wondering if she should have fought for more.

"He wasn't supporting you like a real man, and then he goes off and gets some woman half your age pregnant? How could you let that happen?"

"Jesus, Mom, I trusted him. I thought we were happy. Sure, we had to struggle, but we didn't fight."

"I've asked you not to talk like that!" Before Mary Beth could reply, she raged on. "Your living here is in violation of the covenants, and if anyone reports me, I could get into trouble. You aren't supposed to be here for longer than a vacation. You don't meet the age requirements."

"Damn it, Mom, I am aware of that. Where do you want me to go? The divorce left me nothing, and I lost my job. I need to start over. I need a chance to get myself together."

"Then do it. Quit sitting around feeling sorry for yourself."

"I'm not feeling sorry for myself." Mary Beth swallowed the obvious lie. Of course, she was feeling sorry for herself.

"So your rotten husband left you for someone younger. It happens all the time. Why are you unwilling to move on?"

"I want to move on, Mom. But the divorce wiped me out financially. Now I have to start over. Give me some time, for Christ's sake. I won't stay forever."

"Don't take the Lord's name in vain! I'm trying to tell you that you *can't* stay forever, even if you wanted to. I can't violate the covenants, and besides, this place is too small for both of us."

"You got that right," mumbled Mary Beth.

Back in her bedroom with the door closed, Mary Beth took stock of things. She really didn't want to be here at all. But she had no job, no money and no prospect of income for the future. Her meager savings were nearly gone.

She was 45, had good job skills, but didn't know how to start over. Her back had been giving her more trouble over the years, and the pills only helped so much. She feared becoming addicted to them. She knew she was eating to fill the hole the divorce made, and her self-judgment at gaining ten pounds in the past few weeks only weighed her down further. If she gained more, she wouldn't fit into her clothes, and she couldn't afford new ones. To top it off, she was smoking more than ever.

Every time she thought about starting over, all she could see was a blank wall. It was as if her future were empty, which was how she felt these days. What had she done with her life? All she knew was that she couldn't stay here without making some changes, and she didn't know where to begin.

Mom knocked on her door. "Can I come in and clean your room now? I have other things I need to do soon."

"Sure, come in, Mom. I'll go into the living room." Mary Beth slunk out and settled herself on the couch. Everything smelled faintly of lemon furniture polish. There was no dust on any surface, a real accomplishment in the desert. She didn't know how Mom managed. She just knew she couldn't.

Mom was so different from Dad. Too bad he was gone. He was the one who had loved her unconditionally. If Dad were still around, things would be different. She wouldn't be criticized daily for the failure of her marriage or her lack of plans for the future. But Dad was gone, and this was the life she had. At least it was better than being homeless.

An idea came to her, and she yelled to the back of the condo, "Mom, do I have privileges at the exercise classes here?"

"I could get you a card, but it costs money. Can you contribute anything?"

"I don't have much money. I guess I'll wait. I was thinking of doing an exercise class or something to get fit."

"I think it's a good idea you want to lose weight. You've put weight on sitting around here all day feeling sorry for yourself. But you only need to quit eating so much if you want to lose weight. You don't have to join a class. Or maybe you could go out walking. Lots of people do that here."

Mary Beth considered the walking idea. It annoyed her to agree with her mother, but walking had its attraction. It would get her out of the house and help her get in shape.

Mom appeared in the doorway to the hall. "Walking is a good idea, but what are your plans for the future?" Her voice had taken on the lecturing tone again, and it grated on Mary Beth's nerves.

"How the fuck should I know?" she barked.

Mom's finger was pointed at her like a gun. "Mind your manners, or I'll have to wash your mouth out with soap. And don't think you're too old for me to do that."

"Really, Mom. Get a grip. I try to live by your rules, but you don't cut me any slack. I'm tired of being treated like a loser. And I'm not a teenager anymore. I'm an adult." She couldn't hide the whine in her voice, and she hated it.

"Maybe you feel that way because you *are* a loser. Have you considered that? You lost your marriage and your job and managed to walk away with nothing. Now you're coming back here looking to me, an old woman on a fixed income, to support you? Is that what you call normal?"

Mary Beth didn't answer. It was the same old argument day in and day out. She was too depressed to deal with it. She slouched out of the house and into the bright sunshine. As the door clicked shut behind her, she heard her mother's continuing protests and felt a great relief to be away from her, even if only for a little while.

It wasn't quite the hottest part of the year according to the weatherman, but you couldn't prove it by Mary Beth. Today it was going to be about 110 degrees. She probably should have taken a hat, but she just couldn't face her mother right now. To hell with it. So what if she got sunburn. The sun blazed in a clear blue sky that held no promise of monsoon rain. There was no breeze, and the street was as empty as the world after nuclear armageddon.

None of the sounds Mary Beth associated with summer could be heard. No cicadas. No lawn mowers. No children shrieking as they played in their yards or marauded up and down the sidewalks with skateboards and bikes. The covenants were the foundation of both the appeal and the emptiness of this place. No one under 55 could live here unless married to someone 55 or older. You rarely saw children, because children under 19 were not allowed to live here. She couldn't imagine getting used to this degree of silence. It was deathlike. Yet Mom loved it, as apparently did the other residents.

Mary Beth started walking aimlessly and ended up along the golf course, looking across the neatly groomed grass, seeing the golfers skim by in their carts, chasing their little white balls hither and yon. She had never understood the appeal of golf. But it sure made for lovely open spaces. Only along the golf course could you be guaranteed a view of the distant mountains. The palm trees that gave the development its name surrounded a large manmade oasis. She headed for a bench at the edge of the lake.

She sat for some time watching the pair of swans swimming to and fro like they owned the lake. She stared across the sun-dappled water at the mountains as the small fountain in the center of the lake stabbed into the sharp brilliance of the summer sky. A slight breeze wafted an occasional bit of mist from the fountain her way.

A family of quail crossed the grass in the distance, single file with an adult at the head and tail of the queue. The young ones were nearly full grown now. A plane flew over, shattering the harmony of the scene, and she found the energy to stand up and leave the lakeside.

The grocery store wasn't that far; it was just outside the community. She could extend her walk by going there to pick up items for dinner. Lucky she always had her wallet in her pocket, and she had enough cash for groceries. It was about time she did some cooking. That would get Mom off her back. Well, maybe for a little while.

As she plodded towards the gated entrance of the community, she pondered what she should make for dinner. Homemade spaghetti always hit the spot for Mom. She could afford a cheap bottle of chianti to go with it.

The trek was longer than she had anticipated, having based her judgment on how short a drive it was to the store. As she crossed through the open doorway of the Safeway 25 minutes later, she flinched at the cold shock wave of air that blew into the parking lot, causing her to wonder what their electric bill was. The temperature inside, like everywhere here, was frigid. Her mother would have a word to say about them jacking their prices up so they could air-condition the outdoors. She smiled at the thought.

Covered with goosebumps and having trouble adjusting to the relatively darker interior of the store (she'd forgotten her sunglasses), Mary Beth grabbed a basket and moved through the aisles as quickly as was possible with all the retirees standing in the middle of them. Jesus Christ, she hoped she never got that feebleminded.

She filled her basket with ground meat, pasta, onions, garlic, a bunch of fresh basil and a large can of tomato puree. She considered getting rolls or bread and decided against the extra calories, then chose a cheap bottle of chianti to complement the meal. If she weren't on foot, she might have added some sherbet for dessert, but it was just as well. She needed to cut back. She grabbed a copy of the local paper. She'd been here long enough that it was time she started looking for work. Steady income would be the first step back to freedom.

The clerk rang up her purchases, and as Mary Beth exited the store, she felt as if she'd stepped into an oversized oven, a shopping bag in each hand. Son of a bitch, the wind felt like a blast from hell. She was used to hot back home, but not the extreme, dry heat of the desert. How did anyone get used to it?

The walk back felt a lot longer, probably because of the weight of the groceries. She reaffirmed her commitment to get more exercise. She was too young to be this weak and worn out.

As she neared home, Mary Beth saw the curtain move in the window of the condo across the street. The nosy neighbor was at it again. Mrs. Jameson was a widow with few outside interests other than reporting her neighbors for infractions of the covenants, or so Mom had said. It was possible that the neighbor would report her if she stayed longer than a few weeks.

She toyed with the idea of flipping her the bird but instead got off the street as fast as possible. "Mom, I'm home. I took a long walk and got the fixings for a nice spaghetti dinner. I'm cooking tonight." The silence that greeted her felt wrong. "Mom?"

She dropped the bags where she stood and rushed through the condo, checking rooms and calling, worry growing with each step. When she got back to the master bedroom, she found her mother sitting on a chair, hunched over and clutching her chest, her gray face etched with pain.

"Mom, what's wrong? Do you need a pill? Should I call 911?"

Mom looked up weakly and whispered, "No, I'll be all right. The doctor gave me some medicine. It's just worse than usual. It will pass."

The strife between them forgotten, Mary Beth knelt down next to the chair and put her arm around her mother. "Can I get you a glass of water or anything?"

Mom shook her head and leaned into Mary Beth. "Glad you're here" was all she said.

* * *

Maddie, 1:00pm

MADDIE HAD GOTTEN some work done on the tree during the cooler morning hours. Now, after lunch, the sun was high and beating down on the yard like a hammer, reminding her that she wasn't as young as she used to be. Like she needed a reminder. As she stepped into the front yard and looked at the pruning equipment she'd left under the tree, she felt bone tired.

Crunching across the red gravel, she leaned down and picked up the pruning saw. She stood back and examined the tree, walking around and looking at it from all angles. Just lifting the pruning saw made her shoulder and back ache something awful. Ignoring the pain, she sawed off a small limb. Time was, this would have been a cakewalk. Now it was an ordeal.

She regretted having the mesquite, although it was gorgeous with its spreading 15-foot canopy. A good ten feet tall, it needed frequent pruning now that it was full grown, and she had to admit she just didn't have the energy to do it. There was no way she could wield the long pruning saw required to trim the higher branches. All she could handle was a small saw for the lower ones.

She didn't want to admit defeat to Samantha. The yard work was the only thing she enjoyed doing other than making jewelry. She hated cooking and housework, always had. It seemed wrong that something she got joy from was being taken from her simply because she was getting older. Pruning this tree had become an act of rebellion, but she wondered how long her body would be able to pay the price.

While she was pausing to get her breath, a Posse vehicle drove slowly down the street. As it passed, she saw it was that nice man, what was his name?...Red, that was his name, though there wasn't a red thing about him, all tall and Swedish-looking. He smiled and waved as he drove by. Maybe he was just doing rounds. But she'd seen him a number of times since the incident with Barbara's cat. Was she only noticing him now because she knew him, or was he driving by more frequently?

Maybe it was nothing, or maybe he suspected Owen of something. Word was that Owen had it in for that missing cat. She couldn't imagine anyone harming a helpless animal. Owen never did anything objectionable that she knew of. He never socialized, and he kept his yard neat. He was quiet. All the things she had told Red were true. Owen seemed like a fine neighbor, except for the fact that he went off on Barbara about the cat. But he had a point. Barbara was violating the covenants, and he had a right to complain.

Turning back to the task at hand, Maddie raised the pruning saw yet again and ignored the pain and muscle weakness, determined to get all the way around the lower branches today before quitting and cleaning up the debris. After removing just a few larger branches, she lopped off downward pointing branchlets and focused on a slow, steady rate of progress. Sweat trickled down her face, dripping off the end of her nose. Only in monsoon season did you get enough humidity for that to happen, and it was a deeply unpleasant sensation. She'd have prickly heat under her boobs for sure before the day was out. But she kept pushing on.

A tentative touch on her shoulder sent Maddie into orbit. Was her hearing going, or had she done that thing where she blocked everything out when she was focused on something? Helen was obviously taken aback by Maddie's screech of surprise.

"I'm so sorry I disturbed you, Maddie. I didn't mean to sneak up on you. I just saw you working so hard over here and thought I'd see how you were doing. This is such a lovely tree."

Maddie wiped the sweat from her forehead with her gloved hand, put the pruning saw down and straightened up slowly. She was relieved for the interruption in spite of the shock of it. "It is a real specimen. I just don't want it blowing over like Owen's did."

"Yes, that's a real shame. A lot of trees went down in that storm. Pruning this thing is a big job. I don't know how you do it. And you're out in this sun without a hat. Don't you sunburn?"

"I'm enough in the shade of the tree, and I won't be out here much longer."

"Well, you've sure done a great job."

Maddie was uncomfortable with compliments, so she ignored it. "Your hair looks lovely, Helen, but then, it always does. Are you on your way somewhere?"

"I'll be doing a few errands soon. I just got my mail and saw you and thought I'd say hi. Is there anything I can do to help? I have time on my hands."

"No, no, I'm fine. Why don't you come inside for a minute? I want to show you my latest creation."

Helen gave her a smile. "Sure, Maddie. I'd love to see it."

The pruning forgotten, Maddie led Helen into the house and walked over to the dining room table, which was buried in jewelry-making supplies and projects, and waved Helen over to a less cluttered part where pairs of earrings lay on a white cloth. She clicked the reading light on, illuminating them.

One design was antique gold lizards hanging from French earwires with a clear crystal bead just above the lizard. They were her particular favorites. Others featured carved Zuni bears made of semi-precious stones. Still other pairs were cloisonné beads in a variety of beautiful colors.

"Oh, Maddie, they are just so beautiful!" Helen picked up and examined the different designs. "What is the occasion? Will these be birthday or Christmas gifts?"

"I just like making them. I'll be giving some to Samantha, of course. But I have lots of extras. Take a pair. Take two pairs." Helen was one of the few people, along with Samantha, whom Maddie was convinced really appreciated her jewelry.

Helen seemed reluctant to respond. "You're too kind, Maddie. You've already given me so many lovely things. I shouldn't take anymore." She hesitated, but Maddie was sure she wanted to say 'yes.'

"Nonsense. I have more than enough for everyone. Please take a pair."

Helen reached out and picked a pair of the lizard earrings, looking closely at them. "These speak to me."

"Good choice. They're really special. You know I always put them by Martin's statue after I make them. He blesses them." Maddie pointed to the nearly three-foot-high statue of a black saint which sat on a small table in the corner of the dining room, votive lamp burning in front of it. Helen followed her pointed finger and nodded without saying anything. Maddie bent her head, already immersed in ideas for new earrings, having forgotten all about the pruning out front.

"Thanks so much, Maddie. I need to run. But I'm going home and putting on these earrings right away. Give Stanley my best." Helen patted Maddie on the arm and walked to the front door, waving as she left.

* * *

Helen, 1:40pm

HELEN STROLLED across the street towards her house. She heard the garage door go up at Owen's house, and his sleek BMW slid out. She paused, letting him pass her before crossing to her side of the road. He didn't acknowledge her wave. Following his progress down the street, she noticed Tanya tottering out to her mailbox on 4-inch heels. She seemed to sway a bit, but who wouldn't, wearing those shoes? Tanya arrived at her mailbox just as Owen was passing by. She hollered out to him and waved conspicuously as if trying to flag him down, but other than the briefest pause, he didn't stop. *What was that about?*

"It's not polite to spy," she murmured to herself. She didn't know much about what went on in the neighborhood. But Barbara *was* au courant with events. She'd probably know if there was any gossip about Tanya having an affair. Funny how she was interested in what was going on in the neighborhood now that she was on her own.

Letting herself into the cool house, Helen marched to the bathroom and switched her earrings. Putting on the earrings had a magical effect, like her fairy godmother had dressed her for the ball. Maybe there *was* something to Maddie's blessing ritual, in spite of how eerily Medieval it seemed.

Fact was, she could already see the effects of better eating, more sleep and less wine. Her eyes weren't puffy or bloodshot. Her hair needed a trim, but it was shiny and thick and felt good as she dragged her fingers through it. She must have good genes, as her skin looked years younger than her age.

She went into the bedroom to put her other earrings in her jewelry box and noticed that Sheba had thrown up. Fear stabbed at her when she saw that instead of the expected hairball, it was laced with bright red blood. Sheba had lost weight recently, and she was elderly. Maybe she should take her to the vet. As if she could afford that.

The doorbell rang, dragging her attention away from her worries. Dropping her earrings on the dresser, she ran to the front door. Peering through the peephole, she saw it was Barbara. She unlocked and pushed the heavy wrought iron door open and let Barbara slip through. "How nice of you to come by! How are you doing today?"

"Same old, same old, dear. Not a whole lot going on. Just have a bit of news for you. Thought you might enjoy some company for a few minutes." They walked together into the kitchen.

"Can I get you a cup of coffee or tea?"

"That would be so nice; coffee, please. Sugar and milk or whatever you have." Barbara's beatific smile highlighted a heart-shaped face which was framed by beautifully coifed short auburn hair. She was dressed in casual elegance, as always. Helen had never seen her in worn clothes or colors that were unflattering. Her makeup was perfect, just enough to soften the age lines and allow her to pass for 10 years younger than she was. Without a speck of envy, Helen wished she could be more like Barbara.

After brewing a new pot of coffee, Helen carried the mugs over to the small kitchen table and looked at Barbara expectantly.

Murmuring thanks for the coffee, Barbara dove right into the news. "I heard from the Posse guy, what's his name? Red Johnson? Why is his name Red, anyway? He doesn't have red hair. Did he tell you why he's called Red?"

Helen smiled at the digression. "No, I didn't ask, and he didn't say. It must be a cop nickname. I bet there's a story there."

"Well, he called to apologize that they didn't have anything new to tell me about Fluffy's disappearance and that they thought she probably got taken by coyotes. It's so horrible to think that is what happened to her. He was quite thorough in his investigation. I would never have thought they'd go to that trouble for a cat. So many people told me he'd interviewed them. Not that anything came of it." Barbara paused for a minute, obviously overcome with emotion.

"I'm so sorry, Barbara. I know it's terrible. I'd be lost without Sheba. How is Jack doing?"

Barbara perked up at the change of subject. "Oh, that little rascal? He seems fine. He used to play with Fluffy, but he doesn't seem depressed without her." She paused for a second, shaking her head. "The main reason I came over was to invite you to our party next Saturday. I know you're not a party animal, but it'll be fun. A chance to see the neighbors in a happier setting than the last time we were all together. What do you think?"

"Lou and I never got out much, and I'm pretty shy in groups, but I wouldn't miss it for anything, as long as you don't mind me being a wallflower."

"You'll love it. Just don't let Bernie get anywhere near you. Once he's had a few, he turns into an octopus."

"I am forewarned. Thank you." Helen suppressed alarm and the obvious question.

Barbara flecked a bit of lint off her linen slacks, then focused dark brown eyes on Helen. "So have you had a chance to talk to Shari yet?"

Helen flinched in guilt. "No, I haven't." She contemplated not adding details but then felt an uncharacteristic need to unburden herself. "I keep going back and forth about what the best thing to do is. I want to stay here. I know that. But I've never been in charge of my life or finances, and I'm worried about making a poor choice and ending up having to cut and run after losing lots of money. I'd never hear the end of it from my kids...well, from two of them." She looked down and noticed she was twisting the fabric of her slacks. Forcing herself to stop, she looked directly at Barbara, which took more effort than she would have guessed.

Barbara took a sip of her coffee and paused as if thinking what to say. "Helen, there are no guarantees in life. Things can go either way for any of us. You have to do what feels right for you. If you think it would help, Ben is pretty good with numbers, even though he's only a doctor. I'm sure he'd be happy to look at things and offer an opinion, but in the end, it's your choice."

Something about Barbara's voice calmed Helen. "I think you're right. I'll let Ben look over things after I'm sure what I want to do. He could tell me if he sees any potential problems."

"That would seem to be a good compromise. Of course, he can't anticipate some things, but he could give you a second opinion on how it looks. That might give you some confidence."

"That would be so kind. I don't know what I'd do without you." The anxiety she'd carried around for so long drained away.

Barbara finished her coffee. "I need to run some errands now. I wanted to invite you for dinner tomorrow, but we have a commitment with some friends and won't be eating at home. Can I count on you next weekend for the party?"

"Sure, I'll be there with bells on. Let me know what to bring." Helen smiled and escorted Barbara to the front door.

In the bedroom, Sheba was fast asleep on the bed, and Helen joined her and cooed gently at her, telling her how much she loved and appreciated her. Then she cleaned up the now-dry mess, glancing around the room as she dabbed at the carpet, her eyes falling on Lou's clothes hanging in the walk-in closet. She had a sudden urge to clear it all out and went to survey the scope of the project. She could go by Goodwill when she did her errands. She felt a need to wipe all traces of him from the house.

Before she knew it, she had three large garbage bags full of clothes and shoes. Feeling like she was on a roll, she moved to the dresser. She filled another garbage bag with underwear, socks and t-shirts, then moved on to his 'junk drawer.' There were keys she had no clue about and slips of paper with cryptic notes on them, as well as his wallet (which she'd totally forgotten about). Opening the wallet, she saw it contained a stack of 20s. On counting them, she was shocked to discover they totaled $320.

She put the money on top of the dresser, relieved that this cash would pay for groceries over the next couple of months, but puzzled about the find. She felt like she was on a treasure hunt as she dug through the drawer further. She removed the odd cuff link that had no mate and a few paper clips and a comb that had seen better days. In the back of the drawer amongst bits of fluff and the odd hair, she found a bulging business-sized white envelope. Expecting some kind of document, she dragged the envelope out and opened the flap. She almost dropped the envelope in shock. There was a stack of bills in it. In a daze, she pulled the money out and flipped through it. It was a stack of crisp, new 100s. More money than she'd ever seen in one place in her life.

Her mind was filled with questions that would never be answered. Lou had been secretive, especially about money. Stranger still, he'd always acted like they were poor. How was it possible that he had so much cash lying around? She counted the bills and discovered she had a windfall of $5000. She was stunned. It wasn't enough to keep her in this house, but it would tide her over nicely while she made plans for the future. She could afford to move now, as long as she sold the house. Or, in the unlikely event she took Warren up on his offer, she had her own money she could keep to herself.

Where had this money come from? Lou had retired from an upper management position in a major hotel chain, but he'd started at the bottom and worked his way up, spending his early years as an inspector, which meant he was frequently on the road. She never quizzed him about his trips. And now it was too late.

Then it came to her. What if Lou had more secrets? What if there were other assets she was unaware of? She went back to the pile of stuff from the junk drawer and looked at the keys. Some were for luggage or belonged to things that were long gone. There were his regular keys on his chain; house, car, nothing strange there. Then she picked up a loose key that was shaped differently from the others. She had no recollection of what that was for.

She went and plopped down on the bed. It looked like a safe deposit box key, but to what bank? What was Lou hiding from her? Although part of her was hurt and even afraid at discovering this, another part felt intrigued. This was a mystery, and she was going to solve it.

Saturday, August 19, 1995

Today I found a pile of cash that Lou had hidden in a drawer. I have no clue what it was for or where it came from. I never showed much interest in our financial affairs, and maybe that was a mistake. But it never was a good idea to push Lou. I just left him alone as much as possible and hoped he'd do the same for me.

Lou obviously had secrets, but I'm not sure how to decode them. I found a key that looks like a safe deposit box key, but he never told me we had a safe deposit box. I wonder where it is and what's in it? I'll have to do some detective work to solve this mystery. I wonder if there's more cash or valuables in the box? Wouldn't that be exciting? What if it turned out I was a rich woman? Wouldn't that be a laugh?

She paused and thought about how her life would change if she found a lot of money. There would be no reason at all to consider going to live with Warren if she had financial security.

Just thinking about solving this puzzle has made me aware of how much I really want to stay in Palm Lakes. Life has turned into a big adventure, and it's getting more interesting all the time.

Sheba raked her with her paw, telling her she wanted to sit in her lap. She laid her pen down and picked Sheba up, snuggling her. "What do you suppose we're going to find in that safe deposit box, Sheba? Maybe we'll be rich!"

CHAPTER FOUR

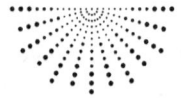

SATURDAY, AUGUST 26, 1995

Helen, 10:30am

"I'm pregnant." Sally looked directly into Helen's eyes as if challenging her to say something judgmental. Sally had arrived on the heels of a phone call the previous night. Helen had known the unexpected visit meant big news; she just hadn't expected something this big.

They sat at the breakfast table, two empty plates between them, having finished a sumptuous brunch celebrating Sally's surprise visit. The food now sat like wet cement in Helen's stomach.

Well, that explained the few extra pounds that looked so good on Sally. She'd always been rail thin and now looked perfect (at least to Helen). Her long blonde hair was caught up in a scrunchy instead of her usual braid, and she had a tan that hinted at time in the sun or maybe a tanning bed. She was always beautiful, but she looked positively radiant, in spite of the tension in her blue-gray eyes. Pregnancy suited her.

"Aren't you going to say anything, Mom?"

Now she wanted Helen to say something? Nothing Helen said would change anything. "I'm just trying to process the news. What does Rafael have to say about this? I'm assuming you didn't plan this?"

Sally frowned. "Of course, it was an accident! It's complicated. I got laid off a few weeks ago. I always made more than Rafael, and he wasn't happy with me not bringing in money. He left. Then I found out I was pregnant."

"So you haven't told him about the baby?"

"Like he'd want to come back to a pregnant, unemployed girlfriend?" Sally rolled her eyes and shook her head.

"Have you decided what you want to do?" Helen got up and started clearing off the table just to have something to do with her hands.

"I want to keep the baby." Sally held up her hands in protest as Helen opened her mouth. "I know you're going to say it's foolish. I know that a baby is a big commitment. But I want the baby."

Helen could see the sincerity in Sally's tear-filled eyes, but she wondered if she had any idea what she was in for.

"So what's next?" Helen started to rinse dishes and put them in the dishwasher.

"I was hoping I could stay with you for a while."

"You know the covenants won't allow you to stay for more than a brief visit because of your age. I'm happy for you to be here for a little while, but what are you going to do after that?"

"I thought it would be nice to live nearby. I need a clean break, and there are probably some job opportunities. I have good references and skills. I was hoping you could take care of the baby when she arrives, so I can work. We could get a place together somewhere else, since I can't live here."

Helen bit her tongue rather than ask Sally why none of her children seemed to think she might want a life of her own now that Lou was gone. Closing the door of the dishwasher and pushing the buttons to buy time, she tried to calm down and think. In the few seconds it took for her irritation to dissipate, she reflected that it would be nice to have Sally and the baby nearby. Maybe there was a way they could both have what they wanted. She screwed up her courage and turned to face Sally.

"I'd love it if you lived nearby. But I'm not leaving Palm Lakes, and I probably need to get a job myself, so what I can contribute will be limited." She took another breath and plunged on, feeling the tremor in her voice. "I'll help as best I can, but you won't be able to rely on me for regular day care. Why don't we make job- and apartment-hunting our project for the next couple of weeks? You can see how things develop and go from there."

Sally nodded slowly in affirmation, looking only a little bit disturbed. Helen was stupefied to have such quick resolution. "So when's the baby due?"

"Mid-March is what the doctor says."

"You have time to sort all this out, and I'll be here to help. Let's try to be positive. I'd like to celebrate my next grandchild. I'm going to call Barbara and see if she minds me bringing you to her party tonight. I'm sure she'll be glad to have you. You'll be the only young person there, but there will be food and drink -- wait a minute, you shouldn't drink alcohol -- but lots of good food, soft drinks and nice people. Let's go out shopping for something to wear. I haven't got a thing that's appropriate, and you could probably use a new dress. How's that?"

Sally brightened up immediately. "That would be terrific!" She jumped up and hugged Helen and then ran from the room to get ready to go shopping.

Helen let out a sigh and finished the dishes. She hoped she was up to the challenge of helping Sally without giving up on her own dreams.

* * *

Owen, 11:00am

OWEN PACED in his living room, rubbing sweaty palms on his jeans. Last time he'd seen her, Tanya had leaned over and given him an eyeful as she told him she hoped to see him at Barbara's party tonight. He never went to parties, and he wasn't used to being hit on by women. She was a drinker and a slut, yet he was strangely attracted to her. And there was something about Mother he couldn't quite place...

"Are you getting ready to do something stupid again?" Mother's shrill voice pierced the knot of confusion he was trying to unravel.

"Go away. I don't have time for you now. I'm trying to think."

"You're getting ready to do something stupid again, just like your father. Can't you use your head? Nothing good will come of going to that party."

"I have a right to make up my own mind. So shut up and leave me alone."

"Or what? What will you do if I don't? It's not like you can kill me again, Junior."

Owen pressed his hands to his temples. He had known that going to the party would upset her, but he had an itch about Tanya he wanted to scratch. He couldn't explain the attraction he felt; it shamed him and got him hot at the same time.

"What do you think that whore has in mind, Junior? She'd sleep with any man who wasn't dead. Just because she's coming on to you doesn't mean you're attractive."

"I don't need you to criticize me, Mother. You were as much a whore as Tanya is. So just let me think. I need to find out if Barbara is suspicious about her cat." The minute he said it, he knew it was a mistake.

"Of course, she is, you numbskull. You should never have killed that cat. You just don't exercise good judgment and foresight. You get that from your father. He was weak and stupid."

"So why did you marry him? Oh, yeah, let me guess. For his money. Quit distracting me."

He sighed and went into the spare bedroom, where he had his weights set up. A good workout would clear his head, and Mother never spoke to him in this room. It had never occurred to him to ask why, but it offered him much-needed peace. He stripped and put on the clean gym clothes that were neatly folded on a chair, then proceeded to do a punishing workout. By the end of it, he was sweating profusely. He loved the sensation of burning in his muscles and how he could block out everything while lifting weights.

When he finished, he grabbed the clothes he'd had on earlier and went into the master bathroom, threw them in the laundry hamper with his gym clothes and showered. Afterwards, he dried off with a big Egyptian cotton towel and wiped the steam off the mirror. Looking at himself critically, he turned this way and that, flexing his muscles. He'd made a decision. He was going to the party.

* * *

Red, 5:15pm

FOR THE PAST TEN DAYS, Red had taken to swinging through Owen Schmidt's neighborhood at least twice a day, often on his own time. Henry's report had been inconclusive but tantalizing. Schmidt had no criminal record, not even a juvenile one. But his mother had died in mysterious circumstances when he was 17.

The autopsy showed she had a blood-alcohol level that would have toppled a horse, and that was consistent with the boy's claim that she fell down the stairs while drunk. But there were some injuries that didn't quite match a fall; not enough that further investigation yielded charges against the boy, but clearly the coroner had questions. Schmidt had no record and there was no history of problems, though, so it had all gone away.

Since he was 17 at the time of his mother's death and had no other living relatives, he had to go into foster care, but it wasn't for long, and being the sole survivor, he inherited everything. It was a surprisingly large estate, built by the late father, who had apparently been quite an entrepreneur. The boy went on to college and a career that had no blemishes as far as Red could tell. Yet Red was still suspicious.

So he found himself prowling through Schmidt's neighborhood, looking for anything strange, unwilling to let go, but not having enough evidence to take action of any kind. As he turned the corner at Schmidt's street, putting the late afternoon sun behind him, he could see there was a party going on at Barbara Blackstone's house. She was the one who had lost the cat. Cars were parked up and down the street, and a trickle of guests entered the house. But what really surprised him was Owen Schmidt striding up the walk to Barbara's house. Schmidt was all eyes ahead and hadn't noticed the cop car. Why in God's name was he going to her party? Weren't they fighting?

Intrigued, he went around the block a few times, watching more partygoers arrive. The second time around, two women sauntered up the sidewalk, arm in arm, one a small blonde, the other a curvy brunette with a rich, sensuous laugh that penetrated his closed windows. She looked like the woman who lived down the street from him. He never spoke to any of his neighbors, so he didn't know her name. On his third pass, he saw Tanya and her husband walking up to Barbara's door. Tanya was tarted up as usual, tottering on spiked heels. The husband was a very unmemorable-looking guy. Red felt sorry for him. He wondered again if Tanya was having a fling with Schmidt. That could explain him going to the party. Or not.

He had to admit he couldn't watch Schmidt enough to catch him at anything except through pure luck, but it wasn't like he had anything more interesting to do. With that thought, he realized he'd slipped back into his old habits. It was always about the job for him. That's what ruined his marriages; his inability to leave work behind. He was supposed to be retired now. He needed to play golf and do things retired people do.

Maybe instead of cruising up and down Schmidt's street, he ought to go to Vegas and have some fun. Play a little black jack, maybe even win. Get laid. Wouldn't that be better than shadowing a potential perp? Why couldn't he just let it go? Tomorrow he'd consider taking some time off.

* * *

Jean, 5:15pm

JEAN PULLED up in front of Lydia's condo. The sun was creeping towards the horizon, but the air outside was still like an oven. The air-conditioning in the car valiantly blasted out cool air on the maximum setting, barely making a dent in the heat.

Lydia's door popped open, and she stepped out and waved at Jean, turning to lock the door behind her. She had on a long, flowing black skirt with a wide leather belt cinching the waist, white peasant blouse with scooped neck, and a beautiful squash blossom necklace. It complemented her coloring and personality perfectly but set her apart from most of the women in Palm Lakes, who dressed more conservatively. Lydia marched down the sidewalk, opened the passenger door and settled into the seat, buckling her seat belt. She must have just washed her hair, because it was slightly damp and curling madly.

"You have such beautiful hair, Lyd."

"And here I always thought my tits were my best feature."

Jean choked on a laugh. "I always feel good when I'm with you."

Lydia looked directly at her as Jean shifted into gear and pulled away from the curb. "How are things going at home?"

"No change. I'm going crazy. All I do is think and think. What should I do? What can I do? What's going to happen? I can't sleep. I have no appetite." She sighed and fell silent.

"Have you tried talking to Richard? Maybe suggest counseling?"

"I'd do it, but you know that won't fly with him. He doesn't talk. And he won't see a shrink. It would be admitting something's wrong with him."

"What about your marriage?"

"That's the thing. We've been living separate lives for a long time, but it wasn't until this porn thing that I realized what that meant. I thought we were doing okay because we didn't fight, but we have nothing in common anymore.

"What's worse is he thinks you're a bad influence on me. I was never interested in New Age stuff until we became friends, and now I'm rabid about it, so of course, it's your fault. As if I have no mind of my own. I can't talk to him about anything I love. He thinks yoga, crystals and energy work are for airheads, and even though he knows I'm level-headed, he treats me like I'm some vacuous blonde."

Lydia giggled. "That's the last word I'd use to describe you. I'm so sorry this is happening. Do you think it might take some pressure off if we took a break? Maybe if I weren't around, he'd calm down."

"Don't you dare suggest that! I don't know what I'd do if we couldn't talk and do things together. It's the only fun in my life right now, and it's keeping me sane. So don't mention that again, unless you're getting tired of listening to my complaints." Jean's voice drifted to a whisper at the end, as if she were afraid maybe Lydia was sick of being around her.

"What, and give up the best friend I've had in years? No way, José. Quit talking like that. And here I brought a surprise for tonight. We're going to par-tee!"

Jean's curiosity got the better of her. "What surprise? Of course, we're going to Barbara's party."

Lydia reached into her generous-sized handbag and pulled out a baggie of some kind of herb. "I got the best pot you can find in this area, and I'm going to share it with you. You need to mellow out, girlfriend, and this is just the way to do it."

Jean's fingers gripped the steering wheel harder as her eyes widened. "Are you kidding? You've got pot? Be careful! We don't want anyone to see that. What if I got pulled over?"

"Calm down, Jean. We're staying in Palm Lakes and you're a great driver. No one is going to pull us over, and they can't search without cause. Besides, it's only the rent-a-cops here, and they're useless."

Jean chose not to argue that point. "But I don't smoke, and I never have. I wouldn't know how. Plus where were you thinking of doing this?"

Lydia put the baggie back into her mini-suitcase. "We'll see how things go tonight. If necessary, we can go back to my place after the party and unwind. It'll do you good."

Jean shook her head skeptically. "I appreciate the thought, Lyd, but alcohol is my drug of choice, and I made myself a promise I'd enjoy myself tonight. So I'm going to have a good time, don't you worry. You just be careful with that. We don't know most of the people who are invited. One of them might even be in the Posse." She frowned as she said it, anticipating that the party might not be so much fun after all.

"I know you're shy, Jean, but don't worry. You won't have to do much. The alcohol will be flowing and people will ask lame questions like 'what's your sign?' and stuff their faces and get plowed. There will be shameless flirting, most of it harmless. Even though Barbara knows how to throw a party and keep it from derailing, there are bound to be a few cases of excess, and I'm looking forward to being a spectator. Who knows, I might even meet a handsome guy who'll sweep me off my feet."

"Yeah, right. With a 10 to 1 ratio of available women to men, that's not likely to happen anytime soon. No offense meant, but most of the attendees will be married."

"Well, that little detail never stopped me before," Lydia purred. They both burst into laughter as Jean grabbed the nearest parking place a few houses down from Barbara's.

They got out of the car and walked up the sidewalk arm in arm, swapping silly speculations about the party, laughing like school girls. Jean flinched and stopped mid-laugh, suddenly fearful of the discovery of Lydia's stash as a Posse car cruised by.

Lydia either didn't notice or didn't care, as she continued laughing and tugged Jean to keep up. They strolled up the walk to Barbara's door. Jean reached up to ring the doorbell but hesitated. The front door was open, in spite of the air-conditioning being on, and a dull roar poured out into the quiet desert evening. Entering would be like diving into cold water.

"No need to ring the bell. Let's go in." Lydia swung the heavy screen door open and waved Jean in.

* * *

Helen, 5:15pm

TWISTING LEFT AND THEN RIGHT, Helen nodded in approval at the reflection of her party outfit in the full-length mirror on the back of the bedroom door. The turquoise silk blouse with boat neck and long sleeves was feminine, and the color complemented her hair. It would be cool, plus it covered her upper arms, which had begun to sag a bit in recent years. The lightweight charcoal-colored linen slacks with narrow leather belt accentuated her flat stomach. Dressy half boots finished the ensemble and gave her just a bit of extra height.

She was so glad she'd splurged with some of Lou's mad money and bought herself and Sally new duds for the party. Thank heaven the atmosphere had turned festive after Sally's disclosure. It gave Helen hope that things would work out.

Sally popped her head around the partially closed door. "Wow, Mom, you look really nice! A bit conservative, but classy."

Helen smiled. "I'm not young like you, missy. And I never was one to go strutting about in flashy clothes. I'm much more comfortable in something elegant but understated. You, on the other hand, are going to be the belle of the ball!"

Sally came in and walked up and down the length of the bedroom, pretending she was on a runway and striking poses. Helen couldn't contain her laughter. She eyed Sally's little black dress. The spaghetti straps showed off her tanned shoulders, and the simple style suited her. The cut of the dress accentuated her narrow waist and long legs. It was shorter than Helen would have liked, but she had to admit, Sally looked great. Her sparkly dress sandals added a touch of color. "I love how you've braided your hair up, Sally. It looks so formal. How are you able to do that yourself?"

Sally smiled smugly. "It isn't that hard once you learn. I got a book on braiding at the bookstore—in the children's section, would you believe? —and it had a bunch of wonderful styles in it. I've really enjoyed trying them out."

"You're going to be the youngest person there. I hope you won't be bored. We don't have to stay for long. You give me a sign if you want to come home."

"Really, Mom, relax. It's about time you got out and mingled. We'll have fun. What's not to like about free food and booze? I know, I'm not drinking any alcohol tonight. I've turned over a new leaf since I got pregnant."

Helen smiled in relief that they weren't going to have to argue about that. Giving a final appraisal to Sally's outfit, she made a decision. "Sally, let's get you some jewelry to wear with that pretty dress. Maddie gave me something that might be perfect."

"Oh, goody, jewelry!" Arm in arm, they giggled their way into the walk-in closet and stopped at the shelf with Helen's two jewelry boxes. Helen searched through the drawers as Sally watched in rapt attention. "What is it, Mom?"

"Maddie gave me a necklace and earrings that are gorgeous, but they aren't in a color I'm likely to wear. Let me find them and show you." She continued to rummage around and then murmured with success. "Here they are."

She pulled out a medium length necklace of graded black onyx beads that had red Swarovski crystals and gold beads for accent. Sally gushed with excitement. "Oh my God, it's beautiful! I love it." She reached for the necklace and put it on. It was just the right length for the neckline of her dress.

Helen held out her hand. "Here are the earrings." A single large onyx dangled from the french earwires with a small red crystal above it, separated by a gold bead. "Now that looks really fancy. They even match your shoes." The dressy sandals had fake crystals, and some were indeed red.

Sally hugged her impulsively. "Thanks, Mom. These are super. Will your friend Maddie be at the party?"

"No, she and Stanley don't go out much."

"I was just hoping I could show her."

"She loves giving away her creations, as she calls them. I have more than I'll ever be able to wear. These lizard earrings are among my favorites. They go with anything." She pushed her hair back from her ears to show Sally.

"Yes, I really like those as well."

"Well, these, I'm keeping. But you can have that set if you like. I never wear black near my face if I can avoid it. It makes me look pasty. Yet it suits you tremendously. I'll tell Maddie I gave them to you. She'll be pleased."

"Oh, thanks so much, Mom. I love them!" Sally bounced up and down like a little girl.

"Well, now that we have our finery on, let's walk to Barbara's and see what's happening at the party."

Helen put her arm around Sally's shoulders and they walked out to the living room companionably. Sheba was curled up on the sofa, and Helen went over to her. "Sheebs, we're going to go next door for a little while. You just relax."

Exiting through the sliding glass doors in back, they crunched across the gravel to Barbara's yard. It was still smolderingly hot, even though the sun was getting lower, its rays painting long shadows in front of them as they approached Barbara's patio.

"She has a really lovely yard, doesn't she?"

"Yes, Barbara has such a good eye for decorating." They stopped on Barbara's patio, surveying the back yard. The bougainvillea bushes were a riot of fuchsia. A spreading desert tree took up a large part of the yard. An empty fire pit was centered in the large, flagstone-paved patio that extended well beyond the patio cover. Lawn furniture was set up in several conversation areas, but they were all currently empty. Turning towards the house, they could see a mass of people through the windows and glass doors.

They entered through the sliding glass door and plunged into the crowd as the sounds of smooth jazz and the buzz of many conversations washed over them. Barbara spotted them from across the room and rushed over to greet them.

"Helen, Sally, so glad you could make it. Isn't it marvelous? I believe almost everyone we invited is going to come. Even Owen, if you can believe that." Barbara gave Helen and Sally each a hug and grabbed Helen's arm to tug her in the direction of the bar. "Ben is on drink duty, so give him your orders and then get some snacks. Oh, but silly me, I want to introduce you to Alexander before we do that. He's our resident travel/food writer—and most eligible bachelor—and even though he's already a world-class chef, he takes the gourmet cooking classes in Palm Lakes just for fun. You mentioned you had enrolled in the next class, and I thought you'd like an introduction to someone who will be in it, so you don't have to feel like a complete stranger going in."

Helen's heart filled with gratitude at the thoughtfulness. "That's so kind of you! Yes, I'd love to meet him."

Barbara guided her and Sally away from the sea of people to the small parlor at the front of the house which was quieter and less crowded than the great room, having only half a dozen people. Barbara steered them towards a couple who were engaged in what appeared to be a lively discussion. As they drew closer, the woman and man stopped talking and looked their way.

Helen's first reaction surprised her. She wasn't one to ogle men. But this man, who must be Alexander, was stare-worthy. At least 6 ft tall, with broad shoulders, wavy silver hair swept back from his high forehead and piercing green eyes, he was so handsome she couldn't take her eyes off him. His clothes looked expensive, even though they were casual. The black and white Hawaiian print shirt seemed to be made of silk, and his black trousers had a sharp pleat. He wore no jewelry except for a thin gold watch on his tanned wrist.

Barbara parked them in front of Alexander and his companion. "Ladies, I'd like you to meet Alexander Stirling and Sophie Forrest. Sophie, Alexander, I'd like you to meet Helen Mueller and her daughter Sally, who's here for a visit. Alexander, Helen is the one I spoke to you about. She's taking the cooking class, and she doesn't know anyone in it. You're such an old hand, I thought maybe you could shepherd her through it."

Helen took his outstretched hand and shook it, still a bit awed. "I really appreciate both of you doing this. I haven't participated in any classes before, and I'm a bit shy about being in a new group of people."

He held her hand just long enough to make her feel he was truly pleased to meet her. "I know how it feels, Helen. You can partner up with me if you like. They always split the class into couples working together. It keeps the cost down for materials. I think you'll enjoy it. I always do." Alexander smiled, showing beautiful white teeth and charming laugh lines around his glittering green eyes.

It was overwhelming to have any man act nice to her, much less one who looked like him, but she managed to respond. "That's very generous of you, Alexander. I accept. I think I'm getting the best of the deal, though. Your reputation precedes you."

He brushed off her self-deprecating remark with a wave of his hand."They're a very welcoming group, and it doesn't matter what experience you have."

Barbara took Helen by the arm again. "Well, I waylaid these ladies on their way to the food and drink, so I'm going to take them back now; just wanted to make sure you two got to meet."

Helen smiled one last time at Alexander. "See you in class, Alexander."

"Looking forward to it, Helen." His smile made her weak in the knees.

They wound their way back to the great room and the bar, where Barbara handed them over to Ben. "I have to run and greet someone else, but I'll be back. Oh, and watch out for Bernie. He's had a few already. Ben, I think it's time you cut him off."

Ben saw Helen's worried look."Don't worry, Helen, you can't miss Bernie. He and I play golf together. He's a bear of a guy, balding, overweight and socially inept, especially after he's had a few. He's annoying but harmless. So, ladies, what can I get you to drink? We have just about anything heart could desire."

Sally spoke while Helen was processing the information about Bernie. "I'll take a Diet Coke, thanks."

Ben reached for a large glass, putting ice cubes into it, then poured the soda. "This is a vintage Diet Coke, Miss Sally. I believe you'll love it. It's bold, but not pretentious." He gave it to her, then turned to Helen. "And what can I get for you, lovely lady?" Helen laughed at his blatant flirting because she knew it meant nothing. "A red wine for me, Ben, any kind is fine. By the way, where's Jack?" She glanced around, looking for a furry whirling dervish.

He grabbed a wine glass and filled it. "This is a delightful merlot that I just know you'll like. Jack's at the sitter's house. Barbara felt it would be better all around if he wasn't under foot."

Helen accepted the glass and nodded her thanks, and she and Sally moved in the direction of the other end of the great room, where a sofa sat invitingly empty. Helen sat down and patted the cushion next to her. "Have a seat. Give yourself time to get the lay of the land."

Sally joined her and sat with perfectly crossed legs, sipping her soda. They hadn't been there a minute when a bearlike creature emerged from the crowd in front of them. *Bernie. It has to be. The receding hairline and combover; the bulging middle hanging over his belt; the clothes slightly disheveled and wrinkled, almost as if he slept in them; the somewhat unfocused eyes. It will cinch it if he does anything obnoxious.*

He looked at Sally and Helen and immediately put his hands out in front of him, though one held a glass with what looked like whiskey in it. The empty hand was making a squeezing motion. Considering he was implying doing it with both hands, his intent was pretty obvious. *Yes, Bernie for sure.*

Before either woman could say anything, he sat down close to Sally. Sally didn't budge, not that there was room to. Helen was annoyed, but wasn't used to remonstrating with a man about his behavior, so she held her tongue.

"I'm Bernie Rivers. R-I-V-3-E-R-S, but the 3 is silent." He laughed at his joke. Obviously, it was one he used a lot and of which he was quite proud. Neither woman laughed, but he did not appear chastised in the least. "I golf with Ben and live a couple streets that way." He exaggeratedly pointed to his left. "What are your names, lovely ladies, and how do you know Ben and Barbara?"

"I'm Helen, and I live on this street, and Barbara and Ben are good friends. This is my daughter, Sally, who is here for a visit."

Bernie ogled Sally, who seemed undisturbed by his attentions. "I can't believe I never met you before, Helen. And how fortunate that Sally was visiting today. Can I get either of you beautiful women a refill?"

Helen sighed to herself. It was obvious neither of them was ready for another drink, though enough time with Bernie might speed that timeline up. "No, thanks, Bernie."

Sally stood up, and Bernie almost fell over onto the vacated spot on the sofa. He must have been leaning on her. "Me, neither, Bernie. Nice meeting you. But I think we're going to have to go now. Mom promised to introduce me to everyone, and we only just got here."

Bernie's face fell. Helen found herself feeling almost sorry for him, but not sorry enough to stay. "Nice meeting you, Bernie," she said, and she and Sally headed for the snacks across the room.

Helen whispered as they plowed through the crowd. "Thanks for saving us, Sally."

"No problem, Mom. He wasn't much of a challenge. You did pretty good yourself, not telling him your last name."

They reached the granite counter that was filled with platters of delicious-looking finger foods, and she and Sally filled their plates with nibbles, commenting on the excellent variety and presentation. Pointing to the small crock pot, Helen told Sally, "I do love hot crab dip, and Barbara makes the best. You'll have to try some." Sally put some on her plate, and they took their refreshments to an area far from Bernie where two chairs were empty. "This should keep Bernie at arm's length," said Helen, laughing. They sat down, putting their glasses on the table between the chairs.

"This dip *is* great, Mom! Do you have the recipe? Where did she get crabmeat here in the desert?"

"Yes, I do, and a specialty grocery store downtown has just about anything you could want for putting on a great party. I'm sure Barbara got it there."

Helen glanced around the room. Tanya and her hubby were standing at one edge of the crowd, Tanya peering predator-like at the other guests. Helen assumed she was scoping the crowd for someone particular. She wondered if it could be Owen. Just as that thought occurred to her, she spotted Owen by following Tanya's now-frozen gaze. He was standing alone in a corner across the room, nursing a drink and looking very out of place. *Hmmm.*

Tanya turned to her husband, said something, then tottered across the room towards Helen. She was wearing 4-inch stiletto heels (did she ever wear anything else?) with black leggings and a very revealing blood-red blouse with lots of ruffles. She'd clearly had work done and liked to flaunt it. Her knuckle-buster rings were garish, and her makeup was applied way too thickly for Helen's taste.

A fake smile plastered to her face, Tanya asked in a singsong voice, "Helen, is this your daughter? What a pretty girl she is! She'll be the hit of the party for sure in that tiny black dress. All the old farts will love it, but watch out for Bernie! What's your name, honey?"

Sally appeared shocked but recovered quickly. "I'm Sally."

"Well, honey, watch out for Bernie is all I can say. In fact, watch out for all of them—or rather, most of them. There's still some life in some of them." She looked pointedly back at her husband with disdain, then turned back with the fake smile. "They rarely see a sweet young thing like you in Palm Lakes. That's one reason the wives like living here. Me included." She didn't wait for a response but lurched away in a direction that Helen couldn't help but see would eventually lead to Owen.

"She's terrible, Mom."

"She lives down the street. I think she drinks, and that doesn't help. I don't think she's a happy person." She kept to herself that she suspected Tanya had Owen in her sights for an affair. It wasn't fair to talk about things she didn't know. Maybe she'd read too much into what she'd seen. But as she chastised herself for making unpleasant assumptions, she saw Tanya weave over to Owen, touch his arm and stand close to him. Her body language said she was coming on to him. His body language was conflicted. He seemed both attracted and repelled. He stayed in place, allowing the contact, but seemed even more tense than usual, if that was possible. Wonder what that meant? And why was he here? Trust Barbara to be so forgiving and include him in the party, but why would he accept the invitation? He didn't seem the party type, but then, neither was she, and she was here.

Helen cast a glance towards Tanya's husband, who could easily see what was going on but showed no signs of concern. There was something nondescript about him that reminded Helen of something she'd read in a spy novel about a good spy not standing out in any way. Tanya's husband could be a great spy, because he seemed to blend into a crowd as if he were a ghost. Poor man.

The tête à tête between Owen and Tanya ended with no obvious outcome, and Tanya moved on to speak briefly to another couple. Shortly after that, Helen saw Owen leave in a rush. Tanya continued to mingle. Maybe Helen was imagining things because she didn't get out enough and watched too much TV. It was silly to imagine illicit romances going on in Palm Lakes. It was a retirement community, after all, not some soap opera.

Just then, Barbara came up to them with two ladies in tow. "Helen, Sally, I'd like you to meet my special friends Lydia and Jean. We're in yoga class together, and we have so much fun. I thought you might like to join us in the next class, Helen."

Helen was touched at being included. "I would love to do that, Barbara."

Barbara smiled encouragingly. "The people are so easy to be around; the teacher is gentle and kind. And yoga just makes you feel terrific." Barbara patted Helen on the shoulder and went back to mingle with the other guests.

The next couple hours were filled with laughter, entertaining stories and a growing sense of closeness to Jean and Lydia. Suddenly for the first time in her life, Helen had friends. She was being included in a group. It had all happened so fast her head was spinning.

After saying goodbye to Barbara and Ben, inviting them to dinner soon (*why did it never occur to me to do that before?*), Helen and Sally walked the short distance across the moonlit yard to the back door of Helen's house and let themselves in.

"That was really fun, Mom. Thanks for inviting me."

"Barbara's the one to thank. You could call her tomorrow if you like. I'm glad you were here. I doubt I could have brought myself to go alone.

I did enjoy meeting Lydia and Jean and Alexander. I hope we weren't too boring for you."

"Ah, Mom, free food and drink in a lovely setting with nice people? What's not to like? And Jean and Lydia were fun. Alexander? He's hot for an old guy! Maybe you and he can go out on a date sometime. He's like movie-star handsome, and he seemed real nice."

"Heavens, Sally, your Dad hasn't been gone that long."

"Yeah, Mom, I know, but you and Dad had nothing, at least as far as I could see. Why not get out and live a little?"

Helen was shocked by Sally's directness, but she couldn't argue. "Maybe someday, but Alexander is way out of my league. He's being nice, but that doesn't mean anything. The women must be beating a path to his door, and I'm no great catch."

"Look in the mirror sometime, Mom. I don't know how you manage to convince yourself you're no catch. You look great for your age. You're a nice person. You put up with Dad for years. You're smart and kind. You're a catch."

"Thanks for the pep talk, Sally. I appreciate the vote of confidence. I agree he is handsome. It will take me time to be willing to go beyond noticing that."

Sally shrugged. "I'm going to hit the sack now. I get tired easier these days." She gave Helen a brief hug and went back to the guest room.

Helen reached down to pet Sheba, who was meowing incessantly. The meows stopped, but Helen knew what Sheba wanted, so she picked her up and snuggled her. "Who's my Precious? Didn't we come back like I promised?" The purring response was loud and strong, but Sheba felt even lighter than usual, her bones sticking out as if she were a rescue cat. "When did you get so skinny, Precious?" Worry stabbed Helen again. She couldn't imagine life without Sheba. Things were still so unsettled, and Sheba was her one true friend. "I'm going to get an appointment with the vet to check you out; Sally's visit distracted me." Then she walked back to the master suite, hugging Sheba and whispering reassurances to her.

Once in the bedroom, she gently deposited Sheba on the bed and changed into her nightgown, an old cotton one with flowers and a scooped neck. They'd never had money for nice clothes, so she didn't have much of a wardrobe, but she didn't really mind. Shopping wasn't her thing, and she rarely went out. It had been fun shopping with Sally today, but she couldn't see herself getting addicted to it.

She went to the walk-in closet and opened a built-in drawer and shoved aside the clothing, exposing her journals. Thank heaven she'd thought to remove them from the office when Sally called unexpectedly. She loved seeing Sally, but she had no intention of sharing her journals with anyone.

Grabbing her pen and the latest journal, she went back to the bed and crawled onto the covers, propping the pillow behind her back to cushion it from the headboard. It wasn't a comfortable position, but she really wanted to write tonight.

Saturday, August 26, 1995

Tonight was the first night in ages that I went to a social function. Lou never liked them, and I have to admit I'm very reserved in groups, so I didn't really mind avoiding them. But today was part of the program to discover the new me. I thought the party would entertain Sally, and I wanted to try to mingle more. I've never been good at mixing with people, especially strangers. And until you mingle, everyone's a stranger.

The night went far better than I could have predicted. I didn't find myself tempted to drink more than a couple glasses of wine. It was fun putting on brand new clothes and going to a real party. Sally looked so pretty. Jean and Lydia were delightful company. I can't wait for that yoga class. And Barbara was so kind to introduce me to Alexander, who offered to partner with me in the cooking class, though I can't imagine why he'd want to be saddled with me. Life is suddenly looking very attractive for the first time in decades.

It's not without its challenges, though. As soon as I began to work out some of my problems, Sally shows up. Her life is in a bigger shambles than mine. I'm still very conflicted about what to do. I find it hard to say 'no' to her. She was always my favorite, but it's more than that. She has no husband, no job, no place to live. She's a grown woman with a good education, and I'm sure she can survive, but somehow I feel it's my job to help her, to say 'yes' to her. I just know that I don't want to leave Palm Lakes and be her child's nanny. How much is a mother obliged to do?

She paused briefly as a scene from the past came back to her in a rush. It had happened years ago. She was sitting in the doctor's examining room, shivering in the chill in a silly paper gown, hoping that

Lou would stay in the waiting room. He'd yelled at her so much that day, and she was terrified. She never handled his rage well. He wouldn't do anything in public; when they got home was another matter. But she wasn't going to give in.

She began to write again.

Sally being pregnant has brought the memories back. It's hard to believe it was nearly 31 years ago this happened...

It was still as fresh as wet paint to her, and she didn't really like to touch it, because of the way it made her feel. She forced herself to continue writing.

It seemed like I waited hours that day in the doctor's office, but finally, he came back. "Congratulations, you're pregnant!"

The doctor had no idea that Lou was going to be angry about the news. Lou had told me he was going to make sure I got an abortion if I was pregnant, that we couldn't afford another mouth to feed. I'd hidden the pregnancy as long as possible; I wore my loosest clothing to cover the bulge.

I smiled faintly at the doc. He probably wrote my bland reaction off to morning sickness. "Shall we bring Lou in and tell him the good news?" I nodded, knowing Lou would be unlikely to overreact in front of the doctor. Anyway, I hoped he wouldn't. He was always so afraid of what people would think.

The doctor brought Lou back and broke the news. Lou's mouth was a savage slit and his eyes glittered with rage. "Can we get an abortion?"

The doctor had looked surprised at the coldness of Lou's question, then after searching both our faces, he must have realized what was what. "No, it's too late for that."

Lou's dark expression darkened further. "Fine." Turning abruptly, he left the room, and it fell to me to smooth things over with the doctor, in spite of my heart being in my throat. I was so relieved I had held out long enough to keep my baby.

I never told Sally how her father had tried to have her aborted. From the moment I conceived, she was my special little miracle, and I wouldn't let anything happen to her. He threw a fit when we got home, saying two kids was enough, but with time, he accepted it. He actually treated her special after she was born, which was a blessing. She was always able to wrap us both around her little finger and often did.

Now that she's in a family way, I find myself asking if an abortion is the best course of action for her. I never liked the idea, and I wouldn't encourage her to, but would I discourage her from it? Fortunately, she never expressed it as an option. It would certainly take me off the hook. The only thing that is making it so hard for me to say 'no' to her is the baby. I want my grandchild to have a good life. But does it have to mean giving up mine?

I wish it were easier to know what to do. I feel selfish, wanting to do what I want. I feel angry that I never really have had a chance to do that. Lou did what he damn well pleased his whole life. I've watched my kids make their own decisions and create their own lives. Sally has lived a carefree, full life until now. I never got that. Of course, it's my own fault for marrying so young, but when will it be my turn?

I want to find a way for both of us to have what we want. I want to help Sally, but I want to stay in Palm Lakes and explore this new life I've been given. I'll go apartment hunting with her if she likes and maybe give her some of the extra furniture when I move. She loves some of these pieces. It will annoy Lena no end, but too bad. I can give them to Sally to help her get a good start here and feel supported. That should soften the blow, and if I can get a decent job and downsize enough, maybe I can continue to give her a bit of money to help out, along with some babysitting. It all comes down to her finding a decent job, which I believe she can.

Helen put the pen down and closed the book. She knew what she wanted to do, but she wasn't sure she'd be able to stick to her guns if Sally couldn't find a good job and place to live. Life had sure gotten challenging the past several months. She got up and put the journal back in its hiding place and bedded down next to Sheba.

* * *

Jean, 12:20am

JEAN AND LYDIA were driving along the moonlit streets, enjoying the quiet, a welcome change after hours of music, talk and laughter.

Finally, Lydia broke the silence. "Want to come in and share a joint with me?"

"No, thanks, Lydia. I really don't smoke. Richard probably wonders what happened to me. It's past midnight, and I never stay out late. Not that I think he'll be jealous."

"Too bad. Maybe we should arrange to make him jealous. We could have gotten you a date with Bernie, I'm certain."

They both tittered. "Yeah, Bernie would be a real catch. Poor guy. Makes me feel lucky to have Richard in a way."

"Sometimes being alone is better than being with someone you're incompatible with," Lydia said with conviction.

"Speaking from experience?"

"Tons of it. I seem to be incompatible with long-term relationships. I've tried often enough. None ever took. But I'm happy on my own, really. I have no one to answer to, no need to compromise and no one to fight with. Life is good."

She didn't sound too convinced, but Jean didn't want to invade her privacy, so she let it slide. "I don't know where my marriage is heading. I'd like to save it, but I'm wondering if there's anything left to save."

"You'll figure it out. Just be true to your heart and be kind to yourself. Whatever you do, I'm here for you."

"Oh, Lyd, I have no idea how I could deal with this otherwise." She pulled up in front of Lydia's condo and parked the car. "Thanks for going with me this evening. I would never have gone on my own."

"It was a blast, wasn't it? There weren't many eligible bachelors, but the food and drink were super, just like the company. I think Helen will be a great addition to our little group. I really like her."

Jean smiled. "I do, too. She seems so sweet, though a little scared in crowds like me."

Lydia patted her on the arm. "It's OK to be shy with strangers. How would it look if everyone wore lampshades at parties? Leave that to us extroverts." They both dissolved into laughter.

Lydia opened the car door and got out, reaching back for her humungous purse. "See you soon! Call me if you need anything." She slammed the door and walked up the sidewalk, digging through her purse for her house key.

Jean sat waiting for her to get in, then put the car into gear and pulled away from the curb.

Moonlight was spilling across the landscape, black shadows

contrasting with pools of otherworldly light. It gave the trees and cacti an alien look, monochromatic and forbidding. No one was out at this time, even on a Saturday. No cars and no people. Typical retirement community. It was as if she were the only person on a movie set.

She enjoyed the quiet and solitude of the short drive home, the car windows rolled down and a warm breeze blowing through them. The garage door went up, splitting the silence eerily as she turned into the driveway. She noticed that Richard had left the light on for her, or maybe he was still up.

The garage door came down noisily behind her and clunked shut. She got out of the car and grabbed her purse from the back seat. The car door sounded louder than usual as it slammed shut in the stillness of the empty garage. *Why do things sound different at night?* Dismissing the odd thought, she went through the office and saw the living room light on through the doorway. Her attention was grabbed by the computer display. It had gone dark like it did when it went to sleep, but there was a small image on the center of the screen, and it caused her eyes to bug out.

It was a picture of a naked woman and man, his genitalia displayed as the main attraction. She couldn't bear to look at it; she barely registered it as her heart pounded in her ears.

Richard's voice snapped her out of shock. "So you're home! How was the party?"

She stepped through the doorway into the hall and stared blankly at Richard, who sat in an armchair in front of the TV in the great room, a book in his hand as if he'd been reading. But clearly, he hadn't. He had just left the office, shutting down a porn site. He wasn't that computer literate, which had led to her discovery of his addiction in the first place. He didn't realize a popup had appeared after he shut the site down. He was in too much of a hurry to get into the living room and look relaxed when he heard the garage door go up.

Her heart pounded in her throat. She had imagined any number of scenarios, but it really hadn't occurred to her that he would lie to her. It felt very much as if a line had been crossed. And it was up to her whether to confront him or let it slide.

"What's the matter, Jean? You look like you saw a ghost. Was the party that bad?" Richard oozed charm, and she marveled at how she would have been taken in if only that popup hadn't appeared and given him away. She couldn't let it pass. This was intolerable.

"I guess I did see a ghost of sorts. The ghost of our marriage. You've been on the computer watching porn again. No, don't deny it. Just go look at the computer. How could you lie to me? I trusted you to keep your promise!" She was annoyed that her voice sounded whiny. Why should she plead, when he was the wrongdoer?

Richard seemed unnaturally calm. "What do you want me to say?"

"You don't know?" She let out a huge sigh of exasperation. It hit her suddenly: he wasn't even going to try. "I'm going to move into the guest bedroom. I need some space and time to sort out this mess in my head. It's late. I've had a few drinks, so it isn't the right time to talk about this." Not that it would ever be.

She stalked back to the master bedroom and grabbed her nightgown and toothbrush and went to the smaller guest room with its adjoining bath. Tears streamed down her face as she realized there probably wasn't any way to save her marriage.

She heard him in the master suite getting ready for bed. She wondered what was going through his mind. Why didn't he come try to talk with her? Didn't he care? She began to cry again.

She could have fought another woman, but this porn thing was impossible. She was actually wondering what she had done to drive him to this. What an idiot she was! She lay down and closed her eyes, and after a while slipped into a troubled sleep.

CHAPTER FIVE

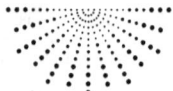

THURSDAY, SEPTEMBER 7, 1995

Helen, 9:54am

Helen sat in her car at the Recreation Center, giving herself a pep talk while letting the cool air blast her face. The first session of the International Gourmet Cooking Club was starting in several minutes. Thank heaven Barbara had arranged for her to meet Alexander at the party, and God bless him for offering to partner with her. That really did take a lot of the panic out of the experience, but it was surprising how the prospect of walking into that room full of strangers still terrified her.

She had always known she was shy, terribly shy, but she'd told herself it was Lou who had kept her home. Now she realized he had merely been a convenient excuse.

Afraid of being late (that would only make things worse), she turned the car off and went into the building looking for Room 107. When she found it, she paused in the doorway, taking in the scene.

In the open part of the room were several islands which each had a sink and countertop. Along one wall was a restaurant-sized stovetop, a couple of wall ovens, a microwave, a large refrigerator, automatic dishwasher, double stainless steel sink and rows of floor-to-ceiling cabinets and shelves, plus plenty of counter space. Everything was spotless and new-looking. There were locks on most of the cabinets, but one set was open, and she could see pots, pans and cooking implements.

The room opened up beyond the cooking area into a dining room with round tables that would seat at least 8 people, each surrounded by comfortable-looking chairs. The far side of the room was a bank of floor-to-ceiling windows that gave a spectacular view of the golf course. Over a dozen people were scattered around the room, talking in small groups.

She spotted Alexander in the center of the largest bunch. She recalled that Barbara had told her he was a writer for a food and travel magazine. It suddenly hit her that her partner was probably the most popular person in the club. The women surrounding him radiated interest, and why not? Alexander was a bachelor. In Palm Lakes, if you were a single man, you had to beat them off with a stick. Unless you were someone like Bernie, she amended. She saw two other men in the room, but most of the students were women.

She propelled herself through the doorway and headed over to Alexander, noting once again how attractive he was. He could make the most casual outfit look like something from a fashion magazine, and he didn't even seem aware of it. His maroon polo shirt, black pants and black leather shoes were a counterpoint to his longish silver hair and emerald eyes. There wasn't an ounce of fat on his frame. She wondered how he managed to stay in shape when so many men his age carried extra weight around their middle. There was no doubt about it; he was gorgeous, and his apparent lack of vanity made him even more appealing.

Finally, his eyes met hers, and he smiled warmly and waved her into the group, introducing her to all the ladies like she was his oldest friend. She shook hands with each of them, swiftly forgetting their names in the tension of the moment.

She got her panic under control as the students began to quiet down and the teacher called the class to attention. "OK, everyone gather 'round me. Let's get started." A few minutes passed as the people stopped their conversations and moved in the direction of the teacher, a grandmotherly woman with gray hair who looked like someone who not only enjoyed cooking, but eating what she cooked, as well.

"I'm Alice, and I'm your teacher. I see the usual suspects are here. Alexander. Nora. Ray. Alan. Welcome back. I hate to make it seem like you're back in school, but I have to take roll call, so we might as well use that as a chance to get to know each other. Let's stick with first names and just briefly say what you hope to get out of this class. That will help me do a better job."

Helen was relieved at the chance to learn names again, and this time, she focused on remembering them. It still went by in a blur, and she was nervous about having to speak, but as she listened to the other students, she relaxed and got into the swing of it. Before she knew it, she was standing with Alexander at one of the islands with several pots and other necessities for their project.

Alexander smiled, the laugh lines around his eyes crinkling his tanned skin. "I saw you taking in the place when you arrived. It's impressive, isn't it?"

"I didn't expect something this grand. What's the dining area for?"

"All the clubs are entitled to have celebrations here, so you'll find that many of them vie for the space around New Year's Eve and other holidays. We have a dinner here annually. You'll have to plan on attending. Assuming you enjoy the club, that is."

"You're so gracious, taking me on not knowing what you're getting into. I'm sure I'll love it. I love cooking, and I really want to expand my culinary horizons."

"Well, this is the place!" Alexander started organizing the implements and looking over the written instructions for today's lesson, but she was too distracted to concentrate.

The room buzzed with conversations, and Alice was teaming unpaired students based on interest and experience, so Helen and the old hands were in a holding pattern.

Ray and Alan were at the island adjacent to theirs, and it was obvious they were going to be the class entertainment. She watched in rapt attention as they did impressions for the people at the next island over, Nora and another woman whose name she had already forgotten.

"Oh, Alan, you know your mother can't compare to mine. *Mine* takes the prize." He was camping it up in a voice that sounded gay, and it occurred to her that maybe Ray and Alan *were* gay.

86

"I beg to differ, Ray, my mother was the *height* of hypocrisy. He posed as if answering a phone... 'Oh Nora, so nice you called. Of course, dear, anything you like will be fine with me...Sure, tomorrow's fine...'" He mimed hanging up the phone and rolled his eyes disdainfully. "Bitch."

It came out such a contrast to the hypocritical niceness that Helen sputtered with laughter. Class was going to be highly entertaining if this was a sample. She looked at Alexander, whose eyes flashed with amusement. "You're in for it, Helen. This is just the beginning."

To her surprise and pleasure, the class passed swiftly. Working with Alexander was how she imagined dancing would be, never having done much dancing. They had a rapport that was...graceful. Though she hardly knew him, it was as if they anticipated each other's thoughts and intentions, and as they worked, the smooth efficiency acted like a balm to Helen's nerves. She'd never imagined working with another person could be so pleasant and rewarding.

They'd created some lovely paté and were busy cleaning up by the time she came back to reality. She hadn't thought to bring something to put food in for later. *Was that in the paper I got about the class? What's the matter with my memory these days?*

Alexander saw her looking around and divined her issue. "It's so easy to forget everything you're supposed to bring the first day of class. Kind of like being a kid again, isn't it? I tell you what. I'm going to make a special dinner tonight because I got some salmon at the store...just couldn't resist, since you don't often see good fresh fish on offer here. Do you like salmon? I can take the paté home with me. You can have dinner at my house and bring a container to take your share of the paté home, or whatever is left after we eat. How's that sound?"

His invitation sounded so normal, so casual, but...why he was asking her to dine with him? She hoped he wasn't asking because he wanted a date. Part of her was intrigued; the other part was petrified. She had no idea how to respond.

He watched her patiently, and she got the distinct impression that he knew she was scared. He'd been so nice, it wasn't fair to act ungrateful.

"That's thoughtful of you, Alexander. I have no plans for this evening, and I would really like that." She hoped she hadn't sounded too wooden, but her vocal cords were partially paralyzed by shock.

"Wonderful. I'll pick you up at 5:30, if that's all right? I want to drive so I can make sure you get home safely, because I have a couple of lovely wines for you to sample." He rummaged through the drawer of the island and found a blank piece of paper. "Why don't you write down your phone number and address for me. If I get lost, I'll call you."

She nodded and numbly began to write on the paper. She knew he was OK because Barbara had introduced them. And he hadn't been at all tactile or forward during the class. He probably was just being friendly, and she could use a friend. She handed him the paper. "It isn't that far from here, and I don't think you'll have a problem finding it. Can I bring anything?"

"No, thanks, I have it covered. But you can help me cook. It will be good practice for class." He chuckled as he said it, and she felt the tension drain from her body. So it wasn't a date. "I hope you don't mind eating later in the evening. I know most people eat early around here, but when you're cooking a nice meal, it takes time. Is a late night all right?"

She wasn't used to being consulted about her preferences and struggled to answer. "I don't keep a regular schedule. It's always a pleasure to have a real meal and someone to share it with."

They walked out to the parking lot, and he pointed at a silver Mercedes a few rows over. "That's my car. I'll swing by and pick you up at 5:30."

"OK. Thanks." She watched as he strode across the tarmac towards his car, then reached into her purse for her keys and walked to her station wagon. It wasn't until she got in the car that she remembered Sally was at home, and she'd have to explain to her why she was going out tonight.

* * *

Samantha, 10:00am

SWITCHING her clipboard to her right hand, Samantha pressed Barbara's doorbell once. Instantly a small dog started yapping. The door swung open, and Barbara smiled in welcome. "Samantha, how nice of you to help me out like this."

"It's my pleasure." Samantha followed Barbara into the large, elegantly decorated great room.

The Jack Russell terrier was hopping up and down around Samantha, so she finally gave him her full attention. "What a cute guy you are. What's your name?"

"He's Jack. Imaginative, right? We can sit down for a minute and talk about my vision for the yard. I'm eager to hear what you suggest. I'm not that knowledgeable about desert landscaping. Oh, and how about I get you a drink? A soda? Lemonade? Iced tea?"

"That's kind of you, but I have water in the car." She wondered if Barbara always put people at ease like this, or if it were just because Samantha was Maddie's girl.

As if reading her mind, Barbara asked, "How are Maddie and Stanley doing? I only see them rarely. They didn't come to my party, but your Mom said they don't socialize."

"That's right. They pretty much stay at home. They don't even go out to eat, which is unusual in this town."

"I'm sure they're happy to have you living here."

"Yes, they were surprised and pleased when my husband said he wanted to retire here. We did enjoy our visits here a lot, and of course, how could anyone complain about the winters? We were pretty tired of snow."

"Ben and I were blessed that way. Winters are mild in Southern California. But Ben wanted to live in a golfing community, and he fell in love with the desert. It's very different from our old home, but I'm getting used to it."

"It certainly does take time to adjust, especially to the summers."

"That's why I called you. I know we've only been here going on five years, but now that I've lived here a while, I'm ready to make some improvements to our landscaping. I really love the hummingbirds. We have a feeder out, but I'd like to put in some plants that would attract them. We spend a lot of time outdoors, and we love watching them. Plus there are a couple bushes I just don't like and want to replace."

"I'll need to look at the various locations before I suggest anything in particular, but there are a number of nice flowering bushes I can recommend."

"Great. Why don't we go out back? That's the main area I'm interested in updating at the moment."

They rose and exited through the sliding glass doors, Jack close behind them, onto a spacious patio with a slatted patio cover. Samantha's eye was caught by the lovely Texas ebony tree which dominated the back yard, its spreading canopy nearly as impressive as a palo verde or mesquite. They walked around the yard as Samantha questioned Barbara about her likes and dislikes.

When they returned to the patio, Samantha eyed the yard for a few minutes as she came up with a new design. "I'm not sure how radical a change you want." She verbally sketched which plantings she'd remove and what she'd replace them with, explaining the pros and cons as she went along.

Barbara nodded, taking everything in. "That sounds exactly like what I wanted, especially those dwarf bottlebrush. We had the full-size version back home, and those sound cute. They'll be perfect around the patio extension."

Samantha looked around as if searching for something. "Where's Jack?"

"Oh, he probably wandered off. He does that sometimes."

"Shall we go find him? People around here get touchy about neighbors' pets in their yards."

"Don't I know it! He'll be back soon. He never goes far. So what do you think about the job? Any further suggestions?"

"I would suggest we do just that much and then go from there. You might not want to do anymore. Or you might. But it's hard to picture huge changes, so why not do it a little bit at a time?"

"I like how you think, Samantha. What will it cost me and what are the details?"

"Give me a minute to work up an estimate."

Barbara turned to go inside. "Let's get out of this hot sun so you can do your math."

Samantha followed her back into the house, smiling that it hadn't occurred to her that it was all that hot. She was still concerned that Jack had run off, but Barbara didn't seem worried.

Ten minutes later, she bid Barbara goodbye and drove the short distance to park in front of Mom's house. Samantha enjoyed doing appointments in her parents' neighborhood because it made visiting much more convenient than finding time outside of working hours. She'd be able to get a couple visits in while doing Barbara's redo, as Julio was very family-oriented and encouraged her to see her folks when she could.

She pressed the doorbell. Right on cue, Beau's deep bark began. It wouldn't stop until he saw her. The door finally opened (Mom was getting slow with her arthritis), and Beau greeted her effusively as she came into the house. A hug for Mom, a pat for Beau. "Where's Dad?"

"In his office, reading."

"I was at Barbara's giving an estimate on some work and figured you'd both be up by now. She's hired me. I'll be able to come by while I'm supervising that job."

"That will be nice."

Mom had obviously been making jewelry, as the light on the dining room table was lit, and bits and pieces of jewelry were lying out on white cloths. "Making a new design?"

"Yes, I got a shipment of some nice tourmaline, and I'm trying to decide what to do with it."

They wandered back to the table together. Samantha really admired her Mom's beautiful and original designs. For this project, she had some lovely gold findings she was mixing with the purple, green and goldish tourmaline chips. "That's going to be really lovely, Mom."

Mom smiled and sat down. "Can you stay a bit?"

"No, I'm still on the clock, and I shouldn't stay longer than to say a quick hi to you both."

"Go see your Dad, then. But come back and say bye before you leave."

"OK."

Samantha straightened her shoulders and walked back to her Dad's small office. As she rounded the corner, she could see him sitting at his desk reading a book. He looked up and waved her in.

"Close the door. I have something I need to talk to you about."

91

She resisted being drawn in. "Dad, I can't stay. I'm just stopping to say hi."

It was obvious resistance was futile. "This won't take long. You need to see this."

She sighed, then hoped his failing hearing hadn't caught her. It was as if he didn't remember that every time she came, he gave her the same unpleasant lecture.

Stanley pulled out a tablet and began to write numbers which he'd obviously committed to memory. "You need to understand the facts because it's likely that I'll be the first to go, since your mother is much younger than me. You need to know what the financial situation is, because she has no interest in it, and someone has to take responsibility. Otherwise, she'll end up in big trouble. She doesn't know the first thing about paying bills or saving. And there's no way she'll ever be able to live on a budget. After I'm gone, the survivor's portion of my pension will be a fraction of what we now get. The house is paid for, and this is how much money will be coming in each month." He pointed to a number on his pad. "This is approximately what the bills cost each month." He pointed to another number. "As you can see, there won't be a lot left. She'll need to use that for food and incidentals."

Samantha stared at the numbers yet again, wondering how her money-obsessed, control freak father had ever gotten into such bad financial condition. He claimed to have very little savings, and he had no life insurance, no catastrophic or long-term care insurance, nothing as a safety net. It was as if he planned to drop dead one day instead of needing special care. If anyone could plan that, he could. But what she didn't understand was why he couldn't have planned better for Mom.

Displaying more confidence than she felt, she offered, "I think she'll do OK, Dad, but of course, I'm here to help."

"She's going to need it. Mark my words." It sounded almost as if he wanted Mom to fall on her face.

"I need to get back to work, Dad. I'm only supposed to take quick breaks to visit you. Arthur and I will come by Sunday. I'll be back a few times over the course of Barbara's redo."

"OK, see you then." Stanley's white head was already bent over his book as he waved a hand at her in dismissal.

Out in the dining room, Mom labored over her project, her jeweler's magnifying glasses like a miner's helmet. Her failing eyes only slowed her down a little; the doctor had said it was macular degeneration, but maybe he was wrong. She was still doing quite well with her jewelry. Samantha hoped it never got too bad. Making jewelry was what kept Mom sane.

"I'm leaving, Mom. I'll come back when I can. Arthur and I will stop by on Sunday. Do you have anything you want me to pick up at Price Club or anywhere?"

"I can't think of anything this time."

"I'll fertilize your citrus trees Sunday. I'll pick up the fertilizer and you can reimburse me."

"OK," Mom said distractedly.

"I have to do mine anyway, and that way you don't have to lug heavy things around and crawl around under your trees."

"I could do it, but if you insist..." Mom's resentment was palpable. Samantha knew that Mom wasn't happy about accepting help with the yard, but she also knew she was getting too infirm to do many of the things she used to do. It made for a mutually unhappy situation.

Samantha patted Beau and left to finish the rest of her workday.

When she got home, Arthur was sitting in a wing chair in the great room, reading the paper. He looked up briefly to acknowledge her return, but said nothing and went back to reading. She registered an inexplicable annoyance towards him.

Her mind went back to her Dad's spiel, and she got the connection. Arthur hadn't mentioned anything about providing for her, yet he was nearly 20 years older than she.

Why hadn't Arthur prepared for the future? Here she was working full time while he played tennis most days, and he had never taken out life insurance or talked about anything that would protect her ability to stay in their home if he died. When he died.

She swallowed her concerns and went back to the bedroom to take a shower.

Sally, 11:10am

SALLY PUT the phone down and did a little victory dance around her Mom's living room. The job offer was everything she could have asked for and more. She could hardly believe she'd gotten such a wonderful job so fast!

Too bad Mom wasn't home to celebrate, but she had her cooking class and then was taking Sheba to the vet. Now would be a good time to rent that apartment they'd looked at yesterday, the one she liked so much. Worried that someone else might get it if she delayed, she decided to go without Mom. It would be easier that way, anyhow.

She got her purse, checking that she had the cash Mom had given her, and headed out to get her new place. The apartment complex was a trying 20-minute drive west on a heavily traveled four-lane highway that was always choked with traffic, or at least had been every time Sally drove down it. Today was no exception.

She arrived at the Desert Palms apartment complex, filled out paperwork and placed a deposit, then let herself into her new home and walked around the apartment, savoring the sense of freedom and the adventure of starting a new life. Her unit on the second floor had two bedrooms and a nice view of the pool and inner courtyard. It even had a stacked washer and drier. Standing in the empty space, she could feel herself expanding and relaxing.

Mom meant well, but 13 days of living with her had shown Sally how ill-suited they were for living together. Once she got into her apartment, she could do what she liked; no prohibitions against alcohol, no worries about bringing a man home with her. She'd forgotten how restrictive living with parents was.

She shuddered to think what living with Mom full time would have been like. Desperation had nearly driven her to do something colossally stupid. Pretense was natural to her (isn't that how everyone manages to live with family?), but keeping it up 24/7 took a toll. After nearly two weeks with Mom, it was clear living with her would mean full-time acting, and she wasn't up for that. Now she wouldn't have to.

She locked up and headed back, stopping for a bite to eat on the way, since she'd missed lunch.

A couple hours later, Mom walked through the door carrying Sheba's travel crate, a sad look on her face.

"What's wrong, Mom?"

"The vet says she has a mass, and it's probably cancer, but they're doing some tests to make sure. At her age, there isn't much we can do about it. Just keep her comfortable for as long as possible." She put the crate down, opened the door and coaxed Sheba out. Sheba walked arthritically towards the master bedroom.

"I'm so sorry, Mom. I know how much Sheba means to you." This was going to take the fun out of her announcement.

"I'm having a hard time accepting it. I know she's old, but I don't know what I'll do without her." Helen picked up the crate and carried it to the garage to put it in a cupboard.

When she came back in, Sally went over and hugged her. "That's terrible news, but I have some good news. Do you want to hear it?"

Mom smiled weakly. "I could use some good news."

"I got a job offer, a really good one. They were impressed with my experience, and they'll give me maternity leave, and they have an on-site day care center. My boss is really cool! It couldn't be better!"

"That's terrific news! Congratulations. Now you can choose your apartment." Mom was making an effort, but her voice was flat.

"Already did that. As soon as I heard, I went and rented that one I liked so much. I didn't want to lose it. I can move in this weekend."

Mom looked stunned. "Wow, it all happened so fast!"

"I can hardly believe it myself." Sally wanted to jump up and down, but tamped down her excitement, since Mom was still reeling from all the news, good and bad.

Mom sat down and sighed. "What are you going to do about your belongings back home?"

"I put them in storage before I left. I was thinking maybe I can coax Warren into loading up a U-Haul and bringing it down sometime. Do you think he'll come for Thanksgiving?" Sally sat down on the sofa and patted Mom's arm encouragingly.

"Maybe. I've suggested they come down, but they haven't committed yet." Mom was looking a bit lost at the pace of change.

"I can make do with minimal stuff for a while."

Mom's blue-green eyes finally sparked with interest. "You need furniture. I'll take you to some estate sales. You can pick up good stuff that way."

It thrilled Sally that Mom was getting with the program. "That's a great idea! We might even be able to do that this weekend since I don't have a lot of stuff to move. I'll get an airbed or futon and maybe a small dining set, some dishes and things like that. But I don't need a lot."

"When I move, you can have furniture I won't need." Sally clapped her hands together in excitement, and Mom smiled. "I have an appointment with a realtor next week, and I'm hoping to find a smaller place here in Palm Lakes."

They walked out to the kitchen, and Mom made iced tea for them to take out to the patio. It was still pretty hot, but Sally liked watching the hummingbirds come to the feeder.

"So how was your cooking class with Mr. Movie Star?"

"Oh, really, Sally, don't dramatize it. We're just partners in the class, which was really fun. We made paté."

"So do I get to try some?"

A look crossed her mother's face. It almost looked like guilt. "Well, I forgot to bring a container with me, so Alexander took it all home...We're having dinner at his place tonight."

"Wow, that was quick! You already have a date with him?" Sally raised an eyebrow appraisingly. "I underestimated you."

"It's not a date, Sally."

"Sure sounds like it to me." Sally started giggling, and Mom smiled.

"Neither of us is interested in dating. He's just a friend." Mom paused, seeming to contemplate something. "It was really strange. I expected to feel awkward, and I did at first, but after a while, it was like we'd known each other forever. We didn't need to talk a lot; we worked together surprisingly well. I felt funny when he asked me to dinner, but he managed to put me at ease about it. Now that I'm talking with you, I'm nervous again."

Sally patted her hand encouragingly. "So what are you having for dinner?"

"He hasn't given me details, but it's salmon, and I have to help cook."

"Is he coming to pick you up?"

"Yes, you'll have to say hi."

"Hell no, Mom. That would spoil the whole thing. He'd feel he had to invite me as well. I'm going to stay out of sight. I'll keep Sheba company. When you get home, if I'm still up, you can tell me all about it."

"There won't be a lot to tell, but I'll be happy to share."

"So what are you wearing?"

Mom looked at her with confusion. "I guess I'll wear what I wore to the party. I don't have anything else."

"That's just wrong! You need something different. You can't let him see you in the same outfit twice in a row!"

"He's coming to pick me up at 5:30. I don't have time to shop, and since it isn't a date, I don't have to worry about rules like that. I'm going to wear what I wore to the party."

They sat in silence for a few minutes, then Mom spoke up. "What do you say we shop the estate sales this weekend and go out for a meal Sunday to celebrate your good fortune?"

"I'd love that!"

"Then it's a deal." She watched as Mom got up and took the glasses back into the house. Alexander would be here in less than two hours. She needed to give Mom a pep talk. She was too timid; no wonder, given what Dad was like.

Eligible men seemed scarce here, and if Alexander was interested, Mom should go for it. Maybe she should give her a safe sex talk...Nah, Mom was too old-fashioned to fall into bed with him on a first date. But it would be nice if it worked out for her, not only because she deserved some happiness. Having a boyfriend would also keep Mom from focusing too much on Sally's life.

Now if only she could find a hunky guy for herself.

* * *

Alexander, 5:29pm

WHEN ALEXANDER PULLED into Helen's driveway, the sun was getting low, but the air was still oppressively hot. She opened the door dressed in the same outfit she'd worn to Barbara's party.

She was a beautiful woman, and there was something about her that hinted at hidden depths and mysteries, which intrigued him. Even more attractive was her total lack of interest in dating him. Her fear of him, or rather, men in general, put him strangely at ease, something he hadn't felt with a woman in a very long time.

"Alexander," she said nervously. "Would you like to come in?"

"Not necessary, Helen. I'm ready to put you to work in my kitchen if you're ready to go. Do you have a container for paté?"

She laughed at his joke while stepping back to get her purse and a small plastic container off a nearby chair. At the car, he held the door open for her. She paused as if she wasn't used to such chivalrous treatment. He almost cracked wise but decided it might unnerve her if she realized he could read her so easily.

She sank into the rich leather seat and reached to touch the dashboard, which had real wood trim. She brushed her fingers over his car phone. It was charming to see her sense of awe at the little luxuries. She broke the silence about halfway to his house. "So, you're going to have to tell me soon what we're eating." It was rewarding to see she was anticipating the evening with interest.

"We're having a coconut seafood curry on jasmine rice accompanied by a very nice bottle of Riesling."

"I thought you said we were having salmon?"

"It's a salmon curry. You said today that you like ethnic dishes with exotic flavors. I took you at your word. Is curry OK?"

"As long as it isn't too hot, I would like it very much."

They chatted about the weather and cooking class and soon arrived at his house. As he pulled into the driveway, he surreptitiously watched her reaction.

Her jaw partially dropped as she took in the grand front entry and the casita nestled next to the house. He drove into the two-car garage that had extra space for his golf cart. The floor-to-ceiling cabinets kept the garage spotless, and the pink epoxy-painted cement made it feel like an extension of the indoors instead of a garage.

"Oh my God! This is beautiful!"

Her admiration tickled him. "Thank you. I'm glad you like it. I'll give you the nickel tour when we go inside."

He got out and rushed around to open her door. She beat him to it, but he offered his hand to help her get out of the seat. She hesitated before accepting. Her hand was cold and dry, and she took it back from him as soon as possible, but instead of offending him, her behavior made him feel more protective towards her. Everything about her said she was frightened of men.

It was a perfect time of day to show her the house. The late afternoon sunlight poured in through the bank of picture windows in the great room. She oohed and ahhed as he led her to the kitchen and showed her the walk-in pantry, wine cooler and 6-burner range plus 2 wall ovens. She ran her hand along the dark granite counter top and touched the oak cabinets briefly.

She opened the refrigerator door and suddenly closed it as if she'd been caught snooping. "I'm sorry. I didn't mean to be nosy. I just got carried away."

"Help yourself, Helen. The kitchen is my favorite room."

She continued to look admiringly at everything. When he felt she'd had her fill, he said, "Let me show you the rest of the place before we cook." He pointed for her to go through the doorway at the other end of the kitchen, and they stepped into the large living room that looked out on the golf course. "I have such a nice view, and that's important to me. I know they say you can't eat scenery, but somehow it feeds my soul."

She sighed in pleasure. "I know exactly what you mean. I've always wanted to live somewhere with a view. This is spectacular." As he guided her across the room, they passed a chair where a large Siamese cat lay sleeping.

"Oh, I love cats. I have one myself. I should have made you come in and meet my Sheba. Who is this?

"That's Fido."

"Not really? That's a dog's name." She looked at him skeptically.

Alexander chuckled. "He's as faithful as any dog ever was. I've had him for seven years. He was a feisty young thing when I moved to Palm Lakes. I was kind of ignorant. I let him run loose. I almost lost him to a coyote through my own stupidity. I'll tell you the story one day. He stays in the house now. He's my best buddy."

"I know just how you feel. My Sheba is much older than Fido. She's my best friend in the whole world," she said with a catch in her voice.

He showed her the rest of the house, and she became more relaxed, asking him questions about his mementos from his travels. When they got into his office, she asked to see his books. He pulled out copies, and she admired them, so he told her he'd give her a signed copy of any one she wanted.

The expansive glow was replaced by embarrassment. "I didn't mean to be hinting for that."

"I know you weren't. I'd be pleased to give you a copy of any of them you want."

"You can't be doing that for everyone."

"I don't." He paused and looked into her eyes. "You're the first person I've had visit."

Her eyes widened in surprise. "You're kidding me!"

"Why would I kid about that? I socialize a lot, but I'm a very private person, and I don't share my home with people. Maybe I'm an urban hermit."

"Then why me?" Curiosity put two small wrinkles between her eyebrows.

"I honestly don't know. It just seemed natural." He nodded to the book she held. "You can let me know anytime, and I'll get you an autographed copy. Let's get to work now."

Back in the kitchen, he pulled all the ingredients and necessary tools out of cabinets, refrigerator and pantry and placed them on the counter and island in a fashion that would divide the labor between them. She watched intently, commenting on the fancy stainless steel pots and pans.

"Would you be willing to do the chopping of veggies while I prepare the fish and measure the spices and other ingredients?"

"Sure, I can do that. Just tell me how much and how you want them chopped."

"I've placed the right number of garlic cloves, onions and serrano chilis there, along with a chunk of fresh ginger. Mince the garlic; chop the onions small; peel and grate the ginger; strip the seeds out of the chilis and then chop them small. A copy of the recipe is on the counter so you don't have to remember. Be careful of the chilis. Wash your hands and use the silver bar by the main sink to remove the juice, or you'll get a nasty surprise later when you touch your eyes or nose."

She seemed a bit overwhelmed, but all she said was, "What silver bar?"

He took her gently by the shoulder and walked her to the main sink, reaching past her to pick up a silver soap-bar-shaped object that lay in a shiny metal container that also held a sponge and vegetable brush. "After you use the soap to wash, pretend the metal bar is soap and wash your hands in water with it, rubbing any surface that touched the peppers. It absorbs smells from fish or garlic and even neutralizes hot pepper juice."

Even though he only had a partial view, he could see her face transform as if he'd given her a magic wand. "I've never heard of such a thing. I can't wait to try it." Her wonder was so joyful, he impulsively patted her shoulder. Instantly, her body tensed up, so he removed his hand, making a mental note to give her more space at the same time as feeling challenged to do whatever it would take to win her trust.

He reached for an open wine bottle that sat way back on the counter by the sink and filled two glasses with red wine. Handing her one, he smiled and said, "Here's to a lovely meal and a great evening."

They clinked glasses. He watched her sip the wine, waiting for her reaction. She didn't disappoint him. "Oh my heaven, this is good! What is it? I don't think I've ever tasted wine this good before."

"This is a good Beaujolais. It will go nicely with some of this fine paté we made." He pointed to a platter of paté and crackers on the counter, and they each sampled some.

"I can't get over how good it is. Did it cost a lot?"

"Yes. But remember, this is what I do, so it's tax deductible." He smiled teasingly at her, but she didn't seem to realize he was pulling her leg.

"Well, I never would have guessed. I confess I thought it was a lot of pretense about expensive wine. Maybe I was being snobbish because I couldn't afford the good stuff. Thank you so much for sharing this with me."

They fell into an easy rhythm as they prepared the meal, and a short while later, he plated the food on elegant china. "Do you mind taking these to the dining room while I open the Riesling?"

"Glad to do that. The sooner I can taste this, the better." She grabbed them and headed for the dining room.

Her enthusiasm was contagious. "I'm really looking forward to it, too. I never tried this recipe, and I'm hungry."

She stopped in the doorway and turned to him, her mouth open in surprise. "You're kidding! Not about being hungry...about never making this recipe before."

"No, I'm quite serious. You're a guinea pig tonight." He turned to the counter to open the wine.

The evening sped by. Dinner was excellent, but then he knew it would be. Helen was rapturous about the whole experience. Obviously, she didn't dine often like this. She was alternately shy and expressive, but both suited her.

She didn't want to leave the cleanup to him, so he had to promise that next time, she could help do dishes instead of being treated like a guest. She seemed surprised at his assumption of a future invitation, which further convinced him she had no designs on him, as if he needed proof. She was the most genuine person he'd met in a long time.

They repaired to the living room to sit in comfortable chairs and chat for a while. He went over to the bar. "What can I get you to finish the evening off? I have a nice sherry if you like that."

"I'm not sure I should drink anything else. I fear I may have overdone it tonight."

"I'll be driving you home, so do whatever feels best to you. I'm going to have a small sherry."

"I'll have one, too, then. But you are leading me into temptation."

He laughed as he carried the two glasses over and set hers by her hand. Almost as if on cue, Fido got up and came to sit in his lap.

Helen's eyes brightened. "He seems devoted to you."

"Yes, he is very affectionate. He sleeps with me and is usually much more talkative. I think he's being reticent because he isn't used to having company."

"That reminds me of Barbara introducing us. It seems like a long time ago we were at her party. I've only just met you, but I feel we've known each other forever...I'm blathering on because I drank so much. Sorry. It's just that I really appreciate your taking me under your wing in the class, and this invitation was so kind and unexpected. I don't get out much at all, and this has been so wonderful." She paused and looked downward.

He pretended he didn't notice the tears welling in her eyes. "I have a bit of a confession to make. I don't mean to brag, but with the ratio of bachelors to single women in Palm Lakes, I'm under siege much of the time, and I've had to develop strategies to avoid getting flooded with casseroles, dinner invitations and even offers of sexual comfort. Barbara's suggestion was a godsend. She told me you're recently widowed, and she sang your praises, and I felt that I would benefit as much as you by the partnership. I assumed you wouldn't be looking for a relationship, and it was an unexpected bonus that we hit it off so well. It's nice to have a friend. It's been a long time for me."

She stayed quiet for a minute, then looked up at him, her damp eyes glistening in the half-light."I'm glad you feel you're getting something out of it. You're right. I'm not looking for another husband. I doubt I'll ever marry again. It was an unpleasant experience. My husband was abusive. I've never told anyone else, but I want to be honest with you." She began to twist her pants leg. "I'm not looking for sympathy. It was my choice to stay with him. But I never had friends, so this means a lot to me." She paused as if wondering what else to say.

That explained a lot. "Anything you say to me stays with me, Helen. And I appreciate your trusting me enough to share that." He was certain something else was bothering her but didn't want to press.

"I'm sorry. I had too much wine tonight. I'm becoming maudlin. I don't want to be bad company."

"You're not bad company. You've been through a lot lately. I'm happy to listen if you feel like talking. I promise to keep whatever you say between us."

She suddenly burst into tears, gulping air like she was drowning. Even though he'd anticipated it, it shook him up to see her so upset. He went to the bar, grabbed the box of tissues and offered them to her. She took them and pulled a couple out, struggling to get control. He wondered if he should put his arm around her, or if her natural shyness would make that a bad move. So he just stood there quietly waiting for a couple of minutes.

"Gosh, I am *so* sorry. I'm not used to being treated kindly." She wiped her eyes delicately and blew her nose. "I'm not usually such a high maintenance person. I guess things have been piling up on me lately, and today the vet told me that Sheba has cancer and there isn't much she can do to help. She wants me to consider euthanizing her, and Sheba is all I have at the moment."

She scrunched up the kleenex in her hand and pulled a new one from the box. "Plus I'm going to have to sell my house. I don't have the money to maintain it. Then my daughter showed up out of the blue; that's a whole 'nother story. There's just been so much change, and most of it very trying. Lou used to say I couldn't handle the real world. Maybe he was right."

She paused as if overcome with emotion, and began to cry again, this time less violently. "Please forgive me for dumping all this on you."

"I'm so sorry to hear about Sheba. I would feel terrible if something happened to Fido. Please let me know if I can help. I can drive you to the vet, so that whatever you do there, you can focus on Sheba and not worry about driving. Would you let me do that?"

"I don't want to impose on you, Alexander."

"It would be my pleasure to help. We're friends, right? Friends help each other through times like this."

"OK. I'll let you know." She seemed embarrassed at her outburst.

He contemplated sharing about himself, but it just seemed too early and too risky. If they remained friends, he'd have to, but maybe he could put it off for a while. Instead, he decided to offer sympathy.

"Years ago, I lost someone who meant the world to me, and ever since, I've wondered if I will ever find love again; in fact, I promised myself I never would, because it hurt too much. The years have dulled the pain, but it's still there. Now and then I still have a good cry about it. Yet I wouldn't give up one moment with my lover. They were the best times of my life. I know it sounds like a platitude, but everything changes, so it won't always be like this for you. I hope you'll let me be part of your support network."

He sat down and reached for his glass and held it up, indicating he wanted to make a toast. She smiled weakly and lifted her glass.

"Here's to good friends."

"Yes," she seconded quietly. They sipped their wine in a

companionable silence. The storm seemed to have passed and left in its wake a deeper sense of intimacy between them. She sighed as if a weight had been removed from her.

He could tell she was wrung out. "Are you feeling tired? It's been a long evening. I'm not trying to get rid of you, but you look exhausted. I can take you home."

She looked at him with gratitude. Nodding in assent, she put her glass down.

"You promise I can help clean the kitchen next time?"

He smiled that she referred to a next time. "Of course! You're family now, and you can't get away with leaving the dirty dishes all to me, woman."

Her laugh was genuine and uninhibited. "I'll be a good helper."

"Let's get you home." He stood up and went to where she had laid her purse and handed it to her. Then he got her container with her share of the paté.

They didn't speak on the short drive, but it felt comfortable. He pulled into her driveway and quickly went around to open the door. This time, he beat her to it. He handed her out and then walked up the sidewalk with her. After a minute fumbling for her house key, she got the door open and turned to him. "Thank you for the best evening I've had in years."

He was flattered and at the same time sad that she felt that way. She was hesitating as if wondering what to do next, so he put his arms around her and gave her a brotherly hug. At first, she flinched; then she leaned into him.

"You get a good night's sleep and pet Sheba for me. Call me anytime, and promise you'll let me drive you to the vet."

"I will." She went into the house, and he waited to hear the deadbolt close.

He walked back to the car and drove home. It was pretty obvious he'd have to tell her soon. First, he'd have to figure out for himself exactly what was going on. She'd dropped into his life as if fitting into a spot made just for her. What exactly *was* the spot? And what would she say if she knew everything about him?

CHAPTER SIX

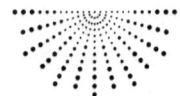

TUESDAY, SEPTEMBER 12, 1995

Tanya, 8:32am

Tanya woke disoriented. Her mouth was dry and tasted like sawdust, and her head felt like a spike had been driven into it. She wanted nothing more than to go back to sleep, but she knew it wouldn't happen. She rolled to her side and slowly pushed herself up.

She needed a pick-me-up to get going. She reached to the bottom of the bed where her red wrapper lay and slipped it on. Padding barefoot from the master bedroom to the kitchen, her bright red toenails flashing against the white of the tiles, she passed the guest bedroom and noted her husband was not in bed. He must have gone golfing this morning. She really didn't give a damn where he was.

Thinking about her useless husband led (as usual) to thoughts of her neighbor Owen. He wasn't tall, but God was he built. He radiated power and strength with all those muscles. He had the attitude of an alpha male who knew his place and wouldn't relinquish it. It made her sleepy body tingle in all the right places just thinking about him touching her. If only he would.

As she mixed her morning orange juice and vodka, she grimaced at how things had gone at Barbara's party. It had been over two weeks, and she hadn't had another chance to approach Owen. He hadn't rebuffed her at the party, but he hadn't encouraged her, either. He must be playing hard to get. No doubt he had his pick of women, just like any single man in Palm Lakes. Speaking of single, that Alexander was a real hunk of a man, but he had an odd vibe. Maybe he was gay. The ones that looked like movie stars often were.

Owen was another matter altogether, simmering with raw male power. She could tell he was attracted to her, but he was holding back for some reason. Maybe he was shy and didn't like the public attempts to connect. Could he be religious and have scruples about her being married? She doubted it. He had an aura of danger that was quite enticing; nothing like that Posse guy, Red what's-his-name, who reeked of straight arrow and treated her like she was trailer trash.

Over the years she'd found it rather easy to cheat on her husband. To her knowledge, he'd never discovered any of her affairs. On the other hand, he was quite vocal about her drinking, though he never had the balls to do anything about it. He was a poor excuse for a man. Unlike Owen. She bet Owen was a man who could assert himself with a woman.

How could she approach Owen in a way that opened the door for seduction? If she went to his house, that was pretty forward. But if she were bringing a gift, that would be OK. As a single fellow, perhaps he'd like some home-baked treat. Neighbors did that for each other, didn't they? She'd seen Barbara carrying food to Helen after Lou died. That should get her in the door.

But what to take? She wasn't that good in the kitchen. That's why she loved getting things from the bakery at the grocery store. They had a remarkable assortment of baked goods that were not only tasty; they looked like works of art. In fact, just yesterday she'd gotten several chocolate croissants that were exceptional. She could put a few of them on a plate and pass them off as her own cooking. Men were dense that way.

Before she had a chance to consider any reservations she might have about the plan, it lay before her fully formed and ready to execute. Her husband never got home until dinner on golf days, so she had hours to burn.

She got dressed for seduction in black tights, high-heeled sandals and a red long-sleeved silk top with a scooped neck. She applied her makeup more carefully than usual, wanting it to pass close inspection, then put on plenty of jewelry. Stepping back a couple of paces to assess herself in the mirror, just enough to fuzz the image, she decided she looked enticing.

Back in the kitchen, she loaded a plastic plate with pastries and covered them with Saran wrap. As an added thought, she made some coffee and poured it into an insulated carafe.

She looked out the front window. As usual, the street was empty. It was a short walk to Owen's house, four doors down on her side of the street.

She'd had just enough alcohol to give her courage, but not too much. She felt alive, and it was getting rarer that she felt this way. She *had* to have him. She had long since lost touch with an awareness of the risks she took and the price she might have to pay for her actions. That part of her mind had been put to sleep by the liberal use of alcohol. She was only aware of the sweet siren song of passion.

She came up to Owen's sidewalk and quickly turned in. Pressing the doorbell, she heard it echo through the house. A minute later, the front door opened, and Owen stared at her through the screen door, his eyes narrowed and his mouth tight. He made no move to open the door.

Even through the alcoholic haze, she could feel the judgment oozing off him. She briefly wished she could hide, as his gaze made her feel like a prey animal, but she shook off the feeling. She wasn't about to give up. "Owen, I made some pastries, and I thought you might like to have some coffee and croissants to start the day. It's too pretty a day to be alone. May I come in?"

He paused just long enough that she could sense his uncertainty, but beyond that, she found him hard to read. While she would have preferred him to open the door right away, at least he wasn't slamming it in her face or cussing her out. She waited more patiently than she normally would, confident of her eventual success.

Without saying anything, he unlocked the screen door and began to open it just as a car drove down the street. Both of their heads turned to see a Posse car, and the driver was looking straight at them. He raised his hand in salute as he cruised by.

For whatever reason, the event spurred Owen into action. He reached out and took the plate from her, then shut the door. "Nice of you to bring these. I'm busy now, but I'll eat them later. You don't need this plate back, do you?" He shut the door in her face, leaving her standing there with the coffee.

It took her a moment to recover. She couldn't make sense of his reaction. It wasn't a "yes," but it certainly wasn't a "no," either. What was his game? And did the Posse guy have anything to do with Owen's behavior? Tanya started back down the sidewalk and headed home, pondering the man's behavior. She'd never had this much of a challenge before.

She didn't let it get her down. The ones that were harder to get were more fun. The sex was always better for having to wait for it. Maybe he knew that, and he was playing her.

She went inside and poured herself some coffee, spiking it with vodka. The Posse guy who drove by was Red, the one who'd interviewed her about Barbara's missing cat. At the time, she'd felt he was trying to implicate Owen in wrongdoing, and she'd done her best to defend him. That explained it! Owen had gotten spooked that the same man saw him with her, and probably thought it wise not to have her seen going into his house. Maybe he was even protecting her reputation. These law guys loved to remember details that later got dredged up, and she preferred to avoid that. She was actually lucky Owen had the presence of mind not to let her in.

She sipped her coffee and wondered if she should phone and thank him. No, that wasn't going to get her anywhere. She needed to do something that would move things forward. She'd invite him to have a drink with her. But it had to be somewhere neutral, outside of Palm Lakes, somewhere residents didn't visit and at a time when it was unlikely they would be seen by anyone they knew.

The best place would be a hotel bar so that they could get a room if things worked out as she planned. There was a nice new hotel just down the road from the entrance to Palm Lakes, and it had a bar. She'd never been in it, but she'd check it out herself, then make a date with him ostensibly to thank him for his sensitivity.

As she pondered the steps to take in her seduction of Owen, she sipped her coffee and fantasized about him touching her. He was strong and powerful, but she wagered she could teach him a thing or two.

* * *

Owen, 9:45am

OWEN PACED BACK and forth in the kitchen, looking at the plate of croissants each time he passed them.

"What was I thinking? Why did I take them? Did that cop see us? Of course, he did. It's not like it's illegal to bring food to a neighbor. But now he's seen me with her."

"You moron. Now you've done it. He's suspicious." His mother's voice, right on cue.

"Oh, shut up, Mother. What could he be suspicious of? Pastry kidnapping? Assault with a croissant?" A bead of sweat trickled down the side of his face, and his fists were clenched as he continued to plow a furrow in the tiles of the kitchen.

"Junior, you know what I'm talking about. You get more impulsive all the time. Killing that cat was a mistake. Now you have a cop watching you. He may even be cruising this neighborhood hoping to catch you at something. All he needs is to remember details that later turn out to be important. I know you've been itching to do something with that bimbo. If something happens to her, don't you think you'll be at the top of the list of suspects?"

"So what? It doesn't matter what he suspects. It matters what he can prove. I'm always careful. I don't leave evidence. Besides, I don't have plans to do anything to that woman. She's the one chasing me."

"You miss my point, Junior. You know you're having a stronger pull to do something to her, and if you lose control, you *will* get caught this time. You can't do something to a neighbor and hope to get away with it the way you do with strangers. What is the matter with you? You're getting sloppy and irresponsible, just like your father. It's going to be the end of you."

Owen clenched his fists over his ears, his elbows on the counter next to the croissants. Suddenly he swept the plate onto the floor and immediately regretted it when the plastic wrap gave way and the pastries tumbled onto his pristine living room carpet, sending a shower of crumbs and bits of chocolate glaze in all directions.

He grabbed his cleaning supplies and went to clean up the mess, dabbing the carpet after spraying it with cleaner. Then he dumped everything into the trash can in the kitchen.

"I can't talk about this anymore." He stalked into the weight room and stripped, putting on his exercise clothes and immersing himself in a workout. Forty-five minutes later, covered in sweat, he sat on the bench with his head in his hands.

She was right. He was becoming more impulsive. When the opportunity came to do the cat, he hadn't been able to resist.

When he thought about Tanya standing at his door with the pastries, he remembered his initial shock. But the shock was quickly followed by a powerful desire to drag her into the house and do things to her. He knew she wanted him, even though she was married. The strong sexual response to her warred with his judgment of her, and suddenly he realized why the conflict was such a familiar feeling. How could he have forgotten?

He sat on the bench twisting his thinning hair. All the times his mother had tried to seduce him when he was a teenager came flooding back to him from wherever he'd buried them, along with overwhelming nausea. He'd never given in, but her warped behavior had filled him with such toxic emotions, he'd finally snapped one day and knocked her down the stairs. And found out how good it was to release his anger. Though the price was listening to her criticize him almost daily ever since.

Tanya did indeed remind him of Mother. He hadn't been so conflicted about a woman since he was 16 and repelling Mother's advances. When Mother got drunk and came on to him was the only time she had ever acted like she loved him. Now Tanya was doing the same thing, even looking like Mother. But she wasn't his mother. He felt a tightness in his chest release as he realized the implications. He could do whatever he liked with her. He just wasn't completely sure what that was.

At some point, he would have to decide. He knew it wasn't wise to take a chance with Tanya. But when she touched him, he felt a current connect them as if they were opposite poles of two magnets and couldn't be pulled apart.

His mother had proven that women were sinful creatures willing to do anything to rule a man. They were all sluts, and they just wanted to bludgeon you with their power to get you to do things you didn't want by using sex as a weapon.

He dealt with them harshly now, but at times, he'd get a flash of desire for something different, something he couldn't articulate. He felt so empty, and no matter how many women he judged, it didn't fill the void, and the hole had been growing and growing lately. Tanya had flashed a light into that darkness, and although he hated her for it, he was nearly overcome with the desire to give in to the unnamed longing he felt.

He wanted her. And she wanted him. He was sure of it. It wasn't like the fake passion he found with hookers at truck stops. This was a woman who knew him and still wanted him. But what if she turned out to be like Mother? It was unpredictable and risky.

Tanya was relentless. He knew she'd be back, and her inability to sense the danger was going to get both of them in trouble. He didn't know how to get around it. He could yell at her or push her away, but the fact was, she was offering herself to him on a platter, and he wanted what she offered.

The only way he could avoid her would be to leave town. That's what he ought to do. Go away for a while and maybe find a woman to judge. Let Tanya find another man to stalk. But even thinking about that made him angry. He didn't want her to turn to someone else. He wanted her for himself.

Back and forth he went, fantasizing about Tanya and what the outcome would be if he gave in to his conflicted fascination with her. He could picture fucking her up against the wall in his bedroom, making her scream. She looked like the screaming type. Of course, that might not be good. The walls weren't insulated that well. They'd have to do it elsewhere. Shit, he was actually starting to plot where to take her. *Stupid!* He needed to get a grip.

He hesitated to leave the weight room, because it was the only place his mother didn't invade, and he needed peace. But he couldn't hide here forever. He knew that waffling about Tanya was going to get him into trouble, but the heady mixture of lust and judgment made his blood sing in a way nothing else could. Prolonging the decision was agonizingly exquisite foreplay, and he wasn't ready to give up this feeling yet, no matter what Mother said. He hadn't felt this alive in years.

* * *

Helen, 10:00am

THE SMALL REAL estate office was buzzing with activity when Helen arrived and announced herself to the receptionist. A minute later, a woman came striding up the narrow aisle between cubicles to where Helen stood waiting. Shari Lopez was a beautiful young Hispanic woman. Well, everyone looked young to her these days, at least outside of Palm Lakes.

They shook hands and smiled at each other. Shari was no more than 35 years old. Her simple blue dress was feminine but not seductive. Her shoes were stylish but sensible for walking around properties. Golden jewelry circled her ears, neck and wrists. The pendant in her elaborate necklace appeared to be lapis lazuli if she was remembering what Maddie had taught her.

"Is that lapis in your necklace?"

"Yes, indeed. I just love the golden matrix that runs through the stone. My husband gave me this for my last birthday."

"Lucky you. It's lovely."

"Thank you. I'm so glad Barbara told you to contact me. I understand you're looking for a condo, and there are a number of nice ones on the market. Let's sit at my desk while I get an idea of exactly what you are looking for, and then we'll see if we can take a look at some. The ones where the owners are not in residence will be easy, and we do have a few of those. For some, we might have to wait for an open house."

They walked back to the small cubicle where Shari worked. It was tidy and decorated with a photo of her with a handsome Hispanic man, no doubt her husband. There were silk flowers in a beautiful vase and some photos of outdoor activities like hang gliding and hiking hanging on the partition.

Shari gestured towards the folding chair wedged into what little space there was beside the desk, and Helen sat down, putting her purse on the floor at her feet.

"Could you give me an idea of what you're looking for, what features and price, etc.?"

"Well, I'm currently living in a house in Palm Lakes. My husband passed away a few months ago, and I can't maintain it financially. I like Palm Lakes, and I was hoping I could find a place within my budget."

"I'm so sorry for your loss." Shari paused with sincerity.

Helen didn't know what to say. She really didn't miss Lou at all, except possibly for the monkey wrench his death seemed to have thrown into her life. The ripples of his passing still threatened at times to overwhelm her, especially with Sheba's recent health problem. Helen struggled to maintain a calm exterior. "Thanks. I want a place with two bedrooms and one bath that also has a little garden area. I need the most economical option you have. At least, I suspect I do. The electric bill alone on my current home is squeezing me. I believe I can manage if I have a smaller place with less overhead."

"That's a wise move, Mrs. Mueller. The cost of air-conditioning in the summer is punitive here, and proper yard care is another huge expense. Downsizing should allow you to live more comfortably without sacrificing the important things. Are you sure you want a 2-bedroom unit? The 1-bedroom units are less expensive."

"I've thought about that, and I'd like to be able to put guests up. My kids sometimes come to visit, and I hate to make them stay at a motel. But you tell me the pros and cons."

"The decision is totally up to you. If you have grandchildren, a second bedroom won't be enough to put up family. It works fine for a single guest or a couple. Still, with one bathroom, that can make the visit a bit strained, with so many vying for the washroom. On the other hand, some residents use the guest bedroom as an office for a home business. That allows it to do double duty."

"I like to write, and I'm hoping to do more of it. So if I can afford the second bedroom, it would be dual purpose. I'm also concerned about the size of the kitchen. I like to cook rather than eat out. So I prefer not to have a tiny kitchen."

"That's very helpful to know. I do believe that at least one of the models could be just what you're looking for. It's called the Sierra, and it has a reasonably-sized kitchen. The second bedroom is small, but I think it would suit you. Let me see my listings...there's one I could show you today, and depending on how you feel about it, we can look at something larger or smaller afterwards. What do you think?"

"Yes, I would very much like to have a look and see how it feels."

They exited the office and went to Shari's car, a gleaming Audi. Shari chattered amiably on the short drive to the condo, which was located fairly close to the entrance gate of the community. As they drove along the road, Helen could see the block wall that marked the boundary of the community ran along the back of the condos' yards. Not that crime was a real problem here, but she felt a little safer in her current location.

Shari seemed to guess what she was thinking. "These condos all have nice but small back yards. The six-foot wall at the back is the boundary of Palm Lakes. We haven't had any instances of anyone scaling the wall to commit a crime. I know you live alone, so your personal safety is a matter of concern. The higher population density here may be a deterrent, but for whatever reason, we don't get much crime, and it's usually because someone left their garage door up and forgot about it. And that happens everywhere in Palm Lakes."

They pulled to a stop right next to a 'For Sale' sign sporting a photo of Shari. The street was quiet and had no cars parked on it other than an old Ford with dented front fenders that sat in front of the condo next door. Helen could see a couple other 'For Sale' signs farther down the street.

She scrutinized the immediate neighborhood. There was a movement in the window across the street; someone was watching. That might not be all bad. She had nothing to hide.

All of the front yards looked much the same, with only minor differences in the landscaping plants. Some had white oleander trees, while others had pink or even red. All the bushes were neatly trimmed and the gravel yards were weed-free.

They walked up the short sidewalk to the front door. The condo was all on one level, and the lot appeared to be long and thin. The door was painted red and contrasted with the white stucco to give it a real Spanish feel.

"Does the condo association care for the front yards?"

"Yes, that will be included in your fee, which also includes some basic maintenance of the condo itself. It's a real blessing not to have to worry about things like a leaky roof, don't you think? You'll be responsible for your back yard, but it's a small space that you won't have much trouble handling."

Inside the condo was dim, because the pleated shades had been pulled shut, and the air was warm and stale. It probably seemed bigger than it actually was, since it was completely devoid of furnishings. Helen tried to imagine it with her furniture and quickly decided she would definitely have to give some pieces to Sally. Not that Sally would mind.

The Berber carpet was a neutral color (oatmeal?) and in good condition. The interior paint job looked recent, the walls a warm off-white. The pleated shades were also neutral colors. She'd need to add some color for warmth, but it would be easy with such a neutral palette as a base. A throw rug here, a bright painting or flower arrangement there would brighten it up. She had some accessories that would work well. She began to be able to picture herself living here.

The living room was small but workable. It was open to the kitchen, the counter and breakfast bar being the boundary between the two rooms. Having the kitchen open to the living room was a very attractive feature. Helen didn't like feeling cooped up in small spaces. The kitchen itself was indeed larger than she had expected. It wasn't quite as big as the one in her house, but it would do. The wooden cabinets were whitewashed, and the light countertop helped give a bigger feel to the room. The appliances were fairly new. She was pleased to see the stove was gas. Continuing through the kitchen, she came to the dining room (more like a breakfast nook) which looked out onto a small concrete patio and a forlorn back yard.

"I was thinking this might be what you're looking for. The open floor plan makes the space feel bigger, and this kitchen is larger than in other models. The bedrooms are nice, too." Shari pointed her to the hallway, and they stuck their heads in the first bedroom, which was the smaller of the two and faced the street. It had a closet with mirrored doors. The bathroom was next. It was more luxurious than she expected, with double sinks of cultured marble and a large bath/shower. A toilet room and linen closet were opposite the sinks.

Finally, they entered the master bedroom, which had a walk-in closet (small, but perfect for her needs). The room appeared to be big enough to have a desk, which would mean she could have her office there instead of in the second bedroom if she chose. It also had a sliding glass door that led to the patio and looked out on the yard.

"This is a fairly large model, with nearly 1300 square feet. Don't you feel they used it well to create a sense of spaciousness?"

"Oh, yes. This is nearly perfect. I don't care for floor plans that are chopped into small rooms just so you can say there are a lot of them." Satisfied with the interior, Helen turned her attention outward. "I'd like to see the back yard next."

Shari took the charlie bar out of the runner, unlocked the glass door and slid it open. She and Helen stepped out into the late morning light. The yard had a southwestern exposure, and the sun would heat this side of the condo in winter and summer. She might need a shade tree or maybe an awning to keep her electric bill down. There were a few miserable-looking bushes and some scrawny cacti in the gravel yard, but no real landscaping.

"The previous owners were elderly and didn't have money for the yard. But that gives you a chance to do it the way you want. It's small, so you wouldn't need many plants, and it already has good gravel. It shouldn't be too costly to landscape it, and you can do it a little at a time."

Helen was already planning in her mind what she'd like to see. A tree for shade, some bushes with color that attracted hummingbirds. She heard the traffic noises beyond the wall, but they were more comforting than annoying. The location was close to the post office and grocery store and about the same distance from the Rec Center as her current home.

Helen was feeling a delicious sense of anticipation. If she could afford this place, it would be perfect. It would be the first place she'd ever lived that was all hers.

"I'd like to find out more about the price, but if it's in my range, I'd like to have it. We'll need to place my home on the market and make buying this one contingent on the sale of mine. I don't have much in savings."

"We can work something out, Mrs. Mueller. I'm glad you like it. Except for the yard, this is a very well-maintained unit, and the yard won't be hard to fix up. Let's go back to the office and look at the details. I can arrange to get your house on the market as soon as you wish."

Before they could go back inside, a woman stepped out from the patio of the condo next door. She waved and walked over to the wrought iron fence that separated the two yards. "Hi! Are you going to be my Mom's new neighbor?"

The woman was not old enough to live in Palm Lakes. She had a half-smoked cigarette in the hand that hung over the top of the fence. Her lush dark hair contrasted with her pale skin and green eyes. She looked to be in her late 30s.

"I'm Mary Beth Jacobson, er, Costello. My Mom lives here. She told me this condo has been for sale for a while. Do you think you might buy it? It would be so great for Mom to have a neighbor. She lives alone. Well, except I'm here for a little while. But she's usually on her own."

Helen was surprised at how forward the woman was, but didn't want to offend a neighbor. "It's nice to meet you, Mary Beth. I'm Helen, and there is a possibility I might buy this condo. I'm just looking at the moment, but between you and me, I really like it."

"It's conveniently located, and most of the neighbors are pretty nice; well, there's a nosy old bat across the street, but everyone else is nice. I'll let you keep looking." Mary Beth waved and walked back to the patio, where there were a small table and two chairs.

After locking up, Shari waited patiently on the front step while Helen stood looking in all directions as if evaluating the neighborhood from the perspective of a homeowner. It really pleased her, but she'd have to look at the numbers and make sure she could afford it.

After looking at pricing details in the office, Helen bid Shari good-bye and went home to think about her options. It was a huge decision, and she'd never made any big ones on her own. Although she was excited at the prospect, she was afraid of making a financial error. Maybe she should take Barbara up on her offer of having Ben look at the numbers.

As she sat at her kitchen table eating a quick lunch and mulling over her options, the phone rang.

"Helen. It's me. Alexander. I was wondering if I could stop by for a brief visit this afternoon. I have something to talk with you about, and I'd love to meet Sheba if that's okay."

Her heart skipped a beat. She liked being around Alexander. When he had dropped her home the other night, she was thinking it was a perfect time for him to plant a kiss on her, and she had wondered what she'd do if he tried. She wasn't sure she wanted him as anything more than a friend, but in spite of her confusion, she was a little disappointed he hadn't kissed her.

His voice shook her out of her musings. "Is this afternoon a bad time?"

"No, of course not. What time shall I expect you?"

"How's 3 o'clock?"

"That will be fine. I'll see you then."

"See you soon."

She hung up the phone wondering what he wanted to talk about that couldn't be discussed in class. Maybe he wanted to offer to help with Sheba again and didn't want to risk her bursting into tears in public. But somehow that didn't feel like something he'd make a special trip to talk about, even though he had said he wanted to meet Sheba. It couldn't be anything bad, so she'd just have to wait and see.

Two hours later, the doorbell rang at exactly 3pm. She ushered him inside.

"Come on in and get cool. Would you like some iced tea or coffee?"

"Iced tea is perfect."

She led him into the kitchen and pointed at the breakfast nook table. "Have a seat. It isn't as grand as your kitchen, but I make a mean iced tea."

He laughed and sat down. He had to stretch his legs out to the side to avoid hitting the support under the center of the table.

"Sorry. It always seemed spacious to me," she quipped.

"I run into this everywhere. I'm good at accommodating."

She brought glasses of ice and the pitcher of tea, then ferried over a sugar bowl and spoons. Rummaging in the cabinet, she found a box of plain butter cookies and laid some on a plate. After carrying everything to the table, she sat opposite Alexander. "Don't be shy. Help yourself."

He poured both glasses of iced tea. "This is nice. Thanks. A small kitchen can be so cozy, don't you think?"

"When you aren't alone, it is." They crunched their cookies and sipped tea. "You have me in suspense. I'll introduce you to Sheba after we eat our snack, but surely you didn't come over just to meet her?"

"I confess I have something else I wanted to talk about. Actually, I have two something elses I want to talk about. I'm a little nervous." His eyes, which normally looked straight into hers, were looking down, and his voice sounded unsure. His nervousness rubbed off on her, and she started to hold her breath as he continued. "I really value our friendship. It was...unexpected that we hit it off so well, and I want to be totally honest with you. I'd like to keep being friends, but you need to know something about me." He paused in the tortured silence. "I'm gay. I don't tell people, and I don't think many have guessed. But if we are going to be friends, you have a right to know. I hope it isn't going to make a difference to you." His green eyes held a hint of doubt as they searched hers.

Helen didn't say anything for a minute simply because she was speechless. She would never have guessed. The fact was, she'd never had a gay person as a friend before, at least, not that she knew. But then, she hadn't had friends of any type.

She hurried to fill the awkward pause. "I'm sorry. I didn't mean to worry you. It doesn't matter a bit to me. I really like you, and I hope we can be friends. I don't mind that you don't want to date me. That actually makes things easier, doesn't it?"

His relief was obvious, and he let out a gusty sigh. "I hadn't asked what your religion or politics were. I was just going with my gut. I don't know why I feel like I've known you my whole life, but I do. I'm glad you don't mind. I haven't had a relationship in years; haven't wanted one."

"Was that because of the person you spoke of the other night at dinner?"

"Yes. He died of AIDS. There's never been anyone else for me."

"I'm so sorry. I've never had anyone I cared that much about; it must be terrible to lose someone you love. Lou and I married young. I was foolish and eager to get away from my family. He was older than I. It turned out badly. I'm actually glad he's gone." She looked at him as if worried he would judge her.

A shadow crossed his face. "You don't deserve to be treated that way...that came out wrong. No one should be treated that way, but especially not you. It fires up my protective instincts to hear you suffered that."

She basked in the unexpected attention. "No one has ever protected me before."

He smiled warmly. "Not to change the subject, but you need to be aware that people will assume we're a couple if we keep doing things together. Is that going to bother you?"

"Why wouldn't I want to be seen on the arm of the most handsome man in town, and a rich one at that?" She laughed in delight.

He shifted in his seat, looking more relaxed by the minute. "Well, now that we have that out of the way, I have something else to talk about. You told me you're looking for a new place to live. I have a suggestion. Why not move into my casita? It's not large, but you could use the main house as much as you like, and the yard is pleasant and spacious. I wouldn't charge you rent unless you insisted. It would allow you to stay in Palm Lakes and save money."

Helen's jaw dropped in surprise. "I don't know what to say. What brought that on? You're a private person who never invites anyone home."

"I am. But you are, too. I don't think we'd get in each other's way. I'm willing to give it a try. I know you'd probably want to have a place of your own eventually, but this could be considered a long term visit while you sort things out." His eyes shone with sincerity, but she still couldn't understand.

"Maybe it's just because I'm not used to grand gestures, but I can't get my head around it."

He leaned forward, an intense look on his face. "I know it's sudden, but it seemed that the clock was ticking. I can't explain why I feel it would work out. I just feel different when I'm with you, and I like it. It could help you through the transition until you get on your feet."

"I don't know how to thank you, Alexander. It's the kindest thing anyone has ever done for me." She felt tears welling up in her eyes.

"I can't imagine that's true." He smiled as if he thought she was joking.

"Imagine." She saw that shadow cross his face again fleetingly as his jaw clenched. She wanted to enjoy the moment, but she needed to tell him about the condo. "This morning I went to a realtor and looked at a condo and put in a bid for it. I've put my house up for sale. I will probably need a part-time job to make ends meet, but it looks like it would work out well for me. If I hadn't already made plans -- I just gave Shari the go ahead 30 minutes ago -- I'd take you up on your offer. I can't tell you how much it means to me."

With a hint of disappointment in his voice, he said, "It's not like you're leaving town. We'll still be able to cook together." Then he gave her the dazzling smile that always took her breath away.

Part of her wished she hadn't already made plans to buy the condo, but now wasn't the time to think about that. "Let me introduce you to Sheba."

He reached across the table and lightly patted her hand. "I'm glad we had this chat."

They stood up and he enveloped her in a brotherly hug. Now that she knew his secret, she felt no fear or ambivalence about letting him touch her. "I don't mind telling you that it's nice to be held. I've missed that my whole life, and I feel so blessed to have found you. And I confess it makes it easy on me not to have to wonder where it goes from here. I think I'm too old for romance."

"Nonsense, Helen, you're a beautiful woman, and no one is too old for romance. Except maybe me." His laugh was tinged with sadness.

She took his hand and led him back to the master bedroom, where Sheba slept on the bed. As they walked into the room, Sheba's head popped up and she meowed just once.

"You should feel honored. She doesn't usually speak to strangers." Helen went and sat down by Sheba.

Alexander stroked Sheba's long fur gently. "She's purring pretty loudly. I see what you mean about her being fragile. She doesn't have a lot of meat on her bones. But she seems in good spirits. It doesn't appear she's in pain. What do you think?"

"I don't think she's in much pain. But she has lost weight and strength. She likes me to carry her rather than jump. It's like she's gone through accelerated aging in the past weeks."

"I meant what I said the other night. I'm here for you. I've had to euthanize a pet in the past, and it isn't easy to do. I can take you if it comes to that, so you don't have to drive."

"I accept," Helen whispered quietly, stroking Sheba's fur.

A few minutes later, she walked Alexander to the door. He gave her a hug. "Let's make a date to have dinner again soon. I love cooking with you."

She felt overwhelmed by his support and generosity. "I don't know how to thank you, Alexander."

"That's what friends are for."

Tuesday, September 12, 1995

I hardly recognize my life. More has happened in the past month than in the previous twenty years. At first, most of it seemed bad. Now it's a mix of happy and sad.

Sally turned up pregnant, no job, asking to stay with me, and now, just three weeks later, she has a great job and a new apartment she loves. I still haven't processed that she intends to live here. I'm grateful to have her close by. And it's good to see her happy. I hope she'll be more careful about the company she keeps. That baby needs a good father, and she has a tendency to pick unreliable men whom she has to support. She promises she's given up drugs, and she said she wasn't drinking during the pregnancy, but sometimes I think she tells me what I want to hear instead of what she means. She's always been light somehow. Maybe that's one reason she's my favorite. I felt weighed down on earth, and she seems to float in the sky, unaffected by earthly troubles. Part of me wants to shelter her and keep her free from those burdens, but part knows that her natural attitude does not make her the most honest person. I love her anyway.

Alexander is a wonder. Imagine at my age having a man like him in my life. He's confided in me, befriended me, offered to help me in so many ways. The closeness and affection I feel for him bewilder me. But he seems as bemused by the whole thing as I am. It just feels good when we spend time together. I've never felt that way with anyone, and I love it. Him being gay actually helps. I'd never admit it to him, but I was finding myself attracted to him, and it made me nervous. Now I can set that aside and just be friends.

But there's still one big shadow. I feel guilty being so happy with Alexander while Sheba faces a death sentence. I can't bear the thought of putting her to sleep. When I had no one else, she was there for me. I had hopes of us spending years enjoying each other now that Lou is gone. How will I get along without her?

She paused, overcome with emotion. Laying the pen down and closing the book, she decided to go hold Sheba a bit. Maybe she'd like to be brushed.

* * *

Mary Beth, 10:45am

MARY BETH SAT OUTSIDE, finishing her second cigarette of the day. *Well, that went really well, stupid! What the hell were you thinking? Mom's paranoid about you being here, and you go announce yourself to the prospective new neighbor. How can you be sure she won't report you? God-damned idiot!*

Berating herself, she crushed the butt into the cheap plastic ashtray, the only one in the whole house. Mom didn't allow smoking indoors, and she didn't want to make it too inviting to smoke outside. In spite of the heat and the way her back hurt after sitting in the cheap lawn chair, Mary Beth liked it out here. Mom didn't come out much, and it was peaceful. The nicotine was doing its job. She just regretted being so effusive with Helen. Well, who knew if she'd even buy the place, or how long it would be before she moved in? No point borrowing trouble. But it did highlight how important it was for her to take some action towards getting on her feet again.

As much as she hated to admit it, Mom was right about that. She couldn't stay here without helping out, and her stay was limited in any case. Plus she was going batshit crazy only having Mom to interact with. She needed to get out and meet people and mingle.

She rose slowly, rubbing her lower back (would it *ever* heal from the accident?), promising herself she wasn't going to take a pill, but knowing she would have to give in eventually.

Back inside, she poured a cup of coffee and sat down to look at the local want ads. Her car wouldn't hold up to serious commuting, but surely there would be a job nearby that could support her. Yet each time she looked, she found nothing that sparked her interest. Maybe she was being too picky.

A while later, she folded the paper and put it down, depressed at the few prospects. There were jobs advertised, but most of them were hourly wage dead-ends. The more professional jobs, the ones that paid better, were aimed at someone with qualifications and experience she didn't have. She'd never really thought about it, but her last job had been a real plum. Old Mr. Watts had thought the world of her and promoted her probably higher than her experience warranted. She knew enough about computers to get around them, but she didn't have qualifications in the fancy programs people were asking for. She was more of a glorified secretary, and there didn't appear to be many jobs like that, at least not that paid anything.

She rubbed her eyes, wishing she had a bar of chocolate, but she'd resisted buying any last time she went shopping. It was her stab at showing will power, but she regretted it now. She really did want to get more fit, though. She'd been walking most days, early in the morning. That in itself was a huge change that had gotten Mom to mellow out. Or else the scare with her heart did. She hadn't had much fire in her since the attack of angina last month. Her doctor had adjusted her meds, and she seemed to be doing better, but she had slowed down noticeably. Mary Beth wasn't sure if it was fear of triggering another episode or just a natural winding down of her energy. Regardless, it had been calmer, and that was a pleasure.

Today was her day to cook. She'd insisted on cooking the main meal every other day, and Mom had relented, which was actually kind of a scary surprise. She'd planned to do a crock pot chili, as that would make a number of meals and was both filling and inexpensive. She needed to make it mild for Mom's digestion, but otherwise, they both liked it. Food was one of the rare things on which they saw eye to eye.

She went into the kitchen, glad to have it all to herself since Mom had wanted to go shopping alone today. After laying all the ingredients on the counter, she got out the large crock pot and began chopping onions, peppers and garlic. Soon the air was filled with the enchanting aroma of sizzling garlic and onions in olive oil. She browned the meat and put all the remaining ingredients into the crock pot and turned it on.

Now came the hard part of the day. Mary Beth didn't know what to do. She wasn't much interested in reading. She'd already scanned the newspaper and gone for a walk. Mom kept the house so clean you could eat off the floor. She didn't have any hobbies. TV was all that was left. Mom didn't have cable or HBO, said it was a waste of money having all those channels, so Mary Beth surfed the few channels she could get and found an old rerun to watch. It was awful and didn't capture her attention.

Fortunately, Mom returned home within 30 minutes laden with grocery bags, and Mary Beth jumped up to help. "Don't carry anything heavy, Ma. It isn't good for your heart."

"Ah, I'm as strong as a horse. Besides, it's just groceries."

"I'll get the rest of them out of the car. You can put things away. You know where you like them better than I do."

"OK."

It was a bit of a jolt when Mom gave in so easily, and Mary Beth wondered if she actually felt worse than she was letting on. Her health was one thing Mom never complained about.

Two trips later, Mary Beth was helping with the unpacking. "We're having chili for dinner, Mom. Just the way you like it. There will be plenty for leftovers. We can freeze them and have them another time."

"That's good, Mary Beth. I do like chili. Just as long as it isn't too hot."

"I made it just the way you like, mild."

"Good girl. It's nice not to have to cook every meal."

Mary Beth's eyes widened at the gratitude. It wasn't like Mom to praise or thank her. She'd be more likely to say 'fuck'. She recovered her composure. "It's the least I can do. I couldn't find a job to interview for today, but I'll keep looking and I'll get something, anything to get enough money so I can pay for my own place."

Mom changed the subject abruptly. "I have an appointment this afternoon with a man about doing the back yard. That darn tree needs pruning. I won't have it falling over in a high wind."

"It does seem to grow fast. Just in the time I've been here, it's gotten really lush."

"Let's get something to eat. He'll be here in less than an hour."

They worked shoulder to shoulder in the tiny kitchen, making sandwiches and a new pot of coffee. At the small dining table, they ate without speaking, the silence a welcome change to Mary Beth, but also laden with an unspoken threat. Was this temporary or was Mom worse off than she admitted? And how much longer would Mom be able to stay here if her health became worse? Worries that had never occurred to her now demanded her attention, but there were no answers.

Later, after filling the dishwasher, Mary Beth wandered back into the living room, wondering what to do, when the doorbell rang. That must be Mom's appointment. "Mom, he's here," she shouted to the back of the condo. "I'll let him in."

She crossed to the door and swung it open to behold the most handsome Hispanic man she'd ever seen. His raven-black hair was a riot of tight waves that ended at the top of his broad shoulders. Unbound and apparently naturally curly, it was hair more suited for a woman than a man, but it looked good on him because it was so well cared for. He wasn't tall...maybe about 5' 9", but you could see he was buff, his slim black jeans hugging narrow hips and t-shirt tight across his muscled chest. He wore an old straw cowboy hat and scuffed cowboy boots. He smiled at Mary Beth, appearing to appraise her figure, and she stepped back, embarrassed at her sloppy clothes and extra ten pounds. Then, getting a grip on herself, she stepped forward again and unlocked the screen door.

In the shade of the porch, his dark brown eyes were hard to read, and his even white teeth flashed in exaggerated contrast to the surrounding shadow and his own coffee-brown skin. He couldn't be more than 35, if that. She shook herself into action. "Hi, my Mom is in the back. She'll be out soon. Why don't you come in and wait for her?"

She opened the screen door and ushered him inside. "My name is Mary Beth. What's yours?"

"I'm Julio," he said in a voice that matched his body: warm and sensuous. He reached out to shake her hand. She slowly responded, and his big hand engulfed her smaller one. He had a firm handshake.

She led him to the couch and pointed for him to be seated. "Can I get you something to drink? Water? Coffee?"

He smiled warmly, sending a shiver down her spine. He was too young for her, but how long had it been since she'd talked to anyone near her own age, let alone a handsome man who smiled at her? "I'd love some ice water."

She nodded and went into the kitchen. When she returned with the glass, Mom was still missing, so she sat in a chair opposite Julio to entertain him.

He accepted the glass and drank it down in a few gulps. "Hot today. That was good."

"Yes, I can't imagine how you stand the heat all summer. You must be acclimated."

"It takes time. Plus you must drink a lot of water. Are you enjoying your stay here in Palm Lakes?"

"Yes, it's very nice. I needed a change of scenery, and I'm thinking of moving here permanently. In fact, I've been looking at the job market, but haven't found anything just right for me."

"What is it you do?" He genuinely seemed interested.

"In my last job, I was an administrative assistant. Actually a secretary. I'm not getting any younger, and people seem to like to hire kids fresh out of school and pay them less."

"You aren't old. You are one of the youngest people in Palm Lakes, I assure you. You have beautiful eyes."

She flinched, wondering why the hell he was flirting with her. "Thank you," she mumbled, not knowing what to say, desperately wishing her mother would show up. If she'd wanted to be alone with this luscious man, her mother would have been sitting next to her from the first minute, but when she wanted some support, Mom was awol. Figured.

"You know, I have an opening at my office for someone with your qualifications. We don't pay a lot, but we have flexible hours and it would be near your Mom's place, so you might want to consider it."

"Really? Tell me a bit about your company." Her self-consciousness evaporated at the thought of maybe finding a job.

"My brothers and I started Palo Verde Landscaping in 1985. We're the biggest landscaper in the area. We recently lost our receptionist. If you would like, you can come to the office and we can discuss the job."

"You're very kind. I'd like that. When's a good time to come by and where's the office?"

He reached into his back pocket and took out a business card. "How about Friday afternoon at 1pm? The office is at this address, and that's our phone number. Turn right outside the gate of Palm Lakes, and we're about a mile down the main road on the right." His liquid brown eyes crinkled with good humor as he stared intently at her.

Having 100% of a man's attention was not something she was used to. "That's perfect. I'll be there for sure. Thanks for the opportunity."

As the business card changed hands, her mother walked into the living room. "Sorry to keep you waiting, but I see my daughter has taken care of you."

"She has, Mrs. Costello. We've had a nice chat. It turns out your daughter will be interviewing for a position at our office later this week. We need a new receptionist."

Her mother's dark eyes looked at her in warm appraisal, as if to say, "That was fast."

This whole approval thing was getting to be too much for Mary Beth.

Mom continued, "That sounds wonderful. She's been looking for something nearby. Shall we go out back so that you can look at the tree?"

"Certainly, Mrs. Costello." He rose and walked with her, gently taking her elbow, as if he knew she was frail. He seemed to have a real respect for older people. Mary Beth followed behind.

Outside, on the back porch, Julio gave them a mini-lecture on desert tree care. "This is a very nice mesquite tree. They provide shade in summer and let the sun through in winter, exactly what you want in this exposure. We didn't plant it, did we?" A frown creased his handsome face.

"No, you didn't," Mom affirmed.

He leaned down and looked at the black bubbler, which was inches from the base of the tree. "You may have seen trees blown over in a storm? It doesn't happen in Nature very often. I am going to recommend that not only do you let our guys prune the tree, but expand the well and move that bubbler out from the trunk and turn the flow of water down. Eventually, you will be able to turn it off. I can give you instructions for deep watering, too. It will cost more than just pruning, but if all you do is prune, you still need to do it several times a year, and it won't guarantee the tree won't blow over, because the roots are what anchor it, and they are not being properly developed to support the tree."

It all made such good sense to Mary Beth the way he said it. She didn't have much experience with local landscapers, but most seemed to be guys who owned a truck and could blow leaves and prune or plant trees. She doubted any of them was trained very well. Julio's knowledge seemed as impressive as his looks. Mary Beth glanced to see if Mom was having the same reaction. She was.

"Well, young man, let me know what it will cost. I don't want to lose that tree. I'm too old to start over. At my age, I don't buy green bananas." They all laughed politely. Mary Beth wondered how many times he'd heard that one.

He stood looking at the tree for a moment, then walked slowly around it. He came back to stand next to Mary Beth, a bit closer than she was comfortable with, but she didn't move as his shoulder brushed hers. "We can do the pruning, the modification to the well and the irrigation for $200."

Mary Beth sucked in a breath. That was a lot of money.

Her mother was stone still, her face betraying no emotion. Finally, after a minute of contemplation, she agreed to the terms.

"We will get this on the schedule for tomorrow or the next day. We guarantee our work, and I will have Samantha come around and train you about the irrigation after the job is done. No charge for that." His confidence made their decision seem all the wiser for seeing things his way. Everyone smiled, and they headed back inside, eager to get out of the sun.

Mom went to her purse and pulled out her checkbook. "I can write you a check today."

"No, thanks, just pay when the job is finished. Whoever is leading the crew will accept the check and give you a receipt if you wish."

That was nice, not having to pay in advance. It seemed to say they could trust him to do a good job. Julio said his good-byes and left for his next appointment, reminding Mary Beth that he was looking forward to showing her his operation on Friday.

After he left, Mom turned to her. "Do you think you might like working for that man?"

"Yes, Mom, I think it could be a good opportunity. I'll have to see what it pays, but if I can get a full-time job, then I can move out. I need to look at the cost of apartments now, but I'm hopeful. I could be close by that way."

Mom looked down at the floor, sighed and sat in a nearby chair as if she were a deflated balloon, alarming Mary Beth.

"Mom, what's wrong? I thought you wanted me out of here. You told me it was against the rules. I'm trying to do what you want."

"I know. It's just that the doctor scared me. He told me I shouldn't exert myself, like doing heavy housework or carrying things that weigh more than five pounds. I've never felt this scared before. If you leave, I don't know what I'll do. I just feel so much safer with you here." She didn't look Mary Beth in the eye.

"Mom, in no time you'll be back to your feisty self, right? He didn't say it was bad, did he? You didn't tell me he did." She leaned in, trying to look directly into her mother's eyes, but failed to make contact.

Mom wrung her hands. Her voice, normally so loud and confident, sounded frightened. "He told me I was in danger of dying if I didn't follow what he said, and he said that the drugs can't restore the heart to how it was. There's too much damage. I didn't want to tell you, but if you're leaving, I want you to know. I don't feel good being here all alone the way things are. Would you please stay a while? Maybe we can keep Mrs. Jameson from reporting you. And if she does, well, maybe I should think about living somewhere I can get more help. What do you think?" She still hadn't looked at Mary Beth, as if she were afraid of the answer.

Mary Beth closed her mouth, which had been hanging open. "Sure I'll stay, Mom. We can take it one day at a time. If worse comes to worse, we can sell this place and get an apartment outside the gates somewhere. I won't leave you if you need me. I'll be able to save money if I get that job. We'll figure it out."

She leaned over and patted Mom on the shoulder, but got little response. She knew this must be tearing Mom up, asking for help after badgering her to leave. They sat in silence for a while, then Mary Beth went into the kitchen and made them both a cup of tea. *Thank God for Julio's offer. Now if only it turns out to be real.*

* * *

Red, 12 noon

RED SAT at the lunch counter of the local diner eating the best hamburger in town, a juicy half-pounder with melted jack cheese, lettuce and tomato, and plenty of ketchup. None of that mayonnaise crap. What was it with putting mayo on burgers, anyway? This was one of the few places locally that didn't use mayonnaise as their default condiment on burgers, which was one reason he frequented it. He certainly didn't come for the outdated decor or chaotic atmosphere. Still, the burgers were super.

He munched contentedly on a few fries as he replayed in his mind what he'd seen earlier. So Tanya was trying to seduce Schmidt. What an odd couple they'd make. Red shook his head in amazement. People were so hard to figure. He would have thought Schmidt would want a mousy, controllable woman, not an alcoholic floozy. Then it hit him. Tanya might remind him of Mom. He didn't have a photo of Owen's mother, but she was a drinker and apparently had a reputation for being loose.

The problem was, it wasn't illegal to have an affair with a neighbor. This was getting him nowhere fast. He was retired, for God's sake. He kept telling himself he needed a hobby beyond golf or running. Or at least a woman. If even Owen Schmidt could land a woman, you'd think he could find companionship.

Truth be told, the women came on to Red pretty consistently. Even Tanya had flirted shamelessly with him. But he wasn't keen on having a fling with someone in Palm Lakes. Especially with his Posse job, it could complicate things. He preferred to have some distance and perspective, which is why now and then he went to Vegas and had a good time. He was overdue for a trip, but somehow this extra cruising had overtaken his free time, and he kept putting off a vacation. He'd even been drinking less, which wasn't a bad thing, but maybe he needed to make a change.

He put money down on the counter for his meal and trudged back to his stiflingly hot car. As he let the air-conditioning blast the hot air out, he mulled over what he had on Schmidt. It didn't amount to anything. Schmidt may have killed the cat...or not. He may be having an affair with a neighbor...or not. He may have made up with Barbara...or not. Why couldn't he just let it go? It was like some karmic die had been cast; his role was to watch Owen Schmidt. But he promised himself he'd back off a bit. Next week, he'd spend more of his evenings at home like he used to.

CHAPTER SEVEN

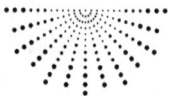

FRIDAY, SEPTEMBER 15, 1995

Maddie, 9:10am

*A*s the hummers buzzed around the feeder, Maddie fretted about all the yard work that needed doing. For years the yard had been her escape. She thought with nostalgia of her home in Moab, three acres of pure red rock bliss. Eleven years was a long time at her age, though, and the things she used to do when she was 'younger' were beyond her now. The "Golden Years"...pah!...that was total crap. Old age consisted of watching everything being taken away from you one bit at a time until there was nothing left to live for.

She had a blower and all the other tools in the garage to get the job done, but the debacle with pruning the mesquite last month had convinced her she wasn't up to it. Samantha did her own yard, but Maddie couldn't ask her to do hers as well. She had a full-time job and did too much for them already. God, how she hated to pay someone else to do it, but she couldn't see any other option. The bitter taste in her mouth had nothing to do with her strong morning coffee.

Moaning inwardly, she remembered it was trash day. After dressing, she went through the house, emptying all the containers into the large garbage bag she dragged from room to room.

As she wrestled the bag down the driveway to the trash receptacle, she tripped. Reflexively, she put her left arm out and heard it snap as her weight fell against her hand, followed by a wave of pain. She yelped, then rolled to her side, cradling her arm. Her biggest concern was that the neighbors might have seen her fall. Whatever could she have tripped over? The embarrassment was almost as bad as the pain.

As if summoned magically, Helen appeared, squatting down and reaching towards her. "Maddie, are you OK? Of course not, what a stupid question. Let me see your arm. Oh, dear, that's swelling already. We need to get you to the ER. You may have broken it."

Maddie squinted, looking up at Helen, the morning sun creating a halo around her pretty face. Maddie's throat felt dry, and the pain was increasing. "I think I heard it snap."

"I'll go inside and tell Stanley, and we'll call the ambulance."

A short while later, Stanley stood over her silently evaluating the situation. Maddie was used to his emotional detachment, but Helen had a confused look on her face. Maddie gritted her teeth at the pain. She felt like screaming at him to do something, anything.

Finally, he spoke. "I'll drive her to the hospital. It's not far, and we'll get there faster that way." Without showing any concern for Maddie, he turned and went into the house to get his car keys. A few minutes later, the garage door went up and the car backed halfway down the driveway to where Maddie still lay. Helen was crouched beside Maddie, speaking soothingly, but Maddie was so overwhelmed by the pain, she wasn't able to respond.

Stanley got out of the car and together they helped Maddie rise. She'd bitten back the pain so much, she had the coppery taste of blood in her mouth. After jockeying to get the right angle, they managed to get her into the passenger seat and the seat belt buckled with only a few cries from her. She could feel Helen jump each time she yelped in pain, so she tried hard to swallow it, but it wasn't easy.

Stanley slammed the door and walked around to the driver's side. As he opened his door, he pointed at the trash bag which sat forgotten on the driveway. "Can you put that bag in the can, Helen?"

Maddie heard Helen agree, and as the car backed out to the road,

Helen's concerned face slipped by the window. Maddie shut her eyes against the pain.

* * *

Helen, 9:35am

BEFORE HELEN GOT BACK across the street, Samantha's red pickup raced down the road from the other direction and slid to a stop at the curb. "Have they gone, Helen?"

"Yes, your Dad just left to take her to the ER. I think her wrist is broken, but it isn't a compound fracture. I happened to be outside, and I saw her trip and fall. She put her arm out to catch herself. She told me she heard it crack."

"Dad called my office and they radioed me. I was close by and thought maybe I could drive them, but perhaps it's better this way. It can take hours for something like this in the ER, and now he has transportation back. I'm so glad you were nearby when it happened. No telling how long she would have lain there. She isn't going to like this. She hates doctors and being incapacitated. Which arm was it?"

"Her left."

"Thank heaven for small favors. She's right-handed."

"Still, only having one good hand is an adjustment. Let me know if I can help. Maybe I could bring food over or do some light housework. I'll go see them after she gets back. Everyone was so supportive of me when I lost Lou; it's the least I can do. Your Mom is always giving me lovely jewelry."

"She's a lot better at giving than she is at receiving. In fact, she can be downright ornery about accepting help...just to warn you..."

"I understand. It isn't always easy to let others do things for you. I'm the same way myself."

Samantha shook her head. "I doubt it. Mom is extreme. But I really appreciate your offer, and it's worth a try. I hope she'll let you help. There isn't a lot to be done, and Dad can do most of it. But I confess, he's never been able to cook, and he hates going out to eat. So I'll be bringing some food over, and you can feel free to pitch in. Well, I'm going to run by the

ER. I expect she'll sit there for a while, and it might calm her to have someone in addition to Dad with her. Thanks so much. See you later!"

Once back inside, Helen went to the kitchen and poured herself another cup of coffee. She'd had her excitement for the day. It was terrible what happened to Maddie. Life had so many unexpected twists and turns, and so many of them seemed to be bad. Like the test results which had confirmed Sheba had inoperable cancer. The vet had called to encourage Helen to consider euthanizing Sheba. She said Sheba probably was in pain, and it would only get worse. At some level, Helen wondered if the doc was trying to make the decision easier by saying all that. She wasn't ready to give up hope that Sheba could be healthy. She didn't think Sheba was that old. Of course, she couldn't know. Sheba had turned up on her doorstep out of nowhere, but at the time, she believed Sheba was fairly young. She thought she couldn't be more than 13 or 14 years old now. And that wasn't really that old, was it?

Agitated by the need to take action to help Sheba, she thought about her options. She didn't want Sheba to suffer, but really, she didn't seem to be in much pain. She was still eating, even though her weight was steadily going down. She interacted pretty much as always, demanding to be brushed and held, though she had to be careful not to be too vigorous with the brushing, as it seemed to hurt her if Helen pressed too hard.

Suddenly she remembered part of a conversation with Jean and Lydia at Barbara's party. Lydia was a real New Ager who was interested in all kinds of off-the-wall stuff. She hadn't paid much mind to it then, but now she recalled that Lydia claimed to be able to heal using crystals. It sounded totally bizarre, but at this point, she'd do anything to help Sheba. What harm could it do? The vet wanted her to put Sheba to sleep. Why not try something unconventional?

She'd had lunch with Lydia, Barbara and Jean once since the party, and she'd enrolled in the yoga class they'd all be in next month, so maybe it wouldn't be an imposition to ask her. Lydia was such a kind person. Surely, she'd be open to helping Sheba, and Helen would offer to pay her. There was still cash left in the envelope she'd found.

Just deciding to do this made her feel better, so she picked up the phone to call Lydia. The phone rang three times, and Helen began to worry she'd have to leave a message. She hated talking to those blasted machines. Just as the fourth ring started, Lydia picked up.

"Hi, Lydia, this is Helen Mueller."

"Oh, hi, Helen. How are you?"

"I'm doing well, Lydia, and I'm looking forward to yoga class next month, but I have a problem I was hoping you could help me with. My cat Sheba has cancer, and the vet wants me to put her to sleep, but I want to try anything that might help cure her. She has lost a lot of weight and the tests say it's cancer, but she's still bright and interactive. I remembered you talked about healing with crystals. Do you work with animals? Can it cure cancer?" Listening to herself, she felt stupid. How could rocks cure cancer?

"I know it seems outlandish, but it can. I haven't worked with animals a lot, but I've done a few sessions with dogs. I'd be happy to come over and work on her."

"I'm willing to pay, Lydia."

"No, thanks, Helen. I do this as a hobby. I enjoy helping however I can. I can't promise anything. I have seen some amazing healing take place, but sometimes there's no change. I'll do my best, but the outcome depends on many factors over which you and I have no control. The one thing I promise is that it won't harm her at all."

"I'm sold, Lydia. I need to be sure I've tried everything. When would be a good time for you? How long does it take?"

"It won't take more than 45 minutes, and I'm pretty free this afternoon. Let me see if Jean can join me. She'll do Reiki while I do the crystals. How about we come over around 2pm?"

"That sounds great. I appreciate your doing this. Let me give you my address. Do you have a pen handy?"

After giving directions to her home, Helen said goodbye with higher spirits than she'd had in a couple of weeks. She knew it was wrong to hope for too much, but she couldn't help it.

The clock in the living room said 2:08 when Helen heard the knock on the door. She opened it to see Lydia and Jean standing in the sunlight, their arms full. Lydia held a large canvas bag stuffed full, and Jean carried a bulging Trader Joe's bag. "Are you guys moving in or what?"

Laughter lightened the mood as Helen ushered them into the living room. "Put your stuff down, and I'll show you around. You can tell me where you want to do this. I wasn't sure what you needed." Helen led them down the hallway, pointing out the kitchen and breakfast nook and the two bedrooms and two baths.

"This is really lovely, Helen," said Jean. "You have a lot of nice space here."

"Too much, which is why I plan to move into a condo soon. I don't need this much space, and frankly, I can't afford to maintain it. It's a good move, though. I just wish Sheba could be healthy for it. I think she'd like the condo I've found."

"You'll be staying in Palm Lakes, won't you?" asked Lydia.

"Of course. My kids are after me to return to Wisconsin, but other than them, there's nothing there for me. I never had friends there, and I hate the cold winters. I'm going to visit them, of course, but I find I'm building a life here, and I like it."

"We're glad you're staying," said Jean, and she sounded so sincere, it touched Helen's heart.

Lydia added, "You'll probably be my neighbor. I live in a condo."

"Is it over by the entrance?"

Lydia smiled and nodded. "Yes, it is."

"Then we'll be neighbors. That's really great!" Helen absurdly felt this was a sign that she was doing the right thing.

"This room will do just fine." Lydia pointed at the desk as she stood in the guest bedroom doorway. "We can use the desk as a healing table. Do you mind moving everything off it? I brought a nice towel for Sheba to lie on. I'd like to light a few candles, if that's okay? And may I spread my stuff on the bed here?"

"Sure, Lydia. Do whatever you need to do."

Helen went to work clearing the desk while Jean and Lydia unpacked on the bed and sorted through things. Lydia got a few votive candles lit, and their jasmine fragrance filled the air.

Her crystals were in a special cloth holder that had a slot for each one, keeping them from chipping or scratching each other. She noticed Helen admiring it. "I made this carrier myself, patterned after the kind you put tools in. I like the purple velvety material."

Jean laid a plush towel on top of the desk and then anchored it with a small brass Buddha statue. "This towel is a little slippery on this surface. It should be OK as long as Sheba doesn't struggle. Do you think she'll be calm?"

"I believe so. She's become more placid lately. She didn't struggle at the vet's, and this is so much nicer. If you're ready, I'll go get her."

"Yes, bring her in," said Lydia as she positioned some crystals at the corners of the desktop.

Helen went and collected Sheba, who was sleeping peacefully on the bed in the master suite. Sheba began purring loudly on being picked up, as always. Helen hugged her to her chest. "Sheebs, I have some nice ladies here who want to help you feel better. They're going to do some crystal healing, and it won't hurt you a bit. I promise."

When she walked into the guest bedroom holding Sheba, she was struck by how peaceful it was. The curtain was pulled shut, making the place soothingly dark, except for the several candles placed around the room whose fragrance had transformed it into a garden. The light was just enough to see the different colors of the crystals Lydia had brought. Purple, rose, brown, clear, green. Most had at least one pointed end and were shaped like wands, but some were just chunks of rock.

She went over to the desk. "What are these clear ones you have at the corners?"

"Those are quartz crystals and help hold the space for healing. You can lay Sheba down in the center of the desk. Stand by if you think she might run off."

"I don't think she will. I'll just pet her for a minute and then step aside." Helen stroked Sheba gently.

"Jean is going to assist me by doing Reiki while I do the crystal work, if that's all right with you."

"I meant to ask. What's Reiki?"

"It's a way of channeling the life force energy of the Universe to allow balancing and healing to take place. You can't make it do things; you just intend to allow healing to occur." Jean smiled encouragingly at Helen as she explained. "I've seen some amazing healings, but most of the time, it's quite subtle."

Jean stepped closer to Sheba and held her hands as if beaming energy to her. Her one hand drew figures in the air, and her lips moved as if she were saying a prayer. After a minute, Jean stepped closer and placed her hands on Sheba.

"She's accepting a lot of energy."

Helen was amazed that Jean could know that. "How can you tell?"

"My hands are buzzing, and they feel magnetized to her body, and she hasn't moved a muscle. Lydia, I think we're ready for you to do your thing."

Lydia stepped up with two crystals and laid one on the desk near the top of Sheba's head and the other near her tail. She paused for a minute, regarding Sheba with intense brown eyes. A shadow seemed to move across her face, but it was so fleeting, Helen wasn't sure. Then Lydia picked up the milky pink crystal.

"How do you know which crystals to use, Lydia?"

"Good question. I don't know how other practitioners decide, but I use a technique called dowsing to help me choose the best crystals for a particular job. My intuition is pretty good, but dowsing allows me to focus it and get an answer to a specific question instead of just waiting for a 'hit'."

Helen tried to process that. It sounded pretty woo-woo, but she didn't want to offend Lydia. "Is dowsing like a psychic power? Isn't that what people use for finding water?"

"No, it isn't psychic, though I know some people present it that way. It's a natural skill anyone can learn. And yes, dowsing for water has been used for at least hundreds of years, probably longer."

Helen could tell Lydia was passionate about this dowsing thing, but it seemed incredible. "How long did it take you to learn to use dowsing well?"

"I'm still learning. It takes a lot of practice to master a particular dowsing application. I'm doing better all the time. Now I'm going to get into a meditative state and do my thing, so I'll be quiet for a little while. Just don't want you to think I'm being rude." Lydia closed her eyes and pointed the crystal at Sheba.

Helen stepped to the side and watched as Jean continued to hold her hands in front of her, sometimes touching Sheba in different places. It was peaceful to watch.

Lydia started humming in a low tone, repeating one syllable over and over. There was no tune, and the frequency was penetrating, yet calming. Helen couldn't see anything happening, but she had to admit, it was the most harmonious her house had ever felt. Maybe there was something to this New Age stuff after all.

Thirty minutes and several crystals later, Lydia turned to her. "You can take Sheba and put her to bed now, Helen. She'll probably sleep well for a while."

Helen stepped forward, picked up the fragile furry body and carried her to the master bedroom. Laying her gently on the quilt, she stroked Sheba. "Please be well. I love you so much." She wiped her eyes as they filled and a tear dropped onto the quilt. Even though she wasn't sure what would happen, she was feeling more at peace than she had in days.

Lydia and Jean had packed most of their gear away by the time she returned. "I'll put the things back on the desk later. You ladies come out and let me make you a drink. Go ahead and put your bags by the front door. If you have time, we can have a snack, too."

When they arrived in the kitchen a few minutes later, Helen showed them their choices. "I have a pitcher of iced tea; I can easily make a pot of coffee; I have some chilled white wine. I have some nice cookies, which I did not bake. But they are delicious."

Lydia spoke first. "After I wash my hands and drink a glass of water, I'd love a glass of wine."

"Same for me, Helen," Jean chimed in.

They went to work in the seamless way that longtime friends often do and soon were enjoying their snack.

Lydia sipped her wine. "Thanks for having us come over and work with Sheba. The methods we used are powerful, and we've seen some great outcomes, but it's unpredictable how a person or animal will use healing energy, or even if they will accept it." She paused for another sip. "And sometimes, if someone is very ill, the healing doesn't bring about a miracle, but it eases pain and helps the transition be smooth. So I don't want you to think we're promising a miracle here, but they do happen sometimes. I hope you'll let us know how Sheba does."

"I certainly will, and I appreciate your honesty. It gives me confidence that what you do is real because you aren't making wild promises."

Though she didn't want to admit it, Helen hoped for a miracle and was disappointed at the dose of reality. "How long does it take to see results?"

"It varies, but if nothing happens within the next three days, it won't. We can come back and do another session if you like. Just let us know."

"I could feel the tranquility in the room while you worked. It's not something I could measure, but I felt it. And I'm sure Sheba felt it, too."

They each sipped their wine and munched on cookies in silence for a couple of minutes. Helen's thoughts went to Maddie's accident. "My neighbor across the way, Maddie, had a fall this morning and broke her wrist. I saw Stanley bring her back with a brightly colored cast on her left arm. Maybe I should tell her about what you do." Helen smiled at the idea.

"Actually, it would be very helpful for the healing of her bone, but we're careful not to push our beliefs on others. Most of the people in Palm Lakes look sideways when you mention energy healing and crystals, even though many of them are from California originally."

Jean laughed at Lydia's observation. "That's so true. Even my husband is looking at me like I'm a witch since I took up Reiki. I'm still the same person, but people look at me differently when I mention Reiki, so I keep a low profile. Is Maddie our age?"

"No, she's older. In her 70s. She probably wouldn't be open to what you do. I have to admit it's a stretch for me, and she's more traditional. But she's so generous. She makes beautiful jewelry. In fact, the lizard earrings I'm wearing are ones she gave me."

Helen pulled her hair back while Jean and Lydia leaned over to look at the earrings. Jean exclaimed, "Those are beautiful! Does she sell them anywhere?"

"As far as I know, she doesn't. Stanley had concerns about tracking sales for tax purposes. Maddie isn't into accounting, and I guess he didn't want to do it. So she just gives them away. Creating them is what she loves to do."

An hour later, she walked them to the door, hugged and thanked them again and waved goodbye as they drove out of sight. After a rough start to the day, it had turned out pretty well.

She went to have a look at Sheba and found her sleeping deeply in the same spot she'd left her on the bed. The afternoon was slipping away, and she wanted to go see how Maddie was. She knew Stanley liked to eat by 5pm, and maybe Maddie wasn't up to cooking.

She walked across the street in the slanting late afternoon light. It was hot, but not nearly as hot as last week. Fall was coming. All two weeks of it.

She knocked on Maddie's screen door, and Beau came barking. Stanley appeared a minute later. "Hello, Helen. Come in. Maddie's doing fine. I assume you came to see her?"

"Yes, Stanley. Just wanted to touch base and see if I can help." She stepped inside and patted Beau. The house was dark, as always. Maddie kept the curtains closed, and her home didn't have transom windows. Lights were on in the dining area and kitchen. Stanley pointed her towards the kitchen, so she preceded him through the small dining area into the kitchen proper.

Maddie was standing at the counter clumsily cutting summer squash into slices as Samantha peeled potatoes at the sink. Maddie looked tired and was so focused on what she was doing that she hadn't noticed Helen and Stanley. When she turned and saw them, she jumped like someone had hit her with a cattle prod.

"You scared the bejesus out of me." Maddie's reaction got Samantha's attention, and she turned to see who was there. "Hey, Helen, thanks for coming by. We're making dinner."

"I just came to see how you are, Maddie. I'm so sorry I scared you."

"They say the break was clean and will heal fine, but they told me I have osteoporosis and am more at risk for breaking bones as a result. They want me to take some pills, but I don't think I'm going to do that. Pills don't set well with me." She went back to trying to cut the squash while she talked.

Samantha stood behind her at the sink, paring knife and potato in hand, and rolled her eyes meaningfully.

Helen wasn't sure what to do. "I don't want to get in the way, but I'd be happy to help. You must be very tired after this ordeal."

Maddie waved her off. "Thanks, but no. I'm fine. I'm making a simple meal. They gave me some pain pills if I need them. So far, I haven't."

"She barely let me help, Helen, and she won't sit down and let us wait on her. We have it in hand." Samantha shook her head and shrugged her shoulders.

"Maybe I could bring you a casserole for tomorrow. Everyone helped me so much these past months, I'd like to give back. I know you and Stanley are careful about what you eat, but I'd be happy to make something that would suit you both."

Maddie paused as if searching for what to say. "I'm going to be fine. But thanks." She went back to chopping as if it took all her focus.

"Thanks for the offer," Samantha said, clearly trying to make up for Maddie's rejection.

Stanley had disappeared, and Helen felt she wasn't getting anywhere, so she decided to leave. "Well, I'm happy to do anything. Just let me know."

Maddie smiled noncommittally and waved. Samantha mouthed 'thank you'. Stanley was on the couch reading and looked up briefly as she walked through. She felt rebuffed, but she tried not to take the stubborn refusal personally.

Friday, September 15, 1995

What a day it's been! So much is happening. I haven't been journaling much. Maybe it's because I'm spending more time actually living. I used to live inside my head, and this journal was the safe place to share all my feelings. Now I find I'm so busy that I'm too tired some nights to sit down and write.

When I do sit down, like tonight, even though I know there are stressful things going on in my life, I don't feel as burdened by them as I once did. I wonder why that is?

I didn't like having to face all those decisions after Lou died. But in spite of everything, I managed to get out of the downward spiral. I was so afraid of making mistakes. I was so afraid of change. Now I get to move to my new place, where I can have things exactly the way I want. I hope the sale goes through, and that I made a good choice.

The only thing really holding me back from happiness now is Sheba's illness. The healing session certainly relaxed her. She's been sleeping peacefully for hours. She didn't even wake up for dinner.

Lydia and Jean are so nice, but I don't know what to make of the strange stuff they did. They didn't act like it was any big deal, but it sure was odd. Yet I could feel a sense of peace afterwards, and they weren't even directing it at me.

I'm afraid to hope that Sheba will get better. I don't know what I would do without her, but at least now I have some other friends whom I know will be there for me.

Alexander and I are cooking dinner together at least one night a week, and he's been sharing with me about his writing career. He's so supportive of my fledgling efforts. He never makes me feel worthless like Lou used to. I'm going to join the Author's Club. He says that there are a few people in town who are real authors, and that the classes aren't bad, and I should join it because he's one of the illustrious members. He wants me to get involved and start writing. I'm not sure where to begin. He says write what you know; write about what you love. I'll have to think about that.

Who would have thought that I'd be learning gourmet cooking and planning to write a book? I've been given a new life to live, and I really like the prospect of it. I don't know exactly where it's going, but so far, it's getting more exciting and rewarding by the day.

She put the pen down and closed the journal. She really was weary. She went back to the master bedroom and checked Sheba, who was still sleeping peacefully. The cricket was serenading from the bathroom again. The bed looked so inviting that she lay down and curled up around Sheba without going through her normal bedtime routine. Within a minute, she was fast asleep.

* * *

Mary Beth, 11:55am

MARY BETH HAD FIDGETED all morning. Her appointment at Palo Verde Landscaping was right after lunch, and it couldn't come fast enough for her. If only it turned out to be a real job offer, maybe she could get her life in gear.

Mom was off getting her hair done, a treat she allowed herself now and then. Mary Beth had enjoyed her morning coffee and cigarettes alone on the back patio in the perceptibly cooler temperature. Fall was coming. Or what passed for fall in the low desert.

She'd spent a lot of time thinking about how to dress for the interview. Not that it was a formal interview. She still couldn't figure out exactly what it was. Julio had made it clear that they were casual, and she didn't want to overdress.

She settled on her best pair of jeans and a loose fitting green top that matched her eyes. Her only pair of cowboy boots completed the outfit. Simple gold hoop earrings and a gold chain were her only jewelry. She liked jewelry, but was loath to spend money on herself (Catholic guilt again), and Jason, damn him to hell, hadn't seen fit to buy her pretty things. Not that she'd minded until the divorce. *Quit moping about that asshole. Mom is right. Get over him.*

It was noon, so she fixed herself a sandwich of leftover ham with some lettuce and tomato, skimping a bit on the mayo as a nod to her intention to lose weight. She'd actually lost several pounds since she started walking every morning. She'd need to rearrange her exercise schedule if she got a job. She sat at the table alone and ate carefully to avoid messing her nice clothes. She was so mixed up, she hadn't thought to eat before dressing.

She almost felt like Julio had decided to hire her the day they met. But that didn't make sense. He didn't know if she was competent to do anything. She had a brief flash of panic that he was interested in her personally. *Get a fuckin' grip, Costello, you're older than he is. He's drop dead handsome, probably married and has to beat women off with a stick. He's not interested in you.* Yet she had to admit she couldn't think of a logical reason why he'd made the offer. Well, she'd find out soon enough.

After loading the dishwasher, she went to the bathroom, brushed her teeth and scrutinized herself in the mirror. Her thick hair was tamed into a pony tail with a scrunchy. She'd used just enough makeup to look perkier than she actually felt. Her back was giving her some trouble, but she was still refusing to take the pain pills until it got too hard to bear. Something told her that today everything was going to change for the better. Her unusually positive attitude surprised her.

The drive to Julio's business was a short one, which would make it an easy commute if she got the job. She turned down the side street towards the open gate on which a weathered, hand-lettered sign announced "Palo Verde Landscaping." A tall chain link fence seemed to surround the entire property, which appeared to be several acres. The land was mostly given over to growing plants of all types and sizes. There were many neat rows of big boxed trees with drip irrigation lines running across them and rows of bushes in black 5-gallon pots. She saw greenhouses in the back, and a couple of golf carts were scooting around on the dusty paths between rows of plants. Otherwise, there was little activity.

She pulled up and parked near what she thought must be the office, though there was no sign. It wasn't much more than a large wooden shack with space to park in front. As she turned off the car, she was overcome by an attack of nerves. *What am I doing here? I won't fit in.* She allowed herself to hyperventilate for a minute and then shoved the feeling aside. *I'm going to find out what this is about. Maybe he's forgotten about me altogether. But I owe it to myself to do this.*

She locked the car and mounted the three wooden steps, the heels of her boots announcing her arrival as they clacked on the wood. She stood at the door, unsure if she should knock or just go in. *Why am I acting so timid? I used to be much more confident.* There wasn't time to think about it further, because the door yanked open from the inside.

Julio stood there, flashing a smile at her. "Come in, Mary Beth. I'm so glad to see you." He held out his hand to shake, and she recovered enough to smile and shake hands. As she stepped inside, he looked her up and down and said, "You've lost weight. You look good."

She did a double take over the fact that he could detect a two-pound difference and then pushed aside her shock. "Thanks."

The office was small, with three desks squeezed into the single open space. They were all empty. He put his hand on her lower back and guided her towards a room at the back of the main office. "I will introduce you to everyone who is here, but many of them are out in the field now."

In the small room off the main office, there was a radio set on the desk. A Hispanic man, older than Julio but just as handsome, sat at the desk with a pile of checks, some of them crunched and folded as if he were organizing the accounts. He looked up on hearing them come to the doorway, and a smile lit up his face. He was dressed more casually than Julio, had a shadow of a beard and hair that was begging to be cut, but the overall effect was still quite attractive. "Alberto, allow me to introduce Mary Beth Costello, who is interested in working with us." Alberto stood up and shook her hand enthusiastically. Once again she remarked to herself that these guys were very big on shaking hands.

"Is Sergio around?"

"No, he's in the field, but I saw Samantha come in. She's in the yard somewhere." Alberto swept his fingers through lush dark hair that was streaked with silver, pushing it out of his eyes. The minute he stopped, it fell back, and for one crazy minute, Mary Beth almost reached over and pushed it aside.

"Great, we'll go find her and tour the yard." Julio guided her back to the front door of the office and out into the bright sunshine. "I'll show you some of the yard, but what we hope you'll do is to be in the office. We need someone to answer phones, coordinate messages and things like that. Right now, whoever is nearby answers the radio and phone, and often there isn't anyone in the office, which means the guys in the field don't get the help they need. We don't have another way of staying in touch with our crews at this time. Mobile phones are too expensive. So we'd need you to stay on top of the radio and the business phone.

"We do have people come by wanting to see plants and buy things. We have a couple guys in the yard plus designers like Samantha and me who sell plants, so you don't need to know plants, but for the occasional person who comes in and wants to buy a plant, we'd need you to do the recording of the sale after the yard guys or we help them pick what they want. And we all pitch in here, so it would help if you knew the layout of the place and some of the basics in case we need you to fill in."

He walked ahead of her down a path between large boxed trees that cast some shade. He found his quarry at the turning of the path. She was sitting on the box of a large palo verde tree, writing on her clipboard. Mary Beth didn't know many desert plants, but the palo verde had a unique green bark that made it stick in her mind.

Julio went up and shook hands with the woman, who was average height, a bit on the thin side and had shiny reddish gold hair in a long French braid down her back. She looked fit and Mary Beth guessed Samantha was about her age. She was decked out in shorts, sandals, a pretty turquoise cotton top and a big straw hat. Though her coloring was Irish, she had a pretty decent tan.

Mary Beth held back, waiting for an introduction. Julio turned to her and pulled her forward. "Samantha, I want you to meet our new staff member, Mary Beth Costello. At least we're hoping she'll join us." Mary Beth held her breath, trying to process that she had the job if she wanted it.

Samantha's eyes smiled. "We sure could use someone in the office. It's been pretty wild since we lost Laura." She reached out to shake Mary Beth's hand. "Are you new to the area?"

"Yes, I just relocated to Palm Lakes. I'm staying with my Mom for a little while until I get settled."

"Palm Lakes? Wow, that's great. You won't have a long drive, and most of our clients are in Palm Lakes. You'll like working here. Everyone is so friendly and helpful." She turned to Julio. "I need to go check a redo now. You can get me on the radio if you need me. Bye for now, Mary Beth. Hope you'll take the job."

Mary Beth was floored at how nice everyone was, and how they were offering her a job without asking for a resumé or references. It was surreal.

Julio showed her the rest of the yard. They were headed back to the office when he said, "You will be perfect for the job. We can only pay you a few dollars over minimum wage, but we would like you to work with us. We do not have benefits, but we are flexible about you taking time off. Just let us know in advance if possible. We are not too picky about when you eat lunch and how long you take; just use your judgment. You could even go home for lunch if you wanted. Dress is casual. We would like you to work Monday through Friday. The hours are early in our business. We start at 6:30am, so we go home at about 3 or 3:30pm, depending on how long we take for lunch. You could come in as late as 7am if you wish, but it would be better if you could be on the same schedule as the rest of us. There is no clock to punch and no time cards to fill out. We assume you will put in 40 hours. This is a family business, and we do our best to take care of our employees. We take pride in being the best landscaping company in the area. What do you think? Would you like to join us?"

Mary Beth's head spun. The pay wasn't that great. No benefits was a downer. But casual dress, flexible hours, no commute and nice people to work with sounded like a dream to her. "I'll take it. When do you want me to start?"

"How about tomorrow?" They shook on it.

A few hours later she was at home sitting on the couch with her feet up, contemplating how much had changed in just a few days. To celebrate her new job, she'd bought steaks and a bottle of good wine on the way home. They'd cook the steaks on the grill out back and have a baked potato and some steamed broccoli.

The doorbell startled her, and she jumped to answer it. "I've got it, Ma," she yelled to the back of the condo.

She opened the door to find Samantha standing there. "Hi, Samantha. Long time no see."

Samantha's eyes twinkled. "Hi, Mary Beth. I came to check on the tree and irrigation job and show you how to care for it. Is now a good time?"

"Yeah, come on in."

They walked out onto the patio. Samantha looked at the tree, the expanded well and the new location of the bubbler. "I'm so glad you took the job. It may not seem glitzy after what you did before, and I'm sure it won't be as much money, but the people are really nice, and you do save a lot in gas and clothing. Plus you'll find it's a whole different culture, and most of it is an improvement over what we're used to." She paused and smiled warmly. "The guys are really flexible. And very family-oriented. They don't mind me stopping to visit my Mom and Dad now and then. I try not to take advantage, because it's way more latitude than I ever had before. No one checks up on how long you take for lunch. You just do your job and get paid for 40 hours a week. It actually makes me want to be more productive; I find myself staying late now and then for no overtime. Weird, huh?"

"Yes, I got that right away. The hand shaking is new to me; they seem so genuine and welcoming. The office isn't fancy, but I'd rather have nice people to work with."

"Me, too. Let's look at your timer." Samantha looked at the back of the house, then walked over to the timer that hung on the wall. Opening the box, she looked at it briefly. "This is a pretty good schedule for now, but plan on changing it every season. Don't change the length of time you water. Change the number of days you water each week. More in summer; fewer in winter. Next spring, remind me to show you how to deep water it so the roots anchor it better. Anyway, this tree looks healthy, so keep up the good work."

They walked back into the house, running into Mom in the kitchen. "You girls want some ice water or tea?"

"No thanks, Mrs. Costello. I need to be on my way, but it's a pleasure to have Mary Beth join our crew at Palo Verde. I believe she'll like it. The money isn't great, but money isn't everything. I love working there." They walked her to the front door and said good-bye.

Mary Beth turned to Mom. "I feel good about this. I'm looking forward to our steak dinner. For some reason, I'm hungry. How about you? You don't seem excited about my getting a job."

"Oh, I could eat something. I'm not that hungry. I'm glad you got the job. I was just wondering...you don't think that man is after you?"

"Nah, Ma, he's too young for me, and he doesn't give off those vibes. It's a whole different culture; they're just more tactile. I feel like a fish out of water, but I have to say I like it. It's very relaxed there, and they seem so trusting. I'm sorry the money isn't going to be great, but if you want me to stay here, it should be more than enough for us to live on and even save some."

"So you'll stay for sure?"

"Sure, I said I'd stay. If they kick us out, we'll find a place on the outside. You don't do a lot of clubs, and I can't participate, so it's not like we'd miss a whole lot, though I do like it here. It's peaceful."

"Yes, it is a good community. We'll just have to be careful no one reports you. Mrs. Jameson is always watching, and she'll catch on soon about you. There's no way to hide that you're living here. Just try to keep out of sight."

They walked back to the kitchen and began to prepare the meal. Mary Beth opened the wine while Mom started on the baked potatoes, since they'd take the longest.

"I've been thinking, Mom, the main thing that is annoying Mrs. Jameson is seeing my junker car out front. It won't help if I park in your garage and you park on the street. She'll still know I'm here. But my job is 6:30 to 3:30 Monday through Friday. I have flexible hours and can come home for lunch. I was thinking that I could sell my car and maybe commute with yours or you could drive me to work and pick me up. That would make it less obvious that I'm here. What do you think?"

"I think you come from smart people. Why don't we sell it right away? I'll be happy to drive you, and on days when I don't need the car, you can drive yourself. With that car out of her face, Mrs. Jameson might not complain. You won't get much for the car, but it will be enough for a nice little nest egg for you."

"Now that I have a job, we can have nicer food and go to the movies now and then. Maybe even plan a vacation. I need to get clothes suited for this climate, and if you don't mind, I'd like to do a little decorating in my bedroom."

"That's OK. You do whatever you like with your room."

Mary Beth's eyes widened, but she said nothing.

Later, after a delicious meal that her mother picked at with little appetite, they clinked wine glasses together and toasted the future. Mom's recent revelation about her health had Mary Beth concerned. She wasn't used to this pleasant, agreeable woman. It was like the aliens had abducted Mom and left a bad copy in her place. She almost missed the cantankerous repartee. Before, it had infuriated her; now, the opposite had her worried.

CHAPTER EIGHT

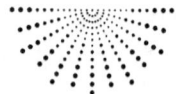

SUNDAY, SEPTEMBER 17, 1995

Helen, 8:15am

*H*elen woke up and immediately reached for Sheba. She was worried because Sheba hadn't eaten much at all since the healing session two days ago. All she did was sleep. She stroked the long gray fur and recoiled. She shot up in bed and looked hard at Sheba, but it was impossible to tell just by looking. She gingerly touched her again. Her body was cold and rigid. She must have died during the night.

She picked Sheba's body up, and even though it was like hugging a wooden toy, she held her and cried. After a few minutes of sobbing, she got out of bed and carried Sheba's body into the bathroom, laying it gently on the counter. She reached into the linen closet and pulled out one of her favorite plush bath towels. She folded it until it was the right size, and then transferred the body to it gently, as if Sheba would be more comfortable that way. She had no idea what to do next. On top of everything, it was Sunday. The vet's office was closed. She couldn't think straight. All that mattered was her best friend was gone forever.

She went to check the clock and saw that it was nearly 8:30am. Alexander was an early riser. Maybe he wouldn't mind if she called. He could help her figure out what to do. Thank God he was home and picked up on the second ring.

"Hello, it's me. Helen."

"Hi, Helen. Is everything all right?"

"No, it's not. I don't know what to do, and it isn't fair to put it off on you, but...Sheba died last night. I woke up and she was gone. I don't know what to do. The vet won't be open until tomorrow morning. Even if I weren't moving soon, you know how hard it is to dig a hole here, and I don't want to bury her in a yard I'm leaving behind, but I can't let her body sit around in this heat for long. I want her near me. Does that sound stupid?"

"Of course not. There has to be a way to solve this. Let's think." He paused for a minute and she silently prayed he could find an answer she could live with. "I know there's no perfect answer, but I have an idea that might work. I'll come over and get Sheba's body. I have a large cooler that I can put it in for now. Then tomorrow, first thing, you call the vet's and tell them I'm bringing the body by for cremation. You can go with me if you like."

Helen thought about it for a while. "I shouldn't be putting you out like this. You're right, we can't just put the body in the garage. It's way too hot. I hadn't thought about a cooler. I have one that might work. I'm just not thinking straight."

"Helen, when will you understand that I want to help? You'd do the same for me, wouldn't you? You know how attached I am to Fido. I'd be broken up if he died. In fact, you can promise to repay the favor someday. Let me at least go with you tomorrow."

"Well, if you don't mind. I can hardly face thinking about it. It would be nice not to have to drive. It's not far, but the traffic can be crazy."

"It's settled then. I'll be over shortly and bring a cooler and ice. You can decide if you want me to keep her or not. But we'll go in my car tomorrow. I'll let you phone them first thing, and I'll pick you up."

"Thank you. I'll see you soon."

She put the phone back in the base and stood in the kitchen wondering what to do next. Looking down at her nightgown, she realized she better dress. Skipping a shower, she put on casual clothes and ran a brush through her hair, not bothering to put on any makeup or jewelry. Then she went through the motions of making a pot of coffee so Alexander could have some when he arrived.

The smell of coffee brewing helped make everything seem more normal. She sat at the kitchen table waiting for the brew cycle to finish, thinking about how different life would be without Sheba. For years, Sheba was her best and only friend. She talked to her, and Sheba talked back. Sheba loved sitting in her lap and sleeping next to her; most of all, Sheba loved getting brushed and being fed tuna as a Sunday treat. There would be no tuna today.

Helen looked down at Sheba's bowls and started to cry again. How could it be that you could get so attached to an animal? To like that animal far better than you liked most humans? To feel she was a better friend than most humans could ever be? Now that she had a few friends, Helen knew it wouldn't be as lonely, but no human could take Sheba's place, and she was sure life would be emptier without her.

When the coffee pot was full, Helen got up and poured herself a mug. Soon Alexander would be here. He was good at taking charge in a way that didn't make her feel incompetent.

At least she didn't have to decide whether or not to put Sheba to sleep. Suddenly, she saw what a gift that was. She'd been agonizing over it ever since she became aware that Sheba was seriously ill. It would have been so hard to euthanize her, and now that wouldn't happen. Maybe Sheba had done her a favor. Lydia had implied that healing came in a number of ways. Sheba wasn't suffering anymore, and that was good, yet Helen just didn't know how she could get over losing her. She was going to need to call Lydia and Jean and tell them the news. But she just wasn't up to it yet.

The doorbell rang, and she rose to answer it. Alexander stood at the door holding a large blue cooler, dressed more casually than usual. She opened the door and stepped aside to let him come in.

He put the cooler down and pulled her into a tight hug. "I'm so sorry, Helen. I know how much Sheba meant to you."

Face buried in his chest, she squeezed back the tears as they spilled out, knowing if she let go, she wouldn't be able to stop. "Thank you, Alexander. She was my best friend."

"I know what you mean. Fido has been that for me, too. Now

maybe you and I can be that for each other." He leaned back to look into her eyes and pushed a strand of hair back from her face. He wiped the tears under her eyes with tenderness. "This is a terrible loss for you, especially with all the changes you've been through this year. I'll help in any way I can." He hugged her close, and then stepped back, still supporting her upper arms with his hands. "Show me where Sheba is."

She led him back to the master bathroom, where Sheba lay in state on the plush red towel. He walked over and looked at her. He stroked her fur and then picked her up, towel and all. He carried her back to the living room like she was a fragile treasure and placed her in the cooler wrapped in the towel on top of several pieces of blue ice. He did everything with an air of respect that warmed Helen's heart.

She couldn't help comparing his behavior with how Lou would have acted. Lou had never liked Sheba. He would have laughed at Helen or criticized her for her grief.

"Have you thought about what you prefer to do? Shall I take her to my place and come by to pick you up tomorrow? Or would you rather leave her here? I'm happy to do whatever you wish." He took her by the hand, and they sat on the couch.

She sat for a minute contemplating. "I'm not sure what to do. Part of me wants her here, but I don't really want to see her dead. Does that seem cold?"

"No, you want to remember her as she was. Why don't I take her and come back by around 8:30 tomorrow, and we'll go to the vet? I would be happy to bury her out back, but like you, I think it makes more sense to lay her to rest in your new home so she can be close by. That means you better have her cremated."

"Yes, you're right. I'll do that. I'll call them first thing tomorrow. I'm so grateful for your help. It would be an ordeal to face this alone." She clung to his hand, fighting off tears.

He looked at her thoughtfully, sympathy in his green eyes. "I have an idea. Don't feel pressured, but what about you come back to my house and spend the day with me? We'll lounge around, drink some wine, make a nice dinner, and you can sleep in my guest room. That way you aren't sending Sheba away, and you'll have some company until this is

all over. You can call the vet's from my house, and we can go from there."
He smiled tentatively.

"I couldn't put you out. It would be silly for me to mess up your guest room and bathroom when I live so close by." She wanted to say 'yes' so badly, but couldn't bring herself to. "Plus, how would it look to your neighbors, if they knew I spent the night?"

"What, are you afraid of ruining my reputation? Don't be silly, Helen. I'm not close with my neighbors, and it isn't like we'll be dancing naked on the back lanai. They probably wouldn't even see you."

Her tears temporarily dried up as she pondered her choices. He peered at her intently but with a patience no one had ever shown her. She looked down and saw that her hand still held his tightly. She couldn't say 'yes' out loud, but she wouldn't say 'no', either.

Feeble objections came to mind. "I'd have to pack an overnight bag. I'd need a change of clothes and my toothbrush."

He smiled gently at her. "Whatever you want. I'll wait here while you pack. Take your time." He released her hand, and she reluctantly let go and left the room.

Back in her room, Helen dug around in the closet for her seldom-used overnight bag. Her mind was in a tizzy. Was it a good idea to accept his offer? Maybe not, but it was obviously sincere, and she felt distraught and lonely. She wasn't sure she could handle being alone tonight; she'd certainly drink too much wine if left to herself, and then how would she drive to the vet's first thing? Being around Alexander grounded her; staying with him would keep her safe.

She still couldn't get over how kind and affectionate he was. She reflected that the old Helen would have sent him away and then collapsed in tears, sobbing all day and feeling miserable. The new Helen wasn't going to feel happy about losing Sheba, but she was willing to accept friendship and support when it was offered by someone who obviously cared.

She pulled some clothes off hangers and out of drawers with little thought as to what she was doing. She threw her toothbrush, makeup kit and hairbrush on top of the clothes and zipped the bag shut. She looked around the bedroom, her gaze lingering on the spot where Sheba liked to sleep, and tears welled up in her eyes again. *It's a good idea to get away for a bit. Maybe I'm a coward, but I can't stand the thought of staying here alone all day.*

She carried her bag down the hall, stopped in the kitchen and turned off the coffeepot. No need to ask Alexander to stay. She could clean up tomorrow when she returned. She glanced around, checking for anything else to do before leaving. He met her in the hall, taking her bag. "Let's put this in my car, and I'll come back for Sheba."

They went outside, and he put her bag in the back seat and handed her into the passenger side of the front. "Give me your keys. I'll lock up."

She handed them to him in a daze and watched as he strode up the short walk and into the house, manhandling the large cooler through the front doors and then depositing it carefully in the trunk of the car. He went back to the front door and locked both locks on the inner door, then found the screen door key on her ring and locked that.

When he got into the driver's seat, she struggled to express herself as she took her keys from his hand. "I'm sorry I'm such a mess. My mind seems to be alternating between totally blank and total chaos." Tears started to flow again, and she wiped her eyes.

He reached into a pocket and wordlessly handed her an immaculate handkerchief. She took it as if she didn't know what to do with it. *Did he expect her to soil this beautiful clean handkerchief?* Suddenly, she started laughing, and it was as if she'd uncorked a champagne bottle, and it overflowed and bubbled out. *Am I getting hysterical? Why am I laughing at a time like this?* But it didn't matter; she couldn't stop. Eventually, she got quieter and the hiccups of laughter were less frequent. All through it, Alexander said nothing.

"Really, Helen, it's for blowing your nose, and I haven't used it, so it's clean."

"I know that." She dabbed her eyes with it, but that's about as far as she could go.

"You don't have to be afraid to use it. You can keep it and return it to me cleaned if you like."

She looked at him like he was from another planet. "How do you know what's bothering me?"

"Maybe I think the same as you do. In any case, please use it however you like. I have plenty and can wait for you to launder and return it." He put the car in gear and drove them back to his house without conversation.

The quiet calmed her. It was as if they didn't need to fill the emptiness with words; besides, there was nothing to say that would make things better. She was beginning to feel good about deciding to go home with him, but by the time they reached his house and entered his garage, she was feeling uncomfortable again. It was wonderful not to face this alone, but what would her kids say if they knew what she was doing? What would anyone say? She didn't dare tell her girlfriends. As worries spun around and around in her head with no clear answer, she decided just to make the best of it. An approximation of peace began to return.

After showing Helen to the guest bedroom, Alexander went back to unload the cooler and left it in the garage. When he returned, she was still standing in the middle of the room, unsure what to do. He filled the doorway and leaned on the frame. "Need help unpacking?" He smiled at his own joke. "Seriously, the dresser and closet are pretty empty. Use whatever you like. You can have the bathroom down the hall this way, right next door. The master suite has its own bathroom, so you'll have plenty of privacy, and it's on the opposite side of the house. If you feel like a soak, though, I suggest you use the jetted tub in the master suite. It's big and a lot of fun. I even have bath salts you can add, if you like. Does that sound good?"

"How do you always know what to say? You're too good to be true."

He smiled at the compliment. "Here, let me show you the tub so you can decide, then you can come back and unpack. Did you bring a bathrobe?" Correctly interpreting her confused look, he pressed on. "No? I have an extra one you can use. It'll be too big, but it will work."

He led her down the hall to the master suite. She remembered being impressed with it the first time she'd come to his house and he'd given her the tour, but she hadn't been looking at it through the eyes of someone who was going to have a soak in his tub.

He walked her through his bedroom, which was spare and had an Oriental flavor, with lacquered black furniture and a beautifully decorated screen at one end of the room. Through an arched doorway was a spacious bathroom with a toilet room off to the side, double sinks and a ridiculously large shower. The jetted garden tub was along a wall made of glass blocks, letting the sunshine in but guaranteeing privacy.

He went to a cabinet and pulled out a jar of bath salts. "Lavender," he said as he held them for her inspection. "Very relaxing." She smiled that he had bath salts. He set them on the counter and then went back into the bedroom and returned holding a large white monogrammed terrycloth robe which he put on the hook next to the tub. It was just about then that she realized there was no door on the bathroom, although the toilet room had one.

He saw her eyeing the doorway and grinned. "Don't worry. I'll stay away from the master suite while you soak. I promise."

He deserved an explanation for her fearfulness, but it was hard to express her feelings. She forced herself to put them into words. "I don't mean to act like a skittish school girl. It's just that the only man I've ever really been around was Lou, so this is kind of difficult to adjust to. I don't mean to seem unappreciative."

"Not at all. Just want to reassure you that your comfort is my priority. So I promise not to worry you. Just go ahead and unpack and have a soak and in a little while, I'll make us lunch. We can sit on the lanai and watch the golfers go by. This afternoon, we can watch TV, or you can read or take a walk; whatever you want to do. I just think it best you not be alone."

"Thanks for understanding, Alexander."

Sympathy filled his eyes. "I'll see you in a bit."

After he left, she stood for a while trying to resolve conflicting feelings that arose again at the thought of soaking in his tub. So she was spending the night with him, and it could be misconstrued. Too bad. She was an adult, and so was he. Life was too short not to be with people you care about.

It was at that moment that she realized how much she cared for Alexander. It was a strange new feeling to love someone who wasn't family, who made no demands on you, who just fit into your life, adding rather than subtracting joy. She'd never felt that way about a man before, nor even had a close female friend. In spite of all the sadness, there was a glimmer of hope and warmth in her heart.

She turned on the water and prepared the bath, marveling at how large the tub was; two people would fit in it easily. She slipped into the lavender-scented water, flicking the switch for the water jets, smiling as the pulsing water began to relax her muscles. She closed her eyes and just floated with the feeling, enjoying it so much that she kept adding hot water so she wouldn't have to get out, but when she began to look like a prune, she decided she better emerge from the cocoon the soak had woven around her.

As she padded back to her room with his bathrobe hanging down to her ankles, she saw Alexander reading a book on the couch. He didn't look up as she passed. Probably trying to give her privacy. She dressed in clothes she would have worn at home, no makeup. She didn't have the energy to worry about her appearance, and it didn't seem important.

She floated through the rest of the day as if anesthetized. Lunch was a work of art, and he served it with a lovely chilled white wine. She had little appetite but made an effort to eat some of it. They watched a movie after lunch, or at least she tried to watch. She couldn't concentrate on the story, even though it was a good one. Her mind kept wandering to the small body in the garage, and her eyes would fill with tears. She kept his handkerchief close, dabbing her eyes when the sadness spilled over. Alexander never let on that he noticed, but she was sure he did.

He put her to work helping with dinner, and that was the best therapy. There were times she even forgot why she was there. Then it would come crashing back like a tsunami. They had more wine with dinner, and she was beginning to feel it since she hadn't eaten a lot.

She pushed her chair back from the table. "I don't want to be a pain. I'm just not that hungry. And I'm beginning to feel the wine. I recently quit drinking as a way of numbing pain, so I'm out of practice. I don't want to overdo it."

He looked hard at her as if evaluating her condition. "I don't want you to have a hangover. You're right; you haven't eaten that much today, and that will make it go to your head. Let's go to the living room and relax a bit. I can come back and load the dishwasher later."

Out in the living room, she sat with him on the couch, enjoying the remnants of another spectacular desert sunset, the reds, oranges and purples splashed across the sky. Then Sheba came back to mind, and she began to cry. She pulled his handkerchief out of her pocket and blew her nose. When he put his arm around her shoulders, she sank into him and wept quietly.

"It's okay. Let it out." He held her tightly as she rocked, sobbing.

"I'll get a grip. I'm sorry to be so weepy."

"You have a right to grieve for your friend. At least you didn't have to put her to sleep. I know that was bothering you."

"More than you can imagine. It was a blessing I didn't have to. I would have carried that around forever. It's terrible she's dead, but that would have been worse." The tears had dried up for now. She wiped her face and blew her nose.

He looked at her solicitously. "Would you like to do something? Take a walk? Watch TV? Talk?"

"I don't feel up to a walk right now. And I'm having trouble paying attention to the TV, but maybe that's the best thing to do. I just need some distraction."

He got up and fetched the remote, and they found a show on HBO that looked pretty good, which was a treat of sorts for her since she didn't have HBO.

Maybe it was exhaustion. Maybe it was the wine. She fell asleep at some point.

Alexander's voice roused her. "Helen, it's late. Would you like to go to bed?"

She looked around, taken aback at where she was, then visibly relaxed. "I forgot I was here."

"Are you ready to go to bed, or would you like to stay up longer?"

"I think I'm ready."

"I'll go load the dishwasher."

"I'll help. I need to feel useful."

They went together into the kitchen, loaded the dishwasher and programmed it, then washed the few items that didn't fit. She found the work soothing, and she didn't have to fight back tears. When they were done, he walked her back to her room and gave her a hug. "Is there anything you need?"

The inviting guest room beckoned her from the doorway. Handmade Navajo rugs hung on the walls next to cowboy art. Native American pottery adorned the surfaces of dresser and desk. Even the night light had a cute cover shaped like a coyote baying at the moon. It was charming, but she hesitated to go in and mess it up. Her bag was on the floor next to the bed. She took another step into the room and stopped.

He seemed to sense her hesitation. "Are you all right? I know it's weird sleeping in my guest room."

"No, it's just that...well, it is kind of weird. I feel displaced and lonelier than I ever remember being. And that's saying a lot." She turned and looked at him.

He smiled sympathetically. "Fido sleeps with me. I know you're going to miss having Sheba with you at night."

She was surprised that his words didn't trigger the waterworks. Maybe she was all cried out for now. She went and sat on the bed. "Don't worry about me. I'll be all right. It just hit me how alone I feel without her."

A pregnant pause filled the air as he seemed to consider what to say next. "I don't want to give you the wrong idea, but you can sleep with me if you like. I promise not to molest you." When she didn't respond negatively, a boyish grin lit up his face.

Unsure how to reply, she blurted out the first thing that came to mind. "I'm exhausted, and I've had too much wine, because that actually sounds good to me."

He adopted a hurt look. "Oh, so that's what it takes for me to look good? Too much wine?" Then he laughed with her.

"Change your clothes and come on back if you like. My bed's a king, and you could be sleeping in another country as far as that goes. It won't force you to be any closer than you want. So if you want to have company, join me. But I get the left side of the bed." He turned and left without projecting any hint as to what he wanted her to do. So she decided to do what she wanted. It was a new and heady feeling.

She put on her nightgown, brushed her teeth and washed her face. Then she went over to the bed and stood for a minute. She felt like a clinging vine even considering his offer, but being near someone who cared sounded so wonderful. She'd never had that before. She knew he had no designs on her, and she felt safe with him. It would be so much nicer than being alone in a strange bed in a strange house.

The alcohol had her brain feeling muzzy, and she needed to crash.

She put his bathrobe on and walked barefoot back to the master suite, where by the night light's glow, she saw he'd already gone to bed. Fido was curled up on the corner near Alexander's feet. Even with a large man and cat in it, there was an ocean of space for her. He wouldn't even know she was there.

He was turned facing away from her, and she couldn't tell if he was already asleep. She slipped out of his robe, lay it across the foot of the bed, and tried to slide under the covers without disturbing him. She lay clinging to her edge of the bed with a vast empty space between them, wondering how she would ever be able to fall asleep.

"Sleep tight, Helen." His voice sounded even warmer and more soothing in the dark, but that only increased the shyness she was feeling at being in bed with someone other than Lou for the first time in her life. *Act normal!* "Thank you for today, Alexander. I really appreciate it."

"Are you comfortable, or are you hanging on to the edge of the bed, trying not to bump into my godlike body?"

Was her discomfort that obvious? "The latter. But don't let it go to your head. I'd be doing that even if your body wasn't godlike."

He laughed. "You don't have to hide. I'll even hold you if you want. I promised not to molest you, and I won't. Sometimes it feels good just to be held at the end of a rough day."

It sounded heavenly, but she couldn't find words to respond. Besides, the old cotton nightgown she had on was thin and ragged, making snuggling up to him inappropriate in more than one way. She didn't respond.

"Come meet me in the center."

He so rarely gave a command, that she didn't even consider refusing. She inched across what felt like miles of bed and bumped noses with him, laughing shyly at the absurdity of it. "I'll never be able to tell anyone about this."

"Why not?" he quipped. Then he became businesslike. "Turn around and make like a spoon." He slid up behind her and put his arm around her, tugging her into his warm embrace. She felt so safe that she sighed. His voice caressed her soothingly, "That's the ticket. Now go to sleep, woman. I need my beauty rest."

She laughed again, in awe at how healing it felt to laugh with someone. The weight she'd been carrying around all day dropped from her, and she felt sleep creeping up, softening all her rough edges. She would have expected it would take her hours to unwind in his arms. Instead, sleep came quickly.

* * *

Tanya, 10:25am

TANYA'S HUSBAND was at a golf tournament in Vegas for three whole days, and she was enjoying being free of his constant criticism. But the silence and solitude had its price. She was champing at the bit to contact Owen. Thoughts of him filled every waking minute, and most sleeping ones, as well. She felt compelled to make a move now, while she was alone, but the debacle with the Posse guy had scared her. She needed a foolproof plan.

She sipped her spiked coffee and reviewed the one she had concocted, examining it for defects. She'd driven by some local hotels and selected one she thought was suitable. It had a bar with low lighting and discreet seating. The hotel had rooms for a decent price, and she had loaded her purse with some of her mad money, cash she had filched from the housekeeping budget.

Today could be the day. If she met him early enough in the afternoon, they'd have several hours together. Her husband never called when he went out of town, so she could even spend the night with Owen if she wanted to.

She hadn't been this horny in years. Of course, the dry spell she'd experienced lately was contributing to her eagerness. It had been nearly three years since her last fling. She was long overdue for some great sex. Seemed to her, if her husband wanted fidelity, he shouldn't refuse to have sex with her.

Certainly, Owen would be up by now. She found her heart fluttering at the thought of talking with him, but she was concerned how he would react to her proposition. It hadn't gotten any easier to read him. She was usually much better at that, but even with the mixed signals, she was sure he was interested, so she'd open the door and see what happened.

She picked up the phone and dialed his number. It rang three times before he picked up.

"Who is it?" His gruff voice temporarily put Tanya off. However, she had to admit he came across as 100% alpha male, and she loved that. She recovered her voice and began her spiel.

"It's me, Tanya. I wanted to thank you for your quick reaction the other day when I came to your house. I'm sorry if what I did caused you discomfort. I just wanted to be neighborly." She'd rehearsed this speech over and over so that she'd sound appropriately submissive and feminine.

He was quiet too long, and she had to bite her tongue. Her patience paid off. His voice was less gruff when he said, "That's all right. I appreciate the gesture."

She hummed like a tuning fork at his compliment. "I'm calling because I was hoping I could thank you in a more concrete way, but discreetly, if you get my meaning. I'm going to have a drink at the Oasis bar in the Traveler Hotel down the road at 2pm today. I'd love to buy you a drink. I'd like to get to know you better." There, she'd gotten it all out, and now the ball was in his court. She held her breath.

Again the long wait. "I guess I could do that. Is that hotel the one at 6th Avenue?"

"Yes, that's the one. I'll be there at 2 o'clock. They have comfortable booths and great nibbles."

"OK. I'll see you there." He hung up without giving her another chance to talk.

She could hardly believe how well it had gone! The next hurdle was to get him into bed, but she had a great deal of confidence in herself where that was concerned.

Now the only hard thing was to wait until 1:45. Maybe she'd get there a few minutes early. She didn't want to appear too eager, but if he got there early and didn't see her, he might leave. She wasn't going to let that happen.

She spent the next two hours bathing, grooming and selecting the perfect outfit for seduction. She found herself obsessing about whether the red silk top was more appropriate than the black one. Both had plunging necklines. She finally settled on the black.

By 1:40, she was sitting and drinking her fourth vodka-spiked coffee of the day, feeling really mellow. She hadn't intended to drink quite that much, but she was nervous with anticipation, and the alcohol took the edge off. Now she felt sexy and mellow, instead of keyed up and anxious. She touched up her hair and put her jewelry on. Assessing herself in the mirror, she felt her chances for landing Owen were very good.

The traffic was hideous, and on the brief drive to the hotel, she found herself struggling to be alert and responsive through her alcoholic buzz. As she turned into the hotel parking lot and cruised towards the bar end of the building, a woman stepped out in front of her. She swerved to the right and instead of hitting the brakes, she hit the accelerator. She rammed a parked car and was thrown forward by the impact. She never wore a seatbelt because they messed her clothes up, so in spite of the low velocity, she was thrown into the windshield, bashing her head badly.

She blacked out for a while. When she came to, a crowd had gathered, and someone had called the police and an ambulance. The EMTs were talking about getting her out of the car in the best way possible to avoid further injury. She could hear them expressing concern about spinal damage. She hurt pretty bad, but other than the blood flowing into her eyes, she couldn't feel any particular injuries. Maybe she was in shock.

"Ma'am, hang in there. We're going to get you out soon. We just want to stabilize you to avoid further injuries. Can you hear me, ma'am?"

She mumbled incoherently, unable to form words. "Grkllb."

"Ma'am, I'm going to look in your purse for your identification so that we can inform your next of kin and get you admitted to the hospital for treatment. OK?"

"Yuss," she whispered. He opened the passenger door to get her purse and went through her wallet to find her driver's license. Satisfied, he put everything back.

"Mrs. Cooper, we're going to get you to the hospital now so you can get treatment. The police will have your car towed. Don't worry about that; the important thing right now is you. I'll take your purse in the ambulance with us. Now bear with us while we get you loaded on the stretcher." He smiled and then went to the other EMTs, and as she watched through the window, she could tell by his gesticulations that he was describing how to get her onto the stretcher.

The direction her car was pointed in gave her a perfect view across the parking lot to the entrance through the spider web of cracks in the windshield. Her eyes were finally focusing, and through the haze of head pain and the blood in her right eye, she saw Owen's car turn in. *Damn! This was supposed to be my lucky day.* His car moved towards the brouhaha very slowly. As the EMTs extracted her from the wreck, she saw he had pulled into a parking space nearby and was watching from his car.

They loaded her into the ambulance, and one of them came and sat beside her as the doors shut, closing out her view of Owen. She'd probably lost her chance with him. She felt more devastated about that than the accident.

"Mrs. Cooper, have you been drinking?" She was startled by the man's impertinent question.

"Why?"

"Ma'am, we are required by law to give full details of the accident, and I can smell alcohol on your breath. If you could tell me what happened and whether you've been drinking, that will go a long way towards resolving any problems. I'm sure that you'll be getting an insurance claim from the owner of the car you hit. It's lucky you were the only person injured. It could have been much worse." Why had he suddenly become so confrontational?

Tanya's throat felt so dry she could barely talk. She wanted to protest his nasty attitude, but didn't have the energy. "Someone stepped out in front of me, and I had to swerve to avoid her. When I did that, my foot slipped off the brake pedal and onto the accelerator by accident. I probably shouldn't drive in these shoes. The heels are too high. I've only had a couple drinks. It was that woman's fault for jumping in front of me."

His look was less than sympathetic. "Do you remember any other details?"

"No."

"What have you been drinking and how much?"

"I had a couple vodka tonics this afternoon."

"Are you sure it was only two?"

"Of course, I'm sure."

The pain was getting to be unbearable. "Can I have something for the pain?"

"We have to let the doc look at you first. Since you've been drinking, we have to be careful about pain medication. We'll have you at the hospital in a jiffy."

Reality was hitting her hard now. When her husband returned, there would be hell to pay. He'd been raking her over the coals about drinking and driving, and now he'd have ample evidence to throw at her. Then she wondered what was going to happen about the damage, and if there would be criminal charges. Maybe she'd lose her license. It was too much to contemplate.

It was only then that her mind went back to Owen. He'd seen the accident and knew it was her. She'd missed the assignation. What would he think? Would he be concerned? Relieved? How could she hope to get a second chance with him? She closed her eyes and tried to find a peaceful space inside where she could hide from the shit storm she knew was coming.

* * *

Jean, 1:30pm

LYDIA AND JEAN were out for a late Sunday lunch at their favorite local restaurant, an Italian place that provided good food and lots of it at a low price. The atmosphere wasn't great, but they were there for the food, not the plastic tablecloths and uncomfortable chairs.

Jean had ordered lasagna, and Lydia got the spaghetti and meatballs. They drank iced tea from the plastic cups and stuffed forks full of tasty food into their mouths. Lydia broke the companionable silence. "You hear from Helen today?"

"Yes, she called me after she called you. I know she hates losing Sheba, but at least she didn't have to put her down. I like to think that what we did helped create a better outcome than if we hadn't."

Lydia nodded. "I agree completely." Jean noted that Lydia didn't appear to be surprised at the outcome with Sheba, and once again wondered how much Lydia really *saw* when she looked at things. But she didn't have the nerve to ask, and Lydia continued, "Helen was hurting pretty bad today, but she had already realized that she'd dodged that bullet. She's a sharp lady. Speaking of sharp ladies, Jean, how are you doing?"

Jean frowned under Lydia's intense brown-eyed assessment. "I don't know. Things aren't getting worse, but they sure aren't getting better. And now I have a wild card in the mix. I can't figure out what to do or what it means."

"Really, that sounds exciting! What kind of wild card is it?"

"Remember I told you that I joined the dowsing email group you recommended? It's so amazing, this world wide web. Imagine me on the computer! There are people from all over the world in the group; well, you know that. The only problem is that even though it's nominally a dowsing group, they rarely discuss dowsing. I mean, they have a lot of interests like we do, but I want to learn more about dowsing."

"That's why I don't visit it very often. I was hoping it would have improved. So how does that relate to a 'wild card'?"

"One of the guys in the group writes intelligent stuff about dowsing. I have no idea of his age or background, but he welcomed me when I joined the group, so I replied and asked if he wanted to correspond directly with me about dowsing, since the group isn't talking much about dowsing. He said 'yes'."

"That's nice! Who is he and where is he located?"

"His name is Ian, and he's in the UK."

"Wow, isn't that something? He's an ocean away, and you can talk about dowsing without phoning or anything, and all for free. How cool is that? I don't remember seeing an Ian last time I was on, but it's been ages."

"All I know is his name and that he seems smart. I don't know any personal details, and I hate to ask. It almost seems an invasion of privacy to want to know about his personal life. But lately, things have developed that make me want to know more about him."

Lydia's eyebrows raised, and she looked harder at Jean. "What kind of things?"

Jean shrank under her scrutiny. "It's really hard to explain, and it's going to sound crazy." She paused as if searching for the right words.

"Try me, Jean. You know I won't judge." Lydia's stare hinted that she already knew what Jean was going to say. Or maybe Jean was just jumpy about her secret.

"His emails are all just about dowsing. Nothing personal or inappropriate, but it's like there's a subtext I can sense. And it gives me the strongest feeling that he's meant to be important in my life somehow. I don't know where to take this. I'm considering inviting him for a visit. No one could complain about that, but with how things are between me and Richard, I'm not sure it's a good idea. I just feel compelled to meet him in person. I feel a strange attraction, if you want to call it that. Maybe it wouldn't be wise to have him visit. How crazy does that sound?"

"Doesn't sound crazy to me. It's all about synchronicity. You know that the Universe will send you things that will help you. Maybe he's here to help."

"It just feels like if I pursue it, it could cause the shit to hit the fan, if you'll pardon my french."

"Maybe that's just what needs to happen. From what you say, Richard isn't likely to change. You two seem to be on separate paths. Is this really what you want from your life? Doesn't being around him have the opposite effect to what you want from a partner?"

Jean considered the question and looked down at the remaining food on her plate. "I just feel guilty. I haven't done anything; I don't even know how old this guy is or if he's single. I just feel such a strange attraction to him. I feel like ignoring it would be a big mistake, but doing anything about it could really mess up my life."

"Maybe your life needs a bit of a shakeup. What's the worst that could happen? Divorce? Would you miss Richard?"

"I hate to admit it, but not really. We have nothing in common anymore. He judges me for my interests in healing and dowsing. I judge him for his addiction to porn. We have less in common every day. But I hate to start over at my age, and like I said, I know nothing about this guy. It's all just intuition."

"Take it slow and see where it goes. I know you're a brave person. But you might have to get braver." Lydia's intense look softened. "Let me know if I can help. You can come stay with me if you need a place."

"What would I do without you, Lyd? You're the best friend I ever had. Thanks! I'm doing OK in the guest bedroom for now."

"Just remember if you need to move out, I have space."

They went back to eating in subdued silence until the waitress came to ask about dessert.

"None for me," said Jean.

"Me, neither," added Lydia. The waitress left their check on the table top.

"Maybe this guy came along to show you that things could be different so that you wouldn't stay in a rut with Richard out of habit or laziness."

"I wondered the same thing. Since I met Ian, I'm looking at things totally differently. I want to have a partner who encourages and supports me, and Richard isn't that. I don't know if Ian is; I don't even want to consider it at this point. For God's sake, he could be 25 and married for all I know. But thanks to him, I'm broadening my horizons."

"Maybe he's just a catalyst. You'll know better later on. Promise you'll keep me informed?"

"Of course. You're the only one who knows. I couldn't tell anyone else; they'd think I was bonkers."

After Lydia dropped her off at home, Jean felt the pull of the computer. Maybe that's how Richard felt about porn. She was beginning to feel guilty about how much she wanted to email Ian. She wondered if Richard ever felt guilty about the porn. She hadn't asked. Maybe she should ask, but it always seemed like such a big effort to confront Richard that she tended to take the easy way out.

Richard had a golf game this afternoon and wasn't at home. He'd probably return no earlier than dinner, so she decided to write Ian.

At the computer, she opened her email up. It was password protected, just as Richard's was. She had no idea what kind of email correspondence he had, and she didn't care. She hadn't thought the password protection mattered when she opened the account, but now it was welcome. She didn't need him snooping in her emails. She hadn't done anything wrong, but she was quivering with potential, and the unnamed feelings she was having made her feel ashamed.

She knew it was evening in the UK. Ian might not see this until tomorrow, but she'd screwed up the courage and was going to follow through before she lost her nerve.

Dear Ian,

I know it's late there, but I wanted to touch base. I've really enjoyed emailing you about dowsing. I'm so interested in it, and there are few opportunities here, as I said. My best friend Lydia loves dowsing, but she's the only other person I can talk to about it.

I know this could be considered intrusive, so please slap me down if I'm out of line, but I keep wanting to picture you as I read your emails. I don't know anything about you, and I would love to hear where you live in the UK and other personal details about you, if you don't mind.

I'll start by sharing a little information about myself. I am 58 years old, married and living in Palm Lakes Retirement Community in the Southwestern U.S. My husband is a retired lawyer, and although I went to college, I never had a career as such. I did a stint teaching in private schools and was a homemaker. We don't have children. As you know, my current interests in Reiki and dowsing are fairly newfound, and my husband doesn't share my interests. Lydia, my best friend, who also lives in Palm Lakes, is my companion and partner-in-crime at various classes we both take. I am short (we call it petite), have naturally blonde hair, blue eyes and am in good health. I am attaching a photo of myself that is not quite up-to-date (it was taken three years ago). It took me eons to figure out how to attach this, so I hope it gets there.

If it doesn't seem intrusive, I'd love to know more about your life, what you like to do besides dowsing, and where you live. We are situated in a very lovely area with many natural attractions nearby. If you ever come to this country, I'd be pleased to have a chance to meet you and show you the sights here. For some reason, I feel like we know each other, and that it is not only reasonable, but necessary, for us to become further acquainted.

Sincerely,

Your Dowsing Buddy, Jean

She reread the draft and then paused as her finger hovered over the Send button. Would she regret this? Would it set some terrible chain of events in motion? It felt portentous to open this door. Some part of her knew that if she didn't open that door, Ian would not. She could keep anything bad from happening by not sending this. But even stronger was the compulsion to ask these questions.

Regardless of the outcome, she'd never forgive herself if she didn't do this. Her mind said, "Maybe it will turn out he's 80 years old or gay. Quit worrying." But she *was* worried, because she had to admit that if he were in any way eligible, she was interested. She pushed the Send button.

CHAPTER NINE

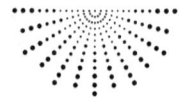

MONDAY, SEPTEMBER 18, 1995

Alexander, 3:25am

*A*lexander dreamed he was wrapped around a woman, his erect penis pressed against her soft bottom and his hand on her breast. Suddenly he realized it wasn't a dream. He was stroking Helen's breast through her thin nightgown and pushing against her backside, consumed with need. He recoiled and rolled to the other side of the bed, praying she hadn't awakened. He had promised not to molest her, and she would surely see that as a transgression, even if it *had* happened in his sleep.

He lay there, trying to calm his heart, which was beating furiously. He listened over its drumming for signs that Helen was awake, but her breathing was even and she appeared to be sleeping peacefully in spite of his manhandling. Thank God for small favors.

Could the timing of his reawakening be any more inconvenient? He'd given up sex when Leslie had died years ago. Unlike many men, he couldn't separate love and sex, so the past trauma meant he gave up both. He didn't want to love anyone; he couldn't face that kind of loss again. He'd found a way to live a fulfilled life without sex. Or so he thought.

Telling Helen he was gay was mostly the truth. His only committed relationship had been a gay one. Since she seemed skittish around him, he knew saying he was gay would allow her to relax. Now he had to admit that his motivation was more about keeping the wall intact around his heart, and telling her that fib made this relationship seem safer for him, as if he weren't changing anything. Now he was in a world of hurt. He couldn't pretend his feelings were platonic anymore.

His mind kept asking, why her, why now, when he'd been dodging relationships successfully for years, but still no answer was forthcoming. In spite of being an intelligent guy, he couldn't explain the way they had clicked. It just felt so good being with her. He didn't want to give that up, so he'd been telling himself they could just be friends.

This morning was a wakeup call. He wanted more than friendship, but he'd painted himself into a corner by not telling her the truth about his bisexuality. Dishonesty was death to a relationship. If he told her the truth, she'd hate him.

What was he going to do now? He couldn't bear the thought of losing her.

He slipped quietly out of bed, dressed in the walk-in closet in the dark and went out to the living room and plopped onto the couch. He couldn't stay in bed with her. The proximity was too provocative. He'd assumed at his age that sex was behind him, but holding her made him feel 30 years old again and forced him to face a previously unacknowledged emptiness in his soul.

He couldn't go on with her as he was. He wouldn't be able to hide his attraction, and it would be torture even if he could. If he told her the truth, she'd think him a liar and would never trust him again. Besides, how would she take his being bisexual? Her tolerance might not extend to that. Worst of all, he couldn't imagine a life without her as part of it.

Sick of going in circles, he picked up a book and tried to read, but gave up after staring at the page for a few minutes. He needed an answer, but none came to him. Thinking only seemed to make things worse.

He was desperate for a way to resolve this. Helen had turned to him in a time of great need, and he wanted to be there for her. He couldn't allow his focus to wander from his mission today. Somehow, he'd have to just act like nothing had happened.

As the sun rose, he still had no answers, so he gave up trying to sort things out and went into the kitchen. He'd make French toast and bacon for breakfast and play things by ear. So much depended on whether she had been awake during the incident.

A while later he sensed her standing behind him in the kitchen doorway. He took some time to put on his best face. He just wanted to see how she reacted. He'd know by looking at her whether she'd been awake during his manhandling of her. Taking a deep breath and holding it, he turned and looked into her eyes and smiled. He felt in that moment that she held his heart in her hand.

There was an attractive glow to her skin. She looked lovely and rested, but there was a question in her eyes. The moment stretched a bit too long, and her smile faded.

He plunged through the silence. "I hope you got enough sleep last night."

"Yes, thank you, I did. Better than I would have thought."

He turned back to the stove top. "Breakfast will be ready soon. I haven't set the table, if you'd like to do that." He heard her go to the cabinet and get plates down, then fish silverware out of the drawer. She carried the plates over and put them on the counter next to him without saying anything, then went out into the dining room with the silver. Something was wrong.

He delivered two plates of food out to the dining room, where she stood lost in thought. There was an air of irritation about her. Was it because she'd been awake in the night, or was it something else?

He set the plates down and they had an unusually quiet meal. Was she grieving over Sheba, or was she mad at him? He couldn't tell, and fear caused him to choose reticence. Finally, they finished eating, and he got up and gathered dishes together to take them to the kitchen. "Would you like to call the vet's? My phone book is in the office, in case you don't know the number."

"Thanks." She left without further conversation, and he went about cleaning up the kitchen, feeling numb and lost. Maybe he should just confess to her. But she didn't seem to be in a good mood, and he didn't feel brave enough to confess he had lied to her when she seemed so irritated. Plus it seemed egotistical to plant himself in the center of a day that should revolve around Sheba.

The morning unraveled from there. He didn't dare touch her, she was so prickly. But she never came out and said why. He felt intuitively that if he asked, it would lead to an explosive exchange that would end their relationship. He just needed to help her through this awful morning and hope for the best.

A couple hours later, when he went to say good-bye on her doorstep, she was so tense when he tried to hug her, it made him feel even more uncertain, so he didn't put his heart into it like he usually did. She didn't wave good-bye or watch him drive away, nor invite him in for coffee. Something was indeed very wrong. Yet if she had been awake last night, wouldn't she have confronted him?

He drove back home, frustrated in more ways than one. He felt he'd lost her, and he'd only just found her. It didn't feel like the kind of situation that time would heal. A profound sense of loss weighed him down, and he had to fight back tears for the first time in years.

* * *

Helen, 7:15am

HELEN AWOKE to the tantalizing smell of bacon. Sunlight poured through the sheer curtains of Alexander's bedroom, confirming that she was alone. How wonderful to have a man make breakfast while you slept!

She stretched luxuriously and then paused in shock as a memory returned to her. Last night, she'd had the strangest dream about Alexander. She never had erotic dreams, so it was doubly embarrassing. She was actually glad he wasn't here, because it made her suddenly feel uncomfortable to be in his bed.

She'd dreamed that he was spooned behind her like he had been when they first went to bed, but instead of just holding her gently, he was gripping her with passion. His hand was on her breast, caressing her nipple, and his enormous erection was pressing into her backside, hot and demanding. In the dream, her body had responded as if awakening

179

hungrily from a deep sleep, while she was a paralyzed observer. That was all she could remember. Whatever had brought that on?

She'd managed to avoid sex altogether in recent years. In spite of being married for decades, her knowledge of sex was mostly limited to what she read in romance novels, and frankly, she didn't believe they were true. That dream she'd had last night was like something out of a romance novel. Maybe that's why she'd dreamt it; being so close to a man she cared for reminded her of those stories.

Just thinking about the dream was causing her to react physically. She couldn't think of Alexander that way! He was gay, and he would be offended if he knew that she'd had an erotic dream about him. He'd made his distaste of predatory females quite clear, and she didn't want him to see her as one. Plus, nothing was more pathetic than a woman trying to 'convert' a gay man.

She was too embarrassed to tell him about that vivid dream. She wasn't even sure she could look him in the eye this morning. It was like it had really happened. If she told him, he'd think she *wanted* it to happen. Now that sex was part of the equation, even in a subconscious form, it wouldn't be the same with him. Having secrets changed a relationship, and never for the better.

Losing Sheba was horrible, but she felt she was also losing Alexander, and tears started streaming down her face. It would never be the same with him again. Why was life so cruel to her?

She got up, put on the bathrobe and went to the guest room to dress. She was too distracted and depressed to bother with makeup, so it didn't take long. She sat on the bed, giving herself a pep talk about just acting naturally. They had a mission today, and she needed his support. She wasn't going to cause trouble. It would all have to work out on its own.

When she went to the kitchen, he had his back to her as he attended the pans of bacon and French toast. She allowed herself to admire his tall frame, broad shoulders and nimble hands as they flew from one pan to the other. The problem was, thinking about his hands brought the dream back to her, and she felt herself flush. She wasn't the type to treat a man as a sex object, and this was her closest friend. *I just need to forget that stupid dream and go back to how it was. I can do that. I know I can.*

But she wasn't convinced. These strange feelings demanded her attention. She was practiced at putting anger and depression into a locked box deep inside herself, but these sexual feelings weren't going to be set aside so easily.

As if he had heard her inner turmoil, he turned and smiled at her. There was something about the smile that seemed different today. A hint of sadness? Uncertainty? What was that about? Or was it just her imagination? Her confusion led to shame, and her own smile evaporated.

"I hope you got enough sleep last night." His comment seemed freighted with other meanings. Maybe she was being paranoid. Was this what she had to look forward to from now on?

She struggled to act normal. "Yes, thank you, I did. Better than I would have thought."

She responded to his request to set the table without talking. There was a conspicuous lack of affection between them this morning, as she felt awkward and unsure what to do. Had she not had that dream and the subsequent feelings, she would have hugged and thanked him again, but she didn't trust herself. She felt the innocent relationship they had enjoyed was now tainted, and it made her anxious and even irritable. She lingered in the dining room, trying to pull herself together so she could get through the morning's ordeal with him. She was beginning to feel annoyed. He was supposed to help her feel better, and she was actually feeling much worse.

After a breakfast she barely tasted, she took his suggestion and went into the office to call the vet. They were very accommodating, which was a relief. She wasn't looking forward to this at all, and being with him made her feel prickly. She was angry that the perfect balance in their relationship had been tilted in a direction that made her so uncomfortable. She wasn't looking for sex, and she felt guilty that he had awakened her to something he could do nothing about.

She knew it was wrong to blame him for her feelings, but logic didn't enter into it. If he hadn't lured her into sleeping with him, she probably would never have had that dream. Maybe he didn't mean to take advantage, but it just wasn't fair. She wanted to yell how unfair it was but stuffed it down deep where she always put the feelings she couldn't express. At least those feelings of injustice stayed put.

She got through the morning somehow. The vet's receptionist promised to phone her when the ashes were ready for pickup. She let Alexander take her back to her empty house and drop her off without offering him coffee. She just wanted to be alone.

He still walked her to the door and gave her a hug, but it was wooden and forced, and it almost made her burst into tears. He was withdrawing from her, and she wasn't sure why. *I want it like it was before.*

She mumbled a weak thank you and unlocked the doors and went inside. She didn't watch as he drove away. The day stretched on interminably. No Sheba to play with or talk to. For the first time since she met him, she felt she couldn't phone Alexander and talk to him. There was a wall between them, and she had no idea how to tear it down, or even if it would be wise to do so.

In fact, as the hours passed, she decided that she was going to be very busy with her upcoming move, and it made sense to withdraw from the remaining cooking classes. She phoned Alice before she could lose her nerve. Alice was very supportive and understanding. That only made her cry more.

The tears weren't just about Sheba now. She felt so bereft about the turn things had taken with Alexander. Finally, she was willing to acknowledge it was all her fault. She should have known better than to be so relaxed. She'd been too open, too willing to jump into the relationship, too everything. It was better just to back off. He didn't need her. She'd been such a leech. He was very self-sufficient and didn't need her plaguing him with her stupid problems.

There was no place for her in his life. She couldn't afford to fall in love with him. His accommodating her was just kindness, and she'd taken advantage. He was pulling back, and she couldn't blame him, even though she wanted to. He owed her nothing. She'd give him the space he needed and throw herself into her move. Thank God she hadn't accepted his offer of living in his casita. What a disaster that would have been!

* * *

Jean, 10:15am

JEAN HESITATED as she stood at Lydia's front door. The door flew open before she could get collected enough to knock.

"Come on in. Were you planning on standing out there all day?" Lydia chuckled.

"I feel funny coming over here to dump on you. I really need a sounding board, and it won't do any good unless I tell you everything, but are you sure you're up for this? I feel guilty making you listen to my sob story." Jane entered and followed Lydia into the cozy kitchen.

"Don't feel bad about me. You're not just having a bitch session; you're trying to figure your life out, and I'm happy to help. How about some coffee?" Lydia stepped over to the coffeemaker, her eyebrows raised.

"Yes, of course, thanks."

Once they were sitting at the table sipping their coffee, Jean felt more relaxed. Lydia sat watching her knowingly, no sign of impatience in her dark brown eyes. Finally, she got up the nerve to spit it out. "Richard is playing golf today, and I wanted to ask you about this thing with Ian. I got an email today that answers some questions and poses some challenges." She reached into her purse and pulled out some paper, handing it to Lydia.

"Just a second. I need to get my reading glasses." After putting her glasses on, Lydia read it aloud, every word plucking at Jean's nerves, but she didn't ask her to stop, because at the same time that the letter disturbed her, it also seemed full of promise.

All hail, Dowsing Buddy Jean,

I received your email and agree that it would be more fun to chat if we knew a bit more about each other, although I'm not a very interesting chap. I'm divorced, 57 years old and am a struggling tarot card reader and healer as well as a dowser.

I spent many years in a corporate job. After nearly 20 years, I wised up and walked out. It was a dramatic change in my life, as I left my wife at the same time. That was almost two years ago, and I love what I do and wouldn't go back to my old life, but it can be a struggle at times to make ends meet, living in what you might call the suburbs of London, where it is rather costly.

I would very much like to travel and see the world. I've spent time in Europe, but never been to the States. I might look at fares and see what it costs.

Of course, you and your husband are welcome to visit here, too. I have lived here all my life, and I know lots of great places like museums and fine restaurants that you would enjoy.

I look forward to your emails, because I also do not have many friends here. I know a few people who have similar interests, but I am not extroverted, so I don't socialize much. I enjoy reading and watching the occasional movie or sport on TV. I'm really pretty boring!

My latest dowsing adventure was to go to Avebury and dowse the energy lines at the site. Are you familiar with it? There are big standing stones there, and the energy is amazing! I wish I could show you. I'll try to get some photos next time I go and figure out how to send them.

Speaking of photos, your picture came through brilliantly! You are a lovely lady. I don't have any recent photos of myself, and so I'll have to figure a way to reciprocate in the future.

Tell me about your latest dowsing adventure.

Your dowsing buddy and pen pal,

Ian

Well, if that don't beat all. So now you have a real problem, don't you?" Lydia looked at her sympathetically over her reading glasses.

"Yeah. He's eligible. Not that I have any clue he's interested, but Lydia, the connection I feel to him gets stronger all the time. I don't know what to do now. Part of me hoped he'd be ineligible. But part of me is excited that he is." She shook her head and looked down at her hands.

Lydia handed the letter back to her as she took her glasses off.

"No, Lyd, throw it out. I can't risk Richard finding it. It's innocent, but I just can't go there with him."

"So what does he say to you about your marriage and his little habit?"

"Nothing. It's like he doesn't acknowledge it's a problem, or he doesn't care that I feel it is. That actually makes me angry."

"Anger can be good sometimes if it prompts you to make a healthy change."

"I feel as if I'm rushing towards a momentous change, and I'm not sure I'm ready. But on the other hand, I'm not happy as I am." She paused for a second, considering how much to say. "Not only has Richard not broached the subject; you know we're sleeping in separate bedrooms, and he hasn't said a word about that. It's like this is the new 'us'. It upsets me."

"It should. That's no way to live."

"I keep asking myself if it's my fault this happened. I know he hasn't liked me pursuing the energy healing and other metaphysical subjects, but I can't imagine that is the problem. Am I that bad at sex? I wouldn't know. We rarely do it anymore, and I haven't had many partners."

"For heaven's sake, don't blame yourself. That's a classic mistake. He did what he did for his own reasons."

"Even if I accept that and decide I don't want to be with him anymore, that's only one big decision. The other one is what to do about Ian. He's never said anything. This is all coming from me. Maybe I'm making it up because my marriage is falling apart." Tears started to fill her eyes.

"You can only take this one step at a time. Don't mingle the two. Ian was a catalyst, but your decision shouldn't be based on whether he reciprocates your interest. Do you really want to stay with Richard for the rest of your life like this? That's the only question now."

"No, of course not."

"Then what's the problem. Divorce him and come live with me for a while."

Jean sighed. "You make it sound easy. But it's so hard. I feel bad about hurting him, not that I'm sure it would. I worry a little bit about money, though we have enough I should be okay. What really bothers me is I don't want to have to explain to people why I left him. It's no one's business, but if I say nothing, they may blame me...I know it's dumb to worry about that, but I do." She sighed again.

Lydia reached over and patted Jean's hand. "Honey, I feel for you. But if you can just be honest and get through it, things will get better. I don't think they will if you stay. That's my opinion, if you want it."

Jean smiled through the tears. "Thanks. I do want your opinion. It makes it easier for me knowing you won't judge me."

"Judge you? I think you're amazing. Most people just stay in bad marriages. You have the guts to consider leaving at our age. I'll help any way I can. I just want you to be happy."

The tears flowed more freely as Jean accepted that she did indeed have a support system. "You don't know how much it means to me that you're here for me. I couldn't do it without you."

Lydia laughed and patted her hand again. "It's going to be all right."

They sipped their coffee for a few minutes in silence. Then Lydia brought up the inevitable. "So what are you planning to do about Ian?"

Lydia's soft eyes held no judgment, but Jean felt herself retreat inward. At last, she responded. "I really don't know. All I do know for sure is I have the strongest feeling that he is important in my life. I can't say exactly how. He lives on another continent. What am I supposed to do? He hasn't even said a word about being more than pen pals." Her voice was tinged with sadness and doubt.

"You'll just have to tell him how you feel."

"Are you nuts? He'll think I'm some psycho. There's no reason for me to be approaching him like I want a date. He doesn't realize my marriage is imploding. He never talks about anything but dowsing."

"So what? What's the worst that can happen if you come clean with him? It's not like you see him every day. You've never laid eyes on him. If he runs screaming, then you know it wasn't meant to be. Don't you think you need something to help settle all the questions in your mind?"

"You're right. But I don't want to take a chance that I'll lose him. Not that I have him. But the way I feel about him is like a delicate flower I don't want to crush. I've had so much disappointment lately. I'm not sure I could take that."

Lydia got up to refill their mugs. "I don't blame you. It's hard. But sooner or later, you need to broach the subject. You can be low-key about it and see what he says. Did it occur to you that he's been circumspect in what he said because he wasn't sure who else reads your emails?"

Jeans eyes flew wide open, and her hand reflexively went to her mouth. "It never occurred to me. Are you suggesting he might be feeling the same way I do?"

"If he's as intuitive as you say, and if you two are fated somehow, then why wouldn't he be feeling much the same thing?" Lydia cocked her head to one side, fixing Jean with an intense brown stare.

Jean mentally cast about, trying to see if that theory could be true."I can't argue with that logic. He may very well be acting cautiously."

Something shifted within Jean like she had finally put down a heavy burden. "I don't know how to thank you, Lydia. I'm not sure I would ever have thought of that, and it makes it a lot easier for me to consider asking him how he feels. Like you say, what have I got to lose? If I do it carefully, we can still be friends."

Lydia nodded. "And if he feels as you do, then what?"

Suddenly Jean smiled. "Then I go to the UK to meet him. After I set the divorce in motion."

"Atta girl."

CHAPTER TEN

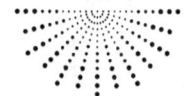

WEDNESDAY, OCTOBER 18, 1995

Owen, 2:15pm

The afternoon sun warmed his back as Owen leaned over the fence talking to his neighbor. He couldn't remember the man's name. Fortunately, the old guy was garrulous. His watery blue eyes squinted in the glare of the sunlight as he told Owen the story.

"I don't know how true it is, but I heard that she nearly ran over a pedestrian in the parking lot of some hotel not far away. She apparently lost control and rammed a parked car. The only person hurt was her. How bad, I'm not sure, but they say she didn't have a seat belt on, and she was taken to the hospital."

Owen nodded encouragingly.

The old guy cleared his throat and continued. "Now I'm not one to spread gossip, but I was told she was drunk at the time. They say her license was taken away, and she's been forced to go into a rehab clinic. Not sure if that's true." The old guy coughed like a cigarette smoker, hacking painfully.

Owen had heard enough. "Well, that's the most excitement I've heard in a long time. Thanks for bringing me up to date." He waved and went back into his house, satisfied that he knew as much as he ever would about Tanya's accident.

Over the past few weeks, Owen had judiciously pumped his few acquaintances for gossip, something he had never done in his life. While not every source agreed how badly she had been hurt -- some said she had a concussion and 32 stitches, while others said she didn't have a scratch -- everyone seemed to agree she'd been drunk at the time and hit a parked car.

He'd been tossing around in a sea of confusion for weeks. He'd lost his taste for judging women. He was disturbed and agitated by this sudden change, this abandonment of anger in all its dark and bloody shades, but not being introspective, all he could do was observe and register surprise. Strange new emotions flowed through him. Their power mesmerized him. He felt like a puppet in someone else's show.

The one blessing out of all this was that his mother had gone silent. He didn't ask himself why that was; he was just grateful and accepted it. With luck, she was gone forever. He hadn't had this much peace since the day he'd pushed her down the steps when he was 17, and that silence had only lasted about 24 hours before she took up residence inside his head.

The ringing of the phone jarred him out of his reverie. Who could that be? Probably a telemarketer. He hated those assholes. "What do you want?" he barked into the phone.

The silence was unlike a telemarketer. They started talking right away no matter how ugly you were to them. "It's me. Tanya." He sank into a chair in the living room, speechless.

"Did I call at a bad time?" Her voice did things to him. Things he didn't understand.

"I'm here." For weeks he'd been telling himself he'd never speak to her again, but when the time came, he found he really did want to talk to her. It didn't seem to matter anymore that she was a drunken slut.

"I called to say I'm sorry for what happened. I saw you drive into the hotel parking lot. I felt so bad about breaking our date. I wanted to call you sooner, but I haven't been able to." She waited as if to give him a chance to say something nice.

"Yeah, whatever."

"I called to give you the details of what happened. I at least owe you that for not being where I promised. It was one of those crazy accidents. A woman stepped off the curb in front of me, and I swerved to avoid hitting her. My foot slipped onto the accelerator instead of the brake pedal, and I hit a parked car. Since I didn't have my seatbelt on, I went into the windshield. They say I got a concussion in addition to nearly 30 stitches. I'm only now feeling almost back to normal. None of it would have happened but for that woman, but they're blaming me instead."

She hurried through the next part. "They gave me a blood alcohol test, and it was over the limit. I'd only had a couple of drinks because I was nervous about our date. They've taken away my license, and so I can't drive anywhere. My husband is being a total asshole, as usual."

She went on without giving him a chance to comment. "The insurance company is hiking our premiums, and the judge has mandated that I have to go to rehab. I'm leaving soon for 30 days at the Twelve Palms Oasis center. It's on the other side of town. Might as well be in another state. I have to leave the 29th.

"They allowed me to stay home while the doctor treated the concussion. I didn't want to leave without giving you an explanation."

On the one hand, he was disgusted by her; on the other, rather admiring of her unwillingness to bend or be broken. "Well, I guess it's lucky you didn't have worse injuries."

"Yes, that's what they said. I wish I could have been there for our date. I was really looking forward to it." Her voice purred seductively now that she had changed the subject to Owen.

"I was there."

"I know, and I appreciate it. And I'm very sorry about missing it. I've been trying to think of a way to make it up to you, but without my license, I can't drive anywhere." She waited as if hoping he had an idea.

He didn't, though he was aware if the opportunity existed, he'd take it. *Surprising.*

When he didn't reply, she continued. "I still want to buy you a drink, even if it's nonalcoholic. I just don't know when or where. They say I can have visitors toward the end of my stay in rehab, but not for the first few weeks. And they'll probably be uptight about anyone coming to see me, and it probably wouldn't be a good idea for you to stop by, even though I'd like it."

"Thanks for the heads up." So it looked like at least 40 days before he could even think about seeing her. "What happens after you get out?"

Her voice perked up. "They won't give me my license back right away, but at some point, I may get it back. That would be an important goal. I'm going stir crazy here."

"Maybe you should give me a call when you get out." He wasn't sure it was a good idea, but he could always say 'no' to her, couldn't he?

"That sounds like a wonderful thing for me to look forward to, Owen. You are so thoughtful, the only man in my life who cares a thing about how I feel. I'll be sure to do that." As if an afterthought, she added, "The doctor insisted I get some gentle exercise daily, and he recommended walking, so that's what I do. I walk around the neighborhood. I'm taking longer walks all the time. Since the weather has cooled off some, I don't have to get up at the crack of dawn. I've been walking late in the morning most days. I like to walk over to that spot near the golf course where there's a bench by the lake that has the swans. Have you ever been there?"

"I don't walk much."

"Well if you ever change your mind, you can find me there most mornings around 10:30."

He knew what she wanted, but resisted giving in too easily. "We'll see."

"All right. See you later." She sounded disappointed.

"Bye then." Owen hung up the phone without waiting for a response.

"You idiot, Junior! Are you determined to end up on Death Row?" His mother's harpy-like voice clawed at him.

He cringed and fisted his hands, wretched that she had returned. "Why can't you stay away from me? You're dead! Go away and leave me alone!"

"I tried, but then you had to talk to that whore. You're under her spell, and it's going to get you caught."

"Mother, I can handle my life. I won't even see her for at least 40 days. What harm can happen when she's in rehab?"

"I don't know, but you'll find a way to screw it up. You're just like your father, incapable of reading the writing on the wall. You're already thinking about meeting her on the golf course. She's no good, and you need to let it go before she drags you down."

"Fine talk from you. All you ever did was drag me down." He stalked into the weight room and began a workout. Blessed silence reigned again. But for how long? His nerves were stretched tight, and unlike in the past, he wasn't sure what to do to release the pressure.

He was beginning to be convinced that the only solution was for him to have Tanya, one way or another. It really didn't matter how. He just needed to purge his system of her, and he was open to any option at this point.

If he could pick her up unobserved by the golf course, it wouldn't matter which way the encounter went. He'd be free of her once and for all. In that past, he never would have considered such a high-risk option, because you could never tell who was looking out the window in Palm Lakes. But if he played it right, he'd get away with it even if someone saw them together.

She was panting for him, and he'd like nothing better than to give her what she was asking for. It just wasn't clear to him exactly what that would be.

* * *

Mary Beth, 2:35pm

HER AFTERNOON at work was nearing an end, and Mary Beth was eager to get home and take a pain pill. The cheap chair at her desk was causing her back to play up like hell, but all the chairs were old and uncomfortable, so she just had to take it. Rubbing her back to ease the pain, she put the last invoice in the Out box. Someone else did the actual accounting. She wasn't even sure who that was. Yet another oddity about working here.

She really liked her job, but it was the antithesis of a typical corporate job. There were no job descriptions, no weekly meetings. Everyone pitched in to get the work done. If someone wasn't around, you did their job as needed. There were no time clocks or cards, just as Julio had promised, and most days she went home and had lunch with Mom. She never heard a harsh word.

She'd seen a lot of practices that would have horrified her old boss. On Pancho's desk, sometimes piles of checks lay around for a day or more, unsupervised and treated almost like ordinary scraps of paper. Samantha had mentioned the other day that she'd gone to finish up on a job and collect payment and once again found some tools the crew had left behind; no one was ever reprimanded, and Samantha assured her it was a common happenstance. And there was the lingering question in her mind of what exactly Ricardo did. All of the brothers were in and out all day doing their appointed tasks, but Ricardo seemed not to have a specific job. He was more of a gofer. And that wasn't the only thing that made him stand out from his brothers. Unlike his handsome siblings, he was short and toadlike, plus he had a slightly creepy vibe about him. The others smiled and assessed her; he leered.

Still, she was glad she'd taken the job, and it was working out well. Her performance seemed to please all the brothers, and she was learning the various tasks quickly.

Samantha came into the office and put her things on the desk by the door, which was where she usually worked. That was another weird thing. No one owned anything. Everything was shared, including desks. Samantha only spent a little time in the office, sketching designs for yards with details that would help the crew do the plantings correctly.

"Hi, Samantha. How's it going?"

"Been busy, but can't complain." Samantha tossed her hat on the end of the desk and turned to smile at Mary Beth. Samantha was so fit and trim. If she didn't like her so much, she'd hate her. Samantha took a tea bag and mug out of her carryall bag, and set them on the desktop.

Mary Beth stood up and twisted her back this way and that, hoping to ease the pain.

"You hurt your back?"

"Nah, I've had problems for a while. Ever since a car accident a few years ago. I'm trying not to take the pain pills. Doc says I can't mix them with alcohol, and damned if I'm giving up drinking." She smiled grimly.

"I'm so sorry to hear that. Have you been to a chiropractor?"

Mary Beth was shocked. "Are they for real? I always thought they were quacks that got you on some kind of eternity plan just to make money."

"I go to mine monthly. With all the hauling I do, I need adjustment regularly. He did X-rays my first visit and showed me how out of whack I was, and I feel so much better since I've been going to him. I used to have neck pain to beat the band. I can give you his name and number if you'd like to give him a try."

"I'd try anything at this point. I don't like being in pain all the time, and it's turning me into a bitch. Pardon my french."

Samantha laughed and wrote the doctor's name on a scrap of paper, then looked up his name in the Yellow Pages and wrote his number down. Handing the paper to Mary Beth, she promised, "You'll be glad if you go see him. More than likely you have a problem that was caused by the accident, and conventional doctors don't see things like that. Trust me." She smiled and went back to her desk and sat down to work on her design.

Just as Mary Beth sat back down, the phone rang. "Palo Verde Landscaping, may I help you?...yes, please hold while I page him." Mary Beth put the phone on hold and yelled, "Alberto, pick up line 1!"

Samantha giggled at her desk. "You crack me up, Mary Beth; 'let me page him'."

"Just trying to sound professional," she quipped.

The door opened and Julio stepped into the office. He noticed the chamomile tea bag on Samantha's desk. "Ah, manzanilla. You like herbs?"

Samantha looked at him and smiled. "Yes, I do. I also study medicinal herbs and make extracts."

Julio looked at her with respect. "You are a curandera?" Mary Beth was wondering what that meant, but from context, it sounded like a healer.

"No, I wouldn't go that far, Julio. I just like using herbs for good health. My background as you know is in Biology, and I love plants. That's one reason I love working here."

"Pancho's wife is looking for a particular herb. Can you buy herbs?"

"Yes, I mail order them. I can tell him where I get them. Do you know what she wants to buy?"

"No, I forget, but ask him."

"OK. No problema." Samantha started back on her drawing, but Julio didn't take the hint.

He perched on the edge of Samantha's desk, one cowboy boot swinging as he leaned towards her and spoke in a stage whisper. "Speaking of herbs, I hear there's a drug operation over on Casino Drive in Palm Lakes. And I'm not talking about medicinal herbs." Mary Beth was entranced. She couldn't imagine her neighbors as drug dealers.

Samantha was dismissive. "Oh, for heaven's sake, Julio, it's probably just a rumor."

He looked at her as if offended. "No, seriously. You don't see Palm Lakes from my point of view. It's pretty wild out there. What do they say? Sex, drugs and rock and roll? There are women in Palm Lakes who like the way my brown skin looks next to their white skin, if you know what I mean." He ran a hand through his lush raven-black hair, pushing it back from his face. Julio was the only man Mary Beth had ever seen who made long hair look attractive. He could have been a gigolo or a male model in other circumstances.

Samantha appeared to be a bit flustered and waved him off dismissively. Mary Beth didn't think Julio was coming on to Samantha, but she'd given up trying to figure out these guys. The other day -- not for the first time -- Julio had complimented her on losing weight. She'd lost all of two more pounds, and it bothered her to think he could see that just by looking at her, or that he was looking that hard.

Julio continued when Samantha failed to respond. "You know, sometimes the residents treat me like I'm deaf or don't speak English. Or maybe it's just that I'm the help, so I don't count. But the other day, a man and his wife were talking about a wife-swapping thing while I was in the room."

That got Samantha's attention. She paused and looked up at him. "Julio, they were just pulling your leg."

"No, they were serious. Trust me." He stood up and brushed off his jeans.

Samantha shook her head as if she wasn't buying it. Mary Beth's mouth was open. She couldn't picture all these people her mother's age selling dope and wife-swapping. It seemed ludicrous but intriguing. She was disappointed when Samantha changed the subject.

"Julio, I'm going to a class at the college soon on desert landscaping plants. It looks really interesting. It's being taught by a guy who has written some books I have. I'll let you know if I find out anything interesting."

He smiled and patted her shoulder but said nothing. It seemed condescending to Mary Beth, but Samantha didn't react negatively. Julio went to the back office.

"Wow, do you believe that shit, Samantha? You've lived in Palm Lakes longer than I have."

"I don't know, Mary Beth. Julio doesn't make things up. He has a pretty big ego, but I've never known him to lie."

"I just can't picture someone my Mom's age in a wife-swapping orgy." Then she giggled. "Yuck!"

Samantha laughed. "It is hard to picture, but I guess just because people get older doesn't mean they stop being themselves, and it might be logical to assume young drug dealers become old drug dealers if they live long enough. As to wife-swapping, I just don't know. You and I work, but lots of these folks are retired and may be bored. We don't travel in the right circles to see what goes on behind closed doors."

"You may be right. It's just weird to imagine that sort of thing going on in Palm Lakes." Mary Beth shook herself as if throwing the thought aside. "Hey, you were talking about taking a class. Does the company subsidize you?"

"Ongoing education is up to me. He might let me out of work if the class were during the day. This one isn't. But I pay for it myself. The guys learn by experience, and that's what they trust. They don't put a lot of stock in a piece of paper or a class. They also aren't that interested in being told how to do things by an Anglo woman, especially the woman part. You and I are outside the family in so many ways. Over time, you learn that there are boundaries you shouldn't cross. For example, the crews that build the block walls make more money than you or I do."

"What? That doesn't seem right."

"They have families to support, so the brothers pay the workers more than us. They figure we have other streams of income. That's true for me.

My husband has retirement income. But it isn't for you. The system isn't perfect, but they have a code, and I respect that. It would be nice to be valued more, but hey, it is what it is." She sighed and pointed at her drawing. "I need to finish this design before I go home, so I guess I better get back to it."

Mary Beth nodded as Samantha bent her head to her design. She was certainly getting a crash course in cultural differences.

* * *

Helen, 4:35pm

HELEN SAT at the dining room table in her new condo, watching the sun dip lower in the sky. The last couple of weeks were a blur. Her house had sold unexpectedly fast for a good price. She was able to hire movers to help her with the things she kept. Sally was thrilled with the furniture Helen no longer needed and came with a few coworkers and hauled it off. At least one of her kids was happy with her.

Lena and Warren were getting on her nerves, constantly expressing disbelief that she had chosen to stay in Palm Lakes, implying that she wasn't competent enough to live on her own, even hinting that she was frittering away their inheritance. Lena was up in arms about Sally getting so many pieces of furniture she'd had her eye on.

Maybe if they could see all of her accomplishments and be a bit less selfish, they would feel different. Maybe not. She wasn't going to live her life for other people anymore. Sure, she was making mistakes. Look what had happened with Alexander. She still wasn't quite certain why they weren't speaking anymore. Drawing away from him had been a declaration of independence of sorts, but it hadn't left her feeling free. She missed him. The course put on by the writing club would be starting soon, and she knew he might be in it. Should she opt out of yet another class just out of fear of seeing him? And what was she so afraid of? He wasn't the type to be ugly to someone in public. Yet even the thought of seeing him shook her up.

She needed to stop obsessing about their failed relationship, but no matter what she told herself, she couldn't stop chewing the situation over and over, playing scenarios, guessing motives. The fact was she just didn't know enough to reach a conclusion she could trust, and it was eating away at her, not having closure and confidence that she had done the right thing.

She sipped her coffee and contemplated the future. The yoga class was a go, and she was excited about starting it next week. Jean and Lydia would be in it, and she enjoyed their company.

The doorbell startled her. She went to the door and looked through the peephole. Mary Beth was standing on the porch.

"Hi, how are you doing, Mary Beth?"

"Just got back from work a little while ago, and I thought I'd come by and see how you were settling in. It's looking really nice. This looks like a different model from Mom's. Would you mind showing me around?"

Helen smiled at how forward she was but welcomed the chance to shift gears mentally. She led her through each room, grateful she had finished unpacking all the boxes. "Things aren't totally the way I want them. I still have pictures to hang. But it's coming along nicely, if I do say so myself."

"What I wouldn't give to have my own place. This is just perfect!"

"You're welcome to visit anytime."

Mary Beth looked at her with a mixture of shock and gratitude. "Don't say that. I'll make a pest of myself for sure, and you'll be left trying to get rid of me without being rude. Sometimes Mom drives me nuts, and I don't have many choices of where to go. My new job is a godsend for both of us. It gets me out of her hair and gives me a chance to feel like an adult for a few hours a day. It's amazing how mothers never see their kids as grown up."

"Guilty as charged. I think it's an occupational hazard. I'm glad you got a job you like. So tell me about it." Helen pointed to the couch, and they both sat down.

"I do like it. It's different from what I did before. You read about culture shock, but until you are immersed in another culture, you just can't imagine. I guess it isn't total cultural immersion, but the atmosphere there is very much Mexican. The owners are Hispanic brothers, and all the workers are Mexican. I suspect some are illegal. Did

I tell you the brothers are total hotties? Every one of them is fuckin' gorgeous, pardon my french."

"I'll have to take your word on it. Maybe you've been living with us old folks too long, and anyone nearer your age looks good." She smiled, uplifted by Mary Beth's enthusiasm.

"Nah, it isn't that, and don't put yourself down, girl. You're a hottie for your age. I know the ratio of women to men is out of whack here, but you could easily get dates if you wanted to."

"I met a guy named Bernie at a party a few months ago who wanted a date. He practically massaged my boobs when we met." She laughed at the memory of Bernie, and Mary Beth giggled with her. Then she felt wistful. "I'm not looking for another husband. I wouldn't mind a friend. I thought I had one, but things didn't work out."

Mary Beth looked at her empathetically. "What happened?"

"I'm not sure. It was probably my fault. I never had friends until recently, and I certainly never had a male friend. I didn't mix socially when I was married, so I don't know how to act. Anyway, something happened and I got spooked. So I withdrew because I was feeling like a total idiot and clinging vine, and it was easier to distance myself than wait for the inevitable rejection." She looked down, feeling sad at the thought of Alexander. "How about a cup of coffee?"

"I'd prefer wine, if you have any. If you really don't mind me stopping by now and then, I'll bring a bottle over for us."

"I'm glad you speak your mind, Mary Beth. Maybe you can teach me how to do that. I'd love to have you come over and visit. It's always fun to have someone to talk to and share a glass of wine or whatever. I don't like to drink alone, and I've cut back recently, but I do like to have a glass now and then. Let's go sit at the dining room table. The view isn't great yet...the yard still needs to be done, but the sunshine is wonderful."

Mary Beth took the glasses she handed her and went to the table. "You know, you need to get Samantha or Julio out here to design you a new yard. They did a great job for us, and everyone raves about their work. They guarantee it. If you get Julio, you can tell me if I was exaggerating."

Helen chuckled. "I'll do that. I got a good price for the house, and I've been accepted for a part-time job at Wal-Mart, so I'm feeling pretty flush.

I'll call them and make an appointment. What's the name of their company? I'm eager to have the yard looking pretty. I know you have to wait for the plants to grow, and I'm the impatient type."

"Palo Verde Landscaping. Just don't tell them you don't buy green bananas anymore. They've heard that one so often they want to puke." Mary Beth pointed her index finger at her open mouth, miming vomiting.

"I don't feel old enough to say that. Yet. I've gotten a little jolt of vitality since I was widowed. I'm feeling younger than I have in years."

"Do you miss your husband?"

The question took Helen totally by surprise. What the heck, she might as well be honest. To a point. "No. I don't miss him at all." She didn't feel ready to add further details and hoped Mary Beth wouldn't ask.

"I don't miss mine anymore, either. He divorced me and married a younger woman, whom I am sure he was banging while we were married, the asshole. Pardon my french. I felt sorry for myself for a while. Mom couldn't stand me moping over him. She always hated Jason, and she said I was lucky he left me. But it isn't always easy to see the truth. Now that I have a job and a place to live, even though the future is uncertain, I feel better about everything. It was rocky for a while there."

Helen sipped her wine, considering how much to reveal. "I went through a period of adjustment, too. I drank too much, but I wised up eventually. It wasn't easy at first to be alone and free and in charge of my life. I was scared. But I've adapted."

"Me, too. If I could get my back feeling better, things would be nearly perfect. Samantha told me about a chiropractor she swears by, and I'm going to go see him next week. At this point, I'd try anything. I don't like taking pain pills. I'm not supposed to drink alcohol when I do, and I am *so* not giving up alcohol." She giggled again and gulped down more wine.

"Do you get to socialize at all? I know you aren't technically supposed to be here. Does that mean you can't be in the clubs or use the Rec Center?"

"Now that I have a job, Mom bought me a guest pass. But I have to be careful about not using it too often. I'm only supposed to visit for brief periods of time. Mom doesn't want me to leave now. I think her heart condition has her scared for the first time in her life. She had an angina attack while I was shopping one day, and it seems to have knocked the legs out from under her. Have you seen Mrs. Jameson, the old bat who lives across the way? She's the Nazi who reports violations to the HOA. Or so Mom says."

"I see her looking out her window from time to time. I have nothing to hide, fortunately. Maybe I ought to start a Tupperware business or do something to distract her from you?" Helen laughed at her own joke.

"Don't kid around. She's serious. I hear she reported someone for having shade cloth over the plants in their front yard. The covenants apparently do not allow that. Can you imagine? And she reported someone else for putting a cute customized mailbox up. They have to be a certain style and color. I had no idea..."

"I never concerned myself with the covenants when Lou was around. I guess I need to educate myself so I don't get in trouble. I had no idea they were so stringent."

"If she turns me in, I'll go find a condo outside and move my Mom if she doesn't want to be alone. Right now, she's begging me to stay, so I will. She may get fed up with me eventually. I kind of hope so." Mary Beth grinned and downed the rest of her wine. "I better get back. Mom'll be wanting to have dinner soon. You know how early dinner is in Palm Lakes." She stood up and headed for the front door with Helen following her.

When they reached the door, Mary Beth turned around and hugged Helen. "Thanks for being so gracious. I look forward to gossiping with you again soon. I'll bring wine next time."

Helen was charmed. "I hope you'll come by again. My work and class schedule are during the day, so I will be here most evenings."

The door closed, and the atmosphere returned to silence. Mary Beth had filled the condo with a joie de vivre that was uplifting. It was good to be around younger people. She needed to remember to call tomorrow for an appointment with Samantha or Julio the hottie. She grinned as she picked up the phone book and scanned the yellow pages for the number to call.

CHAPTER ELEVEN

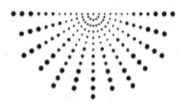

WEDNESDAY, OCTOBER 25, 1995

Samantha, 11:00am

*R*ight on time for her appointment, Samantha pushed the doorbell at Helen's condo. When she stepped inside, Helen hugged her like an old friend. Samantha hugged her back and glanced around the living room. "I like your new place. Are you settling in OK?"

"Yes, it's been crazy busy, but things are coming together. I'm really excited about getting the yard done. Come have a look at it." They walked through the kitchen and dining room and out into the yard.

Samantha looked around for a few minutes, relieved the yard was so empty. "I remember seeing it when I visited Mary Beth a while back. It's been neglected, but we'll soon have it looking great. I think you're better off starting from scratch, because then you can have it just the way you like. At least you have your gravel. That's the biggest single expense."

"I'm eager to have it looking nice."

Samantha smiled to herself. It was always more fun to work with someone who was enthusiastic about the project.

They walked the short distance to the six-foot high block wall at the end of the yard while Samantha bent down and examined the few scraggly cacti. They weren't worth trying to save. Turning around to look back towards the condo, Samantha considered possibilities. "Well, it's a nice small space, but they didn't have an irrigation system, which is why they had mostly cacti. You'll be wanting to put in a system, and I have to warn you, that raises the cost." Samantha always worried that people would think she was jacking up the price when she said that, but hoped Helen trusted her.

"I'm okay with that, but I'm pretty clueless about what to plant. Gardening isn't my thing."

Relieved at Helen's reaction, Samantha pulled a book out from under her clipboard. She flipped it open to a picture of a small tree covered with orchid-like flowers. "This is a desert willow. It's really more a large bush than a tree. For a yard your size, it's perfect."

Helen looked at the picture. "Oh, yes, I'll have that one."

"Then we only need to pick some bushes to fill in the gaps." She pointed at the wall behind her. "A vine will go nicely there and soften the look of the yard." She turned and faced the condo. "I'd put some bushes there and there and along each fence. Here, let me show you pictures."

Helen looked at the pictures and chirped excitedly. "This is just perfect!"

"I want to warn you that we don't overplant. It may look a bit thin at first, but things grow fast here, and you'll be glad if you plant fewer plants. Plus it saves water, maintenance and money."

"That sounds good to me. Can you give me an estimate?"

"Sure, let's go into the house and I'll calculate it for you."

As they walked into the condo, Helen's enthusiasm bubbled over. "When can you start?"

"I believe I can get a crew here within the next several days. We should be able to complete it in one day."

"That would be terrific!"

Fifteen minutes later, business concluded, Helen handed a steaming mug of coffee to Samantha and joined her at the dining room table. "So how is your mother doing? I haven't seen her in a while, with all the ruckus about my move."

"It's kind of you to ask. She hasn't been doing so great. After that fall and the broken wrist, they found she has osteoporosis and wanted her on some drug or other. She isn't much for taking pills, and especially doesn't take orders well, so she isn't taking any medicine.

"A couple weeks ago, the wind blew one of those plastic grocery bags into the top of her citrus tree, and she was trying to get it down by swinging a broom at it, and she cracked a vertebra. Just hitting the tree with the broom was enough to break the bone. She was in the hospital for a few days, but they never keep you long anymore, so she's home now." She didn't try to hide her worry and exasperation.

"I knew Maddie was stubborn, but you make it sound pathological," Helen said sympathetically.

"Well, it *is* pathological. She just won't do what she needs to do, and she resents any kind of help. It's driving me crazy. Dad is mostly unaffected; he lives in his own world. As long as she still cooks his meals, he won't say anything." Samantha sighed and shook her head. "She tries to hide it, but it's clear to me she's in a lot of pain."

"I brought a couple of dishes over to them when her wrist was in the cast. I could tell she didn't want me to, so I quit. I was just trying to pay forward what Barbara and others did for me after my husband died. But I didn't want to make her uncomfortable."

"She told me about that, and she really did appreciate it. The first few days were hard on her. There was a good bit of pain, and pain pills don't work on her. I guess that's one reason she hates pills. Anyway, I want you to know you did help a lot. Thanks."

Helen smiled genuinely. "It was my pleasure. I love the jewelry your Mom makes. I'm going to miss seeing her. I know it's not that far, but you know how it is when you aren't neighbors anymore. Please give her my love and tell her I'll try to stop by and see how she's doing."

"I'm going over there before I go back to the office. I'll give her your message and tell her how nice your new place is." Samantha stood up and took her mug to the kitchen sink, then gave Helen a quick hug and left, promising to call her soon with the date of the installation.

The rest of the day proceeded smoothly, and Samantha got home before 4pm. Tonight was the first day of the class on desert landscaping plants at the local community college. She'd read all of the professor's books, so it would be a real treat to be in his class, an intensive adult education course that lasted four nights over the coming week, plus an afternoon meeting Saturday. She felt it was really going to take her knowledge to the next level.

The simple meal she'd planned got her on the road fast. After finding a parking space at the college and hunting for the room, Samantha slid into the back row of seats in the appointed classroom. There were nearly 40 people milling about, and a man--probably the teacher--stood up front at the desk, talking to a few of them. Five minutes later, just before the class started, another student slipped into the back of the class and looked around for a place to sit.

His longish black hair tied in a pony tail, tanned skin and dark eyes made him look at least part Native American. His chiseled features were handsome, but not in a pretty boy way. He was probably early 40s, nearly 6 ft tall and dressed in jeans and a long-sleeved shirt, all black. The guy was handsome and knew it, and he probably thought he looked hot in black. *Oh crap, he's coming to sit by me. That's all I need.*

There was no way for her to change seats without being obvious, so she stared forward, eyes glued on the teacher, who had just started talking. The guy dropped into the seat to her left and whispered, "Hi, I'm Jack Temple." He held out a hand like the Hispanic guys all did, and she shook it and quickly let go, saying, "Samantha Taylor." Then she looked back at the teacher and prepared to take notes.

She always took a lot of notes in classes, and tonight that habit helped distract her from the strange feeling she got from sitting next to dark-eyed Jack. When the class took a break halfway through, he offered to get her a soda, and she turned him down, pointing to her water bottle. She made a quick pit stop and returned to find him in his seat again, a charming smile on his face.

With five minutes left in the break, she didn't know how she was going to avoid small talk with him, so she decided to grin and bear it.

"So, Samantha, that's a pretty name. Why are you taking this class? I own Temple Landscaping, and I thought this looked like a great resource. If it pans out, I might pay next semester to have some of my staff take it."

"I work at Palo Verde Landscaping near Palm Lakes. You know the area?"

"Yeah, cool. What do you do there?"

"I do designs for new yards and redos mostly. My botany background is from back East, so I'm broadening my base by taking this class. I've read all Dr. Turner's books, and they were very helpful."

"I have his books, too. Where do you live, Samantha?"

Now he was getting personal. Nip it in the bud. "I live in Palm Lakes with my husband, Arthur."

He looked her up and down, apparently assessing her age, then said, "You're not old enough to live there."

She bristled at his presumption. "My husband is."

"Do you like living in a retirement community?" His voice implied she shouldn't.

"My parents live there. They have for years. I enjoy being able to be nearby and help them."

He nodded as if it finally made sense to him. "Your parents are lucky."

Was that some kind of compliment? "They seem to like that I'm nearby and able to do some things to make their life a bit easier." She felt she had to ask about him to reciprocate. "How about you?"

"My business is my life. I'm not married. Came close a few times. I'm always interested in ways not only to expand my business, but strengthen what we offer our clients. Too many companies are not really knowledgeable, and they don't give good service. There are bigger companies than Temple Landscaping, but I like to think mine is the best in our area."

The class started again, and Samantha revised her opinion of Jack. He was full of himself, but it wasn't quite arrogance. She was too quick to judge a handsome man.

As the class finished, the teacher gave instructions for the Saturday afternoon session, which would meet at a local nursery yard. Jack turned to her afterwards. "He said we were going to have to partner up Saturday. Would you be my partner?"

She didn't know anyone here, and he knew it. She didn't see how she could say 'no', and she wasn't sure why she wanted to. "Sure." What harm was there in that? She had to partner with someone.

"Well then, I'll see you Friday night. Same time, same place?" He had a smile to rival Julio's.

"OK. I'll be here." She didn't see any point in changing seats. It would be too obvious she was avoiding him.

All the way home, she wondered why she felt she ought to avoid him and why he made her so uncomfortable.

* * *

Helen, 2:40pm

HELEN HADN'T SPENT as much time in front of a mirror in the past five decades as she had in recent months. She was going out much more than she ever did, and she wanted to look her best, so here she was yet again scrutinizing a new outfit.

She couldn't imagine being seen in public dressed like this, if you could call it dressed. The tights and tank top for yoga were robin's egg blue, a color that flattered her. They looked like they'd been painted on her. She'd rejected the sports bra style tops that were cropped and showed midriff, feeling it was too 'young' a look for her. Her top was a more traditional style tank top that covered her stomach and had wide shoulder straps, but the overall effect was still a bit much for her. It left nothing whatsoever to the imagination. Yet the girls had assured her this was typical wear for yoga class in Palm Lakes. She had to trust them. She just hoped there weren't any men in the class. One thing for sure, it was a comfortable outfit that allowed freedom of movement.

She picked up her purse, yoga mat and the flier for the course and headed out to the Rec Center. Parking close to the entrance, Helen pumped up her courage--it was getting easier--and walked in and found the classroom, which was already filling with students. She spotted Lydia, Jean and Barbara and rushed over to them. After hugs all around, they began to chatter about the class.

"I'm hoping I can handle intermediate yoga. I had a tape on yoga I used to do, so I'm not a total idiot, but it's been a long time. I just so wanted to be in class with you three," Helen said.

Barbara smiled with encouragement. "Don't worry, Helen, the

instructor is a gem. She'll have you up to speed in no time. And we'll all help."

Lydia and Jean murmured their agreement. Helen looked at how everyone else was dressed and had to admit her outfit was mainstream. There were a few students who had loose pants that looked like sweat pants, but mostly people were wearing tights. There was one man in the class, but the rest were women. She was feeling more comfortable by the minute.

Barbara said, "Why don't we plan on getting together for lunch again someday soon? I know it isn't convenient to go out after class, so maybe we should just make a date for lunch? You up for it?"

Everyone chimed in affirmatively. Barbara offered to take the lead on finding a date and place and communicating it to everyone.

Helen thought Jean was looking a bit strained, but then, she'd seemed distracted the last few times she'd seen her. Maybe she'd find out what was going on when they went to lunch. Lydia and Barbara were their usual ebullient selves, such a pleasure to be around, and as they talked, Jean appeared to relax.

It was so good to have friends. They couldn't take the place of Alexander, but they lifted her spirits and made her feel supported. She hadn't yet confided in them that she'd made friends with Alexander. She reflected that if it had happened to Lydia, Lydia would have shared it with all of them easily, but Helen just was too shy to share her deepest feelings. Now she was glad she hadn't. She wouldn't have been able to tolerate their pity over the relationship dying.

The instructor called the class to order, and the students drifted into place. The workout went smoothly, and the hour passed fast. When they finished, Helen assured her friends that it hadn't been too strenuous or challenging to keep up with them. They said their goodbyes until lunch or the next class, whichever came first, and she drove home feeling very satisfied about her day, but looking forward to a nice hot shower.

* * *

Alexander, 3:40pm

ALEXANDER SAT ON HIS LANAI, holding a glass of iced tea and watching the shadows grow longer as the sun dipped towards the horizon. He loved living here and never grew tired of watching the sky. But he had to admit, these past weeks, he'd been sleepwalking through life. He'd even forgotten about the deadline for his book, something he'd never done before. Route 66 diners couldn't compete with Helen for his attention.

He'd tried to move on, allowing her to make her choice, but the lack of closure haunted him. He'd been hurt and shocked when she dropped out of cooking class. Until then, he'd held out some hope that maybe he could patch things up, but she obviously didn't want to see him. Barbara's Christmas shindig was months off, and he didn't know of any other social event at which he could hope to bump into her.

She never called, and he felt it would be intrusive to call her, but what could he do? He couldn't face moving on unless he got closure.

To be honest, it was more than closure he was seeking. When she left, the vitality went out of his life. He still couldn't explain why in such a brief time he'd become so attached to her. He'd gotten so used to seeing things through her eyes, watching her innocence and gentleness touch even the most mundane activity and make it magical. He hadn't realized that he wasn't really living until he met her.

He knew if he confided in someone, which he wouldn't, that they would tell him to get out and meet someone new. But the only person that came to mind when he thought about dating was Helen. And she wasn't going to be happy if she found out he'd lied to her. If he told her the truth, he wouldn't stand a chance with her, and if he didn't, he couldn't picture how the relationship would work. He'd settle for just friendship now, anything but the way it was.

He knew Helen had moved to a condo, but she hadn't told him the address. He had planned to help her move to her new place, and he felt bad that he wasn't there for her and even worse that she didn't feel she could ask for his help. He knew she didn't have many friends to turn to, and it pained him that she wouldn't reach out to him. Why was she so mad at him?

He had to assume it was because she was too shy to admit that she had been awake when he crawled all over her that night. But why hadn't she confronted him? Why didn't she give him a chance to apologize or explain? Did it mean that the relationship meant so little to her? He couldn't believe that. She seemed to really care for him until that day.

All this time, he'd held back, hoping maybe she'd turn to him for help with the move or even get over feeling mad, but not a word. The more he thought about it, the more he felt he needed to go see her. He would apologize. He didn't have to be specific. He wasn't sure what the right thing to do was, but at least he couldn't make things worse. If she said she never wanted to see him again, at least that would be closure. Barbara would know her new address.

Before he could talk himself out of it, he picked up the phone and called Barbara. Barbara wasn't at home, but Ben was, and it only took him a minute to find the address. He didn't act nosy about why Alexander wanted the address or why he didn't know it. Maybe Helen hadn't said anything to anyone about their falling out. That could be a good sign.

He took the time to dress his best and looked at the clock. It was nearly 4pm. She'd be home for dinner probably. He'd go over now.

He didn't want to show up empty-handed, so he swung by the local florist's and picked up a dozen yellow roses. Yellow meant friendship, and since that was what he was aiming for above all else, it was the perfect message, even if she didn't know the language of flowers. At this point, he would give anything to have her back as his friend, even if it never became anything else.

The roses filled the car with their fragrance as he drove to Helen's condo. He was nervous about what to say. What if she slammed the door? No, she wasn't like that. But what if she were cold and turned him away, flowers in hand? She wasn't like that, either. He felt like an idiot going back and forth like this. He needed to be decisive. If he got in the door, he'd apologize first thing and say the truth, that their friendship mattered more to him than anything else, and he wanted it back.

He turned off the car once he got to her condo and sat in it, trying to compose himself. It wasn't going to get any easier. Straightening his shoulders, he grabbed the flowers, walked up to the front door and pushed the doorbell.

The door opened right away, and Helen stood there with a shocked look on her face for about three seconds. Then she recovered and opened the screen door. "Alexander. Come in."

She seemed flustered as she stood there in an exercise outfit that was a robin's egg blue latex that flattered her fit, trim body. She was barefoot, and he noticed her toenails were painted a peach color. Her hair was pulled back into a short ponytail. She was wearing little makeup and no jewelry. She fidgeted as he stepped into the entryway, rubbing her hands on her arms. She looked luscious.

He plunged into his rehearsed speech quickly and urgently. "I'm sorry I didn't call first. I was afraid you wouldn't let me come. I brought you these to help me apologize. I want you to know that our friendship means more than I can ever say, and I am so sorry for whatever I did to cause the breach between us. I was trying to respect your wishes, but life isn't the same without you. I miss you. Will you forgive me?"

She looked nervous, her arms across her breasts. "I just got back from my yoga class, and I haven't had a chance to shower or change. Maybe you should come back later."

"It doesn't matter to me, Helen. If you want, I can wait while you change. I didn't mean to make you uncomfortable." He held his breath, hoping she'd let him stay.

She pointed at the couch, and while she was gone, he put the vase of flowers on the dining room table. When she returned, she was in slacks and a cotton top and still barefoot. She'd let her hair down. She sat on the couch a good distance from him. "Can I get you some tea or coffee?"

"No, thanks. I just wanted to apologize and see if there is any chance we can still be friends. I miss having you in my life." It felt good to get it out in the open.

Her reaction was unexpected. She looked surprised and even a little guilty, glancing down at her hands in her lap. "I've missed you, too."

"I didn't mean to hurt you. Please tell me how I can fix it."

She looked at him like he'd just grown another head, which only confused him. The silence stretched, and then her eyes began to tear up, and she stood and left the room. He was totally bemused. What had he done now?

She returned with a tissue in hand and sat back down, still a good distance from him. Her hands twisted the tissue and she looked at it like

she couldn't stand to make eye contact with him. Then she pulled her
eyes up as if moving against a strong gravitational pull and looked at
him. "I should apologize to you. I didn't mean to be unkind. But you did
so much for me, and I was nothing but a burden to you. I was always
crying or having problems, and you don't need that..." Her voice trailed
off as her eyes broke contact, and again he saw shame. He could tell she
was holding back, but the important thing was that she wasn't mad
at him.

"So we can be friends?"

"No one has ever apologized to me before. No one has ever said they
cared enough to want to fix anything. If you want, of course, we can be
friends."

He tried to catch her eye again, but her gaze was downward. He had
what he wanted. No point in pushing things. "Would you mind showing
me your new place? It looks really nice."

She brightened up at the change of subject. Jumping up, she led him
room to room, obviously pleased with her new home. They went
through the kitchen, which was indeed spacious for a condo, and beyond
to the dining room, where the roses sat on the table. Through the glass
door, he saw the yard.

Her eyes followed his. "Yes, just today I had someone in to look at the
yard. They're going to do some plantings. It's just the right size for me,
and I think you'll like the design Samantha helped me with." *So I'm to be
invited back?* She pointed to a metal tin with colorful paw print design
that sat on an antique hutch. "I want to spread Sheba's ashes in the yard
once the plantings are in place. Would you like to join me for the
ceremony?"

It was all he could have hoped for and more. "Yes, I would be
honored."

"I owe you dinner...actually, more than one. Why don't you come over
and we'll do the ceremony in the afternoon, then we can make dinner
together in my kitchen? It isn't as grand as yours, but we'll make do."

The prospect of being able to do things together again lifted his heart.
"That would be terrific. When?"

She glanced at the calendar that hung on the kitchen wall. "How's

Saturday, November 4th at 4pm? I need to make sure the yard is done, and Samantha promised they'd come next week."

"I'll be here with bells on."

She laughed, and it seemed that the tension had drained from her. Whatever it was no longer seemed to be bothering her.

They went back towards the front door. He was happy to retreat while things were going so well. As Helen opened the door to let him out, the screen door opened and a young woman burst in.

"How did yoga class go, Helen? Was it fun? Oh, sorry, I didn't know you had company." The dark-haired woman, no more than 40 years old, stood in the doorway with her mouth open, staring at Alexander. "Oh, my...I can come back later." She turned to leave.

Alexander spoke up. "It's all right. I was on the way out. I'll get out of your way, girls." He stepped past the woman and held out his hand. "I'm Alexander."

Temporarily speechless, she accepted his hand and forgot to let go. Finally, she spoke up. "I'm the next door neighbor, Mary Beth. Or rather, I'm living at my Mom's for the moment."

"Pleased to make your acquaintance, Mary Beth. I'm glad to see Helen has made friends already." He pried his hand loose and walked down the sidewalk to his car, turning to wave to Helen as he got in.

As he drove off, he marveled at how well things had gone. Suddenly, Helen was back in his life and even making dinner for him. Yet he knew she was holding something back. That didn't really matter. He was holding back, too.

Now that things were going well again, he had no clue how he was going to proceed. He could do the just friends thing for a while, but ultimately, he knew it would begin to pain him. He wanted more. And if he told her that, he might lose her. She had such mistrust of men that even if she could accept who he was, she probably couldn't accept the lie he'd told. He wasn't out of the woods yet.

* * *

Mary Beth, 4:50pm

"NICE CAR," said Mary Beth drily as Alexander drove off.

Helen just laughed. "Mary Beth, I know what you're not saying. I've seen plenty of women look at him. He's just a friend."

"I wish he'd be my 'just friend'. I could use a 'just friend' like him. Boy, howdy."

Helen giggled. "Yeah, he has that effect on women. I'm pretty lucky he wants to be my friend."

"So where was he when you were moving in? How come I've never seen him before?" Clearly, Helen had been holding out on her.

"We had a slight misunderstanding, and I wasn't speaking with him...never mind. Come in and I'll pour you a glass of wine."

Mary Beth noticed the change of subject, but let it pass. "Now you're talking my language." They laughed as they went into the kitchen. As Helen got the wine glasses out, Mary Beth noticed the roses. She went into the dining room and inhaled their rich fragrance. "Oh, my God, he can be my 'just friend' any day. This is so amazing. I've never had a guy friend give me a dozen roses! I'm not much on plants, but I know that yellow roses mean friendship, so you must be right. They'd be red if he had designs on you." She continued to smell and touch the roses with delight. "I wish someone would send me roses."

Helen spoke in a shy voice. "Don't feel bad. It's the first time for me."

"You're shitting me! Sorry, I mean, you're kidding." When would she ever get control of her mouth?

Helen tittered. "I shit you not. No one has ever given me a dozen roses of any color, so this means a lot to me." She came up next to Mary Beth and handed her a full wine glass.

"It would to me, too. My ex gave me roses on a couple of occasions, but sometimes I think it's more meaningful if it isn't an occasion like a birthday or Valentine's Day. You kind of expect it then. You know he meant something by this, right? Are you sure he wants to be 'just friends'?"

"I believe he does. And it's good enough for me." Helen smiled sincerely.

"Better you than me. I'd be having the hots for him constantly. It wouldn't work for me in the long run to be 'just friends' with a man who looked like that. And his voice! His voice is to die for! And those amazing emerald eyes. I'd definitely be dreaming about him..." Mary Beth sighed and sipped her wine.

Looking embarrassed, Helen changed the subject. "Samantha came by today. We had a good time planning the yard."

"Oh, I'm so glad you did that. You'll be pleased with the results. Too bad you didn't get to meet Julio. He's a hottie, too."

"Samantha's mother is my former neighbor, so it was fun seeing her. Speaking of Julio, how's work?"

"It's different, you know? But it's a good kind of different." She sighed in contentment.

"How's your Mom doing?"

Mary Beth frowned. "I don't know. I'm afraid she's going downhill. I guess it gets to that point where you start getting old faster or something. She used to be such a dynamo, and now she doesn't have much energy. Or else, she's afraid of a heart attack. She doesn't confide in me. She's more subdued and less active. She doesn't clean so obsessively anymore. I even saw dust on the furniture the other day. She doesn't yell at me as much as she used to. At least I don't think she's having angina. That's good."

"I'm glad for that. She's so lucky you're here. I'm sure she appreciates it."

"When she's not offering to wash my mouth out with soap for using bad language...yeah, I think she does appreciate my being here."

"The HOA still quiet?"

"It's that bitch across the way I worry about. Sorry, again. Since we sold my car, things have been quiet. I hope it stays that way. That old biddy still watches, and I'm sure she knows I'm here, but I'm hoping it will work out."

Helen reached over and patter her hand. "Me, too."

Mary Beth stared out at the empty yard, wondering what the future held for her. Things were still very tenuous. At least she had a job and an income now, and Mom wanted her to stay. Yet she felt an unpleasant sense of foreboding whenever discussing the future. What could that mean? She shook off the feeling of a chill and sipped her wine. "Helen, I really appreciate having you as a friend. It means a lot to me."

Helen looked at her in shock but recovered quickly. "Until Lou died, I had no friends. Now I'm really blessed. I'm grateful for you, too. We're both having quite an adventure in our lives, aren't we?"

"Damn right!"

* * *

Helen, 9:30pm

WEDNESDAY, *October 25, 1995*

He came back. He gave me roses. I don't know what to think. It's as if I've woken up in some novel. He's too good to be true, and even if he is for real, what does he see in me? Why does someone like that want to be my friend so badly that he'd apologize when he didn't do anything wrong?

It was just a stupid misunderstanding, and it was my fault. I pushed him away. All because that dream scared me. I hurt him because I wasn't able to act like an adult. And he's asking me *to forgive* him!

In my old world, no one ever said they were sorry. No one ever gave me flowers. Good things didn't happen to me. I thought I'd be lucky to live to old age, the way Lou knocked me around. And then he died. And everything changed.

I could have gone back to Wisconsin with my tail between my legs and lived out my days as a burden to my kids. Or I could have had a fatal accident after drinking too much wine, like what nearly happened to Tanya. Instead, I'm living in a great condo, I have more friends than I ever imagined I could have and my finances are getting stable.

Speaking of finances, they're so stable and I've been so busy that I haven't pursued the issue about the safe deposit box key further. I'll get back to researching that soon. At least I know for sure Lou didn't have a box at any of the local banks. I went to all of them with the death certificate.

It's like a mystery, and I intend to solve it. But somehow, living my life has become more exciting than tracking down that box, or whatever's inside it. Who would ever have guessed?

In a few days, I go to the writing class. I'm not sure if Alexander will be there, but either way, it will be fine.

She put the pen down and closed the book. What was she going to do about Alexander? She wanted him in her life, but she wasn't sure she could pretend for long that friendship was all she felt for him. She'd barely been able to resist throwing herself into his arms when he appeared on her doorstep today. All the feelings that had driven them apart were still unresolved. And there was the mystery of why he thought he'd wronged her. Feeling hopelessly confused, she took her worries to bed, and they chased her into a deep but restless sleep.

CHAPTER TWELVE

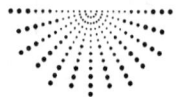

SATURDAY, OCTOBER 28, 1995

Owen, 8:45am

Owen was still lying in bed. Yesterday seemed like ages ago, but it was fresh in his memory, just as fresh as the scent of fear and blood when he was on a hunt. And this memory, although totally different, had exactly the same effect on him. It energized him and made him feel powerful. And horny.

Why had things gone the way they had? He never had success with women until yesterday. After days of scouting Tanya's movements discreetly, he had spotted her near the golf course late in the morning and stopped his car to chat with her. Two minutes later, she was in the car and they were on their way to the hotel bar she'd chosen for their first meeting.

The bar turned out to be perfect. It was dark, intimate and nearly empty at 11am. They slipped into a booth in the back. He'd let out the breath he hadn't known he was holding and looked across the table at Tanya.

Her skin looked healthier. There weren't circles under her eyes, and she was dressed less like a tart than usual. She didn't have roots showing in her blonde hair, and it didn't seem as frizzy. She'd have a scar from where she hit the windshield, but it was healing. Her white blouse had a scooped neck that framed her gorgeous tits, and she had her usual 'big' jewelry on, but somehow she seemed softer and more feminine, more pliable than in the past. She also wasn't as talkative. He liked the new Tanya.

"Thanks for this, Owen. I'd like to buy you a drink."

"Sure. But no more than two for either of us. I don't drive drunk, and you can't afford to be caught drinking."

"You're so kind to think of me, Owen. I'm leaving for rehab in a couple of days, so even if my husband notices, it won't matter. I've been dreaming about this for weeks."

"So have I." Shocked at his candid response, Owen said no more.

The server came and filled the awkward gap. "What can I get you folks?" she asked in an artificially bright voice that made Owen want to hit her.

Tanya answered quickly. "I'll have a vodka tonic."

"Same for me," said Owen. He wasn't a drinker, and he didn't really care what he drank. He never drank alcohol when on a mission. But somehow this wasn't a typical mission. He didn't feel in control, because he had no idea how this would turn out, but he wasn't disturbed by that. Which was unusual.

As they sipped their drinks, Tanya did most of the talking, which was fine by him. She chattered on about her accident, the hospital, her asshole husband (who was currently out golfing) and how much she didn't want to go to rehab. The second round enhanced the effect. Tanya was forever reaching over and touching his arm, but it actually felt good. He didn't usually like contact, but he was feeling so mellow that it was actually pleasant.

Tanya leaned over closer to him. "You aren't listening to me, are you?" She didn't sound critical, but she was right. He'd totally lost the thread of conversation. He was too immersed in the good feelings. It was a novel experience for him.

"You caught me. I was daydreaming." He was surprised at how easy it felt to be honest.

She didn't seem at all upset, unlike Mother, who would have been all over him. She looked at him intensely, with hunger in her eyes. "Let's make a memory, Owen. What do you say?"

He knew exactly what she was implying, and he was ready to jump at the chance. He wasn't even borrowing trouble about outcomes. It was like he was a different person with her. "I'll get us a room. You stay here. But no more booze. OK?"

She looked at him with submission. "Of course, Owen. Whatever you say."

He liked the sound of that. Nodding, he got up and went to the lobby and rented a room. He returned quickly. "I got a room for the night. It's paid for, so we'll just leave the key in the room when we go." Tanya looked at him with smoldering eyes filled with promise. It made his knees wobbly, but he still managed to retain control. "Ready?"

"Yes!" She walked beside him out to the empty lobby, and they took the elevator to the 4th floor. The room was actually spacious and well-decorated, far nicer than he would have expected. It smelled clean, but not medicinal. Owen didn't usually feel comfortable in hotels, but this was OK.

The next three hours were imprinted in his memory forever. Like his own private porn video, he could take it out and replay it in his mind any time he wanted to. And he had replayed it a lot in the last 12 hours. He'd barely gotten any sleep last night for thinking about all the things she'd done to him.

He'd known she would do anything, and boy, did she ever. She was so hot for him that he became insatiable. She praised him for his stamina. She complimented his body. She obviously couldn't get enough of him, and he felt the same way about her. They'd even taken a shower together with interesting extracurricular activities.

He felt six feet tall and as powerful as Superman, but it was a totally different flavor of power from what he experienced when he killed. It was power accompanied by a hunger that just kept going on, unlike the peace and release he got from judging women. He'd never felt like this, ever. And she was going to rehab for 30 days and he wouldn't see her. It was aggravating. Now that he'd had a taste, he wanted more.

He didn't spend time contemplating what this change meant or how it could affect his future. Thirty days was as far as he would look into the future. He'd told her to call him when she could. She promised to, and he believed she would. He felt like the most virile man alive.

But the best thing of all was that his mother wasn't speaking to him. He didn't understand why. She was opposed to him meeting Tanya, yet now that it was a done deal, she was silent. He didn't question it. He was just grateful. Anything that shut that bitch up was worth a gold mine.

He'd never felt so good. Not once during their encounter had he felt like judging Tanya. And all he could think about was when he'd be able to meet her next.

He had to figure a way to continue to see her without anyone getting the wiser. At least what they were doing had no legal implications, so the risk was low. He lay staring at the ceiling and decided to rerun the shower scene again. He liked that one the best.

* * *

Helen, 8:45am

HELEN FINISHED DRESSING for the first day of the writing class and put on her earrings. Alexander hadn't said anything about this class the other day. He'd been so eager to leave as soon as she 'forgave' him. She wanted to see him, but she was still confused about her feelings for him. She was acting like a silly teenager mooning over some boy. It was all pointless, and she needed to move past it.

On the brief drive to the Rec Center, she decided she'd be fine no matter what happened in class. If he was there, it would be a chance to be friendly. If he wasn't, no bother. He was coming to dinner soon.

She was surprised at how disappointed she was when she saw he wasn't in the class. Now she'd have to wait another week to see him.

She soon forgot her musings about Alexander. The class was overwhelming. The instructor dove right into the basics of structuring a story, and she was like a sponge, absorbing all the suggestions and taking copious notes to review later. But then he started talking about word processing and publishers and technical things, and she felt her brain short-circuit. She didn't have a computer or word processor and didn't really want to have one, even if she could afford it, which she couldn't. And thinking about submitting manuscripts to publishers seemed like such a huge project in addition to writing a book. She could feel her confidence slipping.

Maybe when Alexander came over for dinner, she could talk with him about it. Or maybe since he said he wanted to be her friend, she should call him and talk to him about the class. He might have some useful suggestions, and he always made her feel calmer about doing new things. That was one of the things she most liked about him. With him, she felt more courageous.

On the way home, she swung by her old neighborhood. She'd promised herself she'd visit Maddie and see how she was getting on. It was so sad to hear of the bone problems she was having. When she pulled up in front of Maddie's house, she saw a car she didn't recognize parked in the driveway.

A nice-looking stranger answered the door. Towering over her at about six feet tall, he looked to be her age and had graying hair and eyes to match. He was dressed in loud plaid shorts, had slight paunch that hung over his belt and wore black socks with his sandals. In her mind, she couldn't help comparing him to Alexander. Feeling guilty for judging the poor man, she announced her intentions. "I'm here to see Maddie. Is she OK?"

"Oh, sure, she's doing fine, considering. My name's Ethan Westerfield. I'm with The Helpers. Maddie's daughter Samantha arranged for me to come over once a week and do things that her parents shouldn't be doing, like lifting heavy things and walking the dog. The doctor told Maddie not to lift more than two pounds, and that's harder than you might think, not that she's obeying him." A wry smile creased his face. "But you probably know Maddie better than I do. Come on in."

He stepped aside as she entered the house, patting Beau, who had been waiting patiently in the background.

"It's so kind of you to do this. I'm sure Beau appreciates it." She made a point of not including Maddie in that statement.

Ethan spoke barely above a whisper. "Oh, yeah, we get along fine. I like dogs. He's too exuberant for Stanley, and Maddie can't take the risk of having him pull on her. Even she admits that." His eyes went to

Maddie, who was sitting hunched over her project at the dining room table.

Helen followed him the short distance to the dining area and announced herself to Maddie.

Maddie looked up, her magnifying glasses perched on top of her head. "Helen, come over here so I can show you what I'm making for Christmas."

"Wow, you've gotten an early start on the holidays!" Helen couldn't picture Maddie as someone who planned that far ahead.

"I don't usually, but this idea came to me, and I had to write it down and then get materials. What do you think?" She pointed Helen to the piles of plastic beads and gold findings.

Not sure what she was looking at, Helen asked, "Can I see a drawing of the design?"

Maddie handed her a surprisingly clear pencil sketch that showed step-by-step instructions for making angel earrings out of the clear, white and gold beads of various shapes. It was an adorable design, and although the parts were cheap, the finished product was classy-looking. "Oh my, I'd love to buy some of these to give as gifts to my friends. Will you let me do that, please?"

"How many would you like?"

Helen calculated in her mind. Jean, Lydia, Barbara, Mary Beth and of course, herself. "Could I buy five pairs? They would be perfect gifts for my girlfriends."

Standing in the background, Ethan laughed, "I've been over here enough to know what comes next."

Helen flinched because she'd been afraid of that very thing.

"I can't sell them to you, but I'll make you five pairs and give them to you."

"But it costs you money for these materials, and you deserve to get compensated for your creativity and time." Helen knew it was a losing battle, but she had to try.

"No, Stanley doesn't want me to sell things, and I don't, either. You come back in a few weeks, and I'll have five pairs for you." She reached for a pad and pen and wrote "Helen, five pairs of angel earrings" on it.

It was clear that Helen's discomfort at accepting such a generous gift wasn't going to move Maddie at all. So she decided to be gracious about it. "Thank you so much. I can't wait to see them. One of the ladies I intend to give a pair is Barbara, just so you know."

"Thanks for telling me. I'll make sure I give her a different design. I have a plan for a holiday bell earring that's nice; simple, but elegant." Maddie seemed to have no awareness of Helen's discomfort and in typically focused fashion, went back to her work. Helen knew she didn't mean to be dismissive; she was just eccentric.

Ethan spoke up in the pause. "I've walked Beau and taken the trash out. Is there anything else I can do, Maddie?"

"No, thank you, Ethan." Maddie's tone sounded cold and formal, but Ethan didn't appear to be fazed.

"Well, then, I'll be moving on, ladies. More territory to cover today." He waved and patted Beau on the way out the front door.

"He seems like a nice man," commented Helen.

"Hmpf. I don't need help, but Samantha is paranoid about me breaking anything, so she got him through The Helpers. They're residents who volunteer time to help old ladies like me. He told me he volunteers once a week. He got me by the luck of the draw." She didn't seem very appreciative.

"So he lives in Palm Lakes?"

"Yes, his wife died of cancer a few years ago, and he told me the first day he came that this was his way of giving back for all the help they gave during her illness."

Helen found that touching. "Isn't that nice?"

"He ought to be helping people who need it." Obviously, Maddie wasn't touched.

Discretion being the better part of valor, Helen decided to depart. "Thank you so much, Maddie. I'm looking forward to the angel earrings. I love everything you make."

"Then you need to pick one of these to take home."

"Oh, heavens, you've already given me so much jewelry. How will I ever wear it all?"

"Nonsense, look at these and tell me what you think." She pointed to an area of the table that had escaped Helen's notice. There were several pairs of earrings made of what looked like carved bone. Little clever animals hung from french earwires, each pair having a contrasting bead above the carved animal. There was an owl, that was a fox, then a howling coyote. But the cutest one was the rabbit. It had a small, round jade bead above the lifelike rabbit. She picked that pair up and examined them as a brainstorm hit her. "They're all beautiful, but the bunnies are my favorite."

Maddie smiled. "Mine, too. You know how I love the rabbits. Take them."

"I really shouldn't." Helen knew that protest was futile, but tried anyway.

"Take them. They aren't destined for anyone in particular, and you like them."

"OK. You shouldn't, but thank you. See, I have your lizard earrings on today." She pulled her hair back to show Maddie. "They're my favorites. I wear them all the time."

Maddie smiled as she looked at them. "Yes, they turned out well. Everyone loves them."

"So how are you feeling, Maddie. Are you in pain?"

"A bit. Everything hurts these days. You get to be 72, you'll know what I mean. But I'm still hanging in there."

"Did you keep my new address? I have the same phone number. If you need me, just call. I can help if Samantha isn't available. I mean it."

"Thank you, Helen, but we're doing fine. Stanley is 84 now, but we manage. Come by anytime. It's nice to see you."

Helen took her earrings and left without lingering to say hi to Stanley. Usually, he came out when there was company, so he must be busy. She hadn't intended to get more free jewelry, but it was an occupational hazard when visiting Maddie. The earrings were lovely, and she liked to think that Maddie liked her work being appreciated. She'd bring her a bottle of wine next time she came for a visit.

Next stop was lunch at the Italian place with the girls. She was only a tad early. As she turned into the parking lot, she saw that Barbara's car was already there. Good. She wouldn't have to wait alone.

When she walked into the small restaurant, Barbara waved her back to the booth she was sitting in. "Oh good, you came early. Have a seat."

Helen slid into the opposite side of the booth, admiring Barbara's outfit. She always dressed so nicely, and her auburn hair was perfectly coiffed. "You look great, Barbara."

"Thank you. So do you, Helen. So what's up since I saw you last? It's only been a few days, but anything new?"

Helen had been debating whether to tell the girls anything about Alexander ever since his visit. She really wanted to share about him. It was almost like it wasn't real since she'd never told them.

Barbara caught her hesitation and pinned her with sharp brown eyes. "You have something to tell." She didn't give Helen a chance to deny it.

"Yes, actually I do."

"Should we wait so you don't have to tell it again when the others come?"

"Yes, that might be better." At that moment, the door opened and Jean and Lydia walked in and straight back to their booth. Hugs were given and greetings spoken, then the waitress came and gave them menus to peruse.

"I'm having the lasagna," said Lydia. "I've eaten here before, and it's to die for."

"Me, too," said Jean.

Helen added her vote to the lasagna trend.

Barbara made it unanimous. That resolved, they got down to chatting.

"Helen was just going to tell me something when you girls walked in. And it felt like something interesting." Barbara looked at Helen with encouragement.

Helen felt three sets of eyes on her and got shy. "I'm not sure where to begin," she waffled.

"The beginning is always a good place," said Lydia, with a knowing look in her eyes.

Helen plunged in. "You remember Barbara's party in August?"

"Who wouldn't? It was a blast," said Lydia.

"At the party, Barbara introduced me to Alexander Stirling, who offered to partner up with me in the cooking class in September. The class was great, and we had a good time."

All eyes were riveted on her. "Is Alexander the movie star guy?" asked Jean.

"Yeah, he's the drop dead gorgeous one," confirmed Lydia.

Barbara looked at Helen with raised eyebrows. "So it was a good match?"

Helen wasn't sure how to proceed. She wasn't about to share Alexander's secret, but she was busting to tell them about his friendship with her. "It's really weird what happened. We were just so comfortable with each other, we became good friends."

"Just friends?" asked Lydia with a throaty laugh. "Or maybe more than friends?"

"Don't you just wish," sighed Jean.

"Every woman in town has been after him. He ducks them all. I gave up matchmaking for him when it became obvious he wasn't interested," added Barbara with a look of speculation in her eyes.

"We just hit it off right away. I don't know why; neither does he. He did tell me he isn't looking for a wife, and that he figured I wouldn't be looking for a husband. Maybe that's why he let his defenses down."

"So how long has this been going on, and why didn't you tell us?" Lydia sounded indignant.

"There is no 'this'. Nothing is going on. After a storybook start, we had a falling out and hadn't talked in nearly a month until a few days ago."

Barbara perked up. "So that's why he called? Ben said he called and asked for your address, and he assumed it was OK to give it to him."

"Yes, of course it was OK. He came to see me and brought me a dozen yellow roses and asked if we could be friends again. I accepted and invited him to dinner to patch things up. He'll be coming over after my yard is finished, in about a week."

The women were staring at her in disbelief.

"Yellow roses are for friendship, but it sounds like more to me," Lydia observed confidently. *Are my secret feelings for him that obvious to her?*

"He could give me roses any time, and I wouldn't care what color they were," gushed Jean.

Helen felt a bit tired of this type of reaction. "You know, it's kind of weird to be friends with a man whom all the women in town are chasing after. He says they proposition him; even the married ones."

"Get used to it, dear," said Barbara. "He seems to be a pretty special guy, so just ignore the panting women and gloat a bit. There isn't a single woman in Palm Lakes who wouldn't kill to be in your shoes and quite a few married ones. Lucky I'm so happily married or I might be one of them." She grinned at Helen.

Jean's voice interrupted the laughter. "Speaking of happily married, I need some advice. Not that I'm sure I'll take it, but hope I can tell you all something and you won't judge." The strain in Jean's voice was reflected on her face. Helen was glad for the change of subject.

"You're with friends, dear. We're here to support you," Barbara said encouragingly.

"It's a long and sordid story. And I don't think I'm handling things well. Lydia knows all about it." She stopped and looked at Lydia, who nodded in confirmation but said nothing. Jean hesitated for a few moments, then continued. "Richard and I don't fight. I used to think that was a sign of a good marriage. I hated how my parents fought. But recently, I've come to realize that he and I are on separate paths that are diverging further every day. In fact, he's quite negative about my interests. I try to sympathize, because I was never a woo-woo type, sorry Lydia, no offense intended."

"None taken," said Lydia, smiling.

"In recent months I became interested in unconventional things: metaphysics, energy work, Reiki, natural healing methods. I'm fascinated and can't get enough, and he looks at me like I'm a witch when I try to share with him. I ignored it at first, but the looks are more common. He never says anything, just seems more distant. So we have less and less to talk about." So that's why Jean had seemed so strained lately. Helen felt so sorry for her.

Barbara looked at Jean with compassion. "Maybe the problem is that most people aren't interested in growing once they retire. The majority of residents just want to have fun, play golf and eat out. Maybe Richard is like that. It can be unnerving when someone you thought you knew takes a serious interest in something you don't understand. He probably feels threatened."

"You're right, Barbara. He does. But it's more than that. Promise me you won't tell anyone else." Jean's pleading look tugged at Helen's heartstrings.

The atmosphere tensed as they all gave promises of confidentiality.

"OK. It gets worse. A few months ago I stumbled onto something that made me feel differently about Richard. We were never close and in love like you and Ben, Barbara, but we had a contented and peaceful relationship with no conflict. Then I found out he's addicted to pornography."

Helen was dumbfounded as Jean paused and looked at her friends to gauge their reaction. Lydia waited patiently for her to go on, having been in on it from the beginning. Barbara looked at her with sympathy.

"How ever did you discover that?" asked Barbara.

"Just dumb luck. Some article in the paper got me looking on the computer and I discovered his secret. I was floored. I had a picture of him as a wholesome and honest guy, and here he was looking at dirty pictures while I was out of the house. It made me feel ashamed, but it also made me wonder how I'd failed. Then I got mad about his dishonesty. I told Lydia a while back. I couldn't keep it to myself. I've been a mess ever since."

Everyone was silent for a minute. Then Helen said, "Don't feel bad, Jean. You'd be surprised what goes on behind closed doors. It can be even worse than that. I sympathize with how you feel. I'm glad you told us. I wish I had had the courage to ask for help when Lou was alive."

Jean smiled wanly, her eyes damp with tears. "There's more I haven't told you. This is where I start looking like the bad guy, even though I never intended to do anything wrong. It's made me angry with myself. I'm just so confused. Anyway, Richard promised no more porn, but I caught him at it again later, and it was like that was the end. He'd crossed a line, and I moved into our guest bedroom. I don't know how we got to this point, but it feels there's no going back. I don't trust him anymore, and I don't think I ever will. I'm not convinced he isn't still doing it.

"But this is where it gets even worse. While I waited to get my head straight about what to do about our marriage, I was continuing to pursue my interests and got in an email group for dowsers. Lydia's in it and recommended I join."

"Sorry to digress, but what's an email group?" asked Helen.

Lydia answered for Jean, who seemed to be shrinking under the stress of telling her story. "You write the letter on your computer and send it electronically. It's very good for staying in touch with family, and it's easier to use than you might think. There are groups of people who meet online and communicate via email to share experiences."

Jean flashed a grateful smile at Lydia. "So I joined this group. They post comments and stories about dowsing, which I realize is a bit far out for you guys, but it's something I'm interested in, and aside from Lydia, no one I know in Palm Lakes is curious about it. So I figured the group was a good idea."

Barbara spoke up. "I hate to interrupt again, Jean, but what is dowsing? I thought it was about finding water."

Jean glanced at Lydia, who nodded in encouragement. Jean's formerly tense expression was replaced by animation. "Yes, you can do that with dowsing, but you can do so much more. Dowsing is merely asking a question and getting an answer. You use it to get answers to questions you can't rationally answer. In the case of a water dowser, he's asking where the water is. You can use it for health, for finding lost objects, for all kinds of neat things."

Barbara nodded. "Thanks. I had no idea! It sounds intriguing."

Jean pressed on. "So I joined this group hoping to learn more, since I'm new to dowsing, but they weren't talking much about dowsing. And that frustrated me. I noticed that one fellow named Ian seemed very intelligent, articulate and wrote about dowsing more often than other members. So when he contacted me and welcomed me to the group, I asked if we could exchange emails about dowsing, since there wasn't much going on in the group. He said yes."

Jean stopped for a second, and Lydia filled in. "You know, in an email group like this, all you can see is the person's name. You have no idea who they are, how old, where they live or anything else. For all you know, they can be using a pseudonym, though I'm not suggesting that's true in this case. But Jean knew nothing about this Ian guy."

"Thanks for defending me, Lyd, but I have to take responsibility for how messed up my life is. I never intended anything beyond a friendly exchange about dowsing, but it evolved into something else, and I am dead certain that it was me who tipped the scales in the direction it's gone in, and now I have a problem on my hands.

"It started out totally innocent. Well, it's still innocent, but not like it was. The problem was that in reading his emails to me, I kept feeling that he was meant to be important in my life. It was like there was an invisible subtext only I could read. At first, I told myself it was just because he seemed to know so much and was so helpful. I saw him as a mentor. But after a number of weeks, I had to admit that there was another feeling, an undercurrent that didn't make sense, but I couldn't ignore.

"He never said one thing to precipitate this, and if I hadn't asked, we might still be just swapping emails about dowsing. But I opened my big mouth and made it personal. And it took on a life of its own after that. I feel like I'm being swept up in a flash flood that I started. You know, for the longest time, I hoped he was 88 and gay, so it would be safe."

The group went quiet, and Helen reflected on how little protection such details can be when your heart has a mind of its own. She would have agreed with Jean even a few months ago. Now she knew better. Jean would have fallen for this guy no matter what.

Finally, Jean continued. "I made a suggestion we swap some personal details, and he agreed. He's divorced, my age and lives in the UK. Since that time, we've grown closer. We talk about more than dowsing. We have so many interests in common, and I feel like I've known him my whole life."

Helen knew how that felt, but she didn't want to draw attention to her and Alexander, so again she said nothing.

"We talked back and forth for a few weeks about visiting each other. I invited him for a visit, but he said after looking at fares he wouldn't be able to swing it. And I know Richard has no desire to go to the UK. Plus I haven't said anything to him about Ian. After how he hid what he was doing, I feel like a hypocrite for not telling him. But then, why should I? Ian can't visit, and I realized that I'm not sure I want to meet him in person, because I think I'm falling for him."

Lydia looked at Jean with silent, loving encouragement. Barbara was the first to comment. "Jean, thanks for taking us into your confidence. We're here for you, no matter what you decide to do. Don't rake yourself over the coals about this. You haven't done anything wrong. The time to say something to Richard is when it gets to the point that it's permanently affecting your relationship with him. Is it there yet?"

"I think so, but I'm not sure. I felt our marriage fell apart when Richard lied to me, and to be honest, I don't really want to stay married to him, but I'm getting ready to take a step that would definitely kill it, and I'm scared. I feel compelled to do it, yet I know I'm crossing a line, even though it isn't infidelity.

"I wrote and told Ian I'd like to talk on the phone, and that I could get a phone card that would allow me to call him inexpensively. He said he'd love to chat on the phone. So I got the card after scouting where to call from. I didn't want to do it from home and have it appear on the phone bill that I was calling the 800 number to make the call.

"That's when I felt I had crossed the line. I'm doing to Richard what he did to me. It's like I have an addiction I can't let go of, and now I'm hiding it from him. I feel ashamed, yet I must talk to Ian. It's the most powerful connection I've ever felt with another human being. It's scary and exhilarating at the same time."

Helen overcame her reticence. "Jean, I know it took a lot of courage to share this. There were things in my marriage I never shared with anyone. I felt if I did, it would change everything, and for some reason, I was afraid of change. I wish I had reached out. I wish I had had all of you for friends. I feel certain if I had, then I would have made some radical changes for the better.

"Whatever you decide to do, I won't judge you. I believe that if you find someone special, you should do whatever it takes to nurture that relationship. Don't let it go. You'll figure out how to handle the rest."

Jean smiled and reached out to take her hand. "Thank you so much, Helen. I really appreciate you." She let go of Helen's hand and reached out to Barbara and Lydia. "And you two, also. I don't know what I'd do without you.

"So I haven't called Ian, but I'm dying to. I can't promise I'll do what you suggest, but I could use a new perspective. I don't trust my own. Left to myself, I will call him, and if it goes well, I will call him again. And then what's next?" She looked down at the table and put a hand on her forehead.

"I say call him," Lydia voted. "You can decide what's next after that.

Why decide in advance? You're intuitive enough to get a feel during the call. Maybe he just wants to be a friend. Maybe he's lonely. What's the harm in one call? If you get to the point where you feel you want to be with him instead of Richard, that's when to talk to Richard. Not before. And by the way, you can call him from my place anytime. Don't do it in public."

Jean smiled and patted Lydia's hand. "Thank you so much. I accept. It will make it less scary and also remove the fear of getting caught."

Barbara nodded. "You seem to be heaping guilt on yourself when you haven't done anything wrong. So I'm wondering if your intuition is telling you that this man is your future, and that's why you are feeling so ashamed. You haven't admitted your feelings because they aren't rational. But you can't rationalize love, Jean. As long as you're honest with yourself, I trust that you'll be able to be honest with Richard. Call the guy, but don't kid yourself if he is more than a friend. You need to admit your feelings to yourself first of all. Then figure out where to go from there if he feels the same way. Has he given you any inkling?"

"No, but he is very encouraging about me calling, and I take that to mean that Lydia's right. Either he wants a friend, is lonely or also has strange feelings for me like I do for him, feelings he can't rationalize and is afraid to commit to an email. I don't get a creepy vibe from him at all. I don't think he's a serial killer or anything."

Everyone laughed at the outrageous suggestion.

Jean straightened up as if making a decision. "I'm going to call him. I'm going to trust what my intuition says. I didn't embark on this to punish Richard. I'm not looking for a new man. But I'd be lying if I said all I feel for Ian is friendship. It's more than that. It's really a big feeling, like he's fated to be my life partner. So I'll call and we'll see. One step at a time. I am so grateful for all of you."

Just then the food arrived, and they dug in with big appetites. The rest of the meal, the conversation turned to lighter subjects, and they parted with a promise to do it again before Thanksgiving.

Helen drove home pondering Jean's situation and marveling at how timely it was to hear of someone else having relationship complications. She'd felt she was all alone in her quandary, but now it appeared that other people were struggling to make sense of their feelings. She wouldn't want to be in Jean's shoes for anything. Her situation was messed up enough.

By the time she arrived home, she'd decided to call Alexander. In the past, she would have, and she needed to feel like she could still treat him as her best friend. He didn't have to know her secret feelings.

He answered on the first ring.

"Hi, it's me. You ran off so fast the other night I didn't get to thank you properly for the flowers." *I didn't get a hug, either.*

"They're no big deal."

"They are to me. Like I said, no one ever gave me roses."

"I'm glad I'm the first. They were just a way to emphasize my sincerity."

God, he was too good to be true. "I went to the first day of the writing class. I didn't expect you to be there; I know they couldn't tell you anything new. But I was hoping maybe when you come over, we can talk about it. I got overwhelmed. I hadn't considered much more than the idea of writing a novel. I hadn't thought about word processing and submitting to publishers, and now I feel like it's such a big project, and I don't think I have what it takes. I was thinking maybe you could break it down and make it seem more doable to me. I really do want to write."

"Well, although I don't write novels, I might have some things to share about the process. It will be my pleasure to offer guidance in any way I can. You're right. The trick is to just take it one step at a time. There's a huge learning curve. I'll help you. If you have a story to tell, the rest can all work out as long as you commit to it."

"Talking to you always makes me feel better."

"I'm glad I could help. What shall we resolve next? Peace in the Middle East?"

She laughed at how he was able to put things in perspective. Yes, she could do this writing thing with his help. Everything seemed more manageable when he was a part of it.

"Not to be nosy, but how's the landscaping job coming?"

"They'll be doing it next week. It will be done in time for our dinner."

"Great. I wanted to make sure we were still on. If for some reason they don't finish on time, why don't you come over here that evening and we'll do dinner at your place after the yard is done. I don't feel like postponing. Is that all right with you?"

She was pleased that he didn't want to postpone, because she didn't, either. No man had ever treated her so well. Maybe he was sensitive to her needs because he was gay. Gay guys were in touch with their feminine side, right? Maybe that's what made him such a great friend. "I'm sure they'll finish as advertised, but of course we can do that as Plan B."

After hanging up, she sighed deeply. She felt so much more alive when she was talking with him. She knew exactly how Jean felt. She was being swept along by a current that was stronger than she was, and it was scary and delightful at the same time.

* * *

Red, 4:00pm

THE LATE AFTERNOON sun was in Red Johnson's eyes as he slowly drove through the Safeway parking lot, looking for a space. As he turned down an aisle, he noticed a young woman leaning under the raised hood of her car, looking at the insides as if she were totally lost. He drove past, noting that she appeared to be alone.

Damn, he'd just stopped by to get some food for dinner. Technically, he was out of his jurisdiction, and she wasn't his problem. But old habits die hard, and he swung back around the next row and pulled up in front of her car.

She raised her eyes when she heard his car door slam. She was the most beautiful thing he'd seen in ages. Of course, living and working in Palm Lakes didn't give him a lot of chances to see beautiful young women, but she was at least a nine on a scale of ten.

Her blonde hair was pulled back into a ponytail and she had on a simple pink sundress and sandals. She looked to be about 21. It was unseasonably warm at 84 degrees, and looking at her made him more aware of the heat.

As if she'd noticed his assessment, she smiled knowingly and stood up straighter, putting her hand on one hip and cocking her head to the side. Maybe she liked a man in uniform...Maybe he was a fuckin' idiot.

"Are you having car trouble, ma'am?"

"Please don't call me ma'am. My name is Sally, and yes, my car died. I come back out of the store, and it won't start, the piece of shit. Do you know anything about cars?"

"Not much," he admitted. "But I'll take a look." He held out his hand and introduced himself. "Red Johnson."

She took his hand in a firm handshake, holding his hand a bit longer than necessary and looking him straight in the eye as if appraising him. "Sally Mueller." She was a little thing but knew how to make a big impression. He liked her style.

To get to the front of the car and have a look at the engine, he had to squeeze past Sally. He half imagined she was making it hard on purpose (*no pun intended*), though he couldn't imagine why. He had to admit that she gave him a little thrill.

Scrutinizing the engine, he couldn't see any obvious leaks, torn hoses or dismembered parts, but he really didn't know much about cars. "What does it do when you try to start it?"

"Not a damn thing but a bunch of clicking."

"Sounds like the battery to me. When did you last replace it?"

She got a thoughtful look on her face. "I can't remember. It's been a while."

"It's the battery for sure. Around here, you're lucky to get two years, even on batteries that claim they'll last five."

Her eyes widened in shock. "I didn't know that. I just moved here recently."

"Do you have AAA?"

"No. But my Mom lives in Palm Lakes. I was on my way to surprise her. If I could get a ride there, she'd help me sort this out." The pleading look was all he needed.

"As you can see, I'm with the Palm Lakes Posse, so I'll be happy to take you. Lock your car up and let's go." There went his shopping, but he didn't care. She was more interesting than choosing a frozen dinner.

He opened the passenger door for her, and she looked strangely at him (*not used to having doors opened for her?*), then slipped into the seat.

He got into the car and turned to her. "Where does your Mom live?"

She pointed in the direction of the entrance to Palm Lakes. "Just go through the gate and take your first right. She's partway down the block. Thanks for doing this. I'm pregnant, and I'd rather not walk all the way there in this heat."

He couldn't repress his double take. She didn't look pregnant, but what did he know about things like that? Three wives and not one kid. He couldn't help noticing there was no wedding ring on her left hand. Kids these days, always putting the cart before the horse. Belatedly he said, "Congratulations."

She didn't respond at first. Instead, she sighed. "Well, it isn't really that wonderful. I lost my job; my boyfriend split; I found out I was pregnant. I came out here to start over. I got a great new job and a nice apartment. My Mom's nearby to help. So things turned out well, but they don't always turn out the way you expect."

He wasn't sure how to answer that, so he didn't.

"So where are you from, Red?"

"St. Paul, Minnesota. Retired cop."

"But you couldn't really retire? You're still a cop."

"It hardly counts. I need to do something to stay active. I get to meet people and help them, and I never get shot at. At least not yet."

Her blue eyes widened. "You used to get shot at?"

"Yeah, occasionally. I was a homicide detective, and we sometimes managed to get in tight places."

"So what's your wife think of Palm Lakes, Red?"

"Which one?" He laughed weakly. "I have three ex-wives. Nobody currently."

Sally just smiled and nodded.

As they passed through the gate to Palm Lakes, she reached into her purse and pulled out a business card. "Here's my card. Give me a call. I'd like to buy you coffee or a drink to thank you for saving me a lot of trouble today."

He reached over, took the card and put it in his breast pocket without reading it. "You don't need to do that. I'm just doing my job."

She giggled. "You're way out of your jurisdiction, officer. This was above and beyond the call of duty. I owe you."

He had to admit he was tempted, but she couldn't be serious. He must be getting senile to think a woman half his age (a third his age?) would actually want to invite him out for a drink for *any* reason.

She pointed to a driveway, and he pulled in and put the car in park. She looked directly at him with big blue eyes flecked with gray. "Call me." He felt a shiver travel up his spine. Lauren Bacall had nothing on her. Before he could answer, she was out the door and sashaying up the walk. He recovered his senses and backed out onto the street and wound his way back to Safeway to contemplate what he should get for dinner.

* * *

Mary Beth, 4:30pm

MARY BETH WAS restless as hell. Saturday evening approached, and she had nothing to do. She decided to go next door with a bottle of wine. She didn't visit Helen every day, but she was becoming a more regular visitor. She hoped Helen didn't think she was a pest.

She pressed Helen's doorbell, looking around to see if Mrs. Jameson was watching, but there was no telltale movement of curtains at Mrs. J's. Maybe she wasn't home.

Helen answered the door and accepted the wine graciously. "Well, we definitely need to have a glass of this. Thank you so much. I've had a very busy day, and it would be fun to unwind with a friend." *Nice to be called a friend.*

Mary Beth accompanied Helen to the kitchen and helped with the wine, and they sat at the dining room table, as had become their habit. In spite of the age difference, she and Helen had become good friends. She felt herself relaxing. Helen was so genuine and noncritical. Just what she needed.

They sipped their wine in silence for a minute. Then Helen gave Mary Beth a look and stood up. "I have something to show you." She left the room briefly, then returned and put a tiny ziplock bag in front of Mary Beth. Inside it was a pair of cute rabbit earrings. They looked carved, the detail quite charming and realistic. "Where did you get these?"

"A friend here in town made them and gave them to me. I have lots of her jewelry. She's a real artist. I thought you might like to have them."

"Ohhhh!" Mary Beth exclaimed. "A present for me? These are perfect! I wish I could make things like this. I like pretty jewelry, and I've always been fond of beads and gemstones. It must be fun to have talent." She took the earrings out of the bag and replaced the simple gold hoops she was wearing with the bunnies. Then she held her hair back and showed them to Helen. "How do they look?"

"Perfect. The jade complements your eyes. I knew they were yours the minute I saw them. Go look in the bathroom mirror."

Mary Beth wasted no time going to see for herself. "These are so damn nice! Thank you so much!" she shouted from the bathroom.

"Maddie does nice work, and she's so generous. It gave me an idea. You've mentioned you don't have a lot to do outside of work. Maddie once offered to show me how to make jewelry, but it isn't my thing. I was thinking you might enjoy it. It would be good for her, too. I think she could use some company. She has pretty bad osteoporosis, is 72 and a bit eccentric. She's Samantha's mother, by the way, and I know you work together. So she's not a total stranger. Anyway, knowing your Mom, I think you could handle her."

"No one can top my Mom. If I can get along with her, I can get along with anyone."

"Maddie's fine, but you don't want to talk about politics or religion with her. Just talk jewelry. She's passionate about it. I think she'd gladly teach you the craft, and it would be nice company for her. I could introduce you next Saturday."

"I'm dying for something to do. I've always been interested in jewelry, and I'd love to learn if she'll teach me."

"Then let's plan on visiting her next Saturday. I'll call and make sure it's OK."

Mary Beth could hardly contain her excitement. "Thanks, Helen, that's a terrific idea. Small world, isn't it? I work with Samantha, and now I'm going to meet her mother through you. But let's not talk only about me. What's new with you? Didn't you start a new class today?"

"Yes, the writing class started today. It was a bit intimidating, but I called Alexander and he gave me a pep talk. He's a writer, you know."

"He can give me a pep talk any day. So are you sure he's just a friend? I've never thought men and women can be just friends. Sooner or later one party wants more than friendship, and everything goes to shit. Sorry, I didn't mean that was going to happen to you..." Mary Beth looked at Helen to see if she was offended.

"Don't worry, Mary Beth, I know what you mean. I have no experience that way. I married young. My husband and I were anything but friends, and all I can say is that Alexander and I clicked, and I'm glad to call him my best friend."

"Hey, I thought we were best friends," challenged Mary Beth playfully.

"All my friends are best friends." Helen smiled and patted Mary Beth's hand. "I've never had as many friends as I do now, and I feel so lucky."

"My life's taken a turn for the better lately, too. I love my new job, even though it's an eye opener at times, and it's been wonderful getting to know you. I was so cooped up in Mom's condo a few months ago, I thought I was going crazy. I feel like I have a life again."

"I know what you mean. I feel like I have a life for the first time ever."

After finishing her glass of wine and hugging Helen, Mary Beth walked home. She was grateful Helen thought to suggest that she make jewelry with Maddie. It would be fun to have a hobby.

She hoped Mom wouldn't mind all the time she was spending away from home. For the longest time, Mom wanted her out of her hair, and now that she *was* out a lot, it seemed Mom resented all the hours she spent away from home.

It wouldn't seem normal unless Mom gave her a hard time, but lately, Mom's feisty quotient had dropped quite a bit, and that alarmed Mary Beth. So she almost hoped she'd get a rise out of her.

Mom was watching the TV when she returned. "How's Helen?" she asked.

"She just started a writing course and intends to write a novel. Can you imagine? That seems like a big project to me, but if anyone can do it, I bet Helen can. Oh, and she wants to introduce me to her friend Maddie who lives here and makes jewelry. Look at the earrings she gave me that Maddie made."

Her Mom took her glasses off and looked at the earrings. "Those are very nice. She made them herself?"

"Yes, she lives across the street from Helen's old place. She loves to make jewelry and offered to show Helen, but Helen has other interests and offered to introduce me to Maddie when she found out I love jewelry. I was thinking, if Maddie agrees, maybe I could go over for a little bit on Saturdays and learn how to make jewelry. Helen says she's very talented, and I've seen some of the things Maddie gave her, and they are really beautiful."

"All you do is work, walk and take care of me. It's time you found something fun to do. I know you're at loose ends here, and I think it sounds good." She put her glasses back on and returned to her show.

Mary Beth was relieved and surprised, but couldn't stamp out the worry that all this niceness was a bad sign.

CHAPTER THIRTEEN

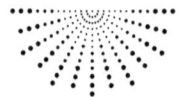

SATURDAY, NOVEMBER 4, 1995

Samantha, 10:20am

*S*amantha sped down the freeway, her stomach tied in knots. Why had she accepted Jack's invitation to see his nursery? More to the point, why hadn't she told Arthur where she was going?

It really wasn't that much of a mystery why she had accepted Jack's offer to show her his workplace. It was one last innocent chance to be together. In the few days they'd know each other, she had discovered they had a lot in common. They had the same passion about plants, landscaping design and how to run a business well. They had worked together in a seamless fashion like old partners on the class project. Working with him was exhilarating, as their mutual passions fed each other. She felt more alive when she was with him than she ever had in her life. And now it had to end.

For so many years, she had kept herself busy working: housework, yard work, helping her parents, Palo Verde Landscaping. She thought she liked her life, because she made a valuable contribution wherever she worked. Now that class was over, though, she wasn't looking forward to going back to her old life. Jack wasn't a part of that life of duty and obligation. The satisfaction of doing what was 'right' wasn't much compared to the sparkle of being with Jack, not that they had a relationship beyond being classmates. Nothing had happened between them. So why did she feel she was missing out on something big and wonderful if he walked out of her life? It was insane to feel as she did, but she couldn't help it. At least she was spared the embarrassment of him knowing about the attraction she felt.

She pulled off the interstate and paid attention to the directions she'd written down. Temple Landscaping was just a short distance down this road. She saw the large sign with a picture of a palm tree declaring Temple Landscaping was just ahead, and knowing that she'd see Jack soon made her heart flip-flop.

As she turned into the parking lot, she admired the small but attractive building. Very southwestern, it resembled an upscale ranch building, lots of rough wood and a covered wooden front porch with nice benches, hanging flower baskets and ristras of red chilis.

After parking, she walked slowly up the steps, getting a first impression of his business, noticing that the plantings out front were well-kept and included some nice solar stick-in-the-ground lighting that he probably also sold. Smart, showing people how they could enhance their landscaping. Very inviting compared to the unadorned shack at Palo Verde.

As she entered the building, she saw it was larger than it looked from outside and opened into a spacious courtyard that flowed out to the nursery itself. In the courtyard was an impressive water feature built from native stone. The waterfall spilled into a 3-foot-wide plunge pool that was 18 inches deep and surrounded by pots of blooming flowers. Another clever marketing technique. One thing everyone wanted in the desert was water, so water features commanded a good price.

As she stood there admiring the beauty, a hand lightly touched her shoulder. She jumped, startled out of her reverie, and turned to see Jack smiling at her. Looking typically handsome in his jeans, cowboy shirt and boots, he grinned at her crookedly, radiating pleasure that struck a responding chord in her. "You're early! Glad you could make it. I can't wait to show you around." He was bursting with pride, and rightly so. It was an impressive operation, and she'd only seen part of it.

She spent the next 45 minutes following him around, listening to him describe where he wanted to be in five years, and asking him questions that made him even more loquacious. He planned to expand, but not so fast that quality would suffer. His company's reputation mattered more than the bottom line. And in the long run, he believed that providing excellent service would make him rich. His attitude resonated with her. She wished the brothers had the same vision.

At the end of the tour, he led her to his office, a small but neat room with just enough space for a utilitarian desk and a couple of chairs, plus a file cabinet and old bookshelf full of reference guides and botanical resources. Framed photos of local desert flora in bloom graced the walls. She glanced at the titles of his books as he offered her the seat next to his desk. "How about I get you a soda or a cup of coffee?"

She wasn't thirsty, but it would give her something to do while they chatted. "That would be nice. I'll take a soda, a diet anything."

"I can do that." He left her alone to peruse the little library, returning a few minutes later with two cans of cold soda. He handed her a Diet Coke.

They popped the tops and drank, enjoying a companionable silence. She broke it first. "You have quite a place here. I'm very impressed."

He beamed with pleasure. "I'm glad you like it."

His smile had a frighteningly powerful effect on her. She focused on drinking her soda, trying to get herself together. She couldn't keep seeing him like this, and already, the thought of never seeing him again hurt. *I'm being stupid. I need to get out of here.* But the attraction of just being with someone who understood her, thought like her and liked the same things was so magnetic, she couldn't tear herself away. *Just a few more minutes.* She stared down at the soda can.

"Penny for your thoughts." He grinned at her guilelessly. He must have no idea what she was going through. Thank God for small favors. At least she wouldn't have to mortify herself.

"You've got a great business here. I thought...no, I *knew* Palo Verde was the best in our area, but we're lucky you're so far away. We couldn't compete with this. The brothers don't have this kind of vision. They have other priorities, which is not to say, bad priorities, just different. This is more in alignment with how I'd do it, but I'm not in charge..." She didn't know what to say without being disloyal, and she didn't want to do that. She'd said enough already.

"Thank you. I respect your opinion, and I'm glad you see my vision and like it. I have a five-year plan, and I intend to be the best small landscaping company and the most lucrative, with the happiest clients and best employees. It's been a lot of work getting this far, but it's worth it."

"You should be very proud of your accomplishments."

"So, you want a job?" His normal confidence seemed to disappear as he looked at her with dark, questioning eyes.

"Are you serious? You know how long a commute that would be?" She laughed; surely he was joking.

"I'm dead serious. I like how you think. You have real talent, and I think we make a good team."

"What do you mean, team? You hardly know me." This couldn't be happening. She'd like nothing better, if only it were closer to home, or if only she weren't married, or both. She felt shame at her traitorous thoughts. There was no way she could accept this.

"Look, I know what you're thinking, but I'll pay you well enough to make the commute worth your while. I'm sure they're paying you peanuts. Aren't they?" His cockiness had returned.

"You're right about that. But they gave me my truck and pay for gas and give me flexible hours, and I work near home and get to see my folks a lot more than I would in another job. It balances out."

"Are you sure of that?" His dark eyes skewered her.

Suddenly his question didn't seem to be about her job. Or did it? She was getting nervous and for some reason almost tearful. Time to go. "It's really very generous of you, Jack, and I would love to work here under different circumstances, but I don't see how it can work out."

"How much of that is because of how you feel about me?" The confident smile was replaced by an even more intense look as his dark eyes bored into hers.

Anger surged through her. The colossal gall of the man! She had never done *anything* to encourage him to think they were anything but friends. He had no right to bring this up. He couldn't expect her to turn her life upside down... Did this mean he had feelings for her? The anger was swept away as she realized maybe he shared her feelings.

He continued to stare at her, demanding an answer. She gathered her wits together. "What do you mean?"

"We clicked right away. You like being with me. We love the same things. I know you're married, and I'm not asking you to do anything you don't want to do, but since you accepted my invitation to come out here, I'm offering you a job. Just that. If you take it, I won't press you for anything else. We can keep it professional. I just don't want you to walk out of my life now that I've found you. I know this is a bad situation, but at least we can see where it leads as colleagues and friends."

She paused at the unexpected offer, unsure what to say. For just a second, she imagined she could make it work, that she could hold her life together if she said 'yes' to him. Then sanity returned. Her shoulders sagged in defeat. "I don't think that's a good idea, Jack. If I took the job and things got messy between us, I'd have no fallback position. We need the income I provide. Your offer is very generous, and maybe you could pay me well enough, but I don't know if spending more time with you is a good idea. I won't lie. I'm going to miss you, but working for or with you is only a further complication to an already difficult situation."

"Don't decide right away. Think about it. The offer is there, and I'm not putting a time limit on it. You have my card and my number. Think about how great we are together and what we could do to make this business even better. I could use someone I trust to do design and field work; someone who could become more of a partner than an employee. You think like me. I trust you."

Samantha had no idea what to say. It was a tempting offer in more ways than one. However, she could see the writing on the wall. If she worked closely with Jack, sooner or later it would come down to a personal relationship, and she didn't think she had the will power to say 'no'; she barely had it now. It would only get worse. Better to cut and run if she wanted to preserve her life as it was.

"I won't lie. I'd love to work with you, but there would be too many complications. I don't have a bad marriage. My parents are very traditional. I'm not the type to have an affair, and anything more would wreck my life completely. It would also hurt a lot of other people. I can't do that." Saying 'no' had never been harder. She swallowed back tears. "I have to go home now. Thanks for the tour."

Looking lost, he nodded and got up to follow her out.

She put her hand up to stop him. "No, I can show myself out. I've taken enough of your time. Thanks."

He stepped around the desk and got between her and the door. Putting his hands on her shoulders, he delayed her escape. "Listen. I didn't mean to upset you. I didn't want to imply I'm a home-wrecker. I have feelings for you, but I would keep my distance. I would treat you professionally. Please don't say 'no'. Just consider it. I don't mind how long it takes for you to decide. Call me." He took his hands away but didn't move out of her way.

"I wish I could accept, but I can't. Maybe I'll see you in class sometime again. I couldn't handle something like this. I'm sorry."

He stepped aside and she brushed past him. The minute she was out of his presence, her control disintegrated. The loss gouged her, and the tears started to flow. She picked up her pace and raced through the building to get to her truck. The ride home was so long. She knew she'd done the right thing, but it didn't feel good at all. She wondered if her life could ever be restored to what it was before she had met Jack.

* * *

Mary Beth, 2:00pm

MARY BETH FOLLOWED SLOWLY in her Mom's car as Helen pulled up in front of her old house, pointing that Mary Beth should park at the house across the way. There was a car in the driveway at what she assumed was Maddie's place, so she parked in front. Helen got out of her car and came over. "Ethan's here. I forget his last name. He helps out once a week, taking Beau for a walk and doing things to keep Maddie from hurting herself. She isn't too appreciative, being so independent-minded; Samantha got him through The Helpers. I'm glad Maddie is letting him come. She needs more help than she's willing to admit, and he's a nice guy."

They walked up the sidewalk, and Mary Beth admired the

247

landscaping with a more experienced eye thanks to her job at Palo Verde. The attractive design had what Samantha called a more 'formal' look, with contrasting color rock in beds that had brick borders.

When Helen pressed the doorbell, a big yellow dog appeared at the screen door, barking deeply. Helen seemed unfazed and said, "That's just Beau. He's a sweetie."

Behind Beau, a man came up to the door. "Hi, come on in, ladies."

"Hi, Ethan. I've brought my friend Mary Beth to do jewelry with Maddie."

Helen preceded Mary Beth into the house. Mary Beth squinted in the darkness, waiting for her eyes to adjust. The brown carpet and closed drapes made it really dark in the great room. The only light came from a study lamp on the table at the other end of the room in the dining alcove, where a small figure sat hunched over, working at something.

As her eyes adjusted, Mary Beth noticed that Ethan was a nice-looking older man with gray hair and twinkling gray eyes. At 6 ft tall, he loomed over both women. "I'm Ethan Westerfield with The Helpers," he boomed. Seeing Mary Beth cringe, he reached out his hand. "Sorry. I get so used to yelling. The old folks don't hear so good. Bad habit of mine."

Mary Beth took his hand, noting he had a firm, warm handshake. "I'm Mary Beth Costello."

"Maddie's gifted. You'll learn a lot from her. I don't know anything about jewelry, but I like what she makes. I'm on my way to walk Beau, so I'll see you ladies when I get back."

Helen interjected, "Oh, you won't see me, Ethan. I'm just staying long enough to introduce Maddie to Mary Beth."

"Well, maybe see you another time, then. See you when I get back, Mary Beth." The screen door slammed shut behind him.

Helen ushered Mary Beth over to the table where Maddie was hard at work, so single-minded she hadn't noticed her guests. "Hi, Maddie, how are you doing today?"

Maddie peered at Mary Beth through her magnifying glasses as if inspecting her. "Doing fine. Is this Mary Beth?"

Wanting to make a good impression, Mary Beth answered before Helen could. "Yes, Maddie, I'm Mary Beth, and I'm grateful you're willing to show me about making jewelry. I've always been interested in it, and you make the loveliest pieces. I'm wearing your rabbit earrings, see?" Mary Beth pulled her hair back and showed her.

A brief, warm smile graced Maddie's face, activating laugh lines that weren't apparent before. "They turned out well, if I do say so myself." Maddie paused and gestured to the chair next to hers, back to business again. "Well, have a seat and let's get started. Helen, come by anytime. I should have your earrings ready in a couple weeks or so. I can give them to Mary Beth if you like."

"That's a good idea. Thanks so much, Maddie." Helen leaned over to hug Maddie gently and left.

Maddie turned to Mary Beth and stared into her eyes. "I understand you work with Samantha."

"That's right. I'm sort of the secretary-slash-receptionist at Palo Verde Landscaping."

Maddie went back to what she'd been doing, stringing some beads. "They do nice work. They did our yard. A bit high-priced, but they know their stuff."

"Your yard is lovely."

"Stanley designed it, if you can believe that. He never had any interest in gardening or landscaping, but when we decided to move here, he was so excited about being able to plant tropical plants, including palms, that he drew up the design himself."

"Wow, I didn't realize that. It's beautiful. You must be proud of him."

Without warning, Maddie changed the subject, leaving Mary Beth little time to wonder why. "We need to get you started out right. So I've put together some things for you." She lay a couple white cloths on the table, and Mary Beth could see they were clean dish towels.

"These are excellent work cloths, and in a hurry, you can wrap your whole project in it and move it from place to place. The white color and smooth texture make it a good work surface. You'll need a few of them. You also need some tools." Maddie reached over to one of many boxes in the shadows at the far edge of the table and began to rummage around.

"Oh, I can buy my own tools." Mary Beth said weakly. Helen had warned her how generous Maddie was, but it was another thing having to deal with it. Already she could tell Maddie was a force of Nature, moreso even than her mother.

"Nonsense. I have extras of everything. You don't need to buy any. I'll show you how to use these, but basically they are for cutting, holding and bending things. A tool for each job."

Mary Beth watched in awe as Maddie laid out each tool on the towels. It was fun to be getting a whole set of jewelry-making equipment, and if these were extras, there was no point in arguing. "Thank you, Maddie. This is so exciting!"

Maddie chuckled with undisguised pleasure. "It is fun. Now, if you decide to pursue this, you might want to get magnifying eyeglasses like I have, if you need them, but for now, you'll just borrow mine. So that's a complete set of tools. You'll want a bag of some kind to transport them in."

"I have something at home that might work. I'll just put them in a plastic grocery bag for now, if you have one I can use."

"I'll get you one when it's time to leave."

Maddie began by showing Mary Beth proper technique for making earrings. Turning her wrist while holding the wire to close the loop took quite a few tries before she got it right, and when she finally did, she trumpeted her success, pumping the air with her left fist. "Yay, I did it!"

Maddie seemed charmed by Mary Beth's enthusiasm. "You're doing great."

Time passed and soon Mary Beth had a pair of earrings she'd made mostly by herself. "I'm going to give these earrings to Mom. She'll love them."

"You're a good girl," Maddie murmured as she continued stringing beads on her own project.

Mary Beth felt strangely glad she'd not been found wanting. "I don't know about that, but I love my Mom. It's been good spending time together. At first, it was kind of tough, but we have a rhythm now and are mostly enjoying living together. It would be less stressful if the covenants allowed me to stay here."

"Damn HOA should mind their own business." Mary Beth flinched. Funny how she didn't expect older women to curse.

"I understand they're trying to preserve the age limits to keep the atmosphere the way everyone wants it, but I don't bother anyone, so I hope I can slip by unnoticed. If only Mrs. Jameson doesn't report me.

She's the only one I'm worried about. She lives across the street, and she's a nosy old biddy."

Maddie patted her hand. "Some people around here have too much time on their hands. Bunch of damn Nazis if you ask me. I hate to admit it, but they intimidate me, too. I wouldn't get my yard done so often if I thought I could get away with it. Too damned expensive. But the covenants say you have to keep your yard nice, so I make sure it looks pretty good."

Mary Beth smiled. "It's nice to meet a kindred spirit. Thanks for keeping my secret."

Just then, Ethan returned with Beau, who galloped over to greet Mary Beth and get petted by Maddie. "Hello, ladies. We're back. What are you making today?"

"I'm making earrings! Look at these. Aren't they wonderful?" Mary Beth couldn't help bubbling over with pride and excitement, in spite of Ethan being a virtual stranger.

Ethan came over and stood next to Mary Beth in the pool of light cast by the study lamp in the otherwise dark room. He leaned down and looked carefully at the earrings she had made that lay on the white cloth in front of her. He was so close that she could smell his after shave and feel the warmth of his body. He turned his face, which was inches from hers as they both looked at the earrings. His gray eyes smiled with encouragement. "You're a quick study. These are lovely." Mary Beth found herself blushing for the first time in years. She looked down, but when she looked back up, his eyes were still locked on her. Were they having a moment? Was her heart palpitating because of him, or because she wasn't used to a compliment? *Christ, Costello, get a grip. Quit imagining things.*

"Thank you," she stammered, embarrassed at her reaction.

Maddie broke in and inadvertently saved the day. "She's a fast learner for sure." Maddie was intently working on her own necklace and obviously hadn't noticed the exchange between Ethan and Mary Beth. That is, if there had been one. Mary Beth wasn't sure.

Ethan stood up. "I'm going to collect the trash now." He went out of the room without looking back, leaving Mary Beth with the feeling that she must have imagined it.

Eager to change the subject, Mary Beth volunteered, "You know, Samantha was a real godsend for me. She recommended a chiropractor, and since I've been going to him, I don't need pain pills for my back anymore for the first time in years. It's a miracle!"

A frown crossed Maddie's face. "I don't hold much with chiropractors."

Silence once again cloaked them as Mary Beth tried to recover. Helen was right. There weren't too many safe topics for conversation with Maddie. "I really appreciate your getting me set up and teaching me today. Would it be all right if I come over next Saturday?"

"Yes, of course. You need to practice if you want to get good at this. Earrings are a fun way to start. Maybe next week we can do some more, or think about designing a necklace."

"You have to at least let me pay for materials."

Maddie waved Mary Beth's objection away with her hand as if it were smoke. "I have a whole garage full of materials. You'd be doing me a favor to use some of them."

Mary Beth didn't feel comfortable being the recipient of such largesse, but she already knew that arguing was a waste of time. "OK. I'll let you be my guide." She knew how to get around it. She'd bring a bottle of wine next week. Samantha had clued her in that Maddie liked wine, even what brand (she didn't like expensive wines; she was fond of the Taylor brand; Samantha had made a joke about it being 'her' brand, since her married name was Taylor.)

"Here, put your earrings in this plastic bag." Maddie handed her a tiny ziplock bag. It was so cute! The earrings fit into it perfectly. She began to gather her tools together and fold the towel around them. "Can I have a plastic bag?"

"Sure. There are some in a box under the sink."

Mary Beth got up and went into the kitchen to get a bag. The light was on in the kitchen, and unlike the living/dining area, this room was brightly lit, some of the light spilling out into the dining area where they were working. Mary Beth was wondering how they managed to eat, since the dining table was covered with materials and boxes stacked 18 inches high in places, then noticed the dinette set in the breakfast nook off the kitchen.

It was obvious Maddie wasn't the housekeeper Mom was. Even now in her less active state, Mom wouldn't have tolerated this mess. The coffee pot was off but still half full. Dishes clogged the sink. There was a sense of chaos and crowding in the kitchen, with very little counter space. Mary Beth felt guilty for judging her; with her osteoporosis, Maddie probably couldn't do much, and Stanley was even older than Maddie. It made her feel lucky to be able to help Mom out.

Under the sink, she found a box with plastic bags of all colors and sizes, each rolled up tightly and knotted to compress the size, a strange spot of order amidst the chaos of the kitchen. The first one she picked had a big hole in it, so she picked through them until she found one that was intact, throwing out the badly damaged ones.

Returning to the dining area, she packed her tools, cloths and the earrings in the bag and sat down in the chair. "I don't know how to thank you, Maddie. I can't participate in clubs and activities here, and I don't have many friends, so this is a real treat for me."

Maddie looked up from the beads she was stringing. "I like having you here. I hope you'll come back." It hadn't taken Mary Beth long to conclude that Maddie always said what she meant, so it warmed her heart to hear she was welcome. "Of course, I will. You've got me all outfitted, and I'm eager to make jewelry." She reached over to a small pad of paper and pen and wrote her full name and phone number down. "Just in case something comes up and you don't want me to come, call me. Otherwise, I'll be here next week at the same time, if that's OK with you."

"Sure." Maddie absentmindedly took the scrap of paper and looked around as if trying to decide what to do with it, and worry flashed through Mary Beth. If it got laid down on the table, it would probably disappear forever.

"I could write my name and number in your address book if you like, so you don't have to worry about losing it."

Maddie paused, paper in hand. "That might be a good idea. It's so easy to misplace things. The green address book is in the drawer by the oven."

Mary Beth jumped up and went to the drawer and found the address book, so ancient that the gold embossed letters on the tabs were nearly rubbed off. As she turned the pages, bits of paper fell out. She picked them up and put them back in. Finding a blank space on the page for "C" (it was a miracle), she added her details in neat, large script. Then she closed the book and replaced it in the drawer, which was obviously a junk drawer and had pens, keys, rubber bands and a flat blade screwdriver in it, among other things. It occurred to her to wonder how helpful doing this would be if Maddie forgot her name. No point in worrying about that, though.

As she closed the drawer, Ethan came around the corner with a garbage bag and emptied the kitchen trash into it. In the dark of the great room, she hadn't noticed his nerdy outfit. He had dark socks on with his sandals, and his Bermuda shorts were a loud plaid. But he was in good physical condition. His legs weren't withered like a lot of the old guys she saw around town, and he wasn't carrying much extra weight, just a little tummy like everyone gets as they get older. He turned around from the trash can and caught her looking at him, so she abruptly looked away.

Had he seen her frank assessment of him? He didn't appear to have registered awareness of her scrutiny. "Well, that's the lot. I'm taking this out to the trash can and moving on to my next assignment."

"Do you come every Saturday, Ethan?" She immediately regretted asking; it sounded so forward.

Ethan didn't seem to mind. "Yes, for as long as Maddie lets me."

"That's nice that you are helping her out."

"It's the least I can do. The Helpers were so supportive when my wife was dying of cancer."

"I'm so sorry." Such an inadequate thing to say. She felt totally lame.

"It was a long time ago." He shrugged his shoulders and cinched the garbage bag tighter.

Suddenly she felt eager to escape. She wasn't making the impression she'd like to, and she felt a craving for a cigarette. "I'll walk out with you. I'm leaving, too." Mary Beth walked back into the dining area and impulsively put her arm around Maddie's shoulders, careful not to squeeze too hard. "Thanks so much for everything."

Maddie didn't look up. "Come back next Saturday." It sounded more like an order than an invitation, and for some reason that made Mary Beth feel wanted.

"I promise." She patted Beau and followed Ethan, who opened the door for her. He went past his car to put the trash into the trash can, then walked her to her car, opening the door for her. She couldn't remember the last time a man had done that. Probably one of the perks of being around an older guy. They had manners.

She leaned into the car and placed the bag of jewelry supplies on the passenger seat, then turned to Ethan. "It was fun today. Maddie sure is a good teacher."

"She is a lonely woman with failing health, and you are doing her as much of a favor as she is doing you, maybe more. It's pretty obvious to me that she doesn't get out much, and Stanley keeps to himself. It will do her good to have a friend." He patted her shoulder, then turned to go to his car.

When she got home and came through the door from the garage, she found Mom watching a rerun on TV. "I'm back, and I have a present for you."

It was fun to see the quizzical look in her Mom's eyes. "It isn't my birthday!"

"I made you something." She reached into the grocery bag and pulled out the small plastic ziplock bag that held the earrings. Handing the bag to Mom, she couldn't contain her excitement as she told her about the afternoon. "Maddie gave me a whole set of tools so I'm all ready to make jewelry, and she helped me make these earrings today. It's lucky your ears are pierced. The big bead is cloisonné, a kind of enamel treatment, I think. Isn't it colorful and artistic?" She held her breath, waiting to see Mom's reaction to her creation.

Her mother stared at the earrings and then opened the bag and replaced those she had on with the new ones. The mainly red color complimented her olive skin and dark eyes beautifully. "I have to look in the mirror." She got up and went to the bathroom and examined the earrings. "These look so expensive. She gave you everything?"

"Yeah, Ma, she's really generous. I'm going to take her a bottle of wine each week. She won't let me pay for anything."

Mom turned around with a big smile on her face. "These are beautiful. Like a Christmas present in November."

Mary Beth hugged her, delighted to see her happy. "I'm so glad you like them. I can't wait to see what she's going to teach me to do next week."

* * *

Helen, 4:00pm

THE ROSES WERE SHRIVELED and drying out in spite of Helen's best efforts to keep them alive. Multiple times a day, she stroked their fading petals and inhaled their lessening scent. Yellow for friendship. She was so grateful, though still confused, that Alexander had come by and apologized. What could he possibly think he had done wrong?

They used to have a level of openness in their relationship that hadn't quite returned. He'd been hiding something that day. It was almost like he was eager to leave once he saw she wasn't angry. He hadn't hugged her, but then Mary Beth had come along as he was leaving. Maybe he had intended to.

The important thing was he was still her friend. The best friend she'd ever had. But Mary Beth was right. A line had been crossed, and she had to admit she had other feelings for him. It was stupid, since he'd been so candid with her about his sexual orientation. Maybe she was one of those women who only wanted men she couldn't have, like priests and gay men.

At least she was finally being honest with herself. Now she just had to get her feelings sorted, or at least shut away somewhere so she wasn't constantly having to acknowledge the inconvenient little monsters. She wasn't going to lose her friendship with Alexander over her silly fantasies. He had gone to a lot of trouble to save their relationship, and the least she could do was be worth that trouble.

She checked her hair in the mirror yet again, pushing it back from her face. If Alexander was just a friend, why was she so nervous about how she looked? Ignoring the question, she admired the new skirt and blouse she'd bought using her employee discount at Wal-Mart. She didn't like most of the clothing there, but these were a find. The long, dark green skirt was a wrinkly-crinkly natural cotton. In fact, the instructions said to tie it when you hang it to dry after washing, so the wrinkles would be restored. The cream blouse was feminine but not overtly sexy. She didn't have cleavage to show off, and she preferred the boat neck on this blouse. The wide belt made of soft, dark brown faux leather accentuated her narrow waist. The outfit set off Maddie's tiger eye necklace beautifully. The matching earrings were the finishing touch. A simple gold C-band bracelet she'd had for years, a gift from her kids, graced her left wrist.

Yet the more she admired the outfit, the more worried she became. Maybe it would be better if she dressed more casually.

Too late. The doorbell announced Alexander was here, on time as usual. She shook off her worries and went to greet him.

When she opened the door, she was glad she'd dressed up. Alexander could make a casual outfit look like a tux. He was a dark study tonight, black pants, black shoes and a maroon and white Hawaiian print shirt, all of which reeked of elegance. His smile lit up when he saw her. "Aren't you looking even more ravishing than usual?" *Has he ever complimented me that way? I guess it's just the skirt. I've never worn one for him.*

She opened the screen door and let him in, feeling nervous about being so dressed up. He stood a bit awkwardly holding a small bouquet of colorful flowers in his left hand, as if he didn't know what to do next. Then he recovered and held out his right hand as if to introduce himself. "The name's Bond. James Bond." He even had the accent right.

His grin set her off in a fit of giggles, as she grasped his hand and shook it. "You're impossible. Get in here and give me those." She took the flowers from him and headed to the kitchen.

"Why did you bring flowers again?" she tossed back over her shoulder.

"You didn't tell me to bring anything, and my mother taught me not to come empty-handed to dinner. I know that if the roses are still alive, they are probably ready to go, and this way, you'll part with them more easily."

"You have no idea. I never got roses before. I might frame them and hang them on the wall."

"I can't believe I'm the first person to ever give you roses!" He sounded inordinately pleased as he followed her to the kitchen.

"Yes, but don't get a swelled head about it," she teased, as she slowly removed the dying roses from the vase. There was something different about him today, but she couldn't put her finger on what it was.

"I'm just pleased to have been the first, though how you made it this long without being showered in roses escapes me." While she busied herself with the flowers to avoid blushing, he went to the door and looked at the new landscaping. "Big change, isn't it?"

"Well, it will take a while to grow. Samantha says people put in too many plants out of impatience, and then the final design is overcrowded. She says it looks small now, but in a few years, it will be perfect. I trust her."

"I like it. It's simple but inviting. Looks like the wire on the wall at the back is to espalier a vine. What type is it?"

"Good eyesight. I think it's called a star jasmine."

She finished fussing with the flowers and moved them to the center of the table. "These are lovely. Thank you."

"When do you want to spread Sheba's ashes?" He put his hand on her shoulder, and she shivered. It was the first time he'd touched her in weeks, and it felt good. Too good.

"Let's do it now. It's a beautiful day, and now the yard is ready for her." She went to the hutch and picked up the metal box, and they went outside.

She stood at a small staked tree in the center of the yard. "This is a desert willow. I want to spread her ashes around the base of it."

"That's a great place." He came and stood next to her, waiting for her to open the box. When she did, the slight breeze stirred the top of the ashes, and they began to come out and float on the wind as if Sheba were leaping out to inspect her new home. Helen bent down and began to circle the tree, sprinkling the contents of the box as she did. By the time she completed the circle, the box was empty.

They stood together in silence for a while. He spoke first. "I think Sheba will like being in this yard. It's a great place."

Helen blinked back tears and nodded her agreement, but couldn't find words to say. She put the top on the box and they turned and went back into the house. In the kitchen, she poured him a glass of wine. "Let's toast our thanks for all Sheba did for me."

He raised his glass and clinked it with hers. "To Sheba." They sipped their wine. He reached over and touched her shoulder again, giving it a squeeze.

"What are we making for dinner?"

"It's a Korean dish called Bulgogi. I got a new cookbook on Asian food, and I'm having fun trying new things out. I hope you like garlic, because there's a lot of it in the marinade."

"Oh, yes, I do."

"Your job as the man of the house will be to grill the meat. That always seems to go with the Y chromosome. Is that all right with you?"

"Aye, aye, Captain." He mock saluted her. "Let me know when to start the grill."

"I have the rice on already, because it will hold in the steamer for a while. The sauces are made up in the fridge, and so all we really need to do is grill the meat, set the table and eat. This kitchen is so small compared to yours, I didn't want to have to do a lot of preparation. You can start grilling while I set the table." They fell into an easy rhythm that gave her hope their relationship was finally mended.

The meal was an astounding success, including the bottle of wine she'd bought at Trader Joe's for the munificent sum of $10. After washing the dishes, they went to the couch in the living room and sat down with a glass of plum wine for dessert, another first for her.

He raised his glass to her. "That was a particularly tasty meal. And you picked a good wine to go with it."

She smiled at the compliment. "I asked the guy in the wine department at Trader Joe's. I told him what I was cooking and what my budget was, and he pointed out that wine. I'm glad you approve. You know much more about wine than I do. I had a lot of fun planning this meal, so I'm happy you enjoyed it."

The silence almost became awkward, but then he broke it, apparently with some reluctance. "I'm not sure whether I'm making a mistake doing this, but I have to tell you something. I know you've been betrayed in the past, and I don't want you to think that of me, and the longer I wait to set the record straight, the worse it's going to look." He paused as if working up the courage to say something.

Her heart began pounding. She didn't want to lose what they had, and it sounded like he was afraid she wasn't going to be happy with what he said. "Don't tell me," she blurted.

"What?"

"Don't tell me if you think it's going to ruin what we have. I can't bear to think of that. The last several weeks have been awful, and I've felt so bad. Now that you're back, I don't want to lose you again. Let's just move forward."

"I have no intention of losing you and I *do* want to move forward, but that's why I need to tell you this. I wouldn't risk what we have for anything, but the truth will come out sooner or later, and I think sooner is better. It will be up to you what to do about it." His strained look pleaded for understanding and maybe something else.

Dread filled her, and she began to twist the fabric of her skirt nervously. *What could this possibly be about?*

After a moment, he began in a soft voice. "I told you early on in our friendship that I was gay."

"Yes, I remember." She looked at him quizzically.

"And that was true...to a great extent."

What could he possibly mean? "What's a great extent? Aren't you gay?" Her voice rose in indignation. "Did you lie to me about being gay so I would trust you more?"

"Yes and no." He winced at the wave of anger that poured off her.

"How can it be yes *and* no?" she snapped. How could he have lied to her? She'd thought he was different from other men.

He reached over and touched her hand briefly, as if to plead with her to understand. "I haven't slept with a woman in decades. My only lasting relationship was gay. I told you about Leslie. He died of AIDS long ago. But that wasn't the whole story. I'm bisexual. I have had relationships with both men and women in my life." He grimaced as if he felt he were making a mess of things.

She paused to process what he said. Her anger turned to curiosity. "Why did you not tell me the whole truth in the beginning?"

"I had no designs on you, and you seemed very suspicious of men. I wanted you to feel at ease."

"It worked. I would have been nervous around you if you'd told me everything. Yet why bother telling me now?"

He sighed deeply and pressed on. "Honesty is necessary for any real relationship. I want to always be honest with you. But you're right. It's more than that. I swear to God it didn't start like this, but I have feelings for you beyond friendship, and I can't hide them anymore."

She stared at him wide-eyed, her mouth open. In a million years, she never would have guessed this. How did she feel about it? This revelation blind-sided her. Part of her was angry that he lied. Part of her was intrigued and confused about his sexual orientation. Part of her was dancing up and down that he cared for her. She wasn't sure which part to give in to.

"So why tell me now?" Her voice was much calmer than she felt.

"Look, I swear when I offered to let you sleep with me that night, I meant no harm. I promised not to take advantage of you."

"And you didn't, so what's the big deal?"

He paused and looked down. "Well, it wouldn't be the same if we slept together again. I had to be honest about my feelings, because I wouldn't want to mislead you, but if I simply refused to be close to you, you might think I didn't care. You wouldn't know I was acting out of respect. I don't want to be another man who hurts you. That's one reason I gave you space all these weeks. I was trying to honor what you wanted. It wasn't because I didn't want to be with you." The pain in his eyes said he was telling the truth.

"There was another reason you stayed away?"

"Yes, but I'm not sure I'm ready to share that quite yet. You haven't flung me out the door yet, and I'd rather end this night not being thrown out. So if you don't mind, I'll wait a bit on that one."

Time passed as she decided what to do next. "If we're getting all honest with each other, I have something to tell you, too. And it was one reason I backed off from our relationship. You deserve to know that what happened wasn't all about you. I had a reason of my own. That night we slept together, I had the most incredible dream about you, and it confused me."

His eyes widened, and then a small smile appeared. "Really. Do tell."

"I'm not sure I can tell you. It's pretty personal."

"By personal, do you mean...erotic?"

"Well...yes." She watched his small grin turned into a broad smile. "Don't you dare laugh at me, Alexander. That's not fair. I'm trying to be honest about an embarrassing event."

"Embarrassing or stimulating?"

"What difference does it make?"

"I'd like to know whether you found my behavior in the dream embarrassing or stimulating. It's a matter of pride."

"Definitely the latter." His smile got bigger, if that was even possible. She knew men could be egotistical about sex, but why did he care about her dream?

"Why were you afraid to share this?"

"I didn't want you to think I was one of those predatory females who are always chasing you, and since you were gay, or so I thought, there was no hope of anything beyond friendship. I was confused and felt bad about my dream. I wasn't trying to convert you or chase you. Sheba had just died. What can I say? I was a coward, and I ran."

"Then that thing I didn't want to share with you, the one I said I'd wait until later to talk about? I think I'm ready to tell you now."

She looked at him quizzically as he held his hands apart in explanation. "You see, you didn't actually have a dream. I have to apologize again. I woke up in the middle of the night wrapped around you wanting to ravish you in the worst way. I promise it happened in my sleep, and when I woke up, I moved away, and you didn't seem to be awake, so I hoped you wouldn't remember. I didn't want you to think I was the type of person you couldn't trust. It just happened. It seems we both had secrets." He grinned sheepishly at her.

She closed her mouth and stared at him as all the pieces fell into place. Thank God they had finally opened up with each other. But where would they go from here? Her head was spinning.

He waved a hand in front of her face to get her attention. "So you aren't going to throw me out?"

"Hardly."

"You aren't mad at me for keeping secrets?"

"If you're not mad at me for keeping secrets."

"Then can we have a sleepover tonight at my house and try for a better outcome this time?" There was that boyish grin she couldn't say no to.

"You had me at the roses."

He leaned towards her and gently kissed her. The spark she'd been trying to deny ignited into a bonfire. As she responded enthusiastically, she realized they were never going to make it to his house tonight.

CHAPTER FOURTEEN

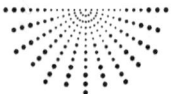

THANKSGIVING DAY, 1995

Helen, 3:50am

*H*elen lay in Alexander's bed, wide awake in the middle of the night. Tomorrow was Thanksgiving, and she wasn't looking forward to it. Warren and Lena had arrived in town at various times yesterday with their families, and she had picked them up at the airport by herself and ferried them to their hotels. She was still stinging at their refusal of hospitality from either Alexander or her. Tears started to fill her eyes, but she refused to give in to them.

Something was going on with Sally, too. She'd cryptically said she was bringing a date to dinner, but wouldn't give further details. Helen was glad Sally had made connections here, but she sure hoped it was someone decent this time. If she was bringing another druggie or failed musician to a family dinner, it would only add to the tension. Alexander had no clue what he was in for.

The clock said 3:55, and she was wide awake and becoming more worried and annoyed as each minute passed. Alexander was another problem. He'd recently suggested she sell her condo and move in with him. Sure, it was the logical thing to do, but she wasn't ready to give up the only place that had ever been hers. It was true that she spent more time here than at her place now. But what if she gave in, and he later tired of her? And how was she going to face her family and have confidence tomorrow when these worries were playing under the surface like annoying background music? They were against the relationship, and she didn't dare show any doubts in front of them. She tried to stop herself from tossing around in an attempt to escape the bad feelings that plagued her.

This was a bad time of night, the time when fears took over. She remembered from the summer how lost and panicked she would often feel if she were awake at this time of night, which was one reason she took to drinking wine, as it helped her to sleep through most of the night. She knew she needed an attitude adjustment. *Try to think about the good stuff.*

All day, every day, was the 'good stuff'. The only time she felt this concerned was in the middle of the night when she couldn't sleep. The rest of the time, she knew she was in the right place and doing the right thing.

Alexander was like water in the desert for her, and when they were together, she felt in her heart that his feelings for her were true and deep. It wasn't just the sex, though, my God, the very thought of what they did together made her tingle all over. He'd opened her up to a whole new way of feeling close, connected and loved. She wondered how long it would take for them to get enough of each other. Passion was a gloriously unexpected thing to experience at her age. But even more important was how supportive and encouraging he was. He treated her like she was special, like he wanted to protect her. So unlike Lou, who'd showered criticism and abuse on her.

But rather than being glad for her, Warren and Lena were skeptical and negative. Alexander hadn't indicated he was offended by her kids' behavior, but she was afraid it might impact their relationship. Irrationally, she wished they could get up and leave town and avoid the impending confrontation she felt was inevitable.

As if responding to her telepathically, Alexander moved up behind her and pulled her close to him. The warmth and hardness of his body felt both nurturing and protective. His hands caressed her gently, not demanding anything, just loving her. Whenever he touched her, she forgot all her insecurities, doubts and fears about the future. She wanted to surrender to him in every way possible, even if it meant losing herself. She was addicted to him, addicted to loving him. And she was afraid to tell him; that was what irritated her most. He had yet to actually tell her that he loved her, and she stubbornly didn't want to change her life for him until he did. Yet she didn't want to act like the insecure person she was and beg for him to say the words she was dying to hear.

His soft kisses on the back of her neck chased away her negative emotions, filling her with the joy of being alive. She turned to face him, filling her nostrils with the scent of him, his cologne overlaying a more primal, masculine fragrance. His voice, his scent, his touch, his taste, even the monochromatic glimpses of his beautiful face in the darkness all contributed to the energy pulsing through her body, needing him, wanting him, driving her crazy with passion. It wasn't possible to think anymore. All she could do was feel.

Later, at exactly 6:38 by the clock, she woke up wrapped in his arms, her neck at an uncomfortable angle. She'd fallen asleep after they made love, and her neck cried out when she tried to move it. *That's the problem with acting like you're a kid when you're not. The old body isn't as flexible as it used to be.* In spite of that thought, she couldn't keep a grin from her face at the ecstasy she experienced in his arms. He completed her. She just wished there was some guarantee for the future and some signposts as to what to do. *Quit being a worry wart. Just for today, be happy and don't let anyone ruin what you have.*

Having made the decision, she felt energized. She wasn't going to let her kids ruin today. In fact, if they acted up, she'd make sure they left early.

Alexander stirred, then snuggled up to her, giving her a kiss on the cheek. "Morning, beautiful. Happy Thanksgiving."

She kissed him back. "You're the beautiful one. And I am so grateful to have you in my life. But I'm not sure I can promise this will be a 'happy' Thanksgiving. My kids are not always easy to be with."

"Nonsense, they're just shocked. We're old folks. We aren't supposed to have sex. It would nauseate them if they knew that last night we were going at it like mink."

She felt herself blush. "You're right about that, and it's kind of you to rationalize for them." She knew he was being nice for her sake, but he needed to know how bad it could get, in case he hadn't already guessed. "I hate to say it, but I'm afraid they're going to embarrass me today...no, embarrass me more than they already have by being so standoffish and refusing to accept our hospitality. They seem determined to pretend that you and I don't have a relationship." She couldn't look him in the eye.

Then suddenly, she realized with horror that he might misinterpret what she meant. "I didn't mean to imply anything about where this relationship is going. I was just saying that maybe they were inferring something, and that they didn't like it." *No, no, that only makes it worse!* Now she was *really* embarrassed. She didn't want him to think she was asking him to marry her. She didn't even know how he felt about marriage.

He held her closer. "Helen, I've been insensitive. I'm sorry."

"You? Are you nuts? Here I am worrying about my selfish kids ruining our Thanksgiving, and you're apologizing?" What had gotten into him?

"I mean it's been unfair that I haven't said anything to you about the future and my feelings for you. I've talked about you moving in here without letting you know exactly *why* I asked you to. That was wrong. It's understandable you're uncertain, and it's my fault for not being more expressive. I can only say that I was terribly traumatized when I lost Leslie all those years ago, and I promised myself I'd never love again. I broke that promise soon after I met you, and not telling you 'I love you' isn't the same as keeping that promise; a promise made in grief that I don't want to keep anymore. I love you. I want you in my life, for as many years as we have. I've never been married, but I'm a reliable, faithful guy, and if you love me, too, I want to marry you."

Helen's head was spinning. He loved her and wanted to marry her! Everything else was just details. For a moment, Helen's mouth was open in shock, but then she threw her arms around him. "Yes! I accept! I love you, too, and I want to be with you always."

They held each other tight and shared kisses laced with joy and promise. After the initial excitement about the proposal passed, Helen whispered in his ear, "Can we run away now?"

He laughed out loud and buried his face in her neck. "Woman, you are everything I ever wanted. Why run away?"

"My kids are just going to ruin today; I know it. I hate to sound selfish, but I don't want to be around anyone who will cast a pall on this day. And if we tell them, they will get worse, if that's possible. I just want to be in a bubble of happiness all day."

"My love, I will do my best to see that no matter what your kids do, today is a happy day for us both. We aren't going to let them spoil anything. First, we won't tell them today. We'll have a great meal, and if they act funny, we can send them packing and come to bed early and lose ourselves in celebrating what we have together."

"Promise?"

"Promise!"

She sighed in contentment and held him for a while longer. "I can't believe this is happening to me."

"You're not the only one. I would never have predicted this for myself. Life is full of surprises, and if you ask me, it makes sense that some of them be good ones."

"So I'm a good surprise?"

"What a silly question! You're the best surprise I never asked for, and I will always be grateful. It's appropriate that I proposed on Thanksgiving, because I am so thankful for you. You broke down the walls I'd put up and helped me to love again, and I feel more alive than I have in years."

She sighed and settled into snuggling him. There was no rush to get up.

* * *

Red, 6:30am

RED'S EYES POPPED OPEN, and for a moment, he didn't know where he was. Then he remembered. He was at Sally's place. Thanksgiving day had dawned, and he badly needed to pee, but he didn't want to wake her by getting up. She was sleeping so peacefully, and they hadn't been asleep more than 4 hours. She needed her rest. Not that he didn't. He was getting too old for nights like last night. Not that he minded. It was worth every bit of the no-boned exhaustion he was feeling.

He blinked his eyes, trying to push his skepticism aside so he could just enjoy the experience of having a young woman treat him like a sex god, but a question kept nagging at him. What did she see in an old guy like him? Sure, he was in decent shape for his age, and he had a good living, but he was no catch, and he had a terrible track record at marriage. She was young, beautiful and obviously intelligent. Surely she could find someone closer to her own age? (Thank God she was older than she looked, but she was still so young.) What was the attraction? He knew why he wanted her; he just had no clue what she saw in him, and that stirred the detective in him.

He didn't want to ask her why him, because he wasn't sure he really wanted to know, and he wasn't sure she'd tell him the truth. Some part of him was afraid if he spoke up, the magic might vanish, and she'd see him for what he was, a guy old enough to be her father.

Maybe she didn't know the truth herself, or maybe she had Daddy issues. She manipulated him shamelessly, and he let her get away with it. He wondered if she knew he was on to her. He just didn't care. He hadn't had such a good time in years.

It's just that he'd never been very good at living in the moment for an extended period of time, and this thing with Sally had lasted over three weeks, much to his surprise. He figured she was new to town, just having fun with someone safe, but that in time, she'd move on and find a guy closer to her age. Maybe she would. At first, it wouldn't have bothered him, but he had to admit, he'd feel the loss if she left now.

He pressed his fingers against his eyelids, feeling the grittiness of sleep deprivation, and wondered if she'd be tired. She was pregnant, after all, though to look at her, even naked, it wasn't all that obvious, just a little bump. That's probably what was bothering him. She'd be showing before long, and that would surely decrease her chances of finding a partner until the baby was born. Why was she still hanging out with him? Could it be she was looking for a father for her baby? He wasn't Daddy material any more than she seemed the stay-at-home Mom type. But what type was she? She seemed to be unique, not fitting any category he could come up with. Which might have explained the attraction, as he was drawn to the mysterious and unusual. And she was certainly that, totally unlike her mother except in her physical beauty.

Which led to him remembering with horror they were going to her mother's for Thanksgiving dinner. Why did her mother have to be Helen Mueller? Thank God she was shacked up with some guy, or so Sally had said, so she probably wouldn't be too harsh to him. He could hope.

Sally began to stir as she woke up, and Red finally gave in to the need to go the bathroom. When he returned, Sally was mostly awake, but still lying naked in bed, not even trying to cover herself with the sheet, as beautiful as any painting he'd ever seen of a naked woman. She had him wrapped around her little finger and liking it. "So are you going to come back to bed and wake me up properly?" she purred as she stretched her long legs out.

He couldn't take his eyes off her. "You must be under the impression that I'm 30 years old. How many times do you think I can do it in a 24-hour period?"

She looked intently at a certain part of him as if to say she knew he had at least one time left in him, and it pleased him, no, *relieved* him, that he was able to respond to her wishes. He wondered how long he could keep up with her appetites. At some level, he was willing to die trying. His rational mind waved a red flag, but he wasn't having any of it.

Later, after they had showered together, he broke down and asked what he'd been wondering all along. "Did you tell your Mom about me?" He continued toweling his wet body, hoping he sounded casual.

She turned as she hung her towel up and gave him a look which included an intense and approving scan of his naked body. "Of course, silly. But I didn't give her your name or details."

His stomach clenched. Just what he was afraid of. "Are you trying to make an entrance of some kind? Give your Mom a heart attack? You should have told her. You know I met her when I was working on a case."

Sally smiled a secret smile. "Yes, I know. You told me. I got her impressions of you without letting on anything about us. She thought you were good-looking and a very serious cop. And you made her nervous. She also wonders why you're called 'Red'. You've never told me. Why do you go by that name?"

He shook his head reproachfully. "Sally, don't try to distract me. Do you want to make trouble at Thanksgiving dinner? Are you using me to get back at your family for something?"

She frowned as if disappointed in him. "Of course not. Wait 'til you see the rest of my family. You could make a movie out of us. My older siblings will claim the spotlight. They're upset about Alexander. I can't imagine why a rich, handsome man would threaten them, but they're both angry at Mom and not trying to hide it. No one will even notice us in the drama they'll stir up."

He was beginning to doubt the wisdom of accepting her invitation to Thanksgiving dinner, but it was too late to back out. "I guess we'll just make the best of it. I wish you'd told her you asked me out first."

She looked wide-eyed at him. "Whatever for?"

Was she serious? "So she wouldn't think I was a pervert or a cradle robber. I threw out your business card. If you hadn't called me, we wouldn't be here." That sounded almost judgmental towards her and surely painted him as insecure. He kicked himself mentally. What was she doing to him?

Locking eyes with him, she came over and wrapped her arms around his waist, giving him a full body hug that surprisingly awakened appetites he thought had been taken care of. She ground her hips against him and looked into his eyes. "I want you. We have time before we have to leave..." She didn't have to ask him twice.

In the car, he decided to answer her question about his name. They'd been together long enough, and it wasn't a big deal, anyway, though he had a tendency to guard personal information like that. "You asked earlier how I got the name Red. My real name is Eric, but no one ever calls me that anymore. Years ago, when I was on a case, we got into a pretty bad situation with a perp who pulled a knife on me and cut me up before I was able to shoot him. By the time the fracas was over, I had blood all over me; mine and his. My partner started calling me Eric the Red, like the Viking, and somehow the name stuck and got shortened to just Red."

Sally reached over and touched his arm tenderly. "So that's how you got those scars? I was wondering, but didn't want to ask."

"Yup. Those are my souvenirs of a crazy homicidal maniac. Whenever

I think I'm bored with what I do or missing the old job, I look at them and tell myself I was lucky to live through that, and it's good to be alive and bored." He almost believed it, too; he'd told himself often enough.

Sally squeezed his arm and said nothing, unlike most women he'd known. It was times like this he appreciated her even more.

As they parked in front of Alexander's palatial house, Red thought of his small condo and had to wrestle with a new type of insecurity. He hoped this wasn't a sample of how the day was going to play out. When they rang the doorbell, an urbane, silver-haired man answered, looking first at him, then at Sally. "Sally, come on in." He opened the door and ushered them inside, hugging Sally (she reciprocated with more enthusiasm than Red felt was warranted, and he swallowed an uncomfortable flash of jealousy). The man who must be Alexander was his height and looked him straight in the eye, holding his hand out as if nothing were unusual. "So you're the mystery date." They shook hands cordially. Maybe it wouldn't be so bad after all. Sally didn't introduce them, so he spoke up. "My name's Red Johnson. Thanks for inviting me."

The meal turned out to be restaurant quality; the company, stilted. Sally was right that no one was going to notice them with the anger pouring off her brother and sister as thick as tar and as poisonous as toxic waste, though everyone tried not to acknowledge it. At least the kids seemed to be having fun, squabbling about who was going to get the wishbone. Helen gave him a look; a strange one he couldn't decipher. It conveyed acceptance, curiosity and... approval? It was almost as if the surprise of him wasn't unwelcome. That gave him pause. There must be a reason Helen didn't seem to object to him as her daughter's lover, and there was no doubt in his mind that she knew he was sleeping with Sally, knowing how Sally liked to flaunt things. So much to figure out.

He was truly in need of sleep by the time dinner was over. On the way home, he wanted to say something pleasant, but was too tired to think of how to say it. "That was interesting."

"You must be either Chinese or ironic." Sally's voice was laced with sadness. "My family is way beyond interesting. You're lucky my Dad isn't still alive. At least Alexander seems to be a decent guy."

He wouldn't go there now, but he'd remind himself to find out later.

"Look, I'll drop you at your place, then I'll go home. I need to get some sleep. I'm on duty tomorrow."

"You can sleep at my place, can't you?" she said in her little girl voice.

"You know damn well I can't sleep at your place." He grinned, and she acted petulant, although he could tell she got the compliment.

Finally, she gave in with a grudging attitude. "All right, go home and sleep. But when will I see you again? Has my family scared you off?"

"Not hardly. I just need some rest. I'm not as young as you are." He was feeling every year of his age right about now and wishing it weren't so. But he wasn't going to give her any more ammunition by telling her how much he wished he could keep up with her.

She reached over and touched his arm. "Promise you'll call me tomorrow."

"I'll call." He was touched and reassured by her insistence.

They drove the rest of the way in silence, and after dropping her off, he wondered just where this was going. At least with one night stands, you knew what was what, but this wasn't a one night stand. And she was too young to be marriage material for him, wasn't she? So what was going on? She acted like she was crazy about him, but he still couldn't get it to compute. Was there some other type of relationship kids her age indulged in? He felt he was playing a game for which he didn't know the rules. And that really bothered him. His cop's intuition was saying it would all end badly, but his hormones were saying go for it. He'd think about it tomorrow. One good thing for sure: he wasn't spending as much time thinking about Owen Schmidt lately.

* * *

Owen, 4:00pm

OWEN LOOKED at the calendar in his kitchen. He'd been marking off the days. In five days Tanya would be released from rehab. Today was Thanksgiving, but holidays meant nothing to him. He couldn't recall a happy holiday in his life. His plans were no more ambitious than a TV dinner, a football game and working on his train set.

The meal was nothing special, but it was easy to fix and clean up after.

The game was a bust, but he was really enjoying working on the scenery in his train set. Everything was to scale like in a museum. The steam engine chugged along the track, going over trestle bridges and through tunnels in mountains while he crafted details of the train station in the little village. The people were dressed in clothing of over 100 years ago. The environment looked like Austria or maybe somewhere in England that had large hills.

Working on the set was therapy for Owen, though he didn't consciously regard it as such. It was peaceful and meditative. It consumed his focus and grounded him. After about an hour, he was satisfied with his progress and quit. Standing in the doorway, he surveyed the world he had created. It was beautiful and orderly. The women knew their place and behaved. He could control every aspect of life in that world in a way he couldn't outside his house.

The phone rang, and Owen was surprised that he hoped it would be Tanya. He had only heard from her once. She didn't get phone privileges often. He ran to the phone and answered. "Hello?"

"It's me, darling. Happy Thanksgiving." Her voice caressed him in a way that soothed and excited all at once.

"I'm glad you called." He wasn't comfortable with talking on the phone or with talking in general. But she had never criticized him, so he made an effort. "I'm not doing anything. I wish you were here."

"Oh, baby, so do I. I know just what I'd do with you if I were there." And she proceeded to tell him in glorious detail that had him so pumped up he thought he'd explode. He no longer thought of her as a whore. She was his woman. She'd made it clear she was his exclusively and thought he was the biggest and best man she'd ever met.

"I'm going to do those things in person as soon as I get out. Will you meet me?"

"You know I will."

"Oh, bother, some asshole ratted me out. I'm not supposed to be on the phone. They're going to come make me hang up. I'll call you when I get out." She hung up. Stunned, he held the phone and looked at it. He'd always been the one to hang up first.

He shook off his discomfort at being hung up on. He had a lot to look forward to. They had the perfect setup; being able to be with Tanya occasionally while still having his own personal space somehow made his life feel complete. He hadn't given a thought to going on the road in a while. Life was just about perfect.

He put the phone in the base and went to watch some TV, but all he could think about was his next meeting with Tanya. She liked to talk about making memories. For the first time he could remember, he felt thankful on Thanksgiving.

* * *

Tanya, 4:15pm

TANYA WAS PISSED about getting caught on the phone by two staff members. They had ruined the rush she got from finally hearing the hunger in his voice. She just wanted to bask in Owen's sexual longing for her. He was so easy to manipulate, like a teenage boy almost. The standoffishness she'd sensed early on had evaporated. It had been so long since a man had treated her the way he did, as if she were a goddess. She intended to keep him on a string for as long as possible. Five more days and she was out of here; she'd find a way to see him.

She was sitting in the common area daydreaming about sex with Owen when her husband walked into the room. She'd forgotten about the stupid family dinner they were having tonight, but she was surprised to see him. He hadn't visited at all during her stay. She closed her eyes and wished he'd be gone when she opened them, but no such luck. He was still there, a blot on her day.

He came and sat down in a chair next to her. "Tanya. I'm not staying for the dinner. I came because I felt it was only fair to tell you in person. I'm filing for divorce. I believe we have enough investments that I can buy your share of the house, and then you're free to do what you wish. I'll offer you fair alimony until and unless you marry or cohabit again. If you prefer, we can sell the house and split the difference. Either way, it's over. I can't take it anymore."

She was speechless. He'd never stood up to her like this. He rarely seemed to have an original thought. Now *he* wanted to leave *her*? What nerve he had! "What am I supposed to do when they release me in five days? Where am I supposed to live?"

"You can live at the house, but we're going to sign a separation agreement about the property as soon as you return. Then either I'll move out or you will. I don't much care which."

"You can't do this to me. I gave you the best years of my life. I worked to put you through law school, and I stayed with you. Now you want to make me homeless. You have an obligation to take care of me."

"I'm tired of killing each other slowly. I want a life. For that matter, this will allow you to choose to do whatever you want to do with *your* life. I doubt you'll pull it together, but this may be your last chance. I don't want to be a part of this train wreck anymore. I'll pick you up the day they release you, and we'll go to a lawyer and settle about the property. Be thinking about the terms you want. I intend to have this over soon. You'll get more by cooperating. You know that I have the ability to either be fair or see that you get nothing. Don't test me." He stood up and left without another word.

She sat shell-shocked at the steel in his voice. Divorce? 'Don't test me?' She never imagined he'd have the balls to do it. Certainly, it would mean less money, and she didn't like that. But the more she thought about it, the better she felt overall. This was actually good news. She would be free to be with Owen publicly. No need to sneak around. She needed to find a sharp lawyer and make sure she got as much as possible from him.

The thought of being able to focus completely on making Owen hers was intoxicating. Yes, maybe this was the perfect outcome. She wished she could call Owen and tell him, but she'd be free soon enough. For now, she needed to think about the property settlement and what she would ask for. She intended to get what was coming to her. It would be a wonderful surprise for Owen to find out she could be with him all the time and in public.

* * *

Mary Beth, 4:20pm

THE FRAGRANCES of a homemade Italian meal swirled around Mary Beth as she stood at the sink washing dishes to keep up with the mess associated with making a banquet. They'd eat leftovers for a week. What the hell; it was worth it.

Mom dozed on the couch in front of the TV, which was blaring so loudly Mary Beth could hardly hear herself think, even a room away. Mom needed a hearing aid, but good luck getting her to admit it. How could anyone sleep through that racket?

There was no use pretending. Mom was fading. Time was, she'd never have allowed Mary Beth to clean *her* kitchen. Every holiday Mary Beth could remember, Mom was busy from dawn until dusk, cleaning and cooking and then cleaning some more. It seemed so unnatural to have her in the next room snoozing, worn out simply from cooking Thanksgiving dinner, even though it was the biggest meal they'd cooked in forever.

It was time to face facts. Mom was old. She couldn't be on her own anymore. She was a shadow of her former self. Sometimes she felt tearful that her feisty Mom was gone, replaced by a weakened, dependent old woman afraid to speak her mind. For years she'd prayed for peace and quiet, and now that she had it, she missed the old Mom.

She opened a bottle of wine and poured a glass for each of them and carried them into the living room. She put the glasses down and turned off the TV. Strangely, the silence appeared to wake Mom, who opened her eyes, closed her mouth and looked around in disorientation. "Hey, Mom, I brought us a glass of wine. The food will be ready in a while, and I thought we could just chill."

Mom smiled at her beatifically, so un-Momlike, then spotted the glass in front of her on the coffee table and reached for it. "We should talk about all the things we're thankful for. I'll start. I'm grateful that you're here with me. I'm sorry your marriage fell apart, but it was a blessing for me. I don't know what I'd do without you." She raised her glass in salute.

Mary Beth's mouth hung open, surprised at such a declaration. She recovered fairly quickly, though, and got into the spirit of things. "I'm grateful I'm able to be here, and I appreciate that you took me in when I had nowhere to go." They clinked glasses and sipped wine.

Mom hadn't finished. "I'm thankful that Mrs. Jameson hasn't turned us in for violating the covenants."

Mary Beth nodded. "Maybe we misjudged her. She's a snoop, but maybe she wasn't turning people in."

"That's possible. And I'm grateful you found a job you like. You still like it, don't you?" Mom looked searchingly at her.

"Yeah, Ma, it's a nice job and gives me a lot of freedom. I'm grateful for it. I'm also grateful that Helen introduced me to Maddie, because I'm having fun making jewelry."

"I love the things you make." Mom reached up to touch her latest earrings in appreciation.

"I guess we're about the luckiest people I know," said Mary Beth, putting her free arm around Mom's shoulders. Mom murmured in affirmation.

The ringing of the phone catapulted Mary Beth from the sofa in surprise.

"Who could that be?" asked Mom.

Mary Beth shook her head. "Maybe it's a wrong number." As she picked up the phone, before she could even say hello, Ethan's voice boomed out. "Happy Thanksgiving, Mary Beth!" She nearly dropped the phone in shock.

Looking at the question in Mom's eyes, she mouthed, "It's for me," which didn't wipe the look of speculation off Mom's face. In a hopeless play for time, she replied, "Happy Thanksgiving! I didn't expect you to call. How are things going?" She couldn't remember which person Ethan was spending the holiday with back East. She let him answer, not listening too carefully, while she cast about trying to figure out how she could explain the call to Mom. There was nothing going on between her and Ethan except that they'd fallen into the habit of standing outside talking every Saturday before leaving Maddie's, and she'd never mentioned him. Now Mom would make all kinds of assumptions and judgments. Damn, shit, hell.

"Mary Beth, can you hear me over this racket? They have the game going in the background." Ethan's voice pierced her confused musings. She wasn't even sure how to explain him to herself, and now this.

"I'm sorry. Yes, I can hear you fine." It *was* good to hear his voice, even if it was going to get Mom going. "I didn't expect you to call me."

"Of course, I wanted to call you and wish you a Happy Thanksgiving. Did I catch you before you ate?"

"Yes, dinner is still cooking. We were just enjoying a glass of wine and sharing all the things we are grateful for that happened this year."

There was a pause on the other end of the line. "I'm grateful I met you." His voice was softer all of a sudden. She wasn't sure how to respond, really not wanting to make any kind of declaration in front of Mom, not sure she was ready in any case. It was like being back in high school. If only she had answered the phone in her room.

"Likewise," she whispered, embarrassed to say more with Mom hanging on her every word. *Now* Mom was wide awake and had perfect hearing. Why couldn't she catch a break? She hadn't even figured out what was going on with her and Ethan, and now Mom would demand to know. Shit!

"Are you having a whole turkey, just the two of you?"

She'd been able to tell from the first that small talk wasn't his thing, and suddenly it touched her that he had gone to this extent to connect with her. It had to mean something. She just wasn't sure what.

"No, we're being unconventional and having a traditional Italian meal. We'll have to eat leftovers for a week. We don't know how to cook for two."

"I'll come over and help eat leftovers. I like Italian food."

It sounded like he was fishing for an invitation. How was she supposed to answer that? If she invited him over for dinner, he'd have to meet Mom, and who knows how that would work out? It wouldn't be kind to him, and it was premature for her. She hadn't decided what to do about Ethan. But that had just been taken out of her hands. She could tell Mom was practically drooling to hear who she was talking to. Might as well take the plunge. "We'll invite you over for a proper meal. You don't have to eat leftovers."

"That would be great!"

She looked at Mom's intense expression. "Maybe it will, and maybe it won't. You don't know what you're in for." She smiled at Mom, hoping she wasn't giving much away.

"I just know I'd like to spend time visiting with you sitting down sometime, instead of standing out by the cars every week. I'm happy to take you out to dinner if you prefer. You don't have to cook for me."

"Nonsense. The women in my family like to cook. If you're up for spending time with me and Mom, we'd love to have you come over some night after you get back here."

"It's a date! I'll let you go. They're hollering at me to come watch the football game."

"OK. Talk to you later. Thanks for calling..." *I think,* she said to herself as she hung up the phone, her head spinning. He was calling it a date. Was that on purpose? Was she dating Ethan now? Jesus!

She walked back the couch and picked up her wineglass, painfully aware that Mom was going to pounce and she had no defenses. So she took the offensive. "That was Ethan."

"Who's Ethan?" demanded Mom, a shade of her former self coming through in flinty tones.

"He's a volunteer with The Helpers. You know, the people who help out residents who can't do for themselves. I met him at Maddie's. He comes on Saturdays, the same time as I do."

"Really? Why haven't you told me about him?" Mom asked accusingly.

"There wasn't anything to tell. We chat a bit sometimes before I drive home. That's all."

"Then what's he doing calling you long distance?"

"I wish I knew, Ma, but it isn't a big deal. Lots of people have free long distance these days."

Mom looked at her in disbelief. "He's looking for some kind of trophy wife, probably. How old is he?"

"He lives here...he's about 60 and a widower. I don't think he's looking for anything, Mom. He's probably just lonely."

"So what's this about him coming over for dinner?" Mom had been waiting to play that card and looked slyly at her.

"He practically invited himself over. What could I do? Besides, he's a nice guy. You'll like him."

"He's after you."

"Really, Mom, he's just a friend."

"Men and women can't be friends."

"Now they can, Mom. At least sometimes." Mom shook her head but seemed too tired to fight about it. "Do you mind if he comes over here? He offered to take me to dinner, but that would be too much like a real date." Mary Beth was embarrassed to admit she was afraid he might be interested in her, though she couldn't see why.

As if she had read her mind, Mom said, "He'd be lucky to get a pretty young girl like you. Why wouldn't he be interested? You shouldn't put yourself down." It seemed strange to have Mom defend her.

"I'm 10 pounds overweight. I smoke. I cuss too much. I have a low-rent job...and, oh, I'm divorced. Yeah, I'm a real catch."

"Enough of that. You invite him over, and we'll make a nice dinner. Then you can see what he wants. They're no good at hiding it for long, and good food will loosen his tongue." Her Mom, the psychologist.

Mary Beth got up and turned on the TV to end the discussion.

* * *

Samantha, 4:55pm

SAMANTHA BUSTLED around the kitchen in final preparations for the Thanksgiving meal. The pecan and pumpkin pies she had made yesterday sat at the far end of the counter. The turkey was nearly ready, and her parents would arrive soon. It was a pleasure to be able to cook holiday meals for them.

The weather was unseasonably warm, and she was dressed in her nicest pair of shorts, sandals and top, her hair in a fancy braid that had taken her 20 minutes to do. Some of her mother's more casual jewelry completed her outfit. The front and back doors were open, the screen doors allowing the gentle, warm breeze to travel lazily through the living area.

Arthur had set the table at her request, God bless him. She'd felt so distant from him lately as she tried to get back into the groove of her old life. Somehow, she had changed. She didn't fit in her own life anymore. It disturbed her terribly, and she had no one to confide in, no sounding board to bounce ideas off of. Most days, she just went through the motions, hoping that she'd change back, but it hadn't happened yet. Arthur hadn't said a word. Maybe he hadn't noticed. Almost three weeks had passed since she turned down Jack's offer, and things weren't getting better.

Once or twice a day, when she was on her own, she took Jack's business card out of her purse and looked at it. She weighed the pros and cons of accepting his job offer. It was a dream job for sure, but the price and risk were too high. People were counting on her. She'd spent her whole life trying to win the approval of her parents. Though she never really felt successful at that, this was something that was almost guaranteed to lead to judgment and rejection.

Her mind came back to the task at hand. Since they had only one oven, the potatoes had to be cooked on the grill, but Arthur was in charge of that and had assured her they were doing well. She opened a can of cranberry sauce, the smooth kind her parents liked, and put in on the small serving dish with a horn of plenty motif. She'd tried to make homemade for them one year, and they hadn't liked it. They liked what they were used to. So instead of the more adventurous meal she would have chosen for herself, she made what she called the traditional O'Neill Thanksgiving dinner. The menu was baked potatoes, a roast turkey with Pepperidge Farm stuffing (not the cubed one, the finer one), homemade gravy, cranberry sauce (not with whole berries), homemade rolls and a green vegetable, which this year was peas, and two kinds of pie for dessert, since not everyone liked pumpkin.

It pleased Samantha to put on a nice dinner for her family, so she did it fairly often, but Thanksgiving was special, so she had pulled out all the stops. She and Arthur didn't decorate much for holidays, but she'd made a centerpiece for the dining room table that was more reminiscent of fall back East than fall in the desert. The cut glass bowl had cute little pumpkin-like gourds and silk flowers in fall colors. The tablecloth was green, and she had candles at each end. She wasn't sure they were going to be used, but they added a touch of elegance. Her good silverware was set with the cloth napkins she reserved for special occasions. She only had one set of china, and it wasn't even china. It was a nice set of stoneware. It would do fine, though.

Arthur came back inside from the patio. "The potatoes are coming along nicely. I think we can leave them there until it's time to serve dinner."

"Thanks. Everything is ready or almost ready here. They should be here any minute."

Arthur came into the kitchen and stood next to Samantha as she checked the peas simmering in a pot on the back burner. She tensed up involuntarily, a defensive posture that was becoming a habit for her. His voice penetrated her defenses. "Are you ever going to tell me what's wrong?"

She cringed at his words. So she hadn't gotten away with it. "What are you talking about?"

"Look, if you don't want to tell me, fine, but I know you've been distracted and upset for weeks. Is it something I did?" Arthur actually seemed concerned about her opinion of him. *How unusual.*

"I'm sorry I haven't been myself lately. I'm just going through a bad patch. It isn't your fault. It's all me." She continued to fiddle with knobs and dials just to avoid looking at him.

"I'm glad I didn't do anything, but since it's been going on for a while, maybe you should tell me. Perhaps I can help." His voice wasn't demanding, but she could tell he was fed up with being in the dark.

"I got a job offer a few weeks ago. There was a guy in class who has a landscaping company, and he offered me a good position. But it would be a long commute that would add at least 90 minutes to my workday; I wouldn't be able to stop by my parents or have lunch with you every day; I'd have to give the truck back to Julio, and I'm not sure I'd get one from Jack."

"Jack who?" Arthur sounded jealous, which was the last thing she wanted. She had turned Jack down, so he had no right to act territorial.

"Jack Temple of Temple Landscaping. We were partnered on the Saturday project, and he liked my ideas. He said he was looking for someone he could trust to take over the design and installation part of his business. It's grown too large for him to do it all himself. I didn't let him go into the details of the offer. All I know is he promised to make it financially worthwhile. But he couldn't give me all the perks I now have, so I turned him down. There was no point considering it." She felt she was being very rational and reasonable, and he should see what a good choice she'd made.

"So why are you upset? If it was such a clear choice, shouldn't you feel good about it? You seem upset because you said 'no'. Are you sure you made the right decision?"

No, of course I'm not. I did the 'right' thing, but I'm not happy with it. Finally, she looked Arthur in the eye. She was shocked to see her fear reflected in his brown eyes. It was as if he knew her secret. Immediately, she was swamped with guilt. She hadn't done anything, but she still felt shame, simply because she wanted to be selfish. How much did he know?

He put his hand on her shoulder. "I know things haven't been the same with us for the last several years, but you stuck with me, even though you could have cut and run. I know how much you love your job. I also realize how stressful it is in some ways. Have you thought that maybe you're upset because you aren't used to doing something just for you? Maybe it's time you did something for Samantha. I think we can all manage to stumble along even if you take a job where you can't be home as much. Your parents and I would miss you, but you aren't exactly good company like this."

She felt tears well in her eyes. She hated how she'd been acting and feeling. He was right. Going through the motions wasn't enough. She needed to want to do what she was doing. She needed to get that motivation back. "You're right. I didn't want to make a selfish decision. I still don't. I just need to get back to my old self."

"I want you to consider taking the job. At the very least, find out exactly what the details are. If it's as good as it sounds, you should take it. Your family should support you. It shouldn't all be one-way."

She was mortified that he was urging her to consider a job that she knew in her heart could endanger their marriage, but she couldn't tell him that. "After the holiday is over, I'll find out the details. But I still don't think I'll want to take the job. I'd have to give up too much, and it's kind of late in life for me to be putting a career ahead of taking care of my family."

Just then the doorbell rang, saving her further rationalization. She and Arthur went to greet her parents. Mom had a bottle of red wine, and

Dad was carrying his ubiquitous sweater, a nod to his sensitivity to cold of any kind.

Samantha was relieved that their arrival had interrupted the conversation, but she knew it wasn't over. Would she really risk calling Jack? If she did, just so she could satisfy Arthur, was that fair to Jack, making him think she was considering the job? Worse yet, if she called him and the terms were favorable, how could she turn it down with Arthur being so intent on supporting her? *What a mess!*

* * *

Jean, 4:55pm

THE PHONE RANG, and Jean ran to pick it up before Richard could get the extension in the other room.

"Hi, Jean, it's me."

She let out a breath she hadn't realized she was holding. "Hi, Lydia. You're still coming, aren't you?" She panicked at the thought of Lydia backing out now.

"Of course. I just wanted to let you know I'm leaving now. Is Richard OK with me coming to dinner?"

"I don't care whether he is or not. You're coming. He won't act up." She whispered so Richard wouldn't hear.

"Have you packed a bag?"

"Yes, I packed it yesterday. It's in my closet. I haven't had the nerve to say anything. Somehow it feels wrong to do this on Thanksgiving."

"There's not going to be any good time to do it, and it's best if you have someone there when you tell him. I'm not saying he'd get violent, but it's just wise not to be alone at times like that. This will work out fine."

"I'll feel better once you're here. I have to admit, I have no appetite at all. I just want this over."

"You're cooking him a real nice meal before you leave, and you aren't running off without telling him. That would be abandonment. We want it witnessed that you are separating rather than abandoning him. That will make the paperwork easier."

"We'll get through dinner and then I'll come to your place. I can't tell you how grateful I am for you offering me a place to stay. I'll get myself sorted out soon. I won't overstay my welcome."

"You can stay as long as you want. I have enough room."

They said their goodbyes and Jean went back to the cooking. The turkey breast was nearly done. It had seemed wise to cook something simple, since she wasn't hanging around to help much after the meal. He was going to have to learn how to care for himself at some point, so it could start today.

It wasn't even a month ago she'd first talked to Ian, yet it seemed like a lifetime. She couldn't wait to get out of this house. She had reservations about leaving Richard on Thanksgiving day, but Lydia was right; there would never be a 'good' day to do it. And she was grateful for Lydia's presence. It would guarantee things wouldn't go off the rails. He wouldn't want Jean to air their dirty laundry in front of Lydia. He wasn't aware she knew it all already.

By the second phone call she'd made to him, Ian had confessed that he felt something between them, too. He even said he'd done a tarot reading that clearly said she was coming to the UK. She found that hard to believe. Not that she'd never traveled abroad, but it just seemed such an extreme thing to do. Extreme, but at this point, it was the next logical step.

Once she'd decided, her mind was overwhelmed with all she had to do before leaving. She would need to set the divorce in motion and remove her possessions and store them before she could go see Ian, but that wouldn't take more than a couple of weeks. She was sure that Richard would be eager to do it quickly and wouldn't put up too much of a fuss. She hoped he'd want to buy her out of her half of the house. She didn't want to live in this house again. It seemed tainted.

She and Ian had only planned to meet and see how things went. He would let her stay at his place, but there were no promises made. She was growing more attached to him each time they spoke, and he seemed to feel affection for her, so she had hopes that her intuition and dowsing were correct, and that he was the life partner she'd always wanted. Her rational mind wasn't totally on board, as she often had fearful thoughts of how her life could turn out if she were wrong about Ian, but she just pushed them aside.

As she mulled all these things while stirring the gravy, Richard stepped into the kitchen. "Is there something you want me to do?" He'd been more solicitous of her feelings lately, almost as if he knew their relationship was on the rocks.

In a way, she felt sorry for him, but she couldn't take it anymore. She felt a pang of guilt for the hurt she knew he'd feel, but pushed it aside. "No, it's all taken care of. We'll be eating in about 15 minutes. Lydia is on her way over. You could pour some wine."

He got wine glasses and a chilled bottle of white wine and opened it. He poured them both a glass and put hers on the counter next to her. Then after being assured there was nothing else he could do, he went out into the living room and sat in a chair to read until the meal was served.

Jean saw Lydia's car pull into the driveway and felt immense relief. Now, things would be easier. She wouldn't be alone.

The meal was quiet but uneventful, and before she knew it, they were gathering dishes to take them to the kitchen to be washed. Richard was once again in the living room, having ceded the kitchen to the women. Lydia and she made fast work of loading the dishwasher, washing pots and pans and putting away leftovers. When it was nearly done, Lydia turned to her and whispered, "Go talk with him now. Then immediately get your suitcase and we'll leave. Do you have more than one packed?"

"No, just the one big one."

"OK. I'll stand by for moral support, but I'll stay out of sight so he doesn't feel we're ganging up on him."

Jean forced herself to dry her hands and go out into the living room. She stood by Richard's chair and waited to get his attention. He looked up at her as if he knew what she was going to say. And maybe he did. They'd been dancing around it for so long. Maybe it would be a relief to him to get it out in the open.

Her mouth was dry and her throat was tense. She had to push the words out. "Richard, I'm moving out. Lydia is letting me stay with her until I find my own place. I'm going to file for divorce. I'll have my lawyer contact you with details about a proposed property settlement."

"Divorce? You want a divorce? Are you sure?" For someone who had appeared to anticipate her, he seemed bemused.

"I can't make it work with you, Richard. Things have gotten too out of hand. You know what I mean. I think we're both going to be better off going our separate ways. I tried to hold it together, but things have changed too much, and there's no getting them back to the way they were. I promise I will be fair, and I won't be hurling accusations as long as you don't; we'll go no fault. I won't ask for unreasonable things. I don't wish you ill. We just don't fit anymore."

He grimaced but kept silent, and she paused only for a few moments, then left to get her suitcase. Lydia met her at the front door, and they went out to her car and loaded her suitcase into the trunk.

Richard stood at the front door, saying and doing nothing. He just stared. She was relieved it had gone so smoothly. She only hoped that the next few weeks would be quick and easy. She wanted to get on a plane to the UK.

Lydia looked at her as they drove down the road. "I know you feel bad, but you did the right thing."

"It doesn't make it any easier. I hate being the one to hurt people."

"People are responsible for their own feelings. He'll deal with it however he deals with it. It isn't your job to make him happy. You tried, and he obviously wasn't. Maybe being shaken up will be good for him. Perhaps it will help him make some positive changes in his life. Either way, it's his responsibility."

Jean sighed. "I'm glad this part is over. I'm calling Ian when we get to your place even though it's late there. I have to tell him I went through with it. This whole thing is like something out of a movie. I can't believe it's happening. I've fallen for a man I've never met. He lives in another country. I'm getting divorced so I can go meet him and see if we belong together like I think we do. How preposterous is that?"

"I think it's romantic."

They drove the rest of the way in silence.

* * *

Alexander, 9:30pm

ALEXANDER POURED a splash of sherry into two glasses, glancing over at Helen on the sofa. In the dim light from the single lamp, she lay back, eyes shut, drained after entertaining her family all day.

Atypically, she'd chosen to wear a dress today, a simple turquoise and white sundress with a Hawaiian theme. Her recently styled strawberry-blonde hair, smooth skin and trim body would be the envy of a much younger woman, but she had an endearing lack of vanity about her beauty. Her grace and elegance must be genetic, because she'd been blessed with few advantages in life. Still, it left her genuine, one of the few he'd ever met, and he was in love with her.

He'd been inordinately pleased today that she wore the necklace he'd bought her. She was fond of her friend Maddie's creations and claimed to need no further jewelry, but he had wanted to give her something as beautiful as she was, and her reaction to the large topaz in an artistic gold setting was everything he could have wished for. It twinkled in the lamplight, giving him a primitive satisfaction of having marked her as his.

He also had to admit to himself that it was a relief to be with a woman who didn't know how to use sex or beauty to manipulate a man. He hadn't realized how much energy he'd expended over the years keeping his guard up. With her, he could relax and be himself.

As he sat down next to her, one glass in each hand, Helen roused and smiled endearingly, reaching for her wine.

"I'm not sure how much more I should drink. I think I'm over my limit due to stress." In spite of her protests, she sipped the sherry with an appreciative murmur.

"At last I have you to myself." He grinned at her with purpose.

She sighed as if the weight of the world had slipped off her pretty shoulders. "To be honest, I wish you'd had me to yourself all day, instead of this circus." She grimaced. "I hope it hasn't changed your mind about wanting to marry me. I didn't dream your proposal, did I?"

His heart melted at the slight wavering in her voice. "Do I seem that fickle to you?"

"Lena and Warren were on the warpath. They were almost rude to you and barely pleasant to me."

He patted her hand. "They just worry about you. They don't want you to get hurt."

She sighed and squeezed his hand. "They aren't worried about me. They don't like the idea of losing control of me...oh, they don't matter. They'll either come around or not. I don't really care." She looked fiercely at him, as if daring him to disagree.

He searched for something positive to say. "At least Sally seemed to be OK about us."

"That was a bit of a shock, wasn't it, finding out she's hooked up with Red Johnson?" She shook her head. "I hope that man knows what he's getting into."

Alexander laughed. "What man does? I think he knows what he wants to know. You're not worried about Sally?"

"I'm worried about *him*. He's not her type. He's not flashy. He's not incompetent. He has a mind of his own and probably will show it once the sex stops being the main attraction. She'll tire of him or think he's too straight-laced. I wish she *would* fall for him, but I can't see it happening."

"You don't mind the age difference?"

"Not at all, but in the end, I think *she* will. And he seems to be such a nice guy. He's in over his head. I hope he doesn't get hurt." She leaned against his chest and sighed. "Love is so confusing and complicated."

"I have to admit I liked him, but I don't know either of them well enough to guess how it will turn out. Seems like she'd be smart to find a man who likes kids and start building a family. But what do I know?" He held her close. "I missed out on a lot in my life by the choices I made, and I'm not missing out on anything else."

Helen kissed him and looked him straight in the eye. "That toast at dinner was excellent. You really took the chill off when you proposed it. I don't think they expected such generosity of spirit. They were thinking you'd be defensive. You disarmed them." Then she kissed him again more thoroughly.

He chuckled and kissed her back. "Remind me to propose a toast more often."

She pushed his shoulder gently. "Stop being so modest. Things would have been much worse if you'd let them get to you today."

That triggered a tangential thought. "Hey, what was that conversation about Lou's financial records about?"

Her left eyebrow shot up. "You don't miss much, do you?"

"You had a real eureka look on your face, but you seemed not to want to share, so I kept quiet."

"I did have a eureka moment. I haven't had a chance to tell you, and I have no intention of telling the kids yet. So much has happened, it slipped my mind. I have a mystery to solve!" Her childlike enthusiasm was contagious.

"A mystery! You have my attention. Tell me or I'll pinch you." He hugged her closer and nuzzled her neck.

"If that's how you're going to be...when I was going through Lou's stuff a while back, I found a safe deposit box key, but he had no accounts here locally. I gave up trying to figure it out when the move happened, and I haven't thought about it since. I believe the box is back home. That's the account Warren was asking about. I'd forgotten all about that one."

Alexander thought about the things people put in a safe deposit box. It could be anything. "Do you know what's in it?"

She play punched him again. "No, silly. That's why I said it's a mystery. But at the same time I found the key, I found an envelope with $5000 cash in it. Can you imagine? Lou always acted like we were so poor. We never had money for anything. So I'm wondering if he had other assets he never told me about." A shadow crossed her face, and she frowned.

What a jerk that guy was, lying to her and hitting her. It got his blood up just thinking about him.

"What?" Helen had a worried look on her face.

"Just thinking what I'd do to Lou if he were still alive."

She laughed. "I'm glad he's gone, because now I have you." Her face became serious. "So I was thinking we need to make a trip to Wisconsin...if you're willing."

He pulled her up into his lap. "Absolutely. I'm ready to solve this mystery. When did you have in mind for this sleuthing trip?"

Her body relaxed, and she leaned against him. "Maybe Christmas? Two birds with one stone? I hate to mention it today after what you've been through, but it would be the most logical time to go." He felt her muscles tense again. So afraid of his displeasure. Maybe a leftover from Lou.

"I'll go whenever you say. It'll be fun to find out what's in the box." He stroked her arm, hoping to soothe her concerns. "And as for your kids, well, we'll handle them. I'm not going to let them come between us. We don't have to spend much time with them, after all."

She sighed deeply and kissed his neck. "Thank you for being you."

He decided it was time to plunge forward. "My pleasure. So let's talk about our wedding. Any thoughts?" He held his breath, hoping she wasn't going to wait for Lena and Warren to change their minds.

She sighed sadly. "I think we ought to have a simple ceremony with just us and maybe a few of our friends from here. The kids aren't going to come around anytime soon, and I don't feel like holding up my life for them."

He hugged her closer. "I'm sorry they're being so difficult, but I agree. Let's get hitched. Who would you like to invite?"

"I was thinking Jean, Lydia, Barbara, Mary Beth...Sally and Red if they want. No presents, of course. Just something very simple. Is there anyone you'd like to invite?"

He thought briefly. "I don't have anyone to invite. I haven't made any deep connections here except you." He kissed her cheek gently. "So do you want to go on a honeymoon?"

"We can go on a honeymoon?" Her voice radiated excitement.

"Of course, woman, I'm loaded. Where would you like to go?"

She paused briefly, then said with conviction. "I've always wanted to visit a tropical island paradise."

He smiled as he hatched the perfect plan for their honeymoon. "I think I know just the place."

Her eyes widened. "Tell me. Tell me."

He looked at her slyly and said, "I'll tell you in bed."

She leaped off his lap and grabbed his hand. "What are you waiting for?"

SECOND CHANCES: A PREVIEW

Monday, December 18, 1995
Mary Beth, 11:15am

The plastic grocery bags slipped from her grasp and landed on the floor of the entryway with a thunk. Mary Beth gasped at the scene before her, deaf to the rattle of a can rolling across the tiles then finally hitting the baseboard. Mom lay sprawled across the couch, her arms hanging over the edge as if reaching for something just beyond her grasp, the surprised look on her face hinting that her last moments had revealed something unexpected.

Recovering from momentary paralysis, Mary Beth dashed into the living room and knelt next to Mom's inert form, reaching for the neck, hoping vainly to find a pulse. Mom was gone, though her skin was still warm.

Seconds or hours later, she couldn't have said which, Mary Beth looked down as if from a great distance at her hands stroking Mom's gray hair, heard a heart-wrenching sob, and realized it was her own voice. "Mom, what happened?" she croaked. "Oh, God, why did I have to be away when you needed me?"

Desperate to do something, she stood and tried to think, but her head felt stuffed full of cotton balls. She closed her eyes to the terrible scene in front of her, pleading for it to disappear, but of course, it didn't. Then her brain finally kicked in. She needed to call 911. Not that they could fix this.

While she waited for an answer, she chastised herself. If she hadn't stopped on the way home, maybe she would have been here when it happened. Maybe she could have saved Mom.

She drummed her fingers on the countertop. *Christ, I need a cigarette!* Then it hit her that even though Mom never allowed smoking in the house, she could have one now if she wished. In typically bizarre fashion, her mind made a link between her desire to smoke and Mom's death, and her craving evaporated in a cloud of guilt. Thankfully, her call was answered quickly, and the barrage of questions distracted her from further self-punishment.

After the 911 call, she opened the front door and stepped into the brisk air to avoid looking at Mom's body. Within minutes, vehicles were pulling up with flashing lights, broadcasting that something bad had happened. Living in the Palm Lakes Senior Community made this type of occurrence fairly common, but it was different when it happened to you. She always said a quick prayer when she saw or heard an ambulance--the nuns had taught her to--but it was so personal now that prayer seemed pointless. Instead of hiding (she knew she couldn't, but the urge was almost overpowering), she steeled herself to facilitate the horrible process as uniformed people were disgorged from the Posse car, ambulance and fire engine.

A few curious neighbors appeared outside the doors of their condos or gathered on the edge of the street, held back as if by an invisible barrier, and Mary Beth swallowed the urge to shout at them for being such damn ghouls. Mom was always on her about her bad language. Then she realized it didn't matter any more what Mom thought. *Shit! Fuck! Damn!*

Across the street, short, plump Mrs. Jameson, a major busybody, stood on her front step, a surprisingly sympathetic look on her face. Funny, Mary Beth wouldn't have expected compassion from her. Mom had said she reported violations of the covenants, and Mary Beth had been avoiding the old hag for months, since she was too young to be a legal resident. In fact, all she had ever seen of Mrs. Jameson was a shadow spying from behind the curtain in her front window. It was hard to picture an elderly plump widow with bluish-silver hair and an outdated housedress as a closet Nazi. It just went to show that you couldn't judge people by how they look.

Mary Beth did her part, woodenly answering questions for emergency personnel and pointing in the direction of the living room, unwilling to go back inside. It was over quicker than she could have imagined. She stepped aside as the EMTs rolled the stretcher back through the doorway. She averted her gaze seconds too late to avoid seeing the body bag. As she listened to the metallic clanking of the stretcher being loaded into the vehicle, she realized that with her Mom dead, she was now technically homeless. Mom owned the condo, but Mary Beth was too young to legally live there or even own it. And certainly someone would notice now. How long would it take them to find out she was living there and make her sell?

The stark desert sunshine cast ugly shadows, the sun being low in the sky even near midday, and a chill breeze tugged at her jacket, reminding her of the season, though it didn't resemble winter back home. She wrapped the jacket more tightly around herself and got into her car to follow the ambulance.

On her return hours later, street lights bathed the empty road and deserted sidewalks, illuminating the chill night. Everything looked as it always did. It was as if nothing had happened. *If only.* She pulled into the garage and walked through the silent house, wishing she could turn back time and be greeted by Mom, even to face criticism for cussing or being late.

She glanced into the living room and wondered how she'd ever be able to sit on the couch again. The condo was so small, she didn't have much choice. Well, selling the place would solve that problem.

She shook her head and went into the kitchen and poured herself a glass of wine. Thank God she had a few bottles, because it was going to be a long, sleepless night. Sitting listlessly at the breakfast table, she stared out through the sliding glass door into the darkness of the back yard and wondered what was going to become of her.

Some time later, she startled back to reality and stared at the wine glass, unaware that she had emptied it, then refilled it and wished she had someone to talk to. That was the problem with being an illegal resident. Her co-worker at Palo Verde Landscaping, Samantha Taylor, had only begun to spend a little time with Mary Beth outside of work, and it didn't feel right to ask her for help, because Samantha was awfully busy with work and caring for her aging parents, who were also residents of Palm Lakes. Helen, her former next door neighbor, had married recently and moved to another part of the community with her gorgeous new husband Alexander. They'd gone on a honeymoon to the South Pacific, and Mary Beth wasn't even sure they were home yet. She missed her visits with Helen, who'd introduced her to Maddie (to her surprise, her coworker Samantha's mother), who had become her jewelry-making mentor. Making jewelry had brought joy into Mary Beth's life, giving her an outlet for her creative energy. But she couldn't turn to Maddie; Maddie was elderly and in bad health, and it wouldn't be fair to impose on her about this. It also wouldn't do to remind her what she had to look forward to at her age. Maybe Ethan, whom she'd met at Maddie's, wouldn't mind if she called him. A volunteer with the Helpers, he came to do things the doctors said Maddie shouldn't do because of her osteoporosis, like walk their big dog or take the trash out, and since they were at Maddie's at the same time, they'd fallen into the habit of standing by their cars before leaving, just chatting. Surely Ethan wouldn't mind if she called; he was a widower and seemed to enjoy her company.

She glanced at the clock and felt guilty calling on him at this hour (anything after 9pm was ungodly late in Palm Lakes, and it was 9:10), but she couldn't stand the thought of bearing this alone for another minute. She found his number and dialed it, holding her breath.

"Hi, Ethan, it's me. Mary Beth."

"Mary Beth! It's good to hear from you. Is everything OK?"

It occurred to her she hadn't planned what to say, but there was no easy way to say it, so she blurted it out. "I came home from work today and found my Mom had died. I've just gotten back from dealing with all the formalities. I'm sitting here at the dining table wondering what to do next. It was sudden, although, I guess it wasn't completely unexpected. She had heart trouble." Mary Beth felt tears threatening for the first time.

"Can I come over? You shouldn't be alone now."

Relief flooded her. "Yes, I'd like that. But I won't be good company."

"You've never given me your address. Tell me how to find you." She cringed that she hadn't followed through on her promise of making dinner for him when he'd called to wish her a Happy Thanksgiving. If she were honest with herself, she knew she was just dreading Mom's reaction. Mom had assumed something was going on between them. Not. Well, that wasn't going to be an issue now.

She gave him directions and hung up, hoping he'd hurry. It was way too quiet and creepy being here by herself, especially after dark. She didn't believe in ghosts, but she almost felt like Mom was hanging around. Probably wanted to give her hell about something or other. When the doorbell rang several minutes later, she rushed past the living room to get to the front door, consciously avoiding looking towards the couch. Ethan stood in ragged jeans and a faded flannel shirt, backlit by a street light.

"Come in here. It's not that warm outside. You should have worn a jacket!" She pulled him into the house and shut the door.

"I was in a hurry and forgot to grab one. It's not so bad. That's one thing about winters in the desert." He stood there towering over her as if uncertain what to do next, looking around the darkened area and shifting from one foot to the other like a restless bear.

Mary Beth turned and walked back towards the light that spilled from dining room. "I can't stand to be out here for long. It was too much of a shock finding her on the couch." She pointed at the offending piece of furniture as he followed her silently past the living room.

"I was having a glass of wine. Actually, another glass of wine. Would you like one?" She indicated the other glass she'd put on the table.

"That would be fine."

She ignored his less-than-enthusiastic response and poured both of them a glass and sat down. Suddenly remembering her manners, she stood back up. "Would you like anything to eat?"

"No, I'm not hungry."

She winced at what she heard in his voice, but pushed past the tightening in her chest. "I'm sorry I didn't get around to inviting you to dinner like I said I would on Thanksgiving, and I'm sorry I never said anything about it until now. I was worried about my Mom. She had some issues with the age difference between you and me, and she could be pretty critical, and I wasn't certain I could take it if she started in on you. That's the only reason I didn't follow through. I was afraid she'd embarrass me. I know that's not much of an excuse, but--"

He reached over and patted her hand. "Don't worry about that now. I'm just so sorry you had to go through this. If I can help in any way, I will. I'd like to come to the funeral once you have it set."

So he wasn't mad at her. "Thanks, Ethan. I didn't know who else to call. I don't have any close friends here, at least not single ones. I shouldn't be so shocked, but I just don't know what to do. We had plans, and things were working out nicely. And now it's all fallen apart." She felt so numb. Where were the tears? What was the matter with her?

His gray eyes held no judgment, just compassion. She put her head in her hands. "I don't want to make this all about me, but I'm worried what to do now. I'm not legal here, and now that Mom's gone, I won't be able to stay. And I was really getting settled here and liking it. Go figure. Who would have thought I'd like living in an old fart community? Oh, shit!" She looked at him apologetically. "Sorry, no offense meant."

"None taken," said Ethan, with a grin on his face. "I'm just pleased you've been enjoying living here. Don't borrow trouble now. The wheels of the community government grind slowly. It will take time for them to discover you're here."

"You think so? That would help. I know I'll have to sell the condo, but I need time to figure out what I'm going to do. With Mom gone, I don't really have anything tying me here. I have my job, but it isn't much, and I don't have many friends. Plus I have nowhere to live." Her voice trailed off as she struggled to face how big a change this was going to be.

"I'm sorry I didn't get to meet your Mom. Tell me about her."

Mary Beth was surprised how grateful she was for the opportunity to talk about Mom. "Mom had heart trouble, but she never liked to complain about her health, so it took me a while to pry out of her that the doctor said she shouldn't be exerting herself and that living alone scared her. She had angina for a while some months back, though that was under control. But the last several weeks or so, she changed. She stopped the obsessive cleaning. She slept more. She wasn't on my case as much as usual.

"I never asked her much, because she didn't seem to want me to. Now I wish I had; it was obvious she wasn't herself. Maybe I could have helped." Mary Beth sighed and put her hands in her lap.

"Mom and I were total opposites. I took after Dad. Poor Mom could never figure me out. She hated that I smoked, cussed and wasn't a traditional woman who cooked and cleaned and raised a bunch of kids. Not that she did. I'm an only child. She couldn't have any after me, due to complications.

"My ex, Jason, and I didn't have children. Mom hated him. Like I told you before, he took up with a younger woman, whom he got pregnant, and then divorced me. I went into a funk and lost my job and ended up coming out here to start over. At first it was terrible. Mom cleaned obsessively and wouldn't let me smoke indoors and complained constantly about me being a burden. I was going batshit crazy, pardon my French. Then things changed overnight."

Mary Beth looked up to see Ethan staring at her with such sympathy, that finally, tears started to flow. She swiped a hand across her eyes. "Julio came here to do some work on the yard and offered me a job, and Helen moved in next door and we started visiting now and then, and she introduced me to Maddie, who was her former neighbor, so I could learn to make jewelry. Which led to you.

"But like I said, lately, Mom became quieter and quit cleaning as much. It was like the aliens had kidnapped her and substituted a poor version. It worried me, even though it was more peaceful, and now I can see it was a sign that she wasn't feeling well. But because I never asked, I have no idea whether she changed because she was in pain, having symptoms or just winding down."

Ethan reached over and held her hand. "Don't beat yourself up. You did the best you could." Then he squeezed it gently. "I appreciate your sharing this with me. I always wondered what caused you to end up like a fish out of water. You've been through a lot this year." He took a deep breath, then stared at her intently. "Why don't you tell me some happy or funny stories about your Mom?"

"You want to hear about my traditional Catholic upbringing and having to wear a uniform to school, or about Mom telling me not to wear patent leather shoes because they reflect up your skirt, nor pearls, because they reflect down your blouse? Stuff like that?"

Ethan sputtered in laughter. "Absolutely! Here, let me do the honors." He grabbed the bottle and refilled their half-empty glasses.

Mary Beth thought about stories she could tell that would help him picture Mom. Once she started, she couldn't stop, because recollections flooded her. Hours later, the dawn lightened her back yard. She shook her head as if waking up and looked at the empty wine bottles that littered the dining table. Her throat was scratchy from nonstop talking. Though Ethan showed signs of being up all night drinking wine, he still looked at her with a softness in his gray eyes. Suddenly, she felt guilty for imposing on him. "I'm so sorry I've been talking all night. You must be ready to keel over. You don't have to stay."

He smiled gently and squeezed her hand, which she only now noticed he had been holding. "I'm glad you called me."

"How about I make us some breakfast? That's the least I can do. We could both use coffee and something to eat after all that wine." She glanced at the empty bottles that littered the table. "I can't believe we drank that much! How about something to eat? One thing the women in my family do well is cook. What do you say? An omelet, bacon and toast?"

"If you don't mind, coffee and something to eat would be very nice." He ran his hand across the stubble on his chin, and she tangentially thought what a domestic scene this was.

It wasn't until she got up to cook that she realized she hadn't smoked a cigarette in nearly 24 hours. And she didn't feel like one. Maybe she was channeling Mom.

* * *

Samantha, 11:59am

Samantha had been putting off calling Jack for a couple weeks, and Arthur was going to become suspicious if she waited much longer. She couldn't bear to call Jack from home, where Arthur could hear her end of the conversation. Yet she couldn't call from work. The phones at Palo Verde Landscaping were not located for privacy, so she couldn't very well call a competitor about a job from there.

So on her way back to work from lunch, she pulled into the parking lot at the Recreation Center and went into the lobby where there was an old-fashioned phone booth. Hopefully she wouldn't run into anyone she knew. Too bad she didn't have one of those mobile phones, but they were just too expensive.

As she remarked to herself about the quiet inside the booth and the comfortable seat, she summoned courage, then extracted Jack's business card from her pocket. It was raggedy from being carried around for weeks and being pulled out of her pocket over and over as she looked at it and debated with herself about calling him. Weeks ago, after they had partnered on a project in a landscaping class at the local community college, Jack had offered her a job. But she still wasn't sure how much the offer was based on their obvious mutual attraction and how much was based on her qualifications. The time for procrastinating was over, though. She dialed his number, half hoping he'd be out for lunch, but he answered on the second ring.

"Temple Landscaping, Jack Temple speaking."

"Hi, Jack. It's me, Samantha."

"Samantha! It's so good to hear you. Are you going to accept my job offer? It's still open."

She was both relieved and disturbed. "I told you I couldn't take the job, but I wasn't very good about hiding my disappointment at home. I ended up having to tell Arthur, and he demanded that I give you a call and ask for full details, because he thinks I should take the job if it's better than what I have now. I still don't think I should, no matter what the offer is, and you know why. I've been putting off calling you, but I have to be able to tell Arthur I followed through. I'm sorry to put you through this, because I don't see any way I can accept your proposal."

There was a pause on his end. Maybe she'd pissed him off. Maybe that would be a good thing and end all this confusion. "Look, Samantha, I need someone with your qualifications to help me with design and managing the planting crews. I promised I wouldn't push for anything else. And I meant it. I think we'd make a great team, and I have my hands full trying to do it all. I won't be able to expand the way I want without your help. Isn't it good that your husband is in favor of it?"

Feeling guilty and annoyed at the same time, Samantha said, "You know as well as I do that if I take the job, sooner or later, things will get personal between us, and I can't afford that. My parents need me. Arthur hasn't done anything to deserve disloyalty; not lately, anyway."

"I understand your concerns, and I respect your values. There must be some way to work this out. What can I do to make you feel safe taking the job?"

Samantha squeezed her eyes shut and rubbed her forehead with her hand. He wasn't making this easy for her. Maybe he didn't understand the power of the attraction she felt for him. Maybe he could be professional with her; she wasn't sure she could be with him. Was he just hoping to wear her down, or did he not feel as strongly? Either way would be bad for her. "Jack, do me a favor and tell me the details. I will report to Arthur. I'm not going to make any promises. I still don't think it's a good idea."

"Fair enough. How can you make a decision without knowing what I'm talking about? I know you get the use of a pickup from Palo Verde, and that they pay the gas for you, and you get to take it home as if it's your vehicle. You would get the same benefit here. I'd give you one of the trucks, a gas card and you could use it to commute. You said the commute bothered you; at least this way, it would not add expense.

"I realize you'd have to give up having lunch at home, and you wouldn't be able to drop by and see your parents during the workday like you do now. I can't do anything about that. Nor can I make the commute shorter. I know it would be a challenge to drive that round trip. The only way I could think to make it balance out was to pay you for 40 hours but only ask you to put in 35 a week. By taking a 30-minute lunch break and doing a 7 hour day, you could get back a lot of the time lost in the commute, which would allow you to spend time with your family."

Samantha was stunned. That was a sweet deal. "So what wages would you pay me?"

"You didn't tell me how much you make, but I'm guessing it isn't a lot more than minimum wage. Am I right?"

"Yeah, I think it's about two dollars over minimum wage."

"I'll pay you ten dollars an hour over minimum wage."

Samantha couldn't believe her ears. A salary like that, with added benefits of gas and car, was an incredible offer. She was wondering how she could ever say 'no' when he interrupted her train of thought.

"I don't offer medical at this time, but I give all employees one week's paid vacation a year. They don't offer that at Palo Verde, do they?" She had to admit, her resolve was crumbling.

"No, they don't," she whispered. "Jack, I'll tell Arthur and phone you back with a decision soon. Thanks for such a generous offer." Her stomach clenched at the no-win situation. No matter what she chose now, she'd lose.

He sighed as if he'd used all his ammunition. "I'll wait for your call. Is there any way I can call you?"

"I don't have a mobile phone, Jack, and there isn't anywhere private you could call. It's for the best this way. I really will call you back." She paused for a second, hating to let him go, sure she was going to turn him down about the job and that she'd eventually never see him again. "I hope you have a nice Christmas."

"I wish I could see you."

"There's no point to it, Jack. And you don't have to hold that job open for me if you find someone else. But I promise I'll call and give you my final decision soon."

"OK. I'll wait to hear from you."

She reluctantly hung up the phone, cracked the door open to turn off the light and sat in the booth trying to compose herself in the shadows. She knew she'd upset him. He'd be staring intently at the phone, his face all sharp angles, his nearly black eyes smoldering. His dark good looks had a powerful effect on her, and she didn't really want him to be her boss. But the offer was way better than she could have hoped, and Arthur was going to insist she take it if she told him the truth. How could she convince him that she shouldn't? They could use the money;

they had so little in savings. And the job would be rewarding for her professionally. He'd never understand why she wanted to turn it down.

She gritted her teeth, trying to ignore the little voice that said she should give it a chance, that she could keep it professional. *Oh, if only that were true.* Shaking her head, she headed back to work, a burning feeling in her stomach.

The high today was going to be 58, pretty typical for winter weather, but to her, it felt chilly, especially with the breeze coming from the north. As usual, she'd worn layers because it had been in the low 40s when she set off to work at 6:30. There was no heating in the office, and she spent most of her time outdoors anyway, so the weather wasn't ideal for her. She'd imagined winter in the desert would be warmer. Still, it was better than Maryland in winter, and she loved what she did.

She parked in front of the ramshackle wooden structure that was the office for Palo Verde Landscaping and went in to finish the design she'd started before lunch. The office was empty. Where was Mary Beth? Probably taking her lunch. No one stuck to rigid hours, so Samantha wasn't concerned. She sat at the desk nearest the door, still in her jacket, and bent her head to finishing the Anderson's yard design.

The door opened five minutes later and two men walked in. One was retirement age, the other, much younger. Probably father and son, as there was a marked resemblance, especially around the eyes. Both wore nothing but t-shirts and shorts. It amused Samantha, who had three layers on top and had been doing a design with fingerless gloves to fight off the chill. The father looked around the office, then at Samantha, since she was the only person there.

"So what part of North Dakota are you guys from?" Samantha asked.

Father blinked his eyes in astonishment. "How did you know that?"

Samantha smiled. "Look at how I'm dressed. Look at you. It's easy to see you don't live here. Residents feel cold this time of year. I knew you were from somewhere that would consider this summer weather. How can I help?"

He shook his head and grinned. "Lucky guess! We *are* from North Dakota, and it *is* pretty balmy today. We're wanting to look at some plants. Can you show us around?"

"Sure thing." Samantha took them on a tour of the nursery and returned to the office a half hour later to write an invoice for their purchase and put their payment in the back office. Mary Beth still hadn't returned from lunch. That was strange. She never took this long. Back at the desk, Samantha resumed the drawing of the Anderson yard.

The phone rang ten minutes later, and Samantha ran over to answer it.

"Palo Verde Landscaping, Samantha speaking."

"Samantha, it's me." Mary Beth's voice was weak and shaky.

"Mary Beth, what's wrong?"

"I came home and found my Mom dead. I won't be back today and probably not until after the funeral. Can you tell Julio or one of the brothers? I'll try to call later when I have a better idea of when I can get back."

Samantha slumped into the nearest chair. "Oh, Mary Beth, I'm so sorry. Please let me know if there's anything we can do. I'll tell Julio. You just do what you need to do. Give me a call at home when things calm down. I'd like to come to the funeral service if that's all right."

"I'll let you know once it's set. Thanks, Samantha." Mary Beth sounded forlorn.

"Just call me if I can do anything at all."

Mary Beth signed off and Samantha went to the radio to contact Julio.

It could just as easily have been her in Mary Beth's shoes. It was becoming obvious that both her parents were teetering on the edge of the precipice these days. Poor Mary Beth. She didn't have a lot of friends, living in Palm Lakes illegally. Samantha's mother spent more leisure time with Mary Beth than she did. Samantha resolved to invite Mary Beth to lunch and try to give her more support. Samantha had been so taken up with her own problems, she hadn't reached out to Mary Beth that often in recent months, even though Mary Beth was her age, making them two of the youngest residents of Palm Lakes.

Back home at the end of the work day, Samantha shared with Arthur. "Mary Beth went home for lunch and found her mother dead. What a horrible thing to have happen."

Arthur frowned. "That's for sure. Let's hope it never happens to you."

His brown eyes looked squarely into Samantha's. "Did you call that Jack fellow about the job?"

"Yes, I did."

"So what's the score? Is it a good offer?"

Samantha sighed, still uncertain how to handle the subject. "It was almost too good to be true. He'll pay me significantly more. I can work 35 hours a week to compensate for the long commute, but he'll pay me for 40. He'll give me a truck and a week's vacation each year."

"So why do you seem so sad? Isn't this just what you've always wanted?" Arthur cocked his head to the side, like he was trying to figure her out. She didn't want to make him suspicious. In fact, it seemed incredible that he wasn't.

"He can't change the fact that taking this job would mean less time with you and my folks. And I'm not a kid anymore." She ignored his raised eyebrow, eloquent in expressing that to him, she was a kid. After all, she was nearly 20 years younger than he. "I'm not looking to build a career at any price. Part of me feels it's too much to ask. My parents aren't getting younger. At some point, I may need to help more, even if they don't want it. What if what happened to Mary Beth happens to me, and I'm working halfway across the city? How will I be able to care for the survivor?"

"Well, I don't see it that way. You ought to take the job. We could use the extra money. Palo Verde is pretty loose. I bet they'd take you back if you decided you wanted to return. You're a valuable employee."

"You may be right." She was galled to think how little they had in savings. It would be foolish to turn down this chance. She let out a sigh of resignation.

He finally smiled. "Of course, I'm right. This is a plum of a job. Give it a shot."

She might as well admit it. The decision was made. "I'll tell him I can start the first of the year. That allows me to give notice at work."

"Go ahead and call him now. You don't want him giving it to someone else now that you've finally decided."

Samantha started to resist, then figured it wouldn't matter. "OK." She got up and went into the kitchen to the phone, pulled out Jack's card and dialed the number, turning her back to Arthur in the other room as Jack answered the phone. "I've decided to accept your offer. I just told Arthur, and he insisted I should call you right away and accept." She hoped he understood she was unable to speak freely.

"I'm glad. When do you want to start?"

"The first of the year. That way, I can give notice at Palo Verde."

"That will be fine. I'll get a truck set up and find you office space."

"OK. See you then." Samantha hung up and turned back to Arthur. "It's done. I have the job."

"Well, I think we ought to go out and celebrate your good fortune. Where would you like to eat?"

Samantha had no appetite at all. "How about the Chinese place?"

Lydia, Noon

Lydia dialed the 800 number on the phone card so she could talk to her best friend Jean. She still had trouble believing Jean was in the UK now, instead of in Palm Lakes. It was currently seven hours later in the day there, making it 7pm. When she got the dial tone, she punched in Ian's phone number. "Brring-brring. Brring-brring." The typical British double ring charmed her. Jean had been expecting the call and answered right away.

"Hi, Jean. How are you doing? I know you've only been there a short while, but I really miss you." Being highly visual, Lydia desperately wished she could see her best friend, as that would tell her anything she wanted to know.

"I'm so glad you called, Lyd. Things are going great! Ian and I are getting along so well, it's like we were meant for each other. Who would have guessed that we'd be matched so well, living on different continents?"

"Well, it is pretty much what you intuitively felt, even though I know it seemed strange to trust yourself given the circumstances."

"Ya think? I meet a guy online and without hardly any facts, decide to divorce my husband and go to the UK to meet the man? It sounds crazy."

"Well, Richard's addiction to porn ended your marriage before you ever met Ian."

"I know, but it was still hard. I beat myself up about it, probably in part because Richard laid on the guilt pretty thickly." Jean sighed gustily. "Enough of that. I did what I thought was best. Best for us all."

"At least it's working out. That's what matters. So what do you two think you'll do?" Lydia held her breath, hoping Jean wasn't planning to relocate to the UK.

"Ian is willing to move to the US, since he has no family here, and he doesn't mind leaving his job. We're researching where to marry and how to get him a green card. It's more complex than I would ever have guessed. It might take a few months to get things sorted so we can come back and know he won't be thrown out by immigration."

"Will you be coming back to Palm Lakes? I could start looking for a place for you if you like. Better yet, why don't you stay with me while you both figure out what you want to do? I have a spare bedroom, and even though my condo is small, we can make it work."

"That is such a kind offer! We're still pretty vague about exactly what we intend to do and how and where to live, other than I want to live in Palm Lakes. Knowing we have temporary accommodations would make it easier, because we wouldn't have to have it all figured out. We can focus on the move, then deal with our future once we get there. I accept. Thanks!"

Lydia sighed in relief. "I'm so glad. I really miss you; you'll get tired of hearing that. It isn't the same doing things by myself. Funny, before I knew you, I was always good as a loner, but now I just can't work up the enthusiasm to do the healing work and go to classes by myself." Then she regretted saying so much, because Jean had a partner now who liked doing the same things, so Lydia was going to be a fifth wheel even if they did come back to Palm Lakes. She had never been more painfully aware of how her single status set her apart from her friends.

"I'm sorry to have deserted you. I miss you, too. It will be good to be back, though we still aren't sure exactly what we'll do. We need to find a way to support ourselves. Ian has been doing Spiritual Healing and tarot readings at a healing center here, and he suggested we consider having a business wherever we end up. I could do Reiki, and he could do

Spiritual Healing, and he could do readings and I could dowse for people. It seems like a huge step to me, but I'm open to it. What about you? Why don't you think about taking your hobby to the next level? You're great at the crystal healing. Maybe we could even find a way to all work together offering complementary services."

Lydia was thrilled to be included in Jean's new life. "There may not be much of a market for such New Age stuff in Palm Lakes, but I'm open to trying. I might even do intuitive readings for people." Lydia knew this would spark questions, but it was time to share her secret with Jean. "I'm just not sure I'm ready to come out yet."

"What are you talking about, Lydia?"

Lydia blew a breath out and took the plunge. "I have this ability to read people visually. I see their energy fields, and that gives me a lot of information about them. I've been doing it since I was a kid. It would be really useful for doing readings. I don't usually tell people about it, but if we're discussing what our talents and gifts are for a business venture, I need to put it on the table."

"Damn it, Lydia, I knew you were psychic! Why didn't you tell me you could read auras?"

Lydia hadn't expected that reaction. "I don't consider it psychic. It's just another way of seeing. But it hasn't always helped me get along with people. In fact, my marriage broke up mainly because of it. It's really hard having a wife you can't lie to." She grimaced at the sad truth of it. "I guess I've been afraid to tell anyone. I don't mind being seen as eccentric, but this is beyond that. I didn't want to ruin our friendship."

"How could you ever have thought that? This is amazing! Tell me how it works and what information you get. I always knew that you could read me somehow."

"I need to see the person to do it. I can't do it with you now. In fact, I rely so much on it that phone conversations are hard for me, because I feel blind. I've been doing this my whole life. I can see colors in your aura and sense what they mean. I can see emotions as well as health problems. And if someone is going to die soon, I can see that. To tell you the truth, it can actually be as much a burden as a blessing."

"I hadn't thought of that. But you could use it to counsel people. It would be a tremendous asset to a healer, too. This makes me think Ian is right. We could set up a business together. Wouldn't that be fun?"

"I can't think of anything I'd like better. Fact is, I'm not desperate for money, so it doesn't have to pay me well. I'd just like to feel I'm doing something meaningful. Since you left, I've been lost. I can't go back to just taking classes. It isn't enough for me anymore. I guess it's time to make some big changes, though I have to admit, I'm not sure how I feel about coming out about my so-called gift."

"Well I was really scared about coming out about Richard, and then later, Ian. You helped me through it. I wish I could be there to support you. But we'll get there as soon as we can."

"It can't be fast enough to suit me," said Lydia.

"I need to ask you a question, Lyd, and please be honest with me. Putting aside the obvious attraction of having a business doing what we love, Ian and I are going to need to make decent money, because even though I got a settlement from Richard, there's no alimony, and I have no pension or other source of income, and Ian doesn't have any money put aside, plus it's a few years before he can draw his pension. Do you think we should start a business, or should we just find regular jobs?"

Lydia was touched that Jean wanted her advice. "My Dad was a successful entrepreneur, but I never had my own business, so I'm not an expert, though I do know some basics. I could check into the process for creating a business entity in this state, and I could also do a little research to see what the market is like in healing and intuitive readings. Would you like me to look into those things with the goal being to go into business together if it sounds reasonable?"

"Sure. If you're willing to do the research, we can figure out a lot before we even get back home. I feel bad putting it all on you, though."

"Jean, honey, it would be my pleasure. If we could work together, that would be a dream come true for me. I've been wondering lately what to do with myself."

"So what else is going on there?"

"Barbara's annual Christmas party is tonight. But it won't be the same without you."

"Yeah, that party in August was so great. It seems like a long time ago. Will Helen be there?"

"Yes, she and Alexander just got back from their honeymoon in Moorea. Can you believe that? I haven't seen the photos yet, but I know I'm going to be green with envy. Helen promised to tell us more tonight. I don't have any other big news to share."

"You'll have to call me again soon. I feel so out of touch. Hardly anyone has email except you, and no one else is phoning me."

"Maybe you should give Barbara and Helen a call sometime. I know they'd like that."

"I'll have to figure out how to get a phone card to use here, like the one you have. And the time difference is a nuisance. It's hard to remember I can't just call when I think about it, or it might be the middle of night there. I'm not much of a letter-writer, and I do want to keep up on things, because I want to come back and be with you all. I want you guys to be a part of my new life."

"That sounds good to me. I'll give everyone your love when I see them. Say hi to Ian for me."

"I will. Call me again soon. Love you!"

"Love you, too!" Lydia hung up. She had lots of work to do. It felt great.

* * *

Helen, 2:35pm

Helen stood in the living room of Alexander's spacious, well-decorated home and gazed out at the golf course with its pale, wintry shades of green and longed for warm tropical breezes and nothing to do all day except eat, sleep and make love. They had returned from their honeymoon a few days ago, and now she felt a chasm between them, one that she knew was of her own making. Still, she didn't know how to bridge the gap.

They'd fit together perfectly on their trip, but faced with living in his house, she was all prickly with not belonging. It was like she'd been dropped into his life to fit an empty slot, and there wasn't room for her to bring anything of herself. They were going to sell her condo, which she had just gotten comfortably decorated and newly landscaped. Her beloved cat Sheba's ashes were scattered around the tree she'd just planted there. They hadn't talked about what to do with her furniture. It wouldn't fit in this house even if she wanted it to. Plus it wasn't nearly as nice as what he had, so it seemed unreasonable to consider keeping it. She'd made friends with the woman next door, Mary Beth, and she knew this move meant that she wouldn't see her often anymore. Why did she have to give up everything to make this new life, when he got to keep everything as it was before?

Then there was the issue with his cat, who was treating her like she was a wicked stepmom. She was usually so good with animals. Why was she the only one having problems adjusting? And why hadn't Alexander noticed? Did Alexander's ignorance of her inner turmoil confirm she was wrong to feel as she did, or was it part of the reason for her negativity?

She had no answers. In truth, she knew he had done nothing wrong. She felt guilty about her attitude but couldn't seem to banish it.

Unlike her, Alexander had returned from the South Pacific energized and eager to get back to writing his next food/travel book. The contract with his publisher demanded he turn in a draft soon. He had such focus and commitment, but she couldn't even decide what she wanted to write about, not that she was a professional like him. For her, writing was merely a lifelong dream. To think that some months back, writing a novel had seemed a good project for her. What colossal ego! After years of faithful daily journaling, she could barely put pen to paper anymore. And that irritated her, too, because she wasn't sure what had happened; she just seemed to have nothing to say anymore. The writing partnership she'd imagined with Alexander wasn't materializing, and it made her worry about how compatible they really were.

She didn't know how to talk with Alexander about her feelings. Big change had always disturbed her. Just as it had after Lou had died suddenly of a heart attack. She'd managed to find her footing then--after a pretty rough patch--and here she was facing a major adjustment again less than a year later. Alexander didn't seem to be aware that anything was wrong.

It occurred to her she was being harder on Alexander than she ever had been on Lou, and that unfairness made her cringe. She had never blamed Lou for not knowing how she felt. She knew he didn't care (why would he beat her if he valued her?), and she had expected nothing good from him. But with Alexander, she thought it would be different, that she'd have a soul mate. Unfortunately, since they married, his intuitive quotient seemed to have dropped to nil. She wanted him to ask her what was wrong, so she wouldn't have to complain, but he seemed unaware that anything was bothering her. The more he didn't notice, the more annoyed she got. And she knew that she was in the wrong, which only made her more upset.

Absorbed in her troubled thoughts, she didn't hear Alexander step up behind her, and when he wrapped his arms around her, she jumped.

"Sorry. I thought you heard me. I saw you weren't in your office, and I wanted to give you a hug." He held her close, and his warmth and the scent of him soothed her frazzled nerves. She held his arms around her fiercely, hoping to drive away the negative feelings. She couldn't bear to tell him. It would make her seem so ungrateful.

"You ready to make a big splash at Barbara's party tonight?" He turned her around and searched her face with his emerald eyes. She buried her face in his chest to avoid scrutiny.

"Yes, I'm ready," she mumbled against his shirt, enjoying the scent of his after-shave mixed with a fragrance that was uniquely him.

"It will be our first public appearance since the wedding. Are you nervous?" She could hear the grin in his voice.

"Why would I be nervous?"

"I know you're not big on socializing. We don't have to stay longer than you want."

"Lydia will be there, and it's always good to see her and Barbara. And Sally told me she and Red were invited."

"Really? That will cause a stir, her showing up six months pregnant with a man twice her age who isn't the father of her baby. She'll be the talk of the party."

"That might be the point. At the last party, she'd only just found out she was pregnant, but she was still noticeable."

"Of course she stood out. She was the only person there who was less than 55 years old, not to mention she's beautiful like her Mom. It should be interesting, as the Chinese say." Alexander pushed back from her and flashed his trademark sexy smile. Then he led her over to the couch and pulled her down next to him. "Maybe it's none of my business, but do you know what's going on between Sally and Red?"

Helen sighed and pushed her hair back from her face. "She never tells me anything. Obviously, they're dating, if that's what you call it these days. I'm worried he's going to get hurt. He just isn't her type. Not that I wouldn't be thrilled if they decided to get married. Her usual type is a young, down-on-his luck artist or musician with a drug habit. Red Johnson is the antithesis of that." Sally was her youngest and favorite child, but sometimes she couldn't figure her out. "I can't say what's motivating her."

Talking about Sally's predicament had calmed her down for some reason. She laid her head on Alexander's shoulder, the earlier storm within her having died.

He sat up straighter and her head came off his shoulder. "Well, enough gossip. I better get back to work. It's so tempting not to. But I need to learn to keep my hands off you so I can meet my deadline." He gave her a sizzling look. "We'll go to Barbara's, but you're all mine after that." He kissed her hard, got up and walked back to his office.

Slightly dazed, Helen wandered into her own little office, the converted former guest bedroom, and sat at the antique desk, the only piece of her furniture in the whole house. Her journals sat on a bookshelf across from her, and her latest one lay open on the desktop, a blank page accusing her of having nothing to say. The irritation began to well up inside her again, and she tamped it back down as she picked up the pen and twirled it in her hand, wondering what to write.

All her dreams had come true. Things she never believed or thought she'd have, she now had. She was married to a rich and talented man so beautiful he made Apollo look shabby. They were going to be writers and travel and cook fabulous gourmet meals and drink fine wines for the rest of their lives. So why was she miserable?

* * *

Red, 4:40pm

Sally had just finished showering and in typical fashion was waltzing around naked. Red suspected she did it on purpose, knowing the effect she had on him. He didn't mind at all.

Her long blonde hair hung loose, way below her shoulders, partly obscuring her breasts. She hadn't gained much weight with the pregnancy, but her breasts were plumper. She was still trim in spite of the expanded belly, and when she moved, she was grace personified. Or sex on a stick. Was it perverted to be turned on by a pregnant lady? He wanted her now more than ever. But lately there was a new emotion to compete with his libido, one he'd never felt before.

He looked at her stomach. "Can I feel the baby kick?"

She rolled her eyes at him, not taking his interest seriously.

"It's just so incredible. He's going to be a real football star." He placed his hand on her swollen belly.

"It's going to be a girl," she assured him stubbornly.

"What makes you so positive?" A sharp kick finally rewarded him. "Wow, that was a big one! Did you feel that?"

She looked at him with disdain. "Of course I felt it. I feel it all the time. And the baby's a girl."

He ignored her scorn and put his cheek on her belly and waited for the next kick. There was something mesmerizing about interacting with the tiny being growing inside her. He was sure it was a fine, strong boy. "I never realized what it was like to watch...I don't know what to call it...watching this baby becoming a real person! You know, I never had kids, and now I see what I was missing."

"You're lucky you dodged that bullet. Wish I had your luck."

Red couldn't believe what she was implying. "Didn't you choose to keep the baby?"

"Yeah, but sometimes I wonder if it was just hormones that made that decision."

He tried to give her the benefit of the doubt. "It can't be easy, working full time and being pregnant."

"It's not. But I manage."

Her independence impressed him, but also threw cold water on the little dream he'd been entertaining. He'd been thinking about what life would be like with a young wife and child. It shocked him to admit he rather liked the idea. He hadn't had the nerve to mention it to Sally yet, especially when she was in this kind of mood, which was most of the time lately.

He lifted his head after not getting another kick and smiled at Sally. Her gray-flecked blue eyes stared at him icily. "You are such a softie. I never would have guessed." A chill went through him. When she acted like this, he didn't know what to think. What pregnant single woman wouldn't want a man to fall in love with her and her baby? Obviously, Sally. *Great.*

He shouldn't let himself become too attached; they'd never made any promises. The red flag he occasionally saw popped up again, waving madly, and he turned mentally in another direction to avoid dealing with it. If she wanted space, he could give her space.

Sensing his withdrawal, she moved closer to him and spoke soothingly, pressing her naked body against him. "I'm sorry. I'm glad you like the baby. You're a hero for putting up with me. I'm just hormonal." Somewhat mollified, he wrapped his arms around her. It was getting harder to ignore the dire warnings from his intuition.

* * *

Lydia 6:00pm

Lydia scanned the crowded great room. The annual Christmas party was obviously going to be as successful as all Barbara's events. Should they even call it a Christmas party anymore? Maybe 'holiday party' was more politically correct. She chuckled to herself at the thought.

A beautiful artificial tree filled a corner of the room, trimmed with flashing lights and southwest-inspired decorations. Mistletoe hung from the ceiling in a few doorways. Christmas-themed platters holding the sumptuous banquet were laid out on the long counter separating the great room and kitchen. Plastic plates and cups in red and green and fine paper napkins with a holly design sat in stacks at the end of the sideboard along with plastic cutlery and pitchers of water and iced tea. Barbara's husband Ben was playing bartender and greeter at the wet bar, his red and white Santa cap sitting at a jaunty angle on his head.

Barbara was making the rounds and had disappeared into the crowd again. She was wearing an ankle-length black skirt and forest green silk blouse with a wide red leather belt, her double strand of pearls providing contrast to the dark colors.

Feeling strangely lost without Jean, Lydia held back from mingling for a little while longer, taking note of the attendees while nursing the glass of exceptional red wine Ben had given her when she arrived. She didn't recognize everyone, but she'd spotted Helen and Alexander, Helen's daughter Sally on the arm of an older man she was sure was her neighbor and of course, Bernie.

She grinned when she remembered how Helen, Jean, Sally and she had struggled to evade Bernie at the last party. He was equally tipsy this time and just as socially inept. Fortunately, he hadn't yet approached her, but she'd seen him lurking under the mistletoe, hitting on various women unsuccessfully.

Information bombarded Lydia as she peered at the partygoers. Maybe theoretically it was possible to filter what came through, but she'd never found a way. A riot of colors danced around each person, the predominant shades revealing emotional state, personality traits and physical health, all through the gift of her enhanced subtle vision. It was practically automatic for her to process the information, but she did her best not to see what was before her, though it took a lot of effort to ignore. If only Jean were here, she'd be able to focus on her best friend and block out much of what was going on around her. Well, she'd just have to make the best of it, exhausting as it was. That's why she always smoked a joint after a party; she just needed to calm down and let go of all she'd seen.

She reminded herself to be an uninvolved observer no matter what she saw (it hadn't gotten easier in all these years) and rose from the chair, heading through the crowd to find her friends. She passed Bernie, who mercifully was focused on someone else, and immediately broke her resolution. The same sadness surrounded him, though his obnoxious behavior blinded most people to his loneliness. He still hadn't recovered from the death of his wife. She wondered if he ever would.

Throwing off his depressive energy, she began to wend her way over to where she'd last seen Helen and Alexander, cursing her dratted talent.

Something wasn't right with Helen, and Helen was trying to hide it. If only Lydia could be unaware like everyone else. She'd just come back from a honeymoon in the South Pacific, and instead of being calm and harmonious, the energy around Helen was tinged with repressed irritation and a sort of confused desperation. Her physical appearance gave nothing away. Though her coloring was fair, she'd tanned on her vacation, and the golden tone of her skin and her reddish blonde hair glistened like sunshine in the roomful of palefaces.

Alexander, on the other hand, seemed calm and relaxed. What a godlike hunk of man he was! Tall, tanned and fit as an athlete. His thick, longish silver hair, green eyes and golden radio voice had women swooning, as usual. Maybe that was what was wrong with Helen. He seemed unfazed by the women playing up to him (his detachment would have been obvious to anyone, with or without special vision), but Helen wasn't used to being married to a man she loved, and maybe she was uncomfortable with all the female attention he drew.

As she approached them, Lydia saw that even Helen's daughter Sally was not immune to Alexander's magnetism. She and her date went up to greet Helen and Alexander, and after hugging her mother, Sally gave Alexander a full-body hug (a real feat, considering she was so pregnant). You didn't have to be psychic to notice the lust rolling off her. Red spikes of anger exploded from both Helen and Sally's date. *Well, this could be interesting.*

Helen turned her focus from Sally when she saw Lydia approaching. "Lydia! It's so good to see you!"

"I want to hear about your honeymoon, or at least the parts you're willing to share." She grinned as Helen flushed slightly. "So what's it like in paradise?"

"The water was the most amazing turquoise, and we went snorkeling and saw fish of all kinds and colors. We went horseback riding on the beach and ate the most incredible meals. I didn't want to come home." She sighed sadly.

Alexander looked at Helen as if weighing what her last statement implied, but said nothing. It was easy to see he lived too much in his head and was missing some signals.

"I'd love to see photos, if you took any."

318

"Are you kidding? I took a zillion. I'm putting them into a big album. I want you to see them as soon as I get them organized."

Sally dragged her date closer to Lydia. "Lydia, I'd like you to meet Red Johnson."

Yup, this was her neighbor. He was handsome, though not the movie-star type Alexander was. His short, graying blonde hair and blue eyes spoke of Nordic genes. He towered over her like a Viking and grinned at her like the neighborhood bad boy. He reached his hand forward. "I believe we're neighbors, Lydia. Don't you live two condos down from me?"

Lydia smiled and shook his hand, pleased at his powers of observation. He had a nice, firm grip. "Yes, that would be me. I'm pleased to finally meet you. Aren't you with the Posse?"

"Yes, I am." He radiated an unusual honesty and groundedness. She turned to Sally, comparing their energies. They were opposites aside from a powerful physical attraction. Amazing how sex held poorly matched people together.

Sally grabbed Red's arm, pulling him away from the group. "Let's get some of the hot crab dip while there's still some left. It's totally awesome." Red gave Lydia one last look (it almost seemed apologetic) and allowed himself to be dragged away. *That relationship isn't going to last much longer.*

Lydia turned her attention to Alexander and Helen. "I haven't bumped into Bernie, though I saw that he's here. Have you had a close encounter, Helen?" She grinned as she said it.

Helen responded with a laugh. "I think being with Alexander warned him off. I haven't had anyone grope my boobs tonight."

Alexander's eyes widened for a second, then he grinned mischievously. "The night is young, dear."

Lydia felt a rare tinge of envy and hurriedly changed the subject. "I didn't get to speak with Barbara yet. Everything has been so crazy. I think I'll go find her now. Helen, can we get together for lunch sometime now that you're back?"

"Sure, Lydia. Let's do that."

"OK. I'll tell Barbara we should set a date after Christmas. See you guys later." Lydia wove through the crowd as "Jingle Bell Rock" played in the background.

She found Barbara talking with a woman near the glass door that led to the patio. No one was outside, in spite of the cheerful fire she could see burning in the fire pit.

She caught Barbara's eye as she drew closer. "Lydia, when did you get here? How could I have missed welcoming you?" Barbara gently touched the arm of the woman she was speaking with, then turned to give Lydia a hug.

"Santa's helper welcomed me." She pointed towards Ben at the bar. "It's quite a turnout you have tonight. You must be pleased."

Barbara's brown eyes flashed warmly. "Yes, it is lovely so many were able to attend. Lydia, I don't believe you've met my new neighbor Emma Lightman. She bought Helen's house. I was just getting acquainted with her."

Emma extended her hand and shook Lydia's firmly. Her shoulder-length, straight black hair was shot through with a few silver threads. Her stunning blue eyes and ivory skin contrasted beautifully with the dark of her hair. She wore no makeup other than lipstick. Brave girl, but it worked on her. Slightly taller than Lydia (who wasn't?), she had the body of someone who was serious about yoga, willowy and trim, but she didn't dress to show off her figure, instead wearing loose blouse and slacks.

Lydia took in the colors that surrounded Emma, who seemed painfully shy and had some kind of health issue that contributed to a subdued aura. "I'm Barbara's partner-in-crime at yoga class and some other pastimes. Welcome to Palm Lakes."

"Thank you," Emma almost whispered. She seemed very uncomfortable being among strangers, and Lydia had to repress her tendency to over-empathize.

Lydia turned her attention to Barbara. "Helen was saying she's almost ready to have lunch with us and tell us all about her honeymoon. Would you like to take the lead on setting that date?"

"Sure. I'll look at my calendar and call everyone. Emma, would you like to join us for lunch next week?"

Emma's eyes widened. The skin around a two-inch-long scar on her left cheekbone flushed pink, a harsh note on her classically beautiful features. Finally she replied. "I don't know if I'm free."

"It's very casual, Emma," assured Lydia. "We just gossip and eat good food and have fun. It would be a chance to get better acquainted." Not that she thought Emma cared for that.

Emma gave a genuine smile. "Let me know, and if I can, I will." In spite of the sincerity, Lydia gave it about a 50/50 chance.

Barbara's attention strayed to the front door. "Oh, Nora and Luke just arrived. I need to go greet them. I'll bring them over to meet you, Emma." Barbara headed off towards the front door in hostess mode.

Lydia turned to Emma, who seemed to have shrunk into herself. "It's not easy being in a crowd of new people, is it? I'm pretty extroverted, but even for me, it can be tiring."

"I'm just really shy, and I don't generally go to parties, but Barbara argued convincingly that I could meet most of the neighbors while having some great food, and how could I turn that down?" A smile graced her face.

"Do you like yoga? We go to a great class. You're welcome to be part of our crew." In response to Emma's shocked look, Lydia amended, "Don't decide now. Get your feet under you and let us know. The next class doesn't start until January, anyway.

"That's very kind of you. I love yoga, but I usually just do it on my own. Maybe a class would be nice, especially if I knew someone in it." Her smile broadened to show even, white teeth.

"Have you had a chance to meet everyone?" Lydia dreaded dragging her around, but it was the least she could do.

"Oh, yes, Barbara is the consummate hostess. She introduced me to everyone. Not that I remember a single name except yours at this point."

Lydia chuckled. "We're all prone to that when meeting lots of people at one time. How about a refill? I see your glass is empty, like mine. Ben is a wizard with cocktails, and they have some terrific wines."

"Yes, that would be nice."

They drifted over to the bar, where Ben's harmless flirting caused Emma to withdraw further. It reminded Lydia of Helen when they first met. After getting refills, they went over to the counter, where Lydia piled a plate with goodies, but noticed Emma picked very few items, only nuts or bits of plain fruit. Lydia led her to an empty couch at the far side of the room, where they could sit and eat in peace. Emma seemed relieved at the choice.

Minutes later, Barbara came over, Nora and Luke in tow. "Lydia, you know Nora and Luke, but I wanted to introduce them to Emma." Emma blinked self-consciously and reached her free hand out to shake hands with each of them. "Emma, I met Nora in the cooking class. We often cross paths in various clubs and activities." Barbara turned to the Nora. "Emma is my new neighbor. She bought Helen's old house. You remember Helen from cooking class? She and Alexander met there--I'm pleased to say I was responsible for them partnering in the class--and they recently got married and just got back from their honeymoon in the South Pacific. Moorea, was it, Lydia?"

Lydia nodded, while Emma's eyes got wider.

"How romantic!" sighed Nora, her hazel eyes dreamy. Luke smiled as if it didn't matter one way or the other to him.

"They are just perfect for each other and so in love." Barbara smiled with satisfaction. It proved that Lydia was alone in seeing Helen's discomfort tonight. Maybe it wasn't as bad as it seemed. It was tricky interpreting what she saw.

Barbara, Nora and Luke drifted off to see other guests, and the rest of the evening passed quickly, with Barbara spending much of her time with them. Emma escaped at ten o'clock, and Lydia left shortly after. When she got home, she grabbed a joint and went out onto the patio. This time of night in winter, no one was outside. Even though Red lived two doors down, she wasn't worried. He was still at the party, and she suspected he was spending more time at Sally's place than his own.

The sky was clear and stars sparkled like diamonds on a jeweler's black velvet cloth. She savored the crisp cold air as she sat wrapped snugly in her winter coat. She started to mellow out, grateful that Digger had such good pot. It could be tricky finding a safe source of quality weed, and Digger lived in Palm Lakes, only selling to people he knew or those referred by people he knew. He got his stuff from a relative in northern California who grew it himself, so she knew it wasn't laced with anything harmful. She giggled at the thought of organic pot.

Lydia felt the cares and emotions of all the partygoers slip away from her, leaving her to contemplate the direction of her own life. The idea of 'coming out' about her 'gift' had sounded good when she was talking to Jean, who not only believed in such stuff, but relished it. The party reminded her why she'd kept it to herself her whole life. Though Barbara and Jean would probably be OK with her ability, Helen might not. She had lived her whole life hiding that her now-dead husband Lou was a wife-beater. Lydia had known the first time she looked at her. If Helen found out, would her need for privacy end their friendship? And Emma? What chance would she have for friendship with Emma, if she knew how much Lydia could 'see' just by looking at her?

She took another toke and tried to let the worried thoughts blow away on the smoke.

* * *

Helen, 11:04pm

Alexander seemed to have enjoyed himself at the party, and that made Helen all the more irritated, because it had been an ordeal for her. Barbara and Ben had outdone themselves, as usual, but seeing her friends and having good food and drink couldn't offset the irritation she felt at all the women throwing themselves at Alexander, Sally included.

She hadn't said a word on the ride home, pretending to be tired, but she was sure he noticed she wasn't herself. Or at least, she hoped he did. Or not. She wasn't sure what she wanted.

As she dressed for bed and brushed her teeth, the frustration mounted. Was she going to have to spend the rest of her life feeling like this? She'd never been the jealous type, and she knew those women meant nothing to him. It wasn't his fault he was so incredibly handsome. She should be mad at them, not him. Why couldn't she just be happy? If only she hadn't gained five pounds since the wedding. Their love of gourmet cooking--well, eating what they cooked--was beginning to make her grow out of her clothes. Why didn't Alexander gain weight? Would he still love her if she turned into a blimp?

It had always calmed her to stroke Sheba when she was disturbed, but her dearest feline friend had died a couple months ago, so she went to pet Alexander's cat Fido, who lay in Siamese splendor on the bed (on Alexander's side, of course). The cat took a swipe at her. No claws, but clearly not interested. "Why do you hate me?" It wasn't the first time she'd asked, but it was the first time she'd said it out loud so accusingly.

Alexander stepped out of the closet. "What's wrong?"

"Your cat hates me," she complained, feeling like a spoiled child.

"Nonsense. He just doesn't know you that well yet. Give him time. He'll grow to love you."

"I miss Sheba. And now her ashes are spread in the yard at my old condo." Helen looked at Alexander accusingly.

"I'm sorry it worked out that way, but I can't think of any way to fix it." His green eyes shone with sympathy, but he just didn't get it.

"Sometimes I feel I don't belong." She knew she was opening the door to an argument, but she'd bottled her resentment up for too long.

He stepped out of the closet where he could see her in the light cast from the bathroom. "What do you mean?" His voice was calm and concerned, but he clearly had no clue how upset she was.

She rocked and held her arms wrapped tightly around her stomach. "I feel like a guest in your house. I barely found myself before we got married, and I feel I've lost myself again. Everywhere I look, I see *your* life, not mine. It's like there's no *me*. You want me to sell my condo, get rid of my furniture, and it makes sense, but I don't want to lose my life. I don't have my cat, and I miss her... Never mind, it sounds stupid."

"It's not stupid, but don't you agree it's logical to sell your place? And I didn't realize you were so attached to your furniture. I know Sheba meant the world to you, and I'm sorry she's there instead of here. What would you have me do?" Frustration had crept into his voice. He didn't understand.

Helen sighed at the impossibility of having what she wanted or even communicating it clearly. "I don't know!" She twisted a bit of nightgown distractedly. "I want a cat who loves me like Sheba did. I want to fit in and feel like I'm not just an appendage of yours. I hate all those women throwing themselves at you."

She saw his eyebrows go up. *Now he thinks it's all about jealousy. And maybe it is.*

"I'm not doing anything to encourage anyone. You're being unfair, and that's not like you."

Helen shook her head, fighting tears. "Even Sally was all over you," she whispered.

His gaze hardened. "Do you consider that *my* fault? If she weren't your daughter, I'd know exactly what to do, but you love her, and I don't want to alienate her. Are you implying I'm doing more than just putting up with her? Maybe you should talk to *her* about her behavior, not me."

Helen knew she was out of line, but now that she'd put it in words, she had to let it all out. "You allow her to rub all over you every time she comes over. That may not be encouraging her, but it isn't dis-couraging her." Helen gritted her teeth, feeling she had stepped over a line.

Alexander closed the distance between them and raised his hand, and Helen flinched and threw her hand up in defense.

His eyes widened in hurt and shock. "Do you think I'd hit you? How could you? I just wanted to reassure you." He slowly reached the rest of the way and touched her cheek, then pulled her into his chest in an awkward hug.

Helen tried to find words to explain her emotions as the tears started to flow. "I can't stand the feeling that I'm competing with every woman on earth for your attention. No, even the men. I've never felt jealous before, and knowing you have a history with both men and women makes me more insecure. Tonight I even found myself jealous of Ray and Alan, and they're a couple. I can't seem to help it. I know you're just friends with them, but I'm no good at being married to a man who is so attractive and...bisexual."

She couldn't see his face, but his voice was stony. "Look, it's late and we're both tired and we had wine at the party. This isn't going to be solved tonight. Let's try to get some sleep and we can discuss it tomorrow."

Helen knew he was right, but it was so hard to put aside the compelling need to resolve the conflicting feelings. She felt guilty, because in her previous marriage, an argument like this would have ended in her being beaten, and instead of being grateful, she was annoyed. It was like nothing he did or said could please her. "OK. Let's

talk about it tomorrow. But don't make me be the one to bring it up."
God, I'm being a total bitch.

"I promise we can sit down after breakfast, or even before, if you like, and talk about whatever is bothering you."

They got into the king size bed, and for the first time, they stayed on opposite sides, as if they were inhabiting hostile countries. Fido stayed on Alexander's side, as always. Helen felt more alone than she ever had in her life, and worse yet, she knew it was her own fault, but she didn't know how to fix it. Tears trickled down her cheeks, silently soaking the pillow.

ABOUT THE AUTHOR

 Maggie McPhee is a writer of contemporary 'boomer' women's fiction. She also writes nonfiction using her real name, Maggie Percy.

www.ingramcontent.com/pod-product-compliance
Lightning Source LLC
Chambersburg PA
CBHW070536260626
47161CB00002B/408